"MR. DARE, ARE YOU ILL?"

Dominic eased gently forward—or did the coach lurch at that precise moment?—and his lips touched hers. It was meant to be a chaste instruction, or so he'd convinced himself, a brief little lesson that he held the absolute power to silence her. But when her lips parted with a surprised gasp, unwittingly inviting him to take more, he suddenly forgot chasteness and the wisdom of forbearance. He was suddenly a starving man offered his first taste of forbidden fruit. He was a man without will.

One lesson, he told himself. He cupped her jaw, eased her head back, her mouth fuller beneath his, and pressed her body up to his. The result was instantaneously, ominously, combustive. Silk and broadcloth sizzled between them, searing skin, setting blood afire. Dominic crushed her against him in an onslaught of lust so startling, he shook with it.

He fell to his knees with her in his arms. He tore his mouth from hers. "Ah, God, Savannah—"

"Mr. Dare," she whispered, gasping for breath.

"Dominic—" He could hardly think. No, he didn't want to think . . . the lesson couldn't end just yet. A minute longer . . .

SR

Dell Books by Kit Garland

DANCE WITH A STRANGER

EMBRACE THE NIGHT

CAPTURE THE WIND

THE PERFECT SCANDAL

The Perfect Scandal

Kit Garland

A Dell Book

Published by
Dell Publishing
a division of
Bantam Doubleday Dell Publishing Group, Inc.
1540 Broadway
New York, New York 10036

ISBN: 0-440-22362-8

Printed in the United States of America

Published simultaneously in Canada

June 1998

10 9 8 7 6 5 4 3 2 1

OPM

Because we snuck out and never got caught, because you had the girls and I had the boys, because of that weekend in Ames, Iowa, because you live and die by children, stray animals, and Greenpeace, because you said to me one day "You've got to do a story set in Newport" and no, they never quite got there, because you're my sister and they thought you were the writer in the family—Victoria, this one's for you.

Chapter 1

New York City
March 1890

Without warning, the bedchamber door burst open.

Before it hit the opposite wall, Savannah Rose Merri-weather stuffed a chocolate creme into her mouth, shoved *The Free Enquirer* under her pillow, and spun around wearing a dutiful and complacent look. Or at least she hoped so.

Penelope Bell Merriweather, looking very much the lampshade in sapphire silk, Valenciennes lace, and a hundred gold tassels, charged past her daughter without seeming to give complacency any notice.

But Savannah knew better.

Penelope waved a newspaper over her head as if it reeked of rotten fish. With one arm she braced herself at the window overlooking Fifth Avenue and with the other rattled the newspaper at Savannah.

"It's come, God save us all. Here, take it. I can't bear to touch it, much less read it."

Thick cream slid down Savannah's throat. Her mother's hard green eyes shot to her. Savannah touched her fingers to her lips and smelled a half pound's worth of chocolate on the tips. It had been a long morning.

1

She reached for the paper, which she knew was the New York society weekly *Town Topics*. Both this and the New York City *Social Register* occupied the hallowed spot on Penelope's night table, right beside her bed. "Remember, Mother, malicious attention from Colonel Sharpe's column is better than no attention at all." She grabbed the paper and swished away before her mother could detect a whiff of chocolate on her breath. She flipped the paper open.

"No, don't."

Savannah understood her mother's need to play out the drama of it. "If you wish."

"Page seven."

"Of course." Savannah smacked the paper flat on a table and braced her hands. Her eyes skimmed the page. "I don't see—"

"Middle right."

"Ah. Right at eye level. How kind of Colonel Sharpe to put it right next to this item about Prescilla Rescott."

"From oil." Her mother sniffed, lifting the drape from the window. The hiss in her breath fogged the pane. "Married that railroad heir. They're building a cottage at Newport. They're calling it Heaven's Gate."

"I hope the view there will console her. Colonel Sharpe writes: 'Seldom does a brunette make a pretty bride and Miss Rescott was no exception.'" Savannah clucked her tongue. "Poor dear. And now all of the Four Hundred know it. I wonder what it would take for Colonel Sharpe and his quilled assassins to stifle their editorial conscience just once." She spotted the bigger, bolder, and thus far more noteworthy item smack in the middle of the page.

"Your lips are moving, Savannah."

"They are? So sorry."

"Dammit, aloud! Read it aloud."

"'. . . still reeking—'"

"From the beginning."

Savannah looked at her mother, a cold pillar of stone in

a room that was a symphony of barbaric splendor. All around them were gold-embroidered draperies and bed hangings, sofas upholstered in Flemish tapestries, Turkish rugs, scrollwork mirrors, and gilding everywhere. Hardly any light stole in through the five layers of curtains. The woodwork and wallpaper were all in dark tones, everything about the room designed to suggest permanence, as if they'd occupied the house and their station for centuries.

The truth of it was that they'd moved into the brownstone less than a year ago. Their money was so new it still gave off the noisome whiffs of the methods by which it was acquired, a sin made unforgivable since their fortune had been made in a Chicago slaughterhouse. The consuming nightmare of anyone immersed in polite East Coast society was to be touched by the Chicago brush. The Merriweathers had been tarred with it.

Her mother's powdered face was taut. "Read it, Savannah."

"As you wish. 'Mr. Stuyvesant Merriweather, still reeking of his newly made Chicago millions, late of Dogberg, Ohio, and society's newest climber, responded to a liquid call of nature in Mrs. Astor's parlor after dinner last evening, retired to her fireplace, and let fly.'" Savannah pursed her lips to keep from smiling. "Well, you know Papa never liked port or Mrs. Astor. He's always said that taking a meal with her was to look dullness square in the eye."

"Dammit, Savannah, your devotion to your father has made you mindless." Like a ship gathering under full sail, Penelope turned from the window. Teeth set, hands clasped below her imperious bosom, she paced the floor with a ponderous grace ill-suited to her agitation. "Damn his smug midwestern contempt. He's proven how ill-prepared he was for the power his wealth conveyed on him. How did anyone know he hailed from Dogberg, Ohio? He told them, that's how, probably right before he took his relief in the flames. Your father is a disgrace, and you and I, by virtue of our unfortunate association, are unfit for society. Thrown out before we're even in." Her hand slashed through the air in front of Savannah's nose. "For over a year our family has sat upon the stool of probation, awaiting trial and acceptance, and now, at the last hour, in Mrs. Astor's very parlor where we should have been so certain of acceptance, our every hope is squashed."

"Actually doused."

"You find humor in tragedy, Savannah?"

"I give it my best, Mother."

"How like your father and every last one of his Irish ancestors."

"Thank you, Mother." Her mother looked sharply at her. Savannah returned a thoughtful look. "Don't you think there's an unnatural insularity to Mrs. Astor's clan? They all talk with the same tone and inflections and in the end say very little."

But Penelope wasn't listening. "I refuse to believe I won't be a member in that pride of lionesses. Good God, I can't be nice to the people-I'm-not-supposed-to-know. I belong to the social sheep, not the unacceptable goats! I will have everyone calling me Bunny."

"But your name is Penelope."

"Indeed! Every lioness has a nickname. At first I wanted them to call me Tookie. But Bunny Bell Merriweather *smells* like old money. Bunny Bell, of the Kentucky Bells. I like it."

"Of course no one suspects that the Bells of Kentucky are chicken farmers." Savannah met her mother's glacial stare with lifted brows. "I've never told a soul, Mother."

"Indeed. You're a good daughter in that regard, Savannah." Penelope looked at her daughter an instant too long and in a way that made Savannah's chest begin to tighten. She suddenly felt every silk-covered button that ran up the front of her dress press deep into her skin. "Open your mouth, Savannah."

Savannah slid her teeth against her tongue and tasted chocolate. She tried not to breathe. Her jaw was gripped in the vise hold of her mother's fingers. Winged nostrils flaring, Penelope leaned near and sniffed. Savannah closed her eyes. Her mother looked like something out of a nightmare with eyes bulging, face mottled, and a vein popping at her temple where her blond hair had grown thinnest. Savannah considered telling her she looked nothing like a lioness.

Penelope released her jaw. "Where are they?"

It was damned hard not to look at the pillow that concealed the half-eaten box of French chocolates. "Who?"

"Look at you." It was the tone that made Savannah's insides shrivel like old bones. The head-to-toe sweep of her mother's eyes was nothing short of humiliating. Savannah felt every jab of lacing in her corset squeezing her waist to its impossible eighteen inches.

"I can see all of your chocolates around your waist all squeezed in and up, and God knows where it's all going but out." Penelope waved a hand at her daughter's bosom and winced. "Virtue, my dear, is almost wholly a matter of appearances. And you are beginning to look a good deal less than virtuous."

"The fault there can't lie with me."

"Is that so? Since you returned from France you've a vague aura of sin about you, Savannah. I can't quite place it."

Savannah felt as if she'd been stuck through with a fork and laid flat on a table for examination.

"It's not only the chocolates and your sudden thirst for wine. It's not even the clothes you've chosen, which scream of your aunt Maxine Beaupre's influence."

"I chose them all myself."

"And there you have it. A nineteen-year-old girl has no taste except what she's told. Let me enlighten you: Pale blondes should never wear low-cut crimson and flounces, especially in the morning. No—it's something else, something you mistakenly believe you can hide from me." Penelope tapped a finger to her lower lip. Savannah felt the fork's prongs dig deeper. "You didn't spend four weeks in Paris just buying gowns at Worth."

"We also walked the Seine."

"A daughter shouldn't keep secrets from her mother."

"Indeed. For such a sin she could be locked out of heaven."

Penelope looked as if she sucked on a lemon. "I warn you, make yourself any more unsuitable than your father already has and you are doomed to be an old maid forced to live out your life with relatives."

A vision of the chicken-farming Bells of Kentucky burst into Savannah's brain. "Am I not suitably modest, pious, accommodating, and submissive?"

Penelope bared her teeth. "There it is again. That vulgar energy and sharp tongue so like Maxine's. Don't you dare lift those brows at me again, young lady. You know what Maxine's vulgar energy got her: two divorces and the affair with that German philosopher who wrote that book about her after she dumped him. The tales he told—why, she should be thankful she was merely banished from New York. I shudder to think what she intends to do now that she's back from France, widowed and titled. I wonder who the poor fellow was."

"Count Henri Beaupre," Savannah said. "He was an artist."

Penelope took this news much as she would the word of a good friend's death: with a wince and a clutching of her hand to her heart. "Only in France, land of immorality and free love, would an artist also be a count." Penelope snapped her eyes open. "Enough of that. I refuse to bear the blame in this. Your father *allowed* me to hand you over to Maxine Beaupre for four weeks! Said it would do you good to get away from me, whatever that means. As if he sees anything but pork prices and market share."

"Do remember you hate ships, Mother."

"Seasickness is a petty price to pay to protect an impressionable and weak-minded daughter. But how could I have known the depths of your deceit? I thought you would do anything to please your father, but even that doesn't seem to concern you. And with his rheumatism bothering him. He worries about you. Works too much, worries too much, the doctors all say. But what man wouldn't fret over his only child, his heir, his legacy?" Penelope sighed and her eyes fluttered low.

Savannah tensed and hated herself for it. She'd heard the words too many times not to hear them now, even in her mother's silence. *If only you had been a son.*

But that's not what her mother said.

"Tell me, this instant, what Maxine Beaupre did to you in Paris."

Savannah knew with absolute certainty that Maxine had done nothing. It had been Jean-Luc the artist. Or was it Jean-Marc the sculptor? Or Jean-Louis the writer? Perhaps all three.

Savannah's cheeks began to throb at the memory. Her chest felt as if it would burst with the passion swelling up inside of her. She wanted to shout to release it but she couldn't. Daughters of millionaires learned to suppress emotion by perfecting proper-decibel voices no matter the calamities they faced or the intensity of their feelings. As a result Savannah had endured the last year of her life and her blossom into womanhood with all her passion and emotion banked down in her chest. Only the huskiness in her voice betrayed her to anyone astute enough to listen. "I was born with this vulgar energy, Mother. Maxine had nothing to do with it and neither did France. But it was only through the exercise of that same vulgar energy that my father put together the fortune that constitutes the entire reason for my existence. And yours."

"He's a man. Men are vulgar."

"Then so are women."

"Suffragists, yes. How like them you suddenly sound." Penelope's eyes shot like little darts around the room. *The Free Enquirer,* the weekly advocating equal rights for women, free nonsectarian education, and, horrors, birth control was still under Savannah's pillow with the chocolates. Penelope had banned both from the house, a minor inconvenience that Savannah had solved by bribing her maid, Patti, to sneak them in. Savannah wondered if the three chocolate caramels she'd paid Patti to hold her tongue stood a chance against Penelope's threats of unemployment. If Patti was anything like Savannah, she would risk a great deal for her chocolate.

Her mother began to pace in the direction of her bed. Savannah held her breath.

"Your main aim in life," Penelope began, "as the heiress of a fiercely undesirable man, is to make yourself desirable as quickly as possible. Hotheaded outbursts, overeating, bad gowns, and independent or deep thought have no place in your life. Exercise self-control and remove them. As for your energies, for God's sake tone them down and think about what you can do to resurrect your father's reputation. If you adore him as you claim, this is high time to prove it."

"Papa is assured of my affections."

Penelope stopped midstride and swung around. "Is he?"

Her mother might as well have abandoned her at sea. Savannah poked out her chin and felt it quiver. "No other daughter ever loved her father more."

Her mother's smile held no warmth. "You're not an aberration, Savannah. It's the only thing fathers expect of their daughters. Now—"

Savannah found herself blinking as she watched her mother pace. "If something's not done to rectify your father's misdeed, we will never be anything in this city except simply very rich. We might as well be dead. What good is a mansion and a corps of liveried servants if you're invisible to everyone of consequence?"

Savannah had several replies she chose to keep to herself. She knew the hardships inherent in managing a large staff of servants would never deter some women from taking a house that couldn't be run without them. A conspicuously splendid house was as essential to upward mobility as a conspicuously well-behaved husband.

"I didn't claw my way from hotel chambermaid to millionairess to be denied my due by your father's coarse Irish upbringing. If it were left to him, the only people interested in us would be scoundrels and fortune hunters." Penelope jerked to a stop. Her head snapped around and she looked at Savannah with lips peeling back over her teeth. "That's it. Oh, God, I'm so clever. Give me that."

Savannah jumped when her mother grabbed *Town Topics* from the table and began to thrash through it with such fury several tendrils of gray-blond hair fell over her eyes. She didn't bother to smooth them aside. She was breathing hard, licking her lips, and smashing through the pages. "Elsebeth Bragg was telling me about her niece Lacey, the one who got herself pregnant by her father's valet—aha! Here they are, all the way at the back." A porcelain teacup from France skidded off the table and fell to the carpet as Penelope slammed the paper flat and began to read. " 'Shipping heiress Miss Lacey Bragg, born 1870, married 1890 to Sir Walworth Hutton, Staffordshire, ninth Baronet, born 1840, Deputy Lieutenant for Staffordshire, seat Wolseley Hall, Rugeley, Staffordshire, creation of title 1628. Family traceable to 1281, alleged to be descended from Sir Kaye, an ancient Briton and one of the Knights of the Round Table.' " Penelope reared up with a satisfied smile. "And there you have it."

Savannah frowned. "I thought I heard Patti say that

Lacey was recently returned from England, without her child or her ninth baronet."

Penelope snorted. "To hell with the child or the husband. She had her title, didn't she? Elsebeth herself lunched with Mrs. Astor not a week ago. You see how easily all was forgiven?"

"Little good that will do Lacey in Morganza. She lost her mind in England."

Penelope began flipping pages. "Did Patti tell you that Lacey Bragg was committed to Morganza because of her marriage?" Her laugh was as brittle as the snap of the newspaper. "Lacey Bragg was a mindless twit long before she had to look to England to save herself. Thank heavens you're nothing like her." Her mother didn't look altogether certain of this.

"Patti says English servants eat American heiresses for breakfast. And the men—"

"Patti has no firsthand knowledge of the servants except that she wishes to be one of them. As for domineering English lords—all fiction. I swear, the day servants work more than they talk will be a liberating one indeed for every matron in this city—ah! Here's one, right under the heading: 'List of Peers Eager to Lay Their Coronets and Incidentally Their Hearts at the Feet of the American Girl.' Listen to this: 'Polish Prince Yablonski anxious to wed an American with a ten-million-dollar dot.' Oh, no, no. That's no good. Polish princes are about as marketable a commodity as last year's hat. Ah, here. Listen to this: 'The right honorable John Fitch, forty-eight years old, educated at Harrow, formerly captain of the Rifle brigade, has no children. Family seats: three castles in Scotland. Entailed estates amount to 16,000 acres'—good heavens—'but do not, owing to mortgages, yield their nominal income of $100,000.'"

"He's broke," Savannah said.

"Inconsequential," Penelope shot back. "If a fabulously wealthy title is to be had for the underpinning of a fabulously broke estate, what better way to dispose of a spare hundred thousand or two?"

"I can think of several but certainly not on a wastrel. The man is auctioning himself off to the highest bidder."

"So? His title is genuine, and titles in New York society are rare. Some can ill afford *not* to pay any price to acquire one." Penelope looked long and hard at Savannah, drilling the scheme with merciless precision into her daughter's brain. "When a woman returns to New York with a title, the sins of the family are forgotten."

"Hypocrisy." The word leapt from Savannah's tongue before she could bite it back. She stood there horrified.

"What did you say?" her mother asked very slowly.

"His pockets weep." Savannah bent to retrieve the teacup from the floor.

Damnable trap. She could feel it like steel jaws clamping into her. She'd been trying to please her father by way of her mother for too long without any success. Any fool knew what was expected of her. But there was this small matter of the elemental yearnings of her heart and soul. Rare was the occasion when the two were the same. Since she'd returned from France, the yearnings were bubbling closer to the surface, and the pressure in her chest was building, like steam trying to escape a boiling pot of water whose lid had been slammed on hard. She stood up. "So now I'm in shameless search of a purchasable baron, count, or marquis, is that it?"

Penelope snorted. "My dear, I'm far too clever for that. You want nothing less than an earl. A few steel-thewed ties to the Prince of Wales would help seal the arrangement. Let's see—earls, earls." Penelope's fingernail slid along a narrow column. "Ah, here's another one. Ooh, this is good. 'An English earl of very old title is desirous of marrying at once a very wealthy young woman. Her age and looks are immaterial but her character must be irreproachable. She must be a virgin—' " Without lifting her chin, Penelope shot her eyes at Savannah, then lowered them. " '—must be willing to purchase the rank of peeress for no less than \$250,000 and have sufficient wealth besides to keep up the rank of peeress. Pleased to communicate with strictest confidentiality through a Mrs. White c/o Number Thirty-five, Belgrave Square, London.' " Penelope beamed. "How helpful Colonel Sharpe is to print such things in our hour of need."

"And why shouldn't he be? He delivered us into need in the first place." Savannah moved to the window. The room felt very warm and cloistered. Beyond the layers of drapery the world looked sun-kissed. "If an American father is to sink his daughter and a large slice of his capital into some broke scion of nobility, he should know everything he's getting in return."

"Nonsense. We know enough. He's an earl, isn't he? I'll post the letter to Mrs. White this afternoon. You'll sail within the month with check in hand."

"What if I don't like him?"

"What? Desperate young women don't pass up a prospect merely on account of possible incompatibility. You can learn to like him. As for any other doubts you might have—well, what is this?" Penelope swooped down on Savannah's bed, seized her pillow, and lifted it as if she uncovered priceless treasure.

Savannah closed her eyes. Not because her mother had found her French chocolate and suffragist paper. Because she'd had to hide them at all.

Penelope swung around, chocolates balanced just beneath her nose, newspaper crushed under one arm. "Your father has sought solace at the Patriarch Club, knowing, of course, that club men will forgive pissing in the fireplace. But imagine his disappointment if I were to tell him that his only child has no control over her appetites or her wicked, extremist thoughts. There's nothing worse for a father than having no sons and only one selfish, senseless daughter." Penelope lifted a chocolate and sank her teeth into it. White cream oozed between her teeth and from the corners of her mouth. She didn't bother to lick at it. "The shock of it could put him in bed for a month. I can't do that to him. You see, we do things for the people we love, because we love them. But you already know that. You're a smart girl. A bit vulgar, but smart just the same."

Savannah stared from the window and listened to the swish of her mother's skirts as she moved to the door. Devotion was perhaps the most inescapable of prisons.

"How stupid you were to trust Patti. She confessed everything to me with only a bit of arm-twisting. Hill will accompany you abroad. She'll keep much better watch on you than even I could."

"Hill." Savannah snorted above the echo of the door slamming. "Hateful old bag." With both hands she jerked at the row of silk-covered buttons. One by one the buttons popped through loops, releasing the pressure on her torso, micro-inch by micro-inch, until she didn't feel as if her ribs would crack when she breathed. In the false bottom of her armoire she found another box of chocolates. She grabbed the first one she touched and lifted it to her mouth. Closing her eyes, she inhaled.

In an instant she was in Maxine, Beaupre's salon in Paris, at a candlelit dining table fit for a bacchanalian feast, wearing no corset, no shoes, and no underclothes. Various Jeans devoured her with their eyes from across the table. Beneath Maxine's watch she'd talked too much, giggled too much, and had fallen desperately in love at least a half dozen times.

She'd even been kissed, not only once but three times, *directly on the mouth*.

Her teeth sank into the chocolate. Having stepped over that invisible threshold into indulgence, how could she possibly go back? Trying to ignore or suppress her desires virtually guaranteed unhappiness. And at barely nineteen, Savannah wasn't ready to condemn herself to an unfulfilling life without one hell of a fight.

The trap, unfortunately, felt all too familiar, pitting Sa-

vannah's desires against her father's happiness. Any loving
daughter would sacrifice her needs. The trouble was, Savannah wasn't yet convinced there wasn't a middle
ground where both she and her parents could be content.
And she was determined to find it.

She threw the draperies wide. Midday sun slammed
into the room, tempting away her doubts. If she'd con-
quered French intellects and artists, how difficult could it
be to charm a crotchety earl and his sour servants? With
her spirit and snap she'd overcome any obstacles. She
could well be the first wife ever to find fulfillment in her
own pursuits. Her father would be proud, his reputation
restored. Women the world over would thank her.

Her chest swelled with satisfaction but her smile wasn't
as forthcoming. There was, of course, one small problem,
easily remedied, but a problem just the same: dear
Charles. Earnest, intelligent, thoughtful Charles Fairleigh
with the warm eyes, soft hands, and poet's words. He was
a merchant's son and a member of the social class her
mother referred to as people-we-don't-know.

He was, therefore, quite perfect. Savannah had decided
to fall in love with him the instant her mother had told her
not to.

Well, duty or not, she had no intention of giving up
Charles. If her instincts served, he had no intention of
giving her up either. She settled herself at her secretary,
took up her quill and paper, and, summoning an appro-
priately stricken look, set about convincing Charles that
the world would end if he didn't accompany her to England. When they arrived there and she married her earl,
she'd have no trouble convincing Charles that he would
be, in the lovely French tradition, her lover.

Chapter 2

Southern England
April 1890

The Black Swan Inn sat a quarter mile off a well-traveled road that led from London to all points south and ended at Killicutt Abbey, a town perched on the chalk cliffs and rumored to be haunted by the ghost of a clergyman who had hanged himself from the church steeple. The sun never seemed to shine on this part of England. The wind whipped in off the Channel with a bone-penetrating chill no matter the season. The landscape seemed washed with muted gray. No one save the lost ever ambled far enough off the main road to reach the Black Swan. Perhaps that was why the Black Swan's owner never closed his doors.

It was also why Dominic Dare had agreed to it for his rendezvous tonight. True, it was close to the port of Plymouth where his ship had docked. But he'd have been a fool to choose a more frequented inn closer to London and run the risk that someone would recognize him as the man who'd seduced Lady Bertrice Hyde-Gilbert out of her Crimson Fire diamond necklace.

It had happened less than a year ago. Poor Bertrice Hyde-Gilbert, daughter of the Duke of Dorcester, well-known philanthropist and art collector extraordinaire. The London papers had made certain that everyone knew that the theft of the Crimson Fire, and Bertrice's unfortunate seduction, had been committed by an American rogue and libertine who'd cleverly escaped his London jail and fled the country. What the papers couldn't have known was that while Dominic might have seduced Bertrice Hyde-Gilbert, his purpose in doing so wasn't to steal the Crimson Fire. He'd wanted information, the kind only a daughter of a preeminent art collector could provide him. The mystery of the missing necklace, Dominic suspected, could be solved in one interrogation of Bertrice's husband, Cecil Hyde-Gilbert, the man who'd thrown Dominic in jail.

But since the English loved to hate Americans, particularly when the reputation of a duke's daughter hung in the balance, attempting to pin the crime on an Englishman, even one of Cecil Hyde-Gilbert's unlikable disposition, would have been pure folly.

Only one prize was worth the risk of returning to England a wanted man. And how great a risk was it, after all? He knew that Hyde-Gilbert summered somewhere in the south of England. But Dominic would have to be miserably unlucky to bump into him here, in the middle of nowhere.

He stepped from his hired coach into pouring rain and ankle-deep muck. He signaled his driver to the stable at the rear of the inn, tugged his hat lower, and dashed for the door. The inn's main room was badly lit and deserted save for an old man dozing on his arm at a near table. A red-cheeked man watched him suspiciously from behind the counter.

Harrigan hadn't yet arrived.

Doffing his hat, Dominic moved deeper into the room, leaving behind a trail of mud and raindrops. He chose a table tucked into shadows with a view of the entrance.

"No coaches to Blithestone or Killicutt Abbey today,"

the man behind the counter said, watching him. " 'Tis the floodin' rains again. Ye'll be needin' a room at least fer the night, guvna, 'til it stops. Roads will be washed out come dusk."

Dominic hadn't planned on staying the night. He certainly hadn't anticipated rivers of mud instead of roads. He'd planned on a quick meeting, an efficient exchange of information for cash, and a speedy return to New York. No delays, not even for sleep. No complications. Nothing that would require the least bit of patience. He was tapped dry of it. He could taste victory, however bitter and poignant. He'd be damned if he was going to be denied it one more night simply because of rain and unnavigable roads.

He worked his shoulders against the confines of his broadcloth coat, resisting the first twinges of doubt. If his coach had made the trip from Plymouth in the rain, then Harrigan's would from London just as well. This was simply an inconvenience.

He muttered his thanks when the innkeeper slid a candleholder and a glass in front of him. The glass was coated with a greasy film, the ale warm and flat, and the man reeked as if he hadn't bathed in months.

Dominic envisioned the bed that awaited him.

Not bad luck. Inconvenience. He listened to his teeth slide together and watched the flame calm. The door burst open and his coachman ducked in. He exchanged a few words with the innkeeper, then retired to another corner of the room with his own warm ale in a dirty glass.

Patience would have been easy enough to come by if the stakes weren't so high. And not only for him. The rain might be all the excuse Harrigan needed to abort the meeting and stay in London. When a man risked his life, his career, and the reputation of an internationally known auction house like Boothby's, he might not require much more than bad weather to rethink selling a man's name to an American.

Hell, they'd both known the stakes when they'd agreed to embark on the scheme over a year ago. Harrigan was determined. No need to worry.

Rain slammed against the casement windows. Lightning flashed. Thunder boomed in response. The inn shuddered like an old woman. Dominic drained his ale, slid his glass to the edge of the table, and glanced at the innkeeper. "Any chance you've a bottle of rum anywhere?"

The innkeeper and Dominic's coachman looked at him then threw back their heads and howled guffaws at the ceiling. Dominic slouched back in his chair, rendered impotent by a pair of fools and Mother Nature. Unlucky as hell, that's what he was. It would take him a good long time to get drunk on flat ale. But he could certainly try.

Three glasses later, he looked up when the door burst open. Quickly he doused his candle flame between two fingers. As if conjured by a nightmare, Cecil Hyde-Gilbert swept into the Black Swan's main room followed by his wife, Bertrice, and two women. Hyde-Gilbert gave the room a cursory sweep of his eyes, which glanced off Dominic without recognition.

Elbows braced on the table, hands clamped around his ale, head tucked between his shoulders, Dominic watched almost in disbelief as Hyde-Gilbert strode to the counter. Bertrice and one of the women remained behind him. The other woman, considerably younger than the others, fidgeted her feet and fussed with her soggy cape as if she found it impossible to stand still. Nervous chit, Dominic decided, watching her glance over her shoulder at the inn's door a second time. He glimpsed a very round face, very large eyes, very full lips, and a great deal of blond hair before she looked quickly at Bertrice and flashed a fake smile. She was waiting for someone and she thought nobody knew it. Or else she was frightened.

What the hell did he care? He had far more pressing problems at the moment. Like staying out of an English jail. Then again, Hyde-Gilbert might decide to shoot him and be done with it. Dominic stuck his nose in his glass and listened to Hyde-Gilbert order up three rooms. Same imperious voice. Same slick veneer. Dominic wondered what the man had done with his wife's necklace.

The innkeeper babbled something about readying rooms and disappeared. Hyde-Gilbert, visibly annoyed, swung around and jerked his chin at the nearest table. The ladies hesitated a moment then moved to the table.

Dominic grabbed his hat, tugged it over his eyes, and left his table. A clear path lay to the door. Only a few chairs blocked the way. Shadows hovered conveniently. While the ladies situated themselves, he'd make his escape unobserved.

And he was certain he would have, had the room not shook again with a booming crash of thunder.

The nervous young woman yelped and leapt like a rabbit from her chair directly into Dominic's path, then spun toward the door. In her clumsiness, she dropped her bag. Items scattered across the floor. She bent over at the waist and began scooping up her things, poking her full-bustled backside up at Dominic and completely blocking his path anywhere around her. He turned right and smashed into the chair of the sleeping man. The man jerked awake, squinted up at Dominic, and began to shout curses at him. Teeth grinding, Dominic contemplated the young woman's backside again and then the world exploded with another crash of thunder.

The young woman reared up and screeched. With no other choice Dominic swung left and bumped smack into Bertrice Hyde-Gilbert as she jumped from her chair. He met her astonished stare.

Her intake of breath was very small, almost soundless at the instant of recognition. She stood absolutely still. Her face paled to a ghostly shade, her eyes became vacant. A raindrop trembled from one of her eyelashes. "Dominic."

"Don't," he said softly. He glanced over her auburn head at her husband speaking to his coachman a mere ten feet away. Hyde-Gilbert glanced at him, briefly, then at his wife. Dominic turned to the blonde. With surprising restraint, given his agitation with her, he clamped his hands around her waist, lifted her from his path and into the consoling arms of Bertrice Hyde-Gilbert, then strode from the inn. Ducking into the rain, he headed for the stable, certain no man had yet been born with worse luck.

"Sign here." Mrs. White tapped an impatient finger at the very bottom of the contract where she'd scrawled an X.

Savannah scanned the minuscule print and chewed at her lower lip.

"It's all there," Mrs. White said crisply.

"But the Earl of Castellane is not." Savannah glanced at Bertrice Hyde-Gilbert.

Bertrice smiled and touched Savannah's hand. Against her own icy fingers Bertrice's felt strong and comforting. Her amber eyes glowed with assurances. "The earl sent us in his stead to meet you in London because he hates traveling any distance in the foul weather. I believe it's the inns he hates even more, and who could blame him? He awaits you at his estate, Ravenscar. See there? He signed the contract, Miss Merriweather. Winthrop Twombley, Earl of Castellane. How kind it was of Mrs. White to secure his signature and meet us here."

"Yes, very kind. I just wish I knew—" Savannah closed her eyes and gathered her fragmented spirits together. Damn the storm. Damn her irrational, childish fears. Women of vulgar spirit didn't cower at thunder! Damn Charles. Where was he? The last she'd seen of him was at a posting inn six hours before when he'd changed horses and given her a solemn look as she rolled away in the Hyde-Gilbert coach. She snapped her eyes open and looked hopefully at Bertrice. "Is the earl handsome?"

Bertrice's smile wavered only slightly. "He's been described as elegant. Not as old as you might think. Not much older than Cecil. He was the youngest of five, and all the rest sisters."

"All sisters," Savannah said, clamping on to this. She'd forever envied anyone who had sisters. And this man had four. How awful could he be? She lifted the quill.

"Cecil favors him."

The quill wavered as Savannah glanced across the table at Cecil Hyde-Gilbert. Her heart sank like falling bread dough. He was watching her and Bertrice. An insubstantial man of few words. Her own father outweighed him by at least a hundred pounds. But he was elegant, in a severely coiffed and starched way she assumed was common to titled gentry. His face was in a perpetual tight clench, as if he had other places to be and other things to do. But Bertrice seemed to like him well enough.

And Bertrice herself was difficult not to like. She'd been so kind to calm Savannah during the storm even though she'd been shaking uncontrollably herself.

Savannah glanced at Mrs. White, then scribbled her signature. "There."

"Both copies," Mrs. White said.

Before the ink had dried, Mrs. White snatched the contracts and handed Cecil Hyde-Gilbert his copy plus the bank draft Stuyvesant Merriweather had made out to the Earl of Castellane for two hundred fifty thousand dollars. For her trouble, Mrs. White was pocketing a ten percent fee. With little more than a curt nod, Mrs. White slid her chair from the table and disappeared up the inn's stairs, business complete.

"Hungry?" Bertrice asked softly.

Savannah caught her teeth in her lower lip, pressed a hand to her belly, and felt her bosom swell up. "Famished."

Bertrice nodded to the innkeeper, and he slid a large plate before Savannah. "Eat, dear, and then to bed. We've an early day of it tomorrow. Cecil is anxious."

"And the earl, I hope," Savannah said, eyeing what

looked to be meat hiding under a mound of boiled potatoes and watery gravy. She slathered butter on bread and
sank her teeth into it.

"Yes, of course." Bertrice's fingers clutched tighter to
Savannah's. "The earl is anxious. We all are, dear. Very
anxious to have you with us at Ravenscar."

Three hours later, from her room's casement window,
Savannah watched Charles pull his horse to a stop in front
of the inn. She checked her pocket watch, the one her
father had given her for her birthday last year. She'd fashioned it into a pin and kept it over her left breast, directly
over her heart.

Eleven-thirty. Only thirty more minutes until their midnight rendezvous. But where?

Lifting the window latch, she pushed the casement
open and leaned out the window, her unbustled backside
high, bare toes dangling inches off the floor. A fine mist
fell from the inky skies.

She called his name in a hoarse whisper just as he dismounted. "Hullo!" She smiled when he glanced up. "My
darling, you're covered with mud. You look quite awful. I
swear I won't meet you in the stable at midnight looking
like that!"

Charles blinked at her, looked down at himself, but
when he looked up again, she was gone.

Dominic jerked awake. "Harrigan—"

Shoving up from the straw, he tried to remember why
he was sleeping in a stall in a pitch-black barn. And then
he remembered and cursed, low and soft and venomous.
Christ, he'd fallen asleep. And with Harrigan coming to
meet him. He started to rise when he heard a creak and a
soft thump, like a door opening, then closing. He froze.

"Perfect."

The sound was low, sultry, and female. Definitely not
Harrigan. Dominic watched soft golden light dance on the
rafters overhead. He leaned up and squinted through the

wooden slats. Two shadows moved on the other side of the stall not ten feet away. One held a lantern. Dominic watched it sway, then stop as they paused. He moved his head an inch right and three inches up and found them through a hole in a plank.

A young man, no older than twenty, faced him. He wore a black topcoat and trousers. High at his throat he wore a stiff collar and tie. It hung limp and looked overworked, as if he'd tried with little success to tie it properly. His hair was mussed and hung over his brow like a dark curtain. Several bloody gashes marked his jaw. He'd either been abused or he'd dressed and shaved in a great hurry. Dominic watched the young man's Adam's apple jerk in his throat. The lantern trembled in his hand.

"I—I'm quite certain we shouldn't be here—"

"Yes, sweet Charles, we should. We must grasp opportunity before it slips away from us."

Something about her voice made Dominic taste honey, sweet and thick on his tongue. As he looked closer, he realized he would have recognized the back of her head and all that bouncing blond hair anywhere. He almost groaned. Same backside, a little less bustled but very full and distinguishable nonetheless.

"Charles, I have a plan."

"My darling angel Savannah, so do I."

Dominic almost winced at the flood of appeal in the man's voice. No man should sound like that, particularly with a woman who made a habit of fouling up men's plans.

"In a minute, Charles. A woman must have a scheme."

"Yes, of course she must."

"Dreams and goals and—"

"Marriage. It is a proud moment in a woman's life to reign supreme within four walls. Her goals are marriage."

"Yes, that too. But her whole reason for being can't be simply loving, honoring, obeying, and amusing her lord and master, managing his household, and birthing his children. She's not some inferior person whose shrinking nature is unfit for life outside of a home. She has sufficient confidence to frame and hold an opinion in the face of opposition!''

Charles paled. "Don't speak of such things just yet, not until we've—.'' His eyes widened. "What are you doing?''

"I'm proving a point to you, Charles.'' She began to pace, her bare feet poking from under her hem, swishing in the straw. Dominic watched her, watched her arms lifting, her hands working at the front of her dress. She was quite spectacularly fashioned in silhouette, as full, round, and precariously high in the bosom as she was in the backside, connected by a sleek and narrow torso. He watched her spin around and felt himself tense. All thoughts of Harrigan evaporated.

Golden curls rippled to her waist. Her eyes glowed like embers about to spark with flame. Roses bloomed in her cheeks. Her lips were plump like cherries. Her tiny hands held her dress together over her breasts. In the course of several moments she'd managed to unfasten the buttons from her collar to her hips. For all her bold talk, she looked dangerously naive.

Dominic felt a drop of perspiration weave down his temple. He suddenly felt as if he'd run ten miles.

"My angel—'' Charles croaked. "I need not tell you the voices of evil spirits speak close to my ear, whispering to the wild beast that lurks in the bottom of all men's hearts! By your woman's virtue and wisdom you must redeem me from weakness and vice, not lead me to it! Please—no more—I cannot bear it!''

She smiled with teeth slightly parted as if she expected him to see her side of it without hesitation. "Why is it that everything we like to do is a sin and that everything we dislike is commanded by God or someone? I'm so damned tired of the everlasting 'No.' Hereafter, Charles, let's act as we choose, without asking permission. Suppose we're punished. We'll have had our fun, and that's better than to mind the everlasting 'No!' and not have any fun at all." Her hands relaxed and the dress parted several inches.

Dominic glimpsed mounds of porcelain-white skin beneath sheer white cambric. He heard shallow breaths, the galloping of a pulse like a brigade in his ears, and realized both were his own.

Charles gave a strangled cry. Dominic didn't take his eyes from Savannah.

"Open your eyes, Charles. Did I tell you that corsets apply an average of twenty-one pounds of pressure to a woman's abdominal area and some, no doubt mine, as much as ninety-eight pounds? Skirts and underskirts weigh an average of twenty pounds. I've known women who were maimed, whose ribs were broken and internal organs damaged, and you want to know why?"

"No," Charles gurgled. "Angel, my angel, marry me and be done with this—"

"I have to marry the earl, Charles. I explained all that to you on the ship. But what I didn't tell you is that I've a plan for you and I promise you'll see my way in this. But that's later. Now, listen to me. The reason women suffer such horrors is because their spirits are in bondage!"

"Good God, have mercy on me! No! Don't come any closer."

"Women have a birthright to self-sovereignty, Charles. It's the height of cruelty to rob an individual of a single natural right. To throw obstacles in the way of a complete education is like putting out the eyes. To deny the rights of property is like cutting off the hands." She stood there, gripping her dress with white fists, chin lifted, eyes flashing, self-righteous and even more self-impressed. Dominic was suddenly certain that the words were not her own but those she'd heard someone else say. But the passion was all hers, and it was glorious to behold. "Someone must inaugurate a rebellion such as the world, or at least England, has never seen before. And I'll be the woman to do it!"

The dress fell to the straw floor.

Charles sank to his knees and began to weep.

From a far corner of the stable, a horse poked its head over its stall, eyed Savannah, and snorted.

Dominic felt his throat go thick as molasses. She wasn't wearing a corset. Only a very thin, transparent white cambric camisole and pantalets. The backside was all her. The bosom, every inch, all her, with no help from whalebone and underwiring, or padding from horsehair. Her waist was whippet narrow, her hips lushly full, tapering to long, long thighs and rounded calves.

Dominic's eyes jerked up to her breasts, then to her mouth, then to the shadowed vee at the tops of her thighs where the cambric had worked up and outlined in excruciating detail the shape of—

"I've got to do this, Charles, for all womankind. Don't you see? Well, of course you can't see. Charles, open your eyes."

"You ask me to sin against God, to sin against you, against the pure woman I want as my own. How easily you condemn me to hell and tortured memories!"

It was the lighting, Dominic decided, grasping at any explanation for his absolute inability to tear his eyes away from her. Something about the way the light colored her skin like the first rays of morning sun, made her more angel than human, more gorgeous than any female he'd ever seen. Or painted. And he'd painted dozens, most without their clothes.

He studied the play of deep shadow beneath her breasts as she moved. Porcelain-smooth arms lifted to Charles. Dominic could smell her now, a heated, lemony musk scent. He licked his lips, tasting it. She was all woman, offering the kind of redemption poor Charles was begging for if only he'd been smart enough to take it.

Looking at her, a man could believe her undeniably

pure, a heaven-sent blank slate on which to impress all his unfair domestic bondage. Even Dominic could imagine wanting to imprison her in a gilded cage and force motherhood and obedience on her. To look at her was to want to possess her, to comfort her when she cowered at storms.

But listening to her evoked something altogether different. The juxtaposition between the impassioned person struggling for independence inside and the woman bursting with domestic promise outside was uncanny. He'd never met a woman like her. Capturing those warring sides on canvas would challenge the most gifted of painters. . . .

The lighting would have to be perfect. Dawn, in his flat on Tenth Street, when the sun broke through the New York skyline and flooded his bed. He would paint her there.

"Charles, you must stop saying no."

With a tortured cry, Charles jerked to his feet and spun away from her. He took a blind step, plowed facefirst into a wooden post, and fell flat on his back.

"Charles!" She was on her knees beside him, wagging his chin back and forth, poking her face close to his. "Wake up. You have to wake up. Foolish, foolish man. You dropped your lantern. The oil is everywhere—oh—my God."

Something in her voice made Dominic stand straight up. He looked over the edge of the stall just as the barn exploded with flame. He knew then he would never meet Harrigan tonight.

Chapter 3

Savannah started to scream. Independence was all well and good when her life wasn't in danger. But when she sensed trouble, she saw every advantage in resorting to female hysterics.

She grabbed Charles's limp arm, braced her legs, and tugged. He didn't budge. She tugged harder, her feet slipped on straw, and she thumped to the hard floor on her backside. She started to cry, and she really hated crying, but the flames were dancing like great big devils around her and she knew she wasn't going to move Charles by herself. Smoke burned her eyes, snaked down her throat, and made her cough. From a far corner she heard a horse's whinny and her heart twisted. Turning onto all fours, she started to crawl toward the horse.

Tears dripped from her nose, mouth, and eyes in an endless gush. She hiccuped and coughed and then she crawled smack into a wall, a warm, hard wall that had long arms and a very solid chest that smelled like damp broadcloth. It smelled like her father.

"Y-you're here—" she babbled, suddenly completely hysterical as his arms wrapped around her and lifted her.

Clinging to his neck, she turned her wet face against the coat and drowned in his comforting warmth. "Y-you've come for me. I—I knew you wouldn't let Mother do this—"

"Easy," he said, but the voice wasn't her father's and neither was the smell of him beneath his coat. She stiffened and tried to look up at him, but one large hand at the back of her head kept her face pressed against him. Away from the smoke, she realized, as they burst from the barn into the chill of the night.

"Charles—" She gasped, trying to look up at him through a soft drizzle.

"I know," he said. *He knew?* "I'll get him."

If he looked as ominous as his voice sounded, he would be like something out of a nightmare. Shadow obscured his features. She glimpsed the face of a medieval warrior, felt the mass of him against and around her, and hoped he hadn't saved her just to harm her. No, something about him made her want to stay forever curled up in his arms and feeling very small.

Her teeth chattered as he sat her on the ground. "The horses—" He yanked off his coat and threw it over her shoulders. Before she could lift her eyes and thank him, he'd turned and was running back into the burning stable.

Flames shot through the center of the roof and danced into the night skies. Smoke churned through the open door. Her rescuer ducked into the smoke and disappeared inside.

Minutes passed like hours. Savannah gnawed at her knuckles. And then he emerged, Charles slung belly down over one shoulder. Behind him, he led a blindfolded horse. Savannah ran to meet them halfway across the yard and fell to her knees in the mud beside Charles. She touched the egg-size lump on his forehead and watched with relief his chest rise and fall. He hadn't yet awakened.

Her rescuer yanked the cover off the jittery horse and slapped it on the rump. His shirt, Savannah realized, star-

ing at the makeshift blindfold in his fist, then at the man's
bare torso. She stared for several long, long moments. Any
woman would feel small against a man like that.

He looked down at her, the medieval warrior silhouetted against smoke and flame. All he was missing was his
lance. It was then that Savannah realized his coat had
fallen from her shoulders. She jerked a hand to her bosom. "I forgot my dress," she blurted, her cheeks and
neck pounding with heat. Her heart felt like it would
burst from her chest. And then: "Oh, God, the pin. My
watch pin. I wore it on my dress—it's from Papa but no,
no!" She jerked to her feet and began to run after him.
"Where are you going? Don't go back in there! I didn't
mean to—oh, damn."

Again she watched the smoke swallow him up. Seconds
later two more horses came zigzagging from around the
back of the stable. Rain began to pour from the sky. Savannah blinked and waited, feeling as if she were going to
choke with frustration. She started to run toward the barn
but someone caught her around the waist. She spun
around, certain that it would be he.

"Good heavens!" Bertrice Hyde-Gilbert gasped, catching Savannah by the arms. She gaped at the barn then at
Savannah. "Miss Merriweather, what are you doing? Look
at you!"

Savannah wanted to scream. "D-don't look at me! He's
in there!" She flung an arm at the stable. Rain flattened
her hair and dripped from her eyelashes. "He's going to
die if we don't get someone."

"Who's in there, dear?"

"I don't know!" Savannah choked as Bertrice forced
her away from the stable. Damn the woman's perpetual
calm. "A man—a warrior. He was a knight. He saved me.
He gave me his coat. He went to get my watch pin. He
died getting my watch pin."

"There's a man here, dear. Come, see—here."

"That's just Charles." Savannah twisted out of Bertrice's grasp. She fought for control of her voice. She could almost hear the flames ravaging. "He bumped his head when I took off my dress. Here—" She bent, retrieved the broadcloth coat from the mud, and shook it at Bertrice. "He gave me his coat. And he died getting my watch pin."

"His coat," Bertrice said. Holding her robe tight at her neck, she moved closer and touched the broadcloth sleeve. "Let me see that—"

Spotting Cecil Hyde-Gilbert and several footmen running from the inn, Savannah quickly put on the coat, shouldered past Bertrice, and ran toward them.

"There's a man in there!" she cried, pointing to the stable. "He saved all the horses. Someone has to save him."

Cecil Hyde-Gilbert's look made her go suddenly, inexplicably cold. "Get inside, Miss Merriweather."

"But he saved your horse as well. He gave me his coat—"

"Now."

"But I—"

Hyde-Gilbert looked as if he were trying to smile, very patiently, which struck Savannah as odd. After all, a man was dying in a burning barn. "If you still intend to become the wife of an earl, Miss Merriweather, I'd suggest you go inside and come up with a story to explain all this."

"Explain what? I didn't—" Savannah paused as a footman came up beside her. Charles was slung against his side, head lolling. She heard him mangle her name and almost winced. Stuffing her hands into the coat pockets, she touched a wallet with one hand and a handkerchief with the other. With a strange sense of loss she withdrew the linen cloth.

"Take him to my room," Hyde-Gilbert instructed the footman without taking his eyes from Savannah, particularly the coat. "What have you there?" he asked, snatch-

ing the kerchief from her hand with a possessiveness that
made her close her fist around the wallet in her pocket.
He spread the handkerchief over his hand, exposing an
intricately monogrammed "Dare" on one corner.

His head snapped up and he looked at her with very
cold eyes, then at Bertrice in the same manner. "You
there!" he barked to the departing footman, and stuffed
the kerchief into his pocket.

While he turned and muttered something to the footman, Savannah gripped the coat closed over her chest. An
instant later the stable caved in on itself with a shower of
sparks. She watched the flames and felt a burst of fresh
tears.

"My wife, Lady Hyde-Gilbert, will assist you to the
inn," Cecil Hyde-Gilbert said, turning to her. "Five minutes, Miss Merriweather. And make it believable."

Savannah curved her palms around a mug, stuck her nose
in the steam, and watched Cecil Hyde-Gilbert settle in the
chair opposite hers in the inn's common room. His eyes
followed Bertrice as she scooted from her chair beside
Savannah's and started up the stairs. Or had his eyes commanded her to do so?

"My dear." Hyde-Gilbert's lips twitched up. For some
reason Savannah was certain he didn't smile often, and
never with mirth. His face was too sharply formed ever to
soften. "We have here a situation of extreme delicacy."

"I know. A man died in the stable tonight. His family
should be notified."

Hyde-Gilbert's gaze intensified. "You didn't know
him."

"No. He appeared like a ghost and saved us. He saved
the horses by blindfolding them with his shirt."

"Resourceful man. I've spoken with your friend Charles
Fairleigh. I gave him one of my wife's powders for his
headache and put him to bed in the room next to mine.

He told me he came all the way from New York with you."

Savannah silently cursed Charles's inability to hold his tongue. No one was supposed to know about Charles, not the earl, not Bertrice, not Cecil, at least not for several years.

"Poor boy asked my assistance in seeing you wed to him." Hyde-Gilbert's lip twitched again. "Am I correct in assuming you had other plans for him, plans that he perhaps has no knowledge of?"

"I—"

Hyde-Gilbert leaned across the table and curved one hand around Savannah's. "You care for him a great deal."

"Yes," she breathed, wanting very much not to be frightened. And yet part of her was and she wasn't sure why. "He's a good man."

"Indeed. Very young and very good. It would be a pity if his youth and inexperience found him in a jail cell for seduction of an earl's intended bride."

His voice was so smooth and innocuous it was several moments before his import sunk in. Savannah blinked. "Charles and I didn't—that is—I'm not certain what you're suggesting."

"Of course you're not, my dear, but you were found hysterical and half dressed outside of the stable after midnight with a young man you intended to be your lover after you married my uncle. These facts can't be refuted. The footmen all saw you. The innkeeper saw you. My own wife saw you. What they saw screamed of indiscretion, of violation, of a criminal act committed against the virgin bride of the Earl of Castellane."

"That's ridiculous."

"Is it? Need I remind you that Mrs. White has scant few men of title willing to overlook the tarnish your father has recently applied to your family name. An incident in Mrs. Astor's parlor, if I remember correctly?" His brows shot up as color crept into her face. "Indeed, were it not for your much-acclaimed virtue and beauty, the earl would never have even considered you for his wife. Your character was and always will be of utmost concern to the earl, so you can imagine his dismay—indeed, his rage—when word reaches him, as it most assuredly will, that his unsullied young bride lay down in hay with another man."

"I didn't lay down in hay. I took off my clothes to prove a point."

"Do you know what the penalty for rape is, my dear?"

"Rape?"

"You'd rather the earl believe you were willing?"

"I was. Charles was quite mortified when I took off my clothes."

"Say that to my uncle in your defense and I can assure you that you will find yourself aboard the next ship bound for New York with no title in your pocket and your father several hundred thousand dollars poorer. I'd wager that you don't want that. Girls so hate to disappoint now, don't they? Here, drink up. You look very pale of a sudden. Don't fret now. I've a plan. We can't have Charles thrown in jail and hanged, can we?"

Savannah choked on her tea. "Hanged?"

"Or castrated."

"You mean cut off his—good heavens. The earl is unreasonable."

"No more than your average man of title. Now, first you must confess."

"To what? Not wearing my corset?"

Again Hyde-Gilbert flashed a smile that made Savannah feel like a small child. "You were coerced to the stable after midnight."

"Charles wouldn't know how to coerce."

"Not Charles. The other man."

"My knight?"

"Yes, that's the one."

"But he didn't—" Savannah felt like something began

to press hard on her chest. "That would be blaming an innocent man for something he didn't do."

"An innocent *dead* man."

Savannah leaned back in her chair very slowly. "I may have fibbed a few times in my life, but to lie outright? It seems a rather ominous way to begin a marriage."

Hyde-Gilbert lowered his voice. "I doubt the stakes have ever been so high for you or young Charles. Indeed, my uncle need never know that Charles Fairleigh exists. I will arrange accommodations for him. I know of a house near Ravenscar we can take for him. He will be well situated and you may see him as often as you wish, just as you had planned, in utter privacy. My uncle will go to his grave believing that a scoundrel attempted to seduce his bride and paid for his folly by dying in a stable fire. Your reputation will be preserved, your character untainted, your virtue beyond reproach, and best of all, the servants won't have anything to talk about. The earl will be satisfied that justice was done, and you will get your title. As for young Charles, he will be safe, grateful, and yours, just the way you want him."

Savannah tried very hard to think of an alternative, but her thoughts were tangled and Cecil so calmly reassuring. She needed reassurance now. She felt very much as if she'd been put to sea in a small boat without oars. She must think of poor Charles. What would happen to him if she didn't agree to Cecil's plans?

Indeed, what harm was there in falsely accusing a man if he was dead? None that she could think of. Poor man. Burned alive, saving the horses and her watch pin. A hero.

Cecil smiled at her and patted her hand in a way that her grandmother had patted her hand when her mother had scolded her for her wild ways. Yes, it made sense. It was, it seemed, the only way.

Dominic had been hunted in his youth. In New York he'd hidden in the maze of tenements and narrow alleys between brownstones. He remembered the smell of his skin perspiring beneath unwashed clothes, the deafening pounding of his pulse, the dry taste of fear in his mouth as he waited, crouched and trembling, sometimes for hours until dark. He knew when he was being hunted. It was a feeling he would never forget. Then his hunters had been the New York police determined to rid the city of pickpockets and immigrant thieves. Once his own padrone, an old Italian man who'd called himself his "grandfather" and kept Dominic in his basement apartment with him, had come after him for pocketing the proceeds from the sale of his corner charcoals. After catching him, his padrone had threatened to amputate his legs so he could bring more money begging. And to ensure that he never ran away again.

Hunted like a fox fleeing the hounds, only now it was Hyde-Gilbert's hounds that were set on his scent. He could almost hear their labored breathing as they came after him in the night. He'd sensed them even before he'd made his escape from the rear of the stable.

He lay on his belly in a dip of sodden grass and lifted his head. He saw nothing but black. Above the distant rush of waves smashing on rocks he could almost hear their footfalls thumping against the earth. Half a dozen of them, at least, half a mile back. Or was it fifty yards to the right?

Rain was falling, steady and straight. His fingers dug into soggy muck. Drops fell into his eyes, pelted his bare back.

Something had given him away. Bertrice? The girl?

The thought brought into his mind a full-blown image of her standing in the middle of the stable in bloomers. And the watch buried in his pocket seemed to press impatiently against his thigh. Clambering to his feet, he turned and something jabbed very hard into his belly. A pistol, he thought. Damn her. And then the world went black as pitch.

* * *

"Milord's steward drowned himself in that pond less than a year ago."

Savannah snapped the drapery closed and turned from the window. Her eyes met those of the sallow-faced servant introduced to her as the housekeeper, Mrs. Spiker. Judging by the lofty jut of the woman's nose, Mrs. Spiker considered herself the nobility of the servants' hall.

Savannah moved away from the window. The day beyond was murky. And the pond that filled her view—well, she could only wonder how they'd dredged up the poor steward through all the reeds choking the banks. A layer of green slime floated over the water. The Earl of Castellane's estate was in dire need of a gardener or two. The landscape needed color to warm it. Perhaps she'd have the pond drained and a field of violets planted there.

"Where is the milord?" She tried a dazzling smile on the stony-faced Mrs. Spiker. "I'm quite anxious to meet him."

Mrs. Spiker stared at her, severe, thin, and gray from head to toes, her white cap and apron starched and unyielding as vellum. Hands folded over her waist, eyes steady beneath a thick, gray sausage curl, she looked very mean, without one kind thought, and Savannah instantly decided the woman meant to intimidate her.

"We're to meet him now. You'll dress, of course."

"I am dressed."

Mrs. Spiker flung open the large armoire. Savannah watched her bony hand move over the row of brightly colored gowns.

"I've one in every shade except white," Savannah announced. "White makes me look like I'm dead."

Mrs. Spiker abruptly left the room. She returned carrying a dress of faded and wrinkled white silk. "You will wear this to meet milord." She tossed the dress on the bed.

Savannah's eyes swept over the torn and soiled hem,

the yellowed lace, the poorly mended rip in the bodice. A wedding dress.

"It was the countess's dress."

"How nice of the earl's mother—"

"It wasn't milord's mother's," Mrs. Spiker snapped as if Savannah had just said something sacrilegious. "It was Millicent's, milord's first wife."

"Ah. He had a wife."

"He had three."

"Three?"

"He was fondest of Millicent. He hasn't left the house since she died. Ten years ago this month."

"Ten years? It isn't healthy for anyone to lock themselves away from life because of grief."

Mrs. Spiker smiled a ghastly smile. "Ah. I see you don't know. Milord fell victim in a peculiar incident. He is not—welcomed outside of his home." Mrs. Spiker held up a length of lace. "You must wear the veil."

Savannah jarred a step back, bumped against the wall and went stiff. "What happened to wives one through three? As number four I think I'm entitled to know."

The house echoed with a high-pitched shriek that made the hairs on Savannah's arms stand straight up. "What was that?"

"Milord awaits." Mrs. Spiker clamped strong fingers around Savannah's upper arm and kept her up against the wall, an amazing feat considering Savannah's youth, vigor, and general dislike for being manhandled. Mrs. Spiker's upper lip, fringed with a thin line of black hairs, twitched into a grim smile. "The wives do what they're told to do at Ravenscar, Miss Merriweather. Milord asks very little of them beyond the reasonable."

"A pity they can't stay alive to enjoy it." Savannah tried again without success to shrug off Mrs. Spiker's grip. "I don't suppose you'll tell me how they all died."

"I believe it was poison, self-ingested. Except Millicent. She died giving birth to twins in this very room. The babies died as well. She bled so much she ruined the mattress." Mrs. Spiker draped the veil over her head and yanked the combs from Savannah's hair. It spilled over her shoulders and fell to her hips. "You look more like her now."

"Millicent was blond, was she?" Savannah asked, trying very hard not to believe that she'd entered a madhouse.

"They were all very young and pale like you. But thin and elegant whereas you are fat."

Savannah took the jab like a fireplace poker deep into her ribs. Damn. This wasn't going at all as she'd planned. She yanked the veil from her head as Mrs. Spiker turned and reached for the gown. "I'll meet the earl in my own clothes."

Mrs. Spiker turned sharply. "Then milord will not have you for his bride."

"That's ridiculous."

"Is it? Ridiculous is the young woman who will not do as she's told and finds herself turned out. Ridiculous is not knowing one's place."

"I know my place."

Mrs. Spiker's face went bleak as stone. "You are a rich American's daughter forced to buy a title to save the family name. It would be stupid to aspire to anything more. As much as milord might need your money to support himself now, do not once believe that he couldn't find another two dozen just like you where you come from. Put the dress on, Miss Merriweather. Milord is not content to be kept waiting. And neither is Mr. Hyde-Gilbert."

Savannah caught the dress against her belly and watched Mrs. Spiker leave the room.

Two babies and a mother had died in this room.

She turned to the window and saw the weeds choking the life from the pond where the steward had drowned himself. And in those slimy depths she saw her father's face deeply lined with disappointment.

She started to yank at the buttons of her gown. Why not do it? After all, who could blame a man for grieving the loss of his beloved first wife and babies? Poor man, tormented and alone, banished from his life outside of his home. Life must be awful with only Mrs. Spiker to offer care. Little wonder Bertrice was so anxious for female companionship at the estate.

Little wonder two young, blond, pale, and elegant women had poisoned themselves to death.

"In here." The voice belonged to Cecil Hyde-Gilbert, but Dominic couldn't see him. After his captors had knocked him unconscious, they'd beaten him up, gagged him, tied a sack over his head and to keep it there they'd looped a rope around his neck. They used the noose as a rein to yank him around the countryside. They'd used the same thick hemp to bind his wrists and ankles, leaving only enough slack for tiny steps. Hyde-Gilbert wasn't taking any chances on his escaping a second time.

They'd entered a very large house, judging by the echo of his boots on the floor. The place felt damp and musty as a cave. Something screeched and the echo seemed to go on for miles.

The rope yanked hard, testing Dominic's neck muscles. He fell to his knees on thick carpet. In a jail?

Someone murmured in hushed tones. The rope around his neck fell slack. An instant later the sack whooshed off his head.

Through swollen eyes he looked up at an enormous man seated in a large, thronelike chair. He was draped in a dressing gown of heavy, scarlet velvet. The pointed tips of red velvet slippers peeked from under the hem. His head was rimmed with a thin line of dark hair and was entirely hairless on top. His face was jowly, round, and ruddy. Tiny eyes seemed sunken in doughy flesh. His mouth was very small and unusually red and his nose abnormally wide, as if it had been broken many times and never set properly. He looked down it at Dominic with an air of odd disinterest, then stuck it in a glass of amber-colored liquid and gulped. On one shoulder perched an enormous black bird that cocked its head one way, then the other, and pierced Dominic with lifeless black eyes.

The man lowered the glass and began to coo to the bird in a queer, high-pitched tone.

A door opened behind Dominic. He heard rustling, like a woman's skirts. He was in a parlor, all shades drawn against the day. Odd place for a judge to be determining a man's fate. Odd-looking judge.

Dominic's head snapped up as a woman moved past him, dressed in a shabby wedding dress and heavy veil that concealed her face. Something about her struck Dominic, and not just the strangeness of it all. He glimpsed blond hair as she moved past and briefly looked at him from behind her veil. Something about the way she moved, the way he couldn't take his eyes from her as she paused in front of the man struck at all his senses with a gnawing familiarity. He expected her to speak but she didn't. She couldn't. He could almost feel the fear that choked her.

"Milord, your bride." A severe-looking woman appeared at the woman's side. She clamped one hand on the girl's arm as if to keep her from running and shoved her a step nearer to the man's chair. "Miss Savannah Rose Merriweather of New York."

Dominic went completely rigid. Hemp bit into his wrists. His mind flew. The spirited woman in the stable, the Madonna, Aphrodite, married to this man? Something was horribly wrong.

The man barely glanced at Savannah. "I can well see that. Cecil, again, do tell me the reason for this man's presence. He's bleeding on my Aubusson."

"Uncle Winthrop." Cecil swept from a far corner. "He's Dominic Dare, the brigand I told you about. I've caught him for you, Uncle."

Winthrop finally glanced away from his bird. He frowned slightly. "Ah, yes, now I remember. How clever of you, Cecil. What is the charge?"

"Attempted seduction, sir. Of your intended bride."

Savannah looked sharply at Hyde-Gilbert. Dominic thought he heard her hissing intake of breath and was certain she would have spoken the truth of it had it not been for the look Hyde-Gilbert gave her. Winthrop turned again to his bird. Dominic felt as if an invisible noose had begun to squeeze his neck.

"He's been wanted for theft and debauchery for over a year, Uncle. He stole Lady Hyde-Gilbert's Crimson Fire diamond necklace at the duke's ball last summer." Hyde-Gilbert turned a pompous look on Dominic. "It seems he's returned intent on defiling us all again. Of course, we can't allow it."

"Indeed. I do so hate being defiled." Winthrop's eyes darted from Dominic to Savannah. The color in his cheeks deepened to intense scarlet. "He looks every inch the blackhearted scoundrel. Tell me, was the seduction accomplished?"

"Indeed not! Miss Merriweather assures me of this. Of course, if you wish, we might have a physician examine her."

"Yes, we might." Winthrop stared at his intended bride with eyes that burned strangely. Dominic watched the man's gaze move slowly over Savannah and was gripped with a staggering desire to smash his fists into Winthrop's face. She was poured into the gown, and had the situation been any less strange, Dominic might have better enjoyed his rear vantage. And yet for all the reasons she had to cower, for all the insanity around her, Savannah stood straight, chin lifted, spirit intact. Dominic wondered how long that spirit would survive in such a place.

Winthrop sighed. "It seems we must do something with him. Is this the man?" he asked, looking hard at Savannah.

"Milord earl." The sound of her voice brought the memory of her in the stable flooding into Dominic's mind. "Actually, I'd rather call you Winthrop. Or is it Earl Twombley? I get very confused with this title business."

The earl and his bird both looked at her blankly. "Winthrop Twombley is my name. You may call me Castellane."

She hesitated. "I see. Castellane, then, though that makes even less sense to me. Nevertheless, I don't know Mr. Dare"—the veil swung out as she turned and looked at Dominic—"and I don't know anything about the jewel thievery and debauchery that's made Mr. Hyde-Gilbert so angry at him. I have to say I'm glad to see that he survived the stable fire. I know I wouldn't want to be burned to death. But I suppose I'd prefer that to having my—you know—cut off, and that's what Mr. Hyde-Gilbert said you would do to him, which seems rather extreme considering that he's not guilty of doing anything with it except—"

"What Miss Merriweather is saying," Hyde-Gilbert interrupted, "is that the punishment should fit the crime."

"No, that's not what I was saying." Savannah looked at Hyde-Gilbert. "You can't tell me there isn't a way to shut all the servants up about me in my bloomers without blaming a man for something he didn't—"

"My dear." Hyde-Gilbert's eyes glowed like hot embers. "Calm yourself."

"I am calm."

"Uncle, Miss Merriweather has yet to understand that in situations such as this an example must be set."

"Then flog him," Savannah said. "Or whatever it is captains do to sailors when they—hey! Ow! Mrs. Spiker, let go of my arm. I'm not finished. We're not savages here! Where's liberty? Where's the judge? I'm the only one here speaking reason—"

Heels scraping on the floor, voice echoing, Savannah

was dragged from the parlor by Mrs. Spiker with a good deal of help from a footman.

Winthrop Twombley, Earl of Castellane, cooed at his bird. "Did you get the money, Cecil?"

"Yes, Uncle. All two hundred fifty thousand, deposited in your account. Of course, Mrs. White took her ten percent."

"Twenty-five thousand pounds used to buy me a place at the Prince of Wales's faro table, Cecil."

"Yes, Uncle."

"I used to win at one time."

"Indeed you did, Uncle."

"They all thought I cheated. I used to say to them—remember me saying this?—why would a man cheat at the Prince of Wales's table, if getting caught would banish him from society? The scandal rocked the kingdom, wouldn't you say?"

"The entire kingdom, Uncle. Some still talk about it."

"Indeed. I suppose it's well and good enough to have known all the best people, even if they no longer care to know you." Castellane waved a pudgy hand at Dominic and yawned broadly. "Do what you will with him, Cecil."

"Indeed, Uncle, it will be my pleasure."

Chapter 4

When the house finally grew quiet enough to register the lone strike of a clock in the lower hall, Savannah left her room in search of Mr. Dare and descended into the bowels of the mansion. Gripping a candle in one hand, she groped along mildewed walls and beneath low beams until she reached a solid door. She lifted the latch and had to shove, hard. The heavy wood budged open mere inches, then groaned still. She squeezed through, tugging her dress when the hem caught on the door.

A musty smell hung heavy in air that was chilled and without comfort. She lifted the candle and saw him, the prisoner, a deeper shadow among shadows. He stood beyond a wall of bars in a cell barely large enough to accommodate him standing. He made no sound, registered no surprise, as if he knew she'd come tonight.

"You have no idea how difficult this was," she said, fishing into her pocket. "Making very little noise is extremely hard for me to do, especially when Mrs. Spiker could pop out at any moment. If it wasn't for Bertrice, I'd have been locked away in my room all night." She withdrew a long hatpin and held it up to the light by its pearled end. "I have Bertrice's assurances that this will work."

She moved to the cell and handed him his topcoat through the bars. "I believe this is yours." The wool was still damp and smelled of smoke. He didn't put it on, nor did he check the pockets. "Your wallet—it's there. I didn't touch it. But the handkerchief—I'm afraid Mr. Hyde-Gilbert took it. I'm—sorry."

He said nothing. She couldn't even hear his breaths. She lifted the candle closer, stuck the pin in the lock, and wiggled. "Nothing's happening." She frowned, wiggled again, poked harder, then froze when his hand closed over hers.

"Wait." He had an exceptionally low voice that seemed to rise up from deep beneath the stone floor. The darkness didn't help the sinister undertones. Neither did his size. Or the fact that he wore nothing to cover his torso. He seemed carved of heavy oak. She suddenly wished he'd put on his coat.

Savannah jerked her wrist as if a bothersome fly had landed on it. Only his hand was much larger and much heavier than a fly and it didn't budge. "I'm sorry, Mr. Dare, but I'm freeing you, even if you don't care to be freed." She looked up at him and saw only shadows. But she smelled him, an earthy, loamy scent as if he'd rolled in warm, rain-kissed soil. "It's because of me that you're in here, and we both know you did nothing to deserve this, at least not recently enough to satisfy me. I thought you died in the fire. Not that I wanted you to die, but Cecil made it sound rather convenient if you had. You see, we needed some explanation for servants talking about me in my bloomers; otherwise everything would have been ruined. You saved my life and now I'm saving yours."

"Are you?"

"I have a plan."

"You have many."

"Don't all women?"

"Gentle," he said, lifting his hand.

She took a breath, eased the pin in the lock, wiggled, twisted, and blew a wisp from her eyes. "Damn. Bertrice made this sound easy. She picked a lock once with this very same hatpin. In a London jail. And it worked."

"Brave woman."

"Well, of course she was. She was freeing her lover."

"Her lover." Not a question. Not a statement.

Savannah's tongue worked slowly along the edge of her upper lip as she probed with the hatpin. She ignored a blond curl that fell past her forehead and dangled over her nose. "Well, she didn't exactly say he was her lover but—" She lifted a shoulder, inclined her head, and gave a shrug she'd perfected in France. "When a woman has tasted passion like that, she's capable of great bravery. I know these things."

"Ah. You're quite brave yourself."

"Indeed I am."

"But we're not lovers."

The hatpin fell to the floor. "Damn." Savannah dropped to her knees. She lay the candle holder aside and skimmed her hands over the damp floor, fingers probing slimy crevices.

"Watch the candle," he said, on his knees beyond the bars.

Their hands collided. Savannah spun in the opposite direction and groped along the floor.

"Where's your Charles?"

His question caught her off guard. "He survived his encounter with the stable. Cecil has taken care of him."

"While you sell yourself to Castellane."

She glanced over her shoulder at him. He'd stopped searching and was on his haunches, watching her. "You're rather impertinent for a prisoner."

"Just curious. How does a recluse like Castellane, who cheats and swindles and is poorer than my great-grandmother, entice an American heiress to marry him?"

"He needs my money. I need his title."

"You're throwing away your life."

"I don't look at it quite that way, Mr. Dare."

"Neither did Bertrice, I suspect."

Savannah suddenly wished the light were better so that she could see his face.

"Why didn't the brave Bertrice come instead?" He sounded as if he already knew the answer.

"I was lucky to get her to speak to me about this. She winced when I even whispered my scheme."

"That afraid of him, is she?"

Savannah swallowed. "Bertrice is a strong woman."

"She's a broken woman. The husband she once thought she needed stripped her of her spirit. Now she's forced to pick locks to free men she thinks she loves." He stood, curled one arm through the bars, and candlelight glinted off the pin he held. He inserted it in the lock until the latch softly clicked. The cell door creaked open.

Savannah scrambled to get to her feet, caught her heel in her hem, and would have fallen to her knees if he hadn't caught her by the arm.

"Easy," he said, as if coaxing a skittish animal.

Skittish. Yes. Instinct screamed at her to get away from him the instant the doors fell open and nothing separated him from her.

"It was you." Her voice sounded thick. "In London. You were the man Bertrice freed."

"Yes, I was."

"Everything Cecil said about you—it was true."

He was staring into her eyes, holding her with very little effort extremely close against him so that she smelled the remnants of smoke on his skin. "Something tells me you thrive on titillation and adventure, Miss Merriweather, a bit of the wicked and unexpected. You enjoy making the servants talk."

"And if I do?"

"Why marry Castellane and sentence yourself to hell?

Why not marry Charles? He would make for a much better husband than he would a lover."

She couldn't disagree with him. And yet she felt compelled to jerk her chin up. "I'm not Bertrice. I have snap and energy, heaps and heaps of vulgar energy. If I set myself to it I could even charm Mrs. Spiker."

"Yes, I don't doubt that you could. But the earl would never make you happy. And women like you—" His voice broke off, husky, and deep, and edged with something that sent a quiver up her spine. His fingers gripped harder around her arm. "What's Cecil holding over you?"

A sharp burst of anger fired in her breast. She yanked on her arm. "It's not Cecil."

"The hell it isn't. He's perhaps the only man in England poorer than Castellane. Ravenscar's a damned fine place to hide out from creditors—at least in the short term. He's unfortunate enough to be married to a woman who will inherit a minuscule part of a very large fortune and watch the rest of it go to her older brother. Unless Cecil does something quickly, he could end up in debtor's prison or dead. But as Castellane's heir, he's destined to get every penny of your money unless Castellane plants his seed in your belly. And we all know that's impossible."

Her gasp echoed around them. Her cheeks started to throb. Somehow the words, coming from him, struck her like the stinging slap of her mother's palm. She stiffened as he lowered his head and looked straight into her eyes.

"Cecil needed a very rich, very desperate woman. Only that kind of woman would agree to marry a monster. Why in God's name did you?"

Savannah swallowed. A monster. Yes, she couldn't help but think of Castellane in those terms. "I'm—" She looked away, horrified that this virtual stranger could touch emotions she'd thought she'd buried beneath heaps of snap and vigor and love for her father. "It's not the money. I have to come back to New York with a title or my family—my father—will be ruined."

He took a moment to consider this. "I know of a half-dozen men of title who would offer for your hand."

"But none that would forgive a tarnished name."

"You might be surprised."

"Really? I have it from a very greedy woman named Mrs. White, who is in the business of knowing such things, that there isn't a man in all of England, except Castellane, who would forgive my father for taking his relief in Mrs. Astor's parlor fireplace."

"Mrs. Astor's fireplace." Was that amusement coloring his tone? He didn't seem the sort that would find humor easy to come by.

Still, she relaxed just a bit. "My mother is determined that I return with a title so that Mrs. Astor will invite her to lunch."

"Ah, lunch. A simple meal, taken every day."

"Oh, this lunch is extremely important. It will tell the world—and you know there is no world beyond the New York Four Hundred—that all is forgiven—that is, regarding the fireplace."

"You've other sins that need forgiving?"

"Me? Mr. Dare, I'm a good daughter."

"You bear more resemblance to a sacrificial lamb, but then again I've known too few heiresses to recognize a good one. You've no brothers to repair the family name? No sisters to help?"

"None. Our entry into New York society depends entirely on me, and Castellane, of course."

"Of course. The title. The man or his character matter very little. Here—" With one hand he tugged the door open and guided her into the hall beyond. "I expected Cecil to be keeping watch."

"Oh, he intended to, but Bertrice took care of that. She planned to give him something in his wine and then—you know—join him and—you know—"

"No, I don't know. Do you?"

Savannah shot him a sideways glance as they moved quickly toward the stairs. "Of course I know."

"Ah."

Damn, but he sounded as if he knew she lied. No matter how many French novels she'd read, Savannah still had too many confusing notions about what exactly went on behind closed bedchamber doors when wives took wine to their husbands.

Just as she lifted her skirts to mount the steps, he caught her arm. "Wait. This is too easy."

"It is?"

"Cecil is no fool."

"Oh, yes, of course. Greedy but not foolish. You can't just walk out of the front door of the house, can you? Perhaps there's another way out from down here. You know, a secret staircase."

"Wouldn't that be convenient? But hell, smugglers along this coast used secret passages years ago to bring in the spoils of scuttled ships. Rum from Spain, jewels from India, spices from the Orient. But you already knew that when you came up with your scheme to free me."

"I—" Savannah flashed a smile. "Why, yes, I did. Here. I'll help you look."

"No." Again, the pressure of his hand on her arm stopped her. He turned her to face him and she was again aware of his uncommon size, and how ominous it made him, especially with his voice rumbling like the low growl of a bear. "Go back to your room and pack your things."

"What?"

"Get it all into something I can carry. Then meet me behind the stable."

"And why the devil would I do that?"

"Because, Miss Merriweather, you're a risk taker perhaps just a bit more than a good daughter should be. What if I told you you could have everything you want without marrying Castellane?"

Her heartbeat tripped along a touch faster in spite of herself. "What are you proposing, Mr. Dare?"

"Meet me behind the stable in fifteen minutes with your bags."

"You can't kidnap me," she warned him.

"I won't have to." He took her hand, pressed something into it, turned and was instantly swallowed by darkness.

She opened her hand and found her watch pin.

Dominic peeked through a window at the rear of the stable. A lantern hanging from a wall hook illuminated the interior of the stable. A stable hand snored on a stool propped against one wall. Not surprisingly, most of the stalls were empty. Horses, servants, and wives, and not necessarily in that order, were usually the first casualty of a man's gambling excesses. Dominic was still surprised that Castellane had any animals to his name. He spotted a chestnut and two matched roans. He decided on the chestnut. The roans might still be winded from their trip from the inn. And neither looked broad-chested enough to carry two people any distance.

Two people. Until he could hire a coach.

He skirted the stable, keeping in the shadows thrown by a half moon. He paused at the stable door and glanced at the house. All the windows were dark. But beyond one of them, a desperate, reckless young woman stuffed gowns into a bag.

She would come. Logic demanded it. His scheme depended on it. There would be no kidnapping tonight.

And by the time the adventurous and spirited Savannah Merriweather realized desperation and duty had seen her from one trap into another, she would be in far too deep ever to escape.

Until he let her.

* * *

With valise held tight in one hand, Savannah eased her bedchamber door closed and took two tiptoed steps down the hall when she realized she'd forgotten her red shoes with the three-inch heels. No adventure could be properly enjoyed without her red shoes. Her mother hated the shoes. Perhaps that was why Savannah loved them so much.

Enough to risk turning back.

She found them in the bottom of her armoire with the corsets she would leave behind. She stuffed the shoes into her bulging valise, managed to secure the latch, and again started down the hall on tiptoes.

The walls seemed to press in around her. The ghosts of the dead wives and the drowned steward whispered to her in the silence.

Run . . . run. . . .

She quickened her step. The staircase loomed in view. Her path stretched before her, lit by frothy moonlight spilling through the windows. She was breathless, her heart a hammer pounding in her chest.

She was fleeing on a stranger's promise. No, not even a promise. Mere temptation from a man who was a self-proclaimed jewel thief and wife seducer. A man who smelled as if he'd sprung up from the earth.

"Miss Merriweather. What are you doing?"

Savannah froze at the top of the stairs, one hand gripping at the railing. Over her shoulder she saw Mrs. Spiker moving toward her from down the hall, slowly at first, then quicker, as if she realized Savannah's intent. The servant wore thin white nightclothes that outlined every jutting bone of her body. The light of the candle she held made her look as if all the blood had been drained from her.

"Stop!" Mrs. Spiker screeched. "No one leaves Ravenscar!"

Except the dead.

Savannah turned and flew down the stairs. She stumbled once, caught herself against the rail, then half tripped down two more stairs. She managed the rest with her skirts hiked to her knees. As if flames were licking at her heels, she ran across the foyer toward the door. And then suddenly Cecil Hyde-Gilbert blocked her path, arms splayed in his silk robes, a look of disbelief twisting his face.

He swiped one arm to catch her. "Shameful girl! No one leaves Ravenscar. You'll be ruined!"

She skidded on the marble, clumsily sidestepped him, then hefted her valise and swung it at him. It was a wild shot, badly aimed, for Savannah was no athlete, but the delivery was passionate and therefore infinitely more punishing. Cecil took the blow fully against the side of his head. He swore and slumped to one knee.

Savannah dashed around him, jerked open the door, and burst into the night air. She stumbled down the porch steps, lost one shoe, kicked off the other, then ran around the side of the house toward the stables. An enormous shadow suddenly loomed from out of the darkness. She shrieked.

"Christ." Dare caught her around the waist with one arm. "Quit screaming. We're not safe yet."

"It's Cecil—" She gasped, unable to catch her breath. Pain sliced through her chest. "He's coming. You have to go now—"

Dare grabbed hold of her waist and lifted her as he turned. She thunked down hard on a horse's back. An ominous tearing sound came from her skirts as her legs were forced astride. Dare mounted up behind her, thighs gripping hard around hers.

"Did I say I was going with you? Mr. Dare!"

"Hang on." He shoved her valise into her belly. The horse leapt forward, and Savannah would have fallen if he hadn't been behind her.

He headed straight for the stable. "Let's make this hard on our friend Cecil." He steered the horse through the doorway, leaned over to unlatch the stall doors, and threw them wide, freeing the remaining horses. In one of the empty stalls, Savannah spotted a stable hand, bound and gagged, watching them. Dare reined the chestnut around and chased the horses across a field of grass that rippled like ocean waves in the moonlight.

A half-mile farther they reached a dirt road that stretched for miles to the horizon. Dare drove the horse at a punishing pace. He seemed to know the countryside well, cutting across fields, choosing lesser-traveled roads, keeping to the shadows thrown by brush and trees.

Of course, he knew how to do this well. He'd fled England once before.

Savannah closed her eyes against the bite of wind, the bone-deep jarring of her body, and became slowly, inevitably aware of the strength in the man behind her. His body curved around hers, almost like a shield. One arm anchored around her waist was all that kept her on the horse as he bent deep into turns and zigzagged around fallen branches. How easy it would be to feel safe and protected. But she couldn't allow herself that luxury, not with this man.

Dare was an exceptional rider. An exceptional thief.

An exceptional seducer of married women.

What felt like an eternity passed before they drew up in the yard of a posting inn. All was quiet, the sky black as pitch. Hours had passed.

Dare dismounted and looped the horse's reins around a post. "I'll inquire about hiring a coach."

Savannah could hardly argue. "Yes, a coach. With a bed." She slumped forward against the horse's neck and closed her eyes.

What seemed like moments later, Dare jerked her awake. "Come inside. We have to be quick."

Savannah's bare feet touched ground and her legs instantly turned to water. Dare caught her as she fell and lifted her in his arms.

"Not much of an athlete, are you?" he said, heading for the inn.

"The innkeeper will get the wrong idea if you carry me in," Savannah replied, keeping both hands planted on her valise and her valise tight against her chest. She couldn't look up at him. "He'll think we're lovers."

"He thinks you're my wife."

"Your wife? I will be nothing but cool and cordial with you, Mr. Dare. Will he believe it then?"

"Definitely. And the colder you are, the more convincing a wife you'll be."

Savannah couldn't argue. Her own parents' relationship was frosty. Rare was the occasion when they displayed warmth or affection for one another. Theirs had become a typical New York marriage, more like a business partnership, with each leading a separate life. Savannah often wondered if such an arrangement could possibly be satisfying for either of them.

With deeply felt chagrin she noticed the innkeeper's sly smile as Dare marched through the common room; she had to close her eyes. But when Dare's boots thumped on stairs she snapped them open.

"I'm not going up there with you."

"I could leave you down here. But there's a bed up there."

"I know. That's the problem."

"And food. Warm wine."

Savannah's mouth watered. "Wine, you say?"

"Mulled and spicy. You'll sleep the entire way to London."

"Is that where you think you're taking me?"

"For starters. Can you stand?" He paused at the end of a hall in front of a closed door. He set her bare feet to the floor and steadied her with his hands at her waist. The door swung open and Savannah saw a bed glowing in soft candlelight.

Her knees tightened against the nudge of his hand at

the base of her spine. "Tell me why I should trust you."
She wanted reassurances. She wanted him to tell her he
went to church every Sunday and visited his mother once
a week. She wanted him to tell her he hadn't seduced
Bertrice out of her necklace.

He said, "Have you any choice?"

She swallowed and wrapped the valise tighter in her
arms.

He nudged and she scooted several paces into the
room. The door thudded closed. Savannah scurried to a
small table and jerked a glass of red wine to her lips. It
tumbled down her throat in a warm torrent.

"Easy." He took the glass from her and lowered his
head to look straight into her eyes. She sank her teeth into
her lower lip. His face was thrown into unidentifiable
shadows and angles, his eyes golden pinpoints of light.
She saw a quiver pass over the heavy line of his brows.
"You don't scare easily, Miss Merriweather."

"No, I don't. But I believe I'm getting there."

"Relax. Cecil is hours behind us, even if he knew exactly where to look." He touched her shoulder and she
flinched. He backed off a pace and turned to the door.
"Rest and eat. The coach should be ready within the
hour."

"And when we get to London?"

"You'll be free to go back to Castellane if you wish."

"That simple."

"No, I don't believe it will be."

Chapter 5

Their hired coach was ready in just over an hour. It was an impressive black conveyance, comfortably appointed, with four matched chestnuts at the fore, a driver and footman. If the weather held they'd reach London by midmorning.

But Dominic wasn't anywhere near satisfied. His impatience festered like an open sore. He'd be damned if he left London without the information he'd come for. Even if he was a twice-wanted man, saddled with a woman who went nowhere quickly or silently.

Watching her shimmy onto the seat opposite him, he reminded himself that she'd demonstrated an astonishing knack for fouling up the best of plans. Particularly if they hinged on her. And wise or not, he was about to make certain that they did.

He worked his neck against the stiff celluloid collar of one of the shirts he'd bought from the innkeeper. She was looking out the window, lips pouty from wine, eyes unblinking, chin just inches above the extravagant upper swells of her breasts. She was squeezed into a dress the color of burnt oranges and wore a matching hat that looked like a squashed orange cabbage with a feather poking out of it that swayed over her forehead. With every lurch of wheels over road she became a bouncing feast of cabbage leaves, blond curls, white breasts. . . .

He shifted in his seat and swung his gaze to the windows. Her doe-eyed reflection looked back at him as if from a framed canvas. Which obsession ruled him at the moment—the avenger or the artist?

"Sorry," she said, after kicking him in the shin. She shimmied again, looked down at her lap, and drew a deep breath. Dominic could almost hear the seams in her bodice screaming. Or was that the sound of his own carnal lusts, dueling with the darker side of his nature, the part of him that intended to use her for his own devices, just as he'd used women many times before?

He couldn't remember wanting to paint any of them with this kind of restless desperation.

"What did you know of Castellane?" he threw out, again shifting for comfort, again getting a toe stabbed in his shin. "Before you arrived in London."

"The paper said he was an earl."

Dominic waited. The dim lantern light glinted off the gold watch pinned over her left breast.

She shrugged as if she didn't give a damn about anything, which wasn't possible for such a passionate creature. "We knew all we needed to know about him to arrange the marriage. He had a title. This sort of thing is done all the time, Mr. Dare."

"That doesn't make it good for you."

She looked at him very hard. "No, it doesn't. But neither of us is much enamored of always doing what's good for us, are we? For me"—she looked down at one hand fussing with a button on the wrist of her orange kid glove—"my responsibilities to my family have always come first."

"Family should be the center of one's life. No bond— hell, no allegiance to king or country could be stronger."

She looked up at him as if his views surprised her. "Yes. Yes, I quite agree. I had responsibilities in Ohio. But they were different. My whole life was different—slower. Things were simple then."

"The past always seems simpler."

"Well, there weren't these blasted rules. I feel penned up like a sheep. It just gets so suffocating sometimes, and I feel like I'll burst if I have to behave a certain way just because some book says that's what 'ladies' do. Tell me how I'm supposed to live the rest of my life without talking above a whisper, without running because I might be in a hurry, or gesturing with my arms because I must to express myself?"

"I know I couldn't do it."

"Well, of course you couldn't. But you've no desire to be a lady. Ladies don't do any of those things. They don't argue or contradict or show anger. They must seem helpless no matter how capable they might be. They can't be intellectual. Ladies, Mr. Dare, are like a crystal-clear pool, quiet, cool, uncontaminated, life-giving. No wind can disturb their deep serenity. They do not sweat. They have a form, no body. Below their waists they're only frilly white petticoats. To be a lady is to quiet the hot, hasty, sweaty male. But you don't understand any of that, do you?"

She didn't lift her eyes, obviously expecting no reply. She thought him incapable of empathizing with her. After all, he was just another hot, hasty, sweaty male. And yet she'd come with him into the ominous unknown.

She was dutiful beyond anyone's expectations of a millionaire's daughter, but perhaps just a bit more reckless.

And swimming in indecision. Which made her quite perfect.

"Tell me about this plan of yours, Mr. Dare. I believe I risked a great deal to hear it."

There was a subtle lift to her nose that he'd seen on every well-dressed woman promenading down Fifth Avenue. It labeled her, and though he might not warm to it, it pleased him. For all her suffragist notions and Midwest roots, she would blend exceptionally well into any New York society drawing room or, for that matter, any private art gallery.

She was, in spite of herself, one of them.

Dominic leveled his tone. "Castellane has been in seclusion for over ten years. It wasn't the wife's death that confined him. He was caught cheating at cards at the Prince of Wales's table."

"Is that bad?"

"Bad enough to get him thrown out of society. I'm sure the prince made certain of it. No gentry suffers cheating at his own table without bearing some of the blame. The scandal must have rocked London."

"Ah, this part of the story you don't know?"

"I spent a good deal of time mingling in London social circles recently. I know my share but not everything." Dominic leaned slightly forward and dropped his voice. "No one beyond Ravenscar's walls would know Castellane if they saw him, particularly on another continent. He could be the fellow at the next table. The man driving this coach. He could even be, say, me."

"You? You're—" She did a quick summation of his torso with her eyes and blossomed a glorious shade of pink, starting at the deepest point of her décolletage. He heard her swallow, or was that him, trying to catch his breath?

She sniffed dismissively. "You're an American. You don't talk British properly."

"I've learned how to Americanize my speech, Miss Merriweather. I can just as easily make it British."

"Is that so? Let me hear something un-American."

Dominic didn't think to hesitate as he so often had in the past. *"Tanti belli cosi."*

He could almost feel her blood warming. "What does it mean?"

"I wish you many beautiful things." He heard the huskiness in his voice and in that instant damned her for being too beautiful, too responsive, damned himself for reacting to it. He should have said something British, something German, something dripping with his friend Bonnie's Irish brogue. Not his mother tongue. Italian love words made women weep with passion.

"Who are you?" She was staring at him.

His face went cold as stone, his lids drooped slightly, and his tongue curled around the words like a pompous English aristocrat's. "Winthrop Twombley, Earl of Castellane."

She blinked. "That was very good. Quite amazing. You must have had lessons."

"Several." Years of lessons. They'd cost him a fortune.

"To forget the Italian?"

Their eyes met. His pulse fired. She was quick. Perhaps too quick. "I'll never forget it."

"But you don't wish to wear it, is that it?"

"Something like that."

"You were born there?"

"In Sicily."

"Dare." She watched him, as if it was all there for her to read. "That's not your family name, is it? You changed it."

"Yes." Why had he answered? Because she was everything soft and cajoling. A man could forget who he was. He could even forget his reasons for doing all that he'd done, especially since he knew what she looked like under all that orange silk. It was impressed on his memory as if rendered in vibrant oils.

"I can accompany you to New York, Miss Merriweather," he said slowly. "I can be your Castellane."

Her face went still. "You mean impersonate him?"

"Think about it. No one in England has seen him in over ten years. He's unknown in New York. No one would have reason to suspect that I'm not who I say I am, your husband, the earl. You'll arrive with your title." He dangled the last bit like a fat bunch of grapes and watched her lick her lips. "And your mother can have her lunch."

For several moments she stared at him, her breaths agitating the ruches running along her bodice. "Yes, Mother needs to have lunch with Mrs. Astor or Papa is doomed. But deceive my parents like that? Papa would know the minute he looked at me."

"Your father spent over two hundred fifty thousand dollars for a title. What do you intend to do when you arrive in New York without one? What do you think he'll do? Send you back?"

She chewed at her lip and glanced at the window as the coach bounced over a deep rut. Dominic stared at her small hand pressed to her breasts. She looked startlingly young. Something twisted in his gut, but he ignored it.

"In my home, Mr. Dare, failure is regarded as the one unpardonable crime. Success, be it business or personal, is the one all-redeeming virtue. The acquisition of social position has been the only aim of my life since we came to New York. To fail in my part of it after my father's worked so hard to get where he is—no, I couldn't do that to my family." Still she looked at him with guarded eyes. "You want something."

"It's never been good business to rescue young women from awkward situations without expecting some token of appreciation."

Her eyes pulsed a fraction wider and she seemed to press deeper against the seat, which made him want to lean forward and take her hand and reassure her of things that he couldn't reassure her of. It all baffled him.

He toyed with his cuff to busy his hands. "Miss Merriweather—"

"I can't marry you, Mr. Dare."

He stared at her. "We don't need to get married."

"But if you pretend to be my husband, we'll have to do things that married people do. Like share a bed."

"Wait a minute—"

"My parents don't sleep in the same room."

"Ah. Very good."

"So it's not required. But to present the illusion—"

"Not of happiness surely?"

"Good gracious no! Married people aren't happy. But they're intimate."

"Some are both." He was thinking of his parents in the small town near Florence where they'd lived before the end of the revolution had come. He'd been very young at the time, but he'd been aware that his father had left his oils and canvases at the Café Michelangelo every afternoon to visit his mother at home. Sometimes they'd gone upstairs. They'd been happy, passionately so. But that same passion had manifested itself in a political unrest in his father that even his mother couldn't control. It had cost his father a magnificent career and all of them their lives. All but Dominic. He'd been left to find his parents, his sister and grandparents with them, lying in rivers of blood in the kitchen where his mother had cooked his meals.

Dominic forced the thoughts from his mind with a chilling efficiency. "An illusion of intimacy can be created, Miss Merriweather. But it can remain an illusion." He forced his lips to soften. "You have my word on that. Your virtue will remain unblemished."

She still looked doubtful. "Then what do you want from me?"

Dominic couldn't help but lean forward in his seat. "Access. To the New York Four Hundred on a social level. Once you return with your title, you'll have it."

Her brows quivered. "Yes, I suppose I will. Once Mother has her lunch and we get called upon. Then we'll be invited to all the lunches and dinners." Her eyes narrowed and she looked every inch capable of scheming something very naughty. "What could you possibly gain by becoming one of them? What could anyone? The Four Hundred"—her laugh was almost too bitter for one so young—"where half the fun of it is getting in and the rest is keeping someone else out. To be in it is merely a bore, to be out of it, simply a tragedy. Are you sure that's what you want, Mr. Dare?"

"Completely sure, Miss Merriweather."

"You don't seem concerned with stature. I doubt you'd like any of them. No, this is all business to you—" She suddenly gasped, but it was a delighted sound, and her eyes popped wide and her smile dazzled as if she'd just discovered something wonderful. "Oh, Mr. Dare, you mean to steal all their jewels."

"I can assure you I don't." Only he wasn't sure if that's what she wanted to hear. Her smile wavered and her eyes lost their mischievous, mesmerizing glitter. He found himself searching for something to say to bring it all back, then caught himself. Damned ridiculous woman. One more of those smiles and he'd spill it all out for her like a man who'd drunk himself silly enough to believe a willful young girl worthy of his most precious trust. His secrets were the kind he'd never part with. Still, it was plain that Miss Merriweather wasn't as enamored of the Four Hundred as a dutiful little heiress should be.

Perhaps she would understand his reasons. A woman who'd freed a thief, then run off with him in the night was capable of a great many things. Perhaps . . .

He grunted with self-disgust and set his teeth, hard. "For your own protection you'll know nothing of the details."

"It's something illegal, isn't it? Something dangerous."

"You won't be in a moment's harm."

"Oh, God, I knew it. And if I refuse?"

His smile was cold. "Go back and marry Castellane. I'm certain you could charm them into forgiving a young bride of prewedding nerves. A few contrite pouts and Cecil Hyde-Gilbert will be more than happy to take your annual allowance."

Her throat jerked with a noisy swallow, but she seemed

to force herself to sit up an inch taller. "At least then he won't be after me. Have you considered that he'll follow us to New York and expose you for the impostor that you are?"

"I've never met anyone eager to admit they were deceived, Miss Merriweather. Least of all the socially elite. Even if Hyde-Gilbert comes after us—supposing he would know where to look and could convince someone to listen to him—would he risk his two hundred fifty thousand to expose me? Not likely. I'd lay odds he's far more greedy than he is vengeful. Even if I'm wrong, it's a risk I'm willing to take."

She looked down at her hands in her lap and fidgeted with the loose thread. "I've never lied to my father, Mr. Dare. Well, that's not quite true. I met Charles once in a bookshop on Seventh Avenue. We arranged it, of course, but Mother was right there, on the other side of a shelf of books while we whispered and held hands and—" She blinked up at him, caught herself, and flushed. "I later told my mother I'd met a friend—a girl, of course. Mother hated Charles. She told me not to fall in love with one of the people-we-don't-know like Charles. But that only made me want to love him even more. You understand, of course."

"Of course."

"That night at dinner with my father I made up a horrible story about the girl I'd supposedly met at the bookshop. I couldn't stop talking, and the lie just kept getting bigger and bigger. I finally had to leave the table, before dessert. And I never leave the table without having dessert. But I had to lie. I couldn't disappoint my father. He has no sons, you see."

"Ah. A damned good reason to lie if I've ever heard one."

"Of course it is. How awful is it for a man to have no sons and only one wild, willful daughter who can't seem to make herself behave? It's mortifying. It will kill him."

"No man has yet died of mortification, Miss Merriweather."

"Of course they have. Dr. Pelton dropped dead two days after his daughter Milly was caught in a closet with a footman at Mrs. Vanderbilt's dinner party last June." She wagged a finger at him. "Mortification, Mr. Dare. It kills men every day in New York City. They just don't tell anyone. They call it heart failure."

Dominic felt his lips twitch. "You make being an heiress sound difficult."

"Isn't it? I have to marry a man I don't know and truly don't like to save the family name. I attend lunches and balls and try to talk to boring people who have nothing to say and think I'm far too outspoken for my own good. I can't do anything I want."

"Little wonder. An heiress hardly has the time to inaugurate a rebellion the likes of which the world has never seen before." He met her astonished look with a quirk of one brow. "Setting women's bound spirits free takes time and energy and a good deal of freedom—something you haven't had in quite some time, if ever."

Anger brightened her eyes. "You were spying on me in the stable."

"No, I was sleeping there. You and Charles woke me up. I could hardly interrupt such an impassioned speech, could I?"

She blinked three times, then jerked her eyes to the window.

Dominic leaned forward and touched the top of her hand where a spray of scalloped lace cuff lay upon the orange kid. She stiffened but didn't pull away. "I can give you the freedom to live your life by your own rules." He felt as if he coaxed a skittish animal from its den, or a shy young woman out of her clothes. Satisfaction leapt through him when she looked at him. The spark of interest in her eyes was unmistakable.

"For all outward appearances we will be husband and

wife," he continued, "living together under the same roof, mingling together in society. A picture of domesticity. But beyond that, you'll be free to come and go as you please. You can pursue your suffragist inclinations. Hell, you can even take a lover."

He expected some kind of sputtering indignation but he didn't get it, only a keen narrowing of her eyes as if she hatched a dozen of her own little schemes in her head. "I abandoned both my corset and Charles at Ravenscar."

"Odd you've spoken of him," he heard himself say, wondering even as he did if she sincerely intended to take the bumbling young man into her bed. "If he loves you as he believes he does, he'll find you. I wouldn't want to stand in the way of true love, Miss Merriweather."

"Very good then. We'll give it six months."

"Six months." He stared at her, jarred to his bones by the ease of his victory. Or was it her decisiveness that rocked him? He could almost believe that the sputtering Charles would have attained the same ease of conquest. "Then you agree."

"On the terms you promised, yes, I believe I do." She stuck out her hand. "We have to shake on it, of course."

"Of course." He grasped her hand, not the least surprised that she pumped his with the energy of a strong young man.

"Freedom," she said, as if saying it set it in stone. "And of course, no—you know—breaching of my—"

"Yes, of course. None of that."

"Or the arrangement is off."

"You should have no fears on that score, Miss Merriweather."

"Very good, then." She smiled and settled back against the corner of the seat, shimmying to get just the right spot. She laid one hand beneath her breasts and touched her fingers to her lips as she yawned. "I'm going to sleep now, Mr. Dare. Wake me when we get to London, will you?"

And with that she closed her eyes and was sound asleep within moments.

"Miss Merriweather."

Savannah opened her eyes. A man with very blue eyes and an exceptionally dark and ominous brow peered at her from beneath the cabbage leaves of her hat. It had slipped lower over her eyes the farther she'd slid down in her seat as she'd slept. She'd obviously slept well and deep despite the cramped coach. Her legs were stretched out and sprawled open. One knee poked right between the thighs of the man on the seat opposite her, so deep the tip of her knee touched something. The seat? No, the seat was cushy and soft and this was hard.

She jerked up, slamming her legs together, and her hat slid over her nose. "Damn," she said. She drew it off, began to smooth her hair, and glanced up. She swallowed and felt her belly flip over. He was even larger and darker and more sinister-looking in the daylight than he was on a moonlit night. He didn't look anything like a knight. He looked like a warrior. "Mr. Dare, you look different in the light."

"So do you."

His voice was deeply unsettling. It sounded as if he'd slept too, with his thighs spread open and her knee deep between them. It sounded intimate.

Savannah poked her face close to the window and directly into a spray of morning sunlight. "Where are we?"

"London. The business district. We have to make one stop here before we catch our ship."

This surprised her. "You've already booked us passage?"

The curve of his lips held no mirth. "We're going on the first ship we can get, Miss Merriweather."

"And yet you dawdle here." She awaited his reply and watched him touch the knot tied high at his throat. For so powerfully built a man his hands were strangely elegant, something about his fingers suggesting gentleness, refinement, not violence, debauchery. She frowned at him. "You won't tell me anything, is that it?"

"I'm glad we understand each other. But I'm not about to leave you alone, either. Are you ready?"

"I'm going with you?"

"Think of it as practice. You're a countess. You should walk like one." He lifted the handle and shoved open the door.

Savannah put on her hat and fussed with the feather to keep it out of her eyes but it refused to comply. She released a hissing breath. "I haven't even had my cup of chocolate for the morning. How can I be expected to walk like a countess? Oh, fine—" She scowled at his extended hand, realized he offered her no choice, and let him help her from the coach. But as she did, she immediately questioned her wisdom in abandoning her corset so soon.

In France, she'd enjoyed a wonderful freedom of movement without it. But in London, she could hardly expect to wear immodestly cut gowns and bend over to get out of coaches without anything to restrain her. It was like trying to keep leaping puppies contained.

"Good heavens." She jerked upright beside him, one hand fluttering like a butterfly at her chest, and glanced up at Dare. With some relief she found him looking off down the street, eyes narrowed against the sun, mouth hard and set. He looked so formidable she had to catch her breath.

"What were you doing sleeping in the stable?" she asked.

"This way." He offered his arm and started off down the street at a pace obviously not intended to accommodate her.

Savannah clamped one hand on her hat to keep it on her head and huffed along beside him. He was becoming increasingly unlikable, and in the cold light of day their scheme tasted far from sweet on her tongue. She reminded herself that she had other options . . . though at the moment, and without her cup of chocolate to rouse her, she couldn't think of any. But she would, very soon, she was certain.

"Boothby's." She craned her neck to read the large sign over the door they paused in front of. An instant later Dare swept her inside in front of him. She felt like a ship blown along before a hurricane's wind, sails full and billowing, incapable of stopping, mere moments from sinking.

The room they entered was quiet, its desks and tables deserted, the hour still early for conducting business. Several of the more ambitious clerks mingled about. The smell of coffee laced the air and made Savannah's mouth water. But Dare had no interest in either coffee or her appetites. And he obviously knew where he was going. He didn't stop to ask assistance from any of the clerks, ignored any who looked curiously at him, and headed instead toward a set of double doors along a side wall. A man with a purpose, unstoppable as a locomotive.

"Are you expected?" Savannah asked, as he pushed the doors wide and began to mount a set of steps, urging her along ahead of him.

"Not quite." He paused at the second-floor landing and glanced up and down a corridor dimly lit with sputtering gas lamps and lined with closed doors, each with a name inscribed upon placards.

Savannah's breaths seemed to echo up and down the hall. She felt like a trespasser. "Perhaps we shouldn't be here."

Dare took her elbow and urged her along, down one corridor and into another. The place quickly became a maze of shadowy passages. Savannah lost her sense of direction almost immediately. And then suddenly Dare drew up before a door labeled "M. Harrigan."

"What does the 'M' stand for?"

But Dare didn't reply. He knocked once, waited, glanced down at her, and a corner of his mouth eased up slightly.

Savannah could almost hear her heartbeat in the silence. Suddenly a door opened directly across the hall. She sucked in a noisy breath when Dare clamped her elbow and drew her around and close to his side. Savannah pasted on a smile.

A white-haired man in oval spectacles and wrinkled black worsted wool suit frowned at them from an office door with "T. Helmsely" engraved on the door. "My mistake," he intoned, but his inflection was almost accusatory. "My hearing isn't quite what it used to be, eh? Looking for Harrigan, are you?"

"Indeed," Dare replied, mimicking the man's British accent.

The man's gaze intensified. "A trifle early for business."

"Never too early for those who want to make money. I'm sure you'd agree." Dare added a sizzling smile to his deeply congenial tone. Savannah stared at him. The man dripped with charm. His words could inspire nothing but understanding and camaraderie, even in an enemy. In an instant the cold warrior had transformed himself into a gentleman with sly, efficient ruthlessness. A chill prickled up Savannah's spine.

The other man grunted his agreement, waved a hand, then shuffled around and closed his door. Dare turned and without hesitating, opened M. Harrigan's door.

Savannah gripped his sleeve. "I don't think we should—" She peered into the dark room. "See there? M. Harrigan isn't here. We should leave."

"Where's all your reckless energy, Miss Merriweather?"

Before she could reply that reckless energy was wasted on trespassing, Dare took her hand, tugged her inside, and closed the door behind them. The room plunged into darkness. Savannah groped in front of her, grabbed something thick and hard between both hands, and realized it was Dare's bicep. He felt stalwart. She hung on. An instant later something scraped and a match flamed. Dare bent and touched the flame to a lamp on the desktop.

"Something about all of this feels illegal to me," Savannah muttered, glancing hesitantly about the room. It was sparsely furnished and extremely tidy, with a very large desk and an overstuffed chair set at an odd distance back on the opposite side of the desk. She glanced at the bookshelves that lined the wall behind the chair, then began to move around the desk to take a better look. "Oh, look. M. Harrigan has a set of Shakespeare's works all bound in gilt. Have you ever seen anything so beautiful?" She kicked something with the pointed toe of her orange silk shoe but she didn't look down, at least not until she all but tripped over whatever blocked her path to the bookshelves. "Blast it, I can't reach because something's on the floor—"

She looked down and saw an arm poking out from beneath the desk. And then she saw that she'd stepped into a pool of deep red blood.

Chapter 6

Dominic clamped his hand over Savannah's mouth before she could scream. He stared at the river of blood flowing from beneath Harrigan's body and closed his lifeless eyes.

"Shh," he hissed into her ear, feeling the softness of her tremble against him, smelling the womanly warmth mingling with the acrid stench of death. She smelled of lilacs and summer grass, a tiny taste of heaven in hell, and he would have lost himself in it had circumstances been any different. His lips touched her ear, his teeth bared. "You have to do as I say. No matter what, keep quiet—unless you want to feel a hangman's noose around your neck. Understand?"

She nodded. He eased his hand away. She turned and looked up at him with a white face and eyes huge with undiluted fear. He wondered if she realized she pressed her hands against his chest in a helpless gesture so uncharacteristic of the woman he knew her to be.

"Easy." He touched her shoulders with his hands.

Her mouth trembled. "W-we should get someone."

His grip on her tightened. "We can't get anyone. We're not going to tell anyone. We're going to walk out of here

and get on a boat to New York. Harrigan's dead. There's
nothing we can do now to save him. Forget you even saw
him."

"How can I forget him? Someone killed him."

"I didn't say they would get away with it. Here—stand
by the door here." She moved as if her limbs were blocks
of wood. He left her leaning against the door and returned to Harrigan. He bent and touched his fingers to
his friend's neck. The skin was cold as hundred-year-old
marble. Dominic tried to remember if he'd had a wife, a
family. No, Harrigan had been a bachelor, consumed with
his work, with exposing the seamy underside of the business.

A fissure of pain and regret sliced through Dominic. He
rose and as he turned, spotted something clutched between Harrigan's fingers—a sheet of paper, crumpled,
something scrawled across it, indecipherable through the
mist suddenly fogging Dominic's vision. He stuffed the
paper into his pocket and mindlessly scooped together
invoices that had scattered on the floor beside an over-
turned file. Harrigan lay in the midst of all of it, the splash
of bedlam in an immaculate office.

Dominic swore, passionately, and only felt worse. He
stood over his dead friend, a man who'd risked as much as
Dominic had, and lost. They'd underestimated their opponent, this much was agonizingly clear. But the stakes
had just been significantly raised. Dominic would find
him.

His chest ached when he tried to breathe. Odd, but
he'd thought men who'd died once felt nothing inside
ever again.

He turned, doused the lamp, and moved to the door.
She was still pressed up flat against it. He touched her
arms and reached lower for her hands. Her fingers in their
kid were cold and stiff and refused to curl into his, even
when he refused to release them.

"You're going to help me find his killer," he murmured.

The feather on her hat brushed under his chin as if she nodded, and then she made a choked sound and rested her forehead against his chest. Every inch of her seemed to go supple as a baby.

It was only for an instant. But in that moment he glimpsed a vulnerability in her that left him oddly breathless.

She pushed back. He felt her breath on his throat and lowered his head until he could feel the warmth of it on his mouth, as if he were hungering for something so badly, needful of it so much he could taste it. His hands curled around her wrists and his body seemed drawn to hers as if by some magnetic force.

"Christ." He reached behind her for the door handle and managed to press her up flush into his chest and belly. She was as soft as he'd imagined under that orange silk, but firm as young fruit, firmer than any imaginings, and he swore again, only more violently, and again he only felt worse.

His body was having a hell of a time remembering that a friend lay dead not six feet away—and that he was partly responsible for it. Lingering was pure stupidity, unless he wished to be charged with Harrigan's murder.

As she turned against him and branded his chest with the imprint of two perfectly round breasts, a part of him conceded that lingering with her in the darkness was worth any risk.

"Come on." His voice was unnaturally rough. He drew the door open and tugged her behind him into the hall, then gently closed the door. Adjusting her hat an inch back on her head, he tried to give her a menacing look and failed. She looked no older than thirteen, pale as a gray English sky, her lips unnaturally rosy and parted as if she couldn't breathe.

"You look guilty as hell," he muttered, anchoring her hand beneath his on his arm and starting off down the hall. He could almost hear the urgency in his step. "Walk now, quicker. That's it."

"I have blood on my shoe."

He glanced down. The pointed toe of her shoe poked from beneath her hem as she walked. It looked dipped in blood. "Keep walking," he said, glancing over his shoulder. An outline of a woman's shoe print stamped in blood followed them down the hall, growing fainter as they proceeded. He quickened his pace. His throat felt tight, very dry.

They passed several men and Dominic nodded, smiled, muttered an incoherent greeting, and continued, even faster. "Smile at them," he ground out.

"I can't smile," she hissed. "I keep seeing M. Harrigan's arm poking out from under the desk. You know who killed him."

"In theory, maybe. Here. Hang on tighter." She managed the stairs very quickly, without stumbling once. "Good," he said, opening the door to the main-floor room. She slanted her eyes at him as if hungering for more reassurances, and he was again reminded of her youth and inexperience. He must have been an idiot to entangle her in his scheme. "Try not to look like anything's wrong," he said as she clamped onto his arm, this time with both hands. She pasted on a smile that would have looked fake from forty yards away. "Don't you heiresses practice that kind of thing?"

"I'm not good at it. I honestly never saw a need for it . . . until now. Oh, God, what are we going to do?"

A shout rang out. Dominic looked over his shoulder and saw several of the men he'd passed in the upper hall standing in the doorway to the stairs, peering into the main room. The white-haired man was behind them, looking right at him.

"You there!" the old man shouted, pointing at Dominic. "Wait! That's them there! Stop them, I say!"

Dominic grabbed Savannah's hand and ran for the

door. He saw a security guard standing his post directly before the door, a menacing look in place on his square face, legs spread wide, the only thing between capture and escape. Dominic drew back and punched him squarely in the nose. The man fell back against the wall and slid to the floor, blood streaming from his nose. Dominic threw open the door and dashed down the steps toward the street.

"My shoe fell off . . ." Savannah tugged on his hand but he didn't stop, even when she stumbled. They reached his coach and he flung open the door, lifting her inside.

"The Number Seven dock and make it speedy!" he shouted to the driver. The coach leapt forward before Dominic could tug the door closed behind him. An instant later it was swallowed up in a tangled web of traffic.

The first ship Dare found leaving London that afternoon bound for New York was a passenger vessel, the *Troubadour*, a small steamer out of Trieste. Dare booked them into the only available accommodation, a first cabin, and listed them on the ship's manifest as Winthrop and Savannah Twombley, Earl and Countess of Castellane.

The ruse had begun.

"Luncheon is being served in the main saloon," he said when he returned to their cabin. For a typical first cabin, the space was exceptionally small, with two wall berths separated by a table less than two feet in width. A bureau stood against one wall next to a small closet. The walls were of lemon-oiled rosewood, the furnishings of mahogany and heavy blue velvet. The tapestries were Flemish. The rugs Aubusson. The china and wash bowl Meissen. All exceedingly elegant for a space that measured less than seven feet in either direction.

And Dare seemed to occupy a disproportionate share of the space.

"I can't eat," Savannah said, turning back to the small porthole that offered a vantage of the diminishing English shores. She pushed the window a fraction of an inch wider and breathed deep. "I keep seeing him. There was a smell in that office. How can you forget it?"

"I'll never forget it."

"And yet you function, eating, talking, perfecting your nasal British tone. I'll bet you'll sleep just fine also."

"Revenge need not be swift, so long as it's certain."

She turned at that.

His lips quirked into his brief and fleeting version of a smile. "Words to live by sometimes."

She was suddenly certain he'd lived by them for quite some time. She wondered how many dead men Dominic Dare had seen in his lifetime, how much blood his pointed-toe leather shoes had stepped in. Only a man accustomed to it could function without any observable distress.

"I feel like I'm going to throw up." She eased onto the bed as the ship lunged deep into the swells. "I want the bed closest to the window. I hope you don't mind. I need to feel a breeze when I sleep."

"You should get some air. You don't look well."

"I'm not seasick."

"It's not a sin, you know." He met her eyes. "Weakness."

"All weakness is a sin. I do my best to try to remember that every day, Mr. Dare."

"Don't call me that, even when we're alone."

"Oh, of course. You're—Castellane." She grimaced at him, her head angling back uncomfortably to get a good look at him. "You don't look like a Castellane."

"Good." He tugged his tie high and tight at his collar. His skin looked like baked leather against the stark white of the shirt. "Call me Winthrop. You're my wife, not my neighbor."

"Winthrop." Savannah rolled the name over her tongue. "You don't look like a Winthrop either. You look like a Mr. Dare." She watched him turn and glance at his reflection in the glass. He shoved a hand through his hair, ruffling it, not smoothing it, a careless gesture, an even more careless look. She got the feeling he didn't look into mirrors often. And yet the cut of his topcoat and trousers suggested he took care with his clothes to choose the very best. A typically arrogant man. She wouldn't be a bit surprised if the shoulders of his coat were padded with horsehair to make his silhouette so startlingly broad. "Maybe I'll call you Winny."

He glanced sharply at her, eyes narrowing to slits, lips curving full and sensuous. "And what will be my pet name for you?"

Savannah stared at him. The room felt suddenly like a closet, small and stuffy. She jerked a swallow and his eyes riveted on her breasts. Her skin started to burn hot, as if he'd scorched her with a torch flame. And somewhere high between her thighs a delicious little spasm quivered. She jerked to her feet, turned, and braced one hand on the wall next to the porthole.

"Yes." She saw nothing beyond the window. "I believe some air will do me a world of good. Yes, indeed, I'll meet my fellow travelers. Walk the decks. Practice up on being a good wife."

"You do all things well, of course."

She glanced at him. He was watching her with his typically glacial look. The predator she'd glimpsed in him a moment before was gone. Perhaps she'd imagined it. "Why bother doing something if you can't do it well?" she replied.

"I agree."

She lifted her chin. "Why live if it can't be on your own terms?"

"Indeed." He was looking into her eyes, his face expressionless, but Savannah felt as if he understood exactly what she meant, without her having to explain any of it. As if he felt exactly as she did.

She indicated her bag, which lay on the floor on the other side of the bed. "I need a hat if I'm going walking."

"And a wrap," he said, moving from her path and back against the wall. But the room was too small, or he too big, or her too round in all directions, because when she tried to go around the foot of the bed, she had to squeeze through a space between him and the bed that was too small even for a child. As she started along, she banged her hip hard on the edge of the bed and decided to face him, which was a cataclysmic error.

Ninety pounds of pressure from a corset was nothing compared to the force of a man's chest. And whalebone was cold, whereas he was warm. Exceptionally warm, particularly where his coat parted over his shirt.

"I'm sorry—" She lifted her arms over her head and tried to shimmy through without an inch of her touching an inch of him, which was impossible. They were squashed together, chest to chest, thighs to thighs, loins to loins. She went hot with embarrassment. "I'm too fa—"

"No-no—" he said quickly. "I'll just—" He groped along the wall for the door handle and looked up at the ceiling. His Adam's apple dipped in his throat. "It's too damned hot in here." He flung the door open so hard against the wall a picture fell from its hook.

"There." She gasped, almost falling as she squeezed through the last inch. Without looking at him, she turned and started to rummage in her bag.

"Let me—" His arm reached around her to lift her bag.

"No!" She arched away from the length of his arm brushing against her side. "I'm—" She heaved and turned and set the bag on the bed. Her smile wavered and she wasn't sure why. "See. I can do it."

He retrieved the picture from the floor and set it on the dresser as she dug deep in her bag for a wrap.

His hand touched hers. He held a pair of French silk stockings in his fist, lace garters attached as if she'd rid herself of them very quickly. They looked very small in his big hand, and very white falling over his long fingers. Without looking up at him, she gave a garbled thanks, stuffed them into the bag, and did a quick survey of the floor to make sure she hadn't dropped anything else in her haste to find the wrap or to leave the room. She wasn't sure which.

She pulled the first thing that looked like a wrap from her bag. It was an ivory silk shawl with fringe, embroidered in an orange and yellow floral pattern. Maxine had bought it for her in Paris.

"Very good," he said, when she'd covered herself to her neck with it and plunked her cabbage hat with the orange feather on her head.

"Time to charm them all," Savannah said as he swept a hand to the door.

As they stepped into the hall and made their way toward the deck and the couples strolling the promenade, Savannah's unease evaporated with each step she took. She had a role to play, one that would bring her everything she wanted. She felt the nudge of Dare's hand at her lower back and realized that he could gracefully assume his role no matter how awkward they'd been not a moment ago, no matter that they'd found a man dead just hours before. Well, if he could do it, so could she. She doubted he had as much to gain by their ruse as she did.

She gave him a cheeky smile that had visibly annihilated Charles on more than one occasion. Dare's gaze deepened, darkened. He looked something less than annihilated.

She looked quickly away, nodded at the passing couples, and listened to Dare's resonant voice offering sedate greeting. The sound of it seemed to vibrate along her spine. She drew the shawl closer and felt his palm flatten to guide her around a man staring up at something in the sky. She looked up and saw a male passenger dressed in trousers and overcoat scrambling up the hemp ropes and ladders that led to the top of the ship's mast. From there a true sailor's view of the Atlantic would be his. Hampered by her long skirts, Savannah felt a stab of envy of the man's freedom. An instant later she had even more reason to envy him his solitary haven when she was jostled against Dare's side by a male passenger trying to get his sea legs.

Dare caught her with one arm that wrapped close under her breasts. But it was the brush of his fingers against her ribs when he released her that left her breathless, strangely curious, and very hot.

Hot? How terribly odd.

Well, they'd get used to each other in a few days, comfortable as well-worn shoes. This strange totality of body awareness would go away.

She was sure of it. Well, almost sure.

Savannah's head swiveled around, she chewed once, swallowed noisily, and blinked watering eyes. "I can't believe what I just overheard," she said in a raspy whisper that wasn't half as quiet as she probably thought it was. "Do you know who that is at that table over there?"

Dominic reached for her glass of water on the table and pressed it into her hand. "Don't eat so fast," he advised softly. "No one's going to take it away from you."

Glancing at the table across the main saloon, he counted six ladies and two gentlemen, recognizing only one of the ladies. He looked at Savannah and saw that her eyes were fixed on the sturdiest of the women, a gray-haired, formidable-looking female who seemed to be holding court over her table with a deep alto monotone. "You mean Frances Trainer?" he asked.

Savannah gulped her water. "You know her?"

"We met shortly after boarding. She made sure I knew who she was."

"Well, why didn't you tell me?"

"Tell you what? That she plowed me over on the promenade deck with her retinue of footmen and luggage? I didn't know you cared, Savannah."

She dismissed him with a scrunch of her nose as if he

were a useless bit of nothing and dabbed at the corner of her lip with her napkin. "You obviously don't know who she is or you wouldn't have minded being plowed over by her. Well, maybe you would have because you're a man, but I wouldn't have. I would have carried all her luggage for her." She gazed at Frances Trainer and sighed like a young girl in the jaws of first love. "I can't believe how lucky we are."

"Ah," Dominic said, reaching for his wine. "She's a suffragist."

"Not just a suffragist," Savannah corrected him primly. "*The* foremost lecturer on the women's rights circuit. She spoke at the women's rights convention last April. In Chicago. I wasn't there, of course. But I read all about it in *The Free Enquirer*. She thinks women suffer a legal death upon marriage." She glanced at him and lifted her brows impressively. "She's dedicated her life to ridding the world of the assumption that women are of value only so long as they are of use to men. Whatever liberty I have I owe to her. Isn't she marvelous?"

Dominic watched Frances Trainer over the top of his glass. She looked a bit too dour and ponderous to suit his definition of marvelous. He reserved the adjective for oil paintings done with almost violent color . . . or a nude woman in dawn's light.

Or Savannah pressed chest to hip against him.

"I have to talk to her."

Dominic clamped a hand on her wrist to keep her in her seat, laid his other arm over the back of her chair, and leaned closer to her ear. Her lilac scent wrapped like soft-gloved fingers around him. "Remember who you are, Countess," he murmured, his eyes straying where he knew they shouldn't, past the shawl clinging to her shoulders, to the soft flesh oozing out of the top of her gown. He watched it swell, recede with each breath she drew. She was excited. Her breaths came short and fast. He swallowed deeply and went instantly, uncomfortably rigid.

He jerked slightly back as if he'd been struck and met the amused look of the woman seated directly opposite him at the table. The stout, middle-age American and her equally stout businessman husband, Mr. and Mrs. Horace Trapp of Philadelphia, had been all but beside themselves to be seated at lunch with "aristocrats." They'd been the perfect pair to practice a first go at deception on. Savannah had slipped only once and had called him "Dar—" After that she'd referred to him as simply "Darling," which pleased him far more than "Winny."

He still hadn't settled on a pet name for her. As he held her chair back from the table and received a slant of her eyes as thanks, he briefly wondered why the idea should plague him at all. Pet names were used by lovers. Not husbands and wives.

Surely not by conspirators. Impostors. Business partners who wouldn't claim to know one another after their six-month charade had passed.

They moved toward Frances Trainer's table for an introduction, and Savannah passed beneath a bright chandelier dripping wax. The flames turned her dress into a mélange of brilliant orange, but her skin, pearlized and opalescent beneath the sun, bloomed with warm rosy hues.

"Rosy."

"What did you say?" she asked, looking up at him.

Rosy. It suited her. Every inch of her, according to his memory of the stable.

He felt his teeth slam together hard. In his ogling he'd forgotten himself and spoken his thoughts. "Nothing. Nothing at all. Enjoy yourself."

"Oh, I intend to. I'll follow her around the ship if I have to. I just want to listen to her."

"Good. Take all day if you like."

"I just might." She looked at him curiously. "You don't think anyone will get suspicious—you know—if we don't act like—like we should?"

"And how is that?"

"Spend time together, perhaps, though I'm not quite sure."

"Then how do you know that they're sure? Maybe they'll all just think we're a progressive, odd sort of couple. A suffragist-minded American woman and her tolerant, titled English husband who lets her do as she wishes."

"Oh, that sounds nice. Maybe they'll talk about us." She smiled at him.

His chest felt like someone squeezed a fist inside it.

"Go on, then," she said, waving a hand, her attention and a dazzling smile riveting on Frances Trainer. "I'll find you."

He released her then, wondering why the thought of a few hours of privacy, which he usually found irresistible, should seem the lesser of his options. A part of him would have been content to linger in the saloon with the dourly monotoned Frances Trainer and her entourage for the rest of the day.

He left the saloon with the thought that an afternoon on the Atlantic would be well spent with pencil and paper in hand. He set out at a determined pace to locate them, musing only briefly on the fact that he hadn't much felt like drawing, or painting, in months. Today, strangely enough, he felt capable of producing a masterpiece.

Chapter 7

Dominic dropped into a deck chair set at some distance from a line of other chairs that stood like obedient soldiers on the promenade deck. The outcast chair for the outcast husband.

And a perfect haven for a man who wished to work undisturbed.

He braced his pad on one knee, glanced up, and began to sketch a woman standing at the ship's rail looking out over the water. The light wasn't as he'd have liked. There was too much color out here on the water, even at dusk when the light should have been best. Nothing mild about it. And his subject—not quite young enough. Not curvaceous enough. Not blond enough.

He listened for the comforting scrape his pencil made on the paper as he worked but could hear nothing above the wash of waves against the bow and the clamor of the steam engines from three decks below. He waited for the calm to come over him as it sometimes did when he worked.

But tonight the calm was going to be even more difficult in coming.

He'd circled the saloon four times in the past hour, peering into windows past fringed red velvet curtains to the corner table where Frances Trainer held court. Savannah sat on her right, deeply situated in her chair and enraptured. Even from across the saloon she looked as if she soaked up every word Frances Trainer breathed. No doubt she had every intention of staying exactly where she was for four more hours.

He'd gone to their cabin, restless with energy. A faint lilac scent seemed to waft along on the porthole breeze. He'd glimpsed a white lace stocking poking out of her bag, tried to tuck it inside and out of sight, and found himself staring at a red silk shoe with startling three-inch heels. He'd left the cabin wondering what the hell he'd done to himself.

He should be damned grateful that Frances Trainer had chosen this vessel to make her crossing. He should be relishing his hours of solitude. He should be thinking about doing his damnedest to present a convincing Earl of Castellane to the Four Hundred and seeing his plans to fruition.

Oddly enough, he was none of these.

Damned restlessness. Perhaps he hadn't walked enough. Once again, the drawing wasn't anywhere near good enough. His fingers curled around the page, itching to crush it.

"Ooh, we've got an artist on board!"

The feminine squeal came from over Dominic's shoulder. Smacking the pad flat on his lap, he swiveled around and met Mrs. Horace Trapp peering down at him from above an imposing shelf of bosom. Something about her big black eyes and broad tilted nostrils was suggestive of a charming toy Boston bull puppy.

His smile never became fully realized. If he'd learned one invaluable lesson since he'd first gone to America twenty-five years before, it was that American women, like his Italian mother, knew how to get their way. They didn't let a bit of protocol or an uncooperative man stand in their path.

"Madam," he said, rising out of his chair and tucking his sketchbook into his inside coat pocket.

"I have to see that," Mrs. Trapp said, her eyes boring holes through his coat, her fingers twitching as if they itched. She flagged her husband down. "Horace, come here. The Earl of Castellane is an artist. I saw it. He was sketching that woman over there and very well, if I might say so. But he made her look younger and thinner than she is. You've a kind eye, your lordship."

"What woman?" Trapp snapped, ambling up to his wife's side.

"That one there."

Horace Trapp watched the woman shove away from the rail and walk off down the promenade, feet braced against the sway of the ship, bustled backside swishing like a mop over the decking.

Mrs. Trapp wagged a pudgy pink-gloved finger at Dominic and dropped her voice an octave. "Your lordship, does the Countess Castellane know you spend your time looking at other women?"

Dominic forced a bland smile. "My wife and I are only recently acquainted, Mrs. Trapp. We've yet a great deal to learn about one another."

"Yes, so you said earlier. And yet the way you looked at her at luncheon—why, Horace hasn't looked at me like that since—well, I don't believe I've ever seen him look at me like that."

"What was that?" Trapp's attention was fixed farther off down the deck.

Mrs. Trapp beamed. "I know a bit about art, your lordship. I have my own personal art agent. All the new rich Philadelphia women do. After all, we need someone to tell us what we should like to hang on all our walls. How else are we supposed to know good art when we see it?"

"Indeed." Dominic was unable to temper the sarcastic

bite in his tone. What a curiously exploitable set these new rich women were, eager to lay their trust and their money into the hands of any self-proclaimed art connoisseur. The possibilities for defrauding them exploded through Dominic's mind.

"Just some French bastard," Trapp added, frowning at Dominic as if he'd sized him up as nothing better than that same French bastard.

"He's not from France." Mrs. Trapp sniffed. "He's actually from New York." She leaned several inches closer to Dominic and whispered, "His accent is fake."

"Ah," Dominic said in his fake accent.

Mrs. Trapp tapped her ear. "I can tell, of course. But if it weren't for him I could pay a fortune for forgeries and never even know it. He's worth every penny of commission I pay him. Will you sketch me, your lordship?"

"Call me Castellane," Dominic said. He should have left his sketchbook in his room with Savannah's red shoes. The less attention he drew to himself the better. But Mrs. Trapp had all the signs of a basset hound hot on the trail of fresh meat. He doubted she would give up the hunt without a hell of a fight.

He envisioned sneaking around the ship for the next eleven days, trying to avoid Mrs. Trapp, and didn't like the thought in the least.

She turned slightly right, poked up her chin, and pushed out her bosom. She stared off at some distant horizon, her face a mask of serenity. "I sat for the portrait painter Caroline Duran about a year ago when we first came to Philadelphia from Des Moines. I know how to pose. Horace liked the painting, didn't you, Horace? We had it mounted above the fireplace in the parlor."

Her husband scowled off down the deck, jerked his mustache, and grunted something under his breath. But Mrs. Trapp's chin only shifted higher, firmer, more determined. "Caroline said I have a lionesque grace. Do you think so, Mr. Castellane?"

"Without question, Mrs. Trapp," Dominic said, profoundly unable to deny this woman a compliment, as unable as he was to correct her improper address of him. "It would be a pleasure to capture such grace on paper." In opting for a directly overbearing manner instead of quiet charm, Mrs. Trapp had somehow managed to make Dominic do what he hadn't wished to do.

He felt somewhat turned around by it all but had no explanation or remedy for it, particularly when she gasped with delight and gushed her thanks. Then like any true American woman who'd gotten her way, she took the direction of the matter entirely into her own hands.

"By the railing!" Mrs. Trapp instructed, hurrying over to the rail as if she feared it would suddenly evaporate. "Just like the other woman. Right here. No, you stay there, Mr. Castellane. On the chair, right where you were. The angle was so advantageous to the woman's backside. Or maybe it was the lighting. Do hurry. Oh, and you must sign the sketch. Something sweet, of course." Mrs. Trapp giggled. " 'To my dearest Dolly' would do just fine."

"Of course," Dominic said.

Horace Trapp anxiously departed, with a muttered reminder that he would look for his wife before late supper, some three hours later.

Savannah's heels tapped like a staccato drum on the decking. Only her hand clamped on top of her hat kept it from flying off into the jaws of the dark Atlantic. The other pressed her shawl to her bosom. She jostled against one woman, breathed a smiling apology in the face of the woman's scowl, and continued on even faster.

Well, who the devil could blame her for being excited? She'd spent an entire eight hours, dinner included, with Frances Hopewell Trainer, and tomorrow she would attend her first "conversation." There, under the supervision of Mrs. Trainer, a select group of women would get together on the promenade deck, *in full view of the gentle-*

men, and converse in a way that was designed to free them from all sense of intellectual inferiority.

The idea made Savannah giddy. How long she'd craved relief from the glittering artifice of her life! She was sure she wouldn't sleep tonight. But what good was being a giddy insomniac if she didn't have anyone to share it with? And Mr. Dare seemed the perfect prospect. After all, it was he who'd afforded her with this opportunity.

As she pushed open the door to her cabin, she was sure she would explode with excitement. She drew up with a disappointed "Oh."

The cabin was empty. Where was Mr. Dare?

She returned to the promenade deck, glanced fore then aft and spotted at the farthest point aft a large group of men and women assembled around something. Never content to be left out of the fun, she hurried toward them, realizing as she drew nearer that it was the women who were gathered like a flock of squawking geese around a crumb of food. The men stood several paces behind them and to the side, muttering among themselves and shaking their heads as men are wont to do when their women are otherwise occupied in something they have no interest in.

"What's the curiosity?" Savannah asked the nearest gentleman.

"Some artist." He jerked his head at the throng. "The ladies all want appointments to have their portraits done."

"An artist!" Savannah ran her tongue over her upper lip. "Is he from France?"

"My bet," another man put in, making Savannah go warm from the inside out at the memory of all her dark, young French artists. "Haven't been able to catch a glimpse of the bastard," the man said. "Damned Bohemians should stay in their own country."

"The trouble with artists," added another, "is that the wife will meet them, like them, and invite them to dinner. Writers are bad enough to have at a man's table. Painters, even worse. I say, throw him down in steerage. He has no business on this deck with polite society."

"It seems he has more business than he can manage in a single crossing," Savannah quipped. With a nod at the startled gentlemen, she turned and gently elbowed her way through the outer fringe of women. She wanted a good look at him. Perhaps even have her portrait done. Something pouty and passionate.

To her dismay the crowd was at least four deep, all the way around. She had no idea this many women were on board, and so young and fashionably dressed in flounces and bustles and low-cut evening dresses. Judging by the yardage of the gowns, these women's husbands had done very well for themselves financially.

Hushed whispers rose around her. Several women giggled. Others strained on tiptoes and gave breathless sighs. Savannah could see nothing but the backs of the coiffed heads in front of her. Even if the artist had wished to escape, he wouldn't have been able to. But what man would want to flee a prison of trembling females?

"Ladies—" A male voice rang out above the whispers, so deeply masculine and commanding every woman went suddenly silent. "Ladies, step back just a bit, please."

Savannah poked her head between two women and strained up on tiptoes. Mr. Dare? How good of him to come to the artist's aid. Yes, he seemed the sort that could look beyond the invisible barriers of class. After all, in assuming his new persona, he'd effortlessly breached those barriers.

"He's British," the beautiful blonde on Savannah's right whispered. "An earl. Do you think he paints too?"

"With those hands?" Another sighed, this one a slender brunette with exquisite eyes. "I hope he sculpts."

Savannah frowned. She didn't like the way these two women were discussing her "husband." Besides, Mr. Dare wasn't the artist. She blinked. Or was he? It was positively chilling to realize she'd put her faith in the hands of a man she knew next to nothing about.

"Castellane is his name," the blonde purred. "I wonder if there's a wife somewhere."

Savannah suddenly looked at these women with new eyes, and a vision fully blown and unexpected burst into her mind: the blonde and the brunette offering themselves like ripe fruit on a platter to the commanding artist's brush of Mr. Dare. To capture their likenesses, any man would have to spend hours staring at them.

Savannah didn't know precisely why but that thought made her spine as tight as new leather. Did it really matter what Mr. Dare did with his time? His enjoyment of his particular pastime shouldn't lessen her enjoyment of her own.

After all, he was a business partner. Nothing more.

Well, he was also an artist, and her time in France had proven she had a profound weakness for them. Something about all that brooding passion and tortured soul kind of thing made them irresistible as chocolate cremes to Savannah.

Irresistible. No, that wouldn't do at all.

She scooted to the rear of the throng and retreated back up the promenade toward her cabin. If she intended to contribute tomorrow to a rousing conversation of uninhibited female intellects, she needed a good night's sleep. She was determined that nothing clutter her mind. No distractions. No wandering curiosity. No unanswered questions . . .

Like what did a mysterious Italian artist have to gain by infiltrating the Four Hundred? Who was it that murdered poor M. Harrigan in his London office . . . and why did Mr. Dare's voice seem to echo out of the night skies long after she'd turned down the lamp and drawn the quilt to her chin?

* * *

Before Dominic even opened his eyes, he sensed that something had changed. Some time during the night, the ship's gentle forward roll had become a pronounced side-to-side pitching, as if the ship labored against a turbulent ocean. The engine's clamor had diminished to a distant hum. The cabin was so quiet he could hear the drone of Savannah's breath as she slept. Gentle inhale, soft snore exhale. It sounded surprisingly peaceful.

Murky skies offered little light to the cabin. The hour was still early. He just might be able to sneak to the saloon for coffee without encountering any overzealous art lovers.

He sat on the edge of his berth massaging a tightness from his neck and watched Savannah sleep. She lay with her back toward him, her hair tangled on the pillow behind her. She hadn't moved since he'd entered the cabin late last evening. Her nightgown was a long white cotton thing with a scalloped hem, full and modestly cut, but he doubted Savannah would look modest in anything, particularly when it clung to all those swells and dips. The cotton robe she wore over the gown was bunched up to her thighs. The sheets looked as if thcy'd been kicked to the foot of the bed with great impatience. Her legs were long, curvy, and pearly-pink, just like the rest of her.

The light was exceptionally mild, perfect for painting.

He picked up the orange dress that lay at his feet and tossed it over his bed. She'd left a trail of clothes from the door. Orange shoes upended just inside the door; shawl draped over the foot of the bed, one fringed corner dangling to the floor. A filmy heap followed. He stared at the chemise and was besieged by a vision of her in it.

He reached for it and stared at his hand through the transparent linen. He could almost feel her body's warmth still clinging to the fabric. A scent drifted up to him. His manhood sprang to life as if from a hundred years' slumber.

He flung the linen aside and headed for the wash basin.

Cool water splashed over his face and neck and ran in icy streams over his bare chest and into the waistband of his trousers, which he'd slept in. No wonder he was so damned hot, his skin almost steaming beneath the trickles of water. He usually slept naked.

He wondered if Savannah Rose Merriweather usually slept without her nightdress to let any wayward breezes play over her flesh.

Grabbing a towel, he vigorously rubbed his face. He didn't realize he snarled into the cloth until she made a sound. He froze, then glanced at his pelvis. Damn.

He'd never thought there'd be a time when he'd curse the fit of his trousers or the abundance of his blessings.

"Good morning," she murmured. The sheets rustled. The bed squeaked, as if she were getting up.

He spun around to find his shirt, giving her his back. "Uh—yes, good morning," he tossed over his shoulder. He shrugged into his shirt, buttoned it as fast as he could, and left it hanging loose past his hips, well past his pelvis. Satisfied that he could face a virgin without shocking the hell out of her, he turned to the wash basin again, reached for his razor, and glanced at his reflection in the mirror. Again he froze.

The angle was ruthlessly perfect. He had her directly in his sights. She sat on the edge of the bed but her eyes were still closed. She rocked with the pitch of the ship, blond curls swaying like a heavy curtain to her hips, toes dangling an inch above the floor, like a child's. Her cheeks were rosy and her lips looked sleep-swollen and red as ripe cherries.

The knot at her waist had loosened and the robe had slipped off one shoulder. So had her nightgown. And the row of buttons that should have run straight up to her high collar now veered sharply toward her shoulder. But the cloth was stretched, caught low somewhere between her thighs, and the fabric between the buttons gaped open, right over the plumpest part of her breasts, and higher, over one large pink nipple.

Dominic swallowed. Coffee. He needed something to clear his head. Something to take the fire from his blood. It seemed to rage with a madman's fury this morning.

He looked at himself, saw the demon in his eyes, but had to look at her again. This wasn't the studied disarray of an artist's model. There wasn't a hint of guile in her pose or artifice in the crooked tangle of her clothes. She could barely stifle her yawn and did it broadly and with gusto, ending it with a groan. And yet he couldn't have imagined anything that screamed more of sex and sensuality than her at that moment.

His lust took his breath away.

She slipped off the bed to her feet and opened her eyes. The gown fell straight. The instant before she jerked the robe closed he glimpsed two perfectly erect nipples.

Their eyes met. And he suddenly felt as if he'd taken something that wasn't his to take.

He had to get coffee. All he wanted was coffee, and he couldn't make himself leave to get it. Heat swarmed into his face.

"I'm going to get coffee," he said into the mirror, feeling stupid and tongue-tied for the first time in his life.

"What's wrong with the ship?"

"Bad seas." He busied his hands and his eyes with shaving, aware that he made more noise than he might have otherwise, swishing his brush around in a porcelain cup of water, staring grimly into the mirror at himself, perhaps to prove that his attention was fixed decidedly away from her.

"How am I supposed to walk?"

"Hang on to something."

"I'm trying. God, I hope I don't get sick. I'm having a conversation this morning on the promenade. With several ladies and Frances Trainer."

"Ah."

"While you do portraits."

His hand drew the blade slowly down his right cheek but he glanced at her in the mirror. She was bent over at the waist and rummaging through her traveling bag, tossing stockings and shoes to the floor. "Sketches," he corrected her, wincing as the blade scraped hard over his jaw.

"Remember, you can't be too good at it or it will seem more than a pastime and people will get suspicious of you."

"How so?"

She jerked up and turned to him, her scarlet shoes in her hands. "They'll likely think you're an artist, not an earl. And the Four Hundred will flee in body from a poet, a painter, a musician, or a clever Frenchman. Artists, Mr. Dare, like art, are considered articles to be bought for display."

"I'll try very hard to be mediocre."

"Did you study art in Italy?"

He swished his blade in the water. "In Florence."

"At an academy?"

"The Café Michelangelo was as good as any academy in Paris. My father and grandfather painted there. With the rest of the Macchiaolli." He poked out his jaw, turned his face, and slid the blade slowly over his left cheek, offering nothing more. He'd already said too damned much. His past wasn't a subject he liked discussing, his talent—his curse—something he rarely invited inquiry into. The trouble was, he seemed to forget all that when she asked her questions.

"Macchiaolli. It sounds like a men's club." She watched him, eyes spitting curiosity, hands holding those red silk shoes.

"You won't walk well in those on a pitching deck," he said.

"I have to wear them. They go with my red dress, and I have to wear my red dress today for Frances Trainer. We're discussing her *Letters on the Equality of the Sexes*."

"No man ever wore red shoes with three-inch heels to discuss anything."

"I know of one that does. Templeton Snelling is his name. You'll meet him once we get to New York. He's Mrs. Astor's pet."

"I can hardly wait."

"Ah, here it is. Not too wrinkled." She drew a long scarlet satin dress from the bag and shook it out. "My mother hates me in this dress. She says pale blondes shouldn't wear low-cut red dresses and flounces. What do you think, Mr. Dare?"

He rubbed a towel over his wet face. The dress she held up to her chest looked like it had been born in the Seven Sisters' bordello on West Twenty-fifth. He slung the towel over his shoulder.

She lifted her brows. "You don't like it."

On the contrary. Perversely self-punishing, he wanted very much to see all of her in it. "I like it," he said.

"Well, I wouldn't care if you didn't. You said I could do what I pleased, with whom I pleased, just as you will—" He caught the subtle arch of her brow as she turned and spread the gown on the bed. "It's best that we both keep busy. What the devil would we do cooped up in this cabin all day?" She glanced at him when he could come up with no suitable response, many unsuitable and entirely self-serving, but none that he could say.

If he was anything less than a gentleman he would have.

"You're bleeding—" She pointed to her jaw. He pressed the towel to his jaw. She frowned. "No, other side. You missed it again. Here." She moved toward him and he had a mystifying desire to back away from her. He bumped back against the dresser.

When had he ever fled a beautiful woman?

She took a corner of the towel and pressed it to his jaw. "You misbuttoned your shirt." She was frowning at his chest. "Really, Mr. Dare, you must miss your manservant dreadfully."

"I don't have a manservant," he said, his voice oddly husky.

"Do you want me to fix it?" And before he could scream that she shouldn't touch him, her fingers were pushing open the row of buttons, very quickly moving lower and lower, closer and closer to his pelvis.

And nothing down there had improved over the course of the last few minutes. She was standing so close he could feel her body warmth mingling with his, and the situation worsened to almost painful proportions.

He looked over her head out the porthole at the scudding clouds, tried to focus on the bounty of magnificent gray hues, and all he could think about were those two pink nipples.

"Are all Italian men covered with so much hair on their chests?"

He closed his eyes. She'd paused in her unbuttoning to spread open his shirt and was examining his chest with her eyes, her hands, the tips of her fingers, as if she were a curious little anthropologist noting the odd physical characteristics of an exotic tribe.

Why couldn't he stop her?

Stop her? He couldn't even fill his chest with enough air. Her palms were curved around his ribs, and her thumbs gently probed the center ridge of muscle, lower, lower, like the touch of an angel. Her breaths stirred the hair on his chest, the heat of her body pulsed into his, and his agony became exquisite.

"Oh, there's where you misbuttoned it," she said, her voice so calm and controlled, so without realization of what she was doing, he almost groaned. "Right down here at the bottom." His eyes slammed open and then her innocent's fingers brushed completely over the length of his erection.

She jerked but he caught her by the upper arms and kept her close, God help him.

"Good heavens," she breathed, staring up at him. "Is

there something wrong with you down there, Mr. Dare? Perhaps you should see a doctor."

"Listen," he managed, feeling much like a man who'd crawled across ten miles of desert and still had twenty to go. He looked deep into her eyes and felt his resistance begin a horrific crumbling. "I can't do this."

"Do what? What can't you do? I told you I'd button your shirt for you if you find it so hard."

"Hard," he rumbled, staring at her mouth, the petal-pink softness, the heaven that could be his. Her skin beneath his hands felt womanly smooth, as if coated with heavy cream. "Didn't anyone ever teach you anything about men?"

"Oh, I know a great deal about men. I know that they have their feet on women's necks so that we can't stand upright on that ground which God designed us to occupy, beside them, not behind and below them."

"I'm talking about their lust."

"Their *what?*" Her eyes were enormous. She sucked in a great breath and her breasts lifted against his bare chest. "I—I've been told that lust is an appetite not governed by reason and that young men should subdue those appetites by means of exercise, cold baths, hard beds, and religion."

"I could almost believe you've never experienced it," he murmured, shifting her subtly yet infinitely deeper into him, and he felt the fit of her loins plainly against his. Her lower lip trembled open with a soundless gasp. "Yes, I could almost believe you've managed to escape it for this long. Don't you think it's high time for a lesson?"

Chapter 8

He was like a heavy oak tree. Savannah felt every inch of him pressing into her. His hands were huge and strong on her arms. The feeling was something like smothering, but she was enjoying it. The rock of the ship seemed to anchor her against him, or maybe she just imagined it was impossible to move away from him.

"I have no need for lessons," Savannah said proudly. "I've already been kissed."

Dare kept staring at her mouth. "Where?"

Savannah's brows quivered. "On my cheek, of course. And twice, no, three times right on my mouth." He watched her, as if he was waiting for her to continue. She blinked. "That's all. Are there any more places?"

His eyes glinted like fine steel. "Who was he?"

"There were three of them."

"Three."

"All French." He didn't look impressed, which disappointed her a bit. "Jean-Luc, Jean-Marc, and Jean-Louis. One a writer, one a sculptor, one a painter. Or was Jean-Louis an actor? How strange that I don't remember."

"Strange indeed. A woman's first three loves should be memorable."

"Well, it's been awhile. I met them all several months ago when I was in France buying gowns with my Aunt Maxine. You see, it's extremely important for a girl to go abroad, Mr. Dare. If you've gone twice, a certain very prestigious woman in New York named Mrs. Nesbit will receive you clear into her parlor. One trip abroad will get you to the dining room. If you *expect* to go in the near future, you make it into the hall. And if you have no hope of ever going, you don't get anywhere beyond the front porch. I've been twice."

"And how is her parlor?"

"Why, I haven't been there yet! I expect we'll go together. You can see it then."

"And what makes her so very prestigious?"

"I'm not quite certain, but I believe she's descended from no fewer than fourteen Revolutionary soldiers. She's also a member of the National Society of Americans of Royal Descent and of the Order of the Crown in America. I expect she'll appreciate your English accent and your tweeds. Americans so admire English tweeds and their thin watercress sandwiches."

"How did you like Paris?"

"Well, with Maxine you enjoy yourself. She invited the three Jeans to dinner, night after night, and they would sit across from me and stare at me until I couldn't even eat—" His stare was suddenly so intense, or perhaps just discussing this with him seemed abruptly not the thing to do. Heat throbbed in her cheeks. "I—she's quite wonderful. Very elegant. She's returned to New York intent on expending her money, her imagination, and all her powers on showing society exactly what she thinks of it. I can't wait to find out what she's done since I've been away. You're still bleeding, Mr. Dare." Gently she pressed the tip of her finger to his jaw, retrieved the drop of blood, and held her finger up for him. "See? You shaved too quickly."

His face went cold and hard, like a mask. Savannah felt a chill creep through her. "Listen," he said, setting her firmly away from him. For an instant she felt abandoned, as if he'd yanked a blanket off of her in a freezing rainstorm. She blinked at him, and he scowled at her and shoved a hand through his hair as if he was angry and frustrated. His shirt billowed away from him as he moved, and she got an eyeful of the dramatic breadth of his chest and the startling taper of his torso to his hips. Her legs felt strangely weak.

And the tingling seemed to have settled in the very tips of her breasts.

"We made a deal," he said, looking hard at her, his fingers jerking the buttons closed along his shirt front.

"Yes, we did."

"And I mean to stand by it—" He glanced at her breasts in a way that made the tips tingle even more. His face grew a shade deeper red-brown. "We need to make some rules."

"Should we write them down?" She wanted to be helpful. He looked so beside himself.

"Yes. Write them down. That way I can remind myself of them as often as I need to."

"Do you have paper?"

"Yes, yes, paper—" He located his topcoat and dug his sketch pad and pencil from his pocket. He handed both to her and watched her sit on the edge of the bed. She crossed her ankles and swung her little feet. The robe gaped open and the buttons slid crooked again and he turned and gnashed his teeth.

Coffee was all he needed.

"You should get dressed in something besides—" He waved a hand at her and stood in front of the porthole gulping big breaths.

"What about the rules?"

"Make that the first one. You need to be dressed first thing in the morning."

"Dressed in the morning," she repeated, flipping a page. "Oh, look at this. Why, this is quite good. It's a lady—standing at the ship's rail."

"You're not writing." He stuffed his hands into his trouser pockets, resisting the urge to yank his sketchbook out of her hands. He snarled at the porthole, the artist who'd scorned the critics, and God knows why, but he wanted her approval.

"You reveal yourself in your sketches, Mr. Dare. I don't suppose you want to hear that. Yes, there's a flesh-and-blood truthfulness about this sketch, no posturing, no artifice. Very anatomical. And yet it's full of mysterious and haunting images that suggest something unsuspected lurks behind the reality we see. Now I understand the fascination. Will you sketch me?"

"No." He said it with a cutting finality.

"Why not? Am I not interesting enough?"

"The rules, Miss Merriweather, sometimes require no explanation. Number one: Clothes worn at all times. Let's make this simple. You be in bed by ten, up by seven. I'll come in later, rise earlier, and leave before you wake. Privacy ensured. Agreed?"

"That sounds reasonable. I like to be in bed early."

"Number two: No sketching between us. Number three: Physical contact besides the sort required when we're out of this cabin taking our meals together and mingling as husbands and wives do should be severely limited."

"I see. We don't touch."

"Exactly. And if we're never both awake in the cabin at the same time, that won't likely happen."

"Do I offend you, Mr. Dare?"

He looked at her. She looked at him, cocooned in her innocence. For all her French artists, she'd left France dangerously naive. She didn't have one inkling what the hell he was talking about. He'd assumed most beautiful women knew how to use their charm and looks. Not Savannah.

She was like an untouched canvas, waiting for the sullying mark of his brush.

Not *his* brush. Some other brush, belonging to some repressed young nob who even now drowned his lust in cold baths, a hard bed, and religion.

There was no explaining it to her. Best that she remain uneducated until he set her free. Six months. But how the hell would he survive it?

"No," he said, thinking seriously about finding himself a woman at the Seven Sisters the instant his feet met with land. "You don't offend me."

At first she didn't look satisfied. But after a moment she seemed to brighten with realization. "Ah. You must be one of those men who doesn't like women. I've met several in New York. You know, the sort that prefers men."

"What?"

"I promise not to breathe a word of it to anyone."

Dominic stared at her and wondered why the urge to straighten her out in her thinking more than outweighed the advantages in letting her believe the impossible.

"And if we break the rules, Mr. Dare, is there a punishment?" She charged on, apparently comfortable with her newfound discovery. "After all, what good is a rule if you don't have something to fear by breaking it?"

"Right." He looked pointedly at her. "Food."

"What?"

"If you break the rules, you go without the next meal."

"Good heavens, you *are* serious about this, aren't you?"

"I believe, Miss Merriweather, that I'm simply being wise."

Her eyes flew wide. "Oh, God, what time is it? I smell coffee. Damn—" She tossed aside his sketchbook, leapt from the bed, and started to flutter around like an agitated bird. "I can't be late. It's my first conversation and I still don't know which part of the cause I'm going to champion. I have to be there right from the start so I can get a good seat. Promptly at seven."

He glanced at her watch pin on the dresser. "You've got ten minutes."

She froze. "Ten? Yes, I believe I can do it in ten, if I don't snag my stockings."

"No," he almost shouted, when her fingers fumbled with the robe's tie, but the knot slipped free, she shrugged, and then the cotton robe billowed and fell to the floor. He spun around and couldn't reach for his topcoat fast enough. One hand started to stuff his shirt into his trousers. The other groped around on the floor for his shoes. He kept his eyes on the far wall. Then the ceiling. He felt a shoe. It had three-inch heels.

"Here." Blindly he handed it to her, contorting himself around to keep from touching her. He found another shoe, this one his own, and had never known such relief. He found the other but didn't pause to put them on.

"I'll just—" He reached around her upthrust backside toward the bed as she searched beneath it for something. He patted the bed, couldn't find his sketchbook, and finally had to look. He got an eyeful of plump, cotton swathed backside, grabbed his sketchbook, and only then realized he held his breath.

Jerking to his feet, he spun toward the door. "I'll see you at some point—" he tossed over his shoulder, yanking open the door. He slammed it closed behind him. Only when he met the curious stares of a passing couple did he realize that he was trembling.

Ten minutes later, dressed, tucked, and under control, he poured himself a third cup of coffee in the main saloon and looked out over the churning Atlantic. Assuming a stiff, wide-legged stance, he donned a scowl that was sure to put off even the most determined young woman. As it was, today and every one thereafter was crammed with appointments to sketch nubile young women. He sipped deeply and hoped the ship's lurching would keep most in their cabins bent over their chamber pots.

He caught sight of Frances Trainer lumbering up to a semicircle of young women seated out on the deck. An ambitious group to take on the wind and the pitching decks in the name of women's sovereignty. His eye passed over the small group. All wore dark, demure dresses, feathered hats, and intense expressions. There wasn't a smile or a crimson dress among them.

He dug his watch out of his pocket, flipped it open and frowned. A quarter past seven. Frances Trainer took a seat at the table and began to speak. Every woman at the table leaned closer to her.

Setting his coffee aside, he left the saloon and moved through the short hall to their cabin. He hesitated at the closed door, knocked once, and entered.

Savannah was sitting on her bed. When he entered she turned abruptly away from him and sniffed. She sniffed again. Then she hiccuped and looked down at her hands clamped in her lap.

"The conversation is stalling without you," he said, lingering at the door, half in, half out of the room. His fingers toyed with the handle and he contemplated his sudden feeling of ineptitude.

She sniffed again and lifted one shoulder in a shrug.

"You're crying." There, stating the obvious ought to fix it.

"Of course I'm crying," she said, in a child's cracking voice that made him feel even more incompetent. "And you want to know why?"

"Yes, then I can help."

"Help?" She spun around, her face splotchy, her eyes filled with tears. Her bottom lip trembled open. "You can't do anything, Mr. Dare. Look at me. I'm so fat my dress doesn't fit without my corset to hold me in. Look. Right here—" She waved a hand over the row of crimson-covered buttons that ran the length of the front of her dress. She'd left the top half dozen or so open, revealing the lacy trim of a cotton garment beneath and a cavernous depth of décolletage that had swallowed one blond curl. "The buttons are pulling every time I breathe or move or sit down, and here—" She sounded as if she choked on something awful as her hand fluttered over the stupendous swell of her bosom. "It's all getting squeezed up and out. I can't even lean over, and I feel like I'm suffocating. Do you want to tell me why I have to have an eighteen-inch waist? Who made that rule?"

"Some very rich man who invented the corset, I'd wager. Here. Stand up."

"I don't want to stand up. I want to cry only I can't really because I can't breathe all that well. I can't meet Frances Trainer looking like this. Mother was right. I'm wearing my chocolate. Please, just sew my mouth closed until we get to New York."

He abandoned the door, abandoned the rules that required him to keep his distance, and sat on the bed beside her. She looked away and a tear slipped to her cheek. It occurred to him that he'd thought her impervious to the afflictions of vanity that tortured most other women. For so stalwart a defender of women's liberty, she was still a vulnerable young girl.

Strange that her self-consciousness didn't tire him. Her vanity didn't put him off. Indeed, it troubled him a great deal to see her this way, the bird suddenly caged, unable to do anything to save itself but flap its clipped wings. For a man who'd determined to mingle very little into the lives of other people, particularly those of vain women, he wanted very much to fix it all for her, and he didn't know why.

But looking at her—how could he explain to her that it seemed only right that a woman so abundantly blessed in spirit should be as extravagantly blessed in body? That to look at her and not paint her was torture for him, every single moment that his eyes rested on her? That the fullness of line and curves to her silhouette made her an angel among whalebone-narrow mortals? That next to her every woman looked frail, cold, sterile.

He reined in his thoughts. "You yourself wanted to bend the unspoken rules that all suffragists wear gray and frown most of the time. Can't a woman be an advocate of women's rights and still be dramatically feminine, in every sense of the word? Can't she shed her corset and fill out her red silk dresses and still stand beside the men of this world?"

She lifted her eyes and Dominic's heart did a little stutter.

"I think so," he said. "What could be more compelling to the cause, or more daunting to the male populace, than a thinking suffragist who looks like any man's version of Aphrodite?"

She blinked. "Really? You think so?"

His voice seemed to come up from below his feet. "You're exceptional in that regard, Savannah."

"No, not that," she said quickly, distractedly, as if she didn't give a damn whether he thought her body the most magnificent he'd ever beheld. She sat a bit forward, her face lighting with animation. "Do you think Frances Trainer would appreciate that? I mean, such audacity. I don't want to shock her, or do I?" She bit her lip and angled her eyes at him. "She'd well remember me, wouldn't she?"

"Few are likely to ever forget you."

"Good!" She leapt to her feet with such enthusiasm Dominic had to follow. Her chin lifted, her shoulders thrust back. "So my dress is tight. So my bosoms don't fit some snobbish French designer's vision of a proper size. Perhaps that vision has long been in need of a bit of an adjustment. Perhaps the notion that bosoms shouldn't be shown before five in the afternoon should be amended. Let acreage of bosom be displayed, I say, and let it be at any time of the day. What the devil is wrong with the body that God gave me? I ask you, Mr. Dare, shouldn't I be proud to show it in its unfettered state?"

"I know of no man who would argue that with you, Savannah."

"Very good, then. I believe I've found my topic for the conversation. And what better way to initiate discussion on the subject than to appear in my ill-fitting dress? It's the dress that's the problem, Mr. Dare, not me. Oh, thank heavens, and to think that I was going to forgo food! Thank you!" And then she rose up on tiptoes and pressed her lips to his cheek.

He stood frozen to the floorboards, palms sweating against his thighs, heart thudding along like a seventeen-year-old's.

"You look pale, Mr. Dare," she said, stepping back and looking not the least bit disturbed. "Perhaps a turn around the decks will help you."

"I'll consider it."

"Very good then. I imagine I'll see you—sometime—"

"Sometime." He didn't want her to leave. He suddenly didn't want her to go anywhere dressed like that without him. He stood still and steady as the Rock of Gibraltar.

She looked expectantly up at him, hesitated, leaned a bit right, then left, and decided getting past him was impossible. Her brows lifted. "Did you need something, Mr. Dare?"

No, it wasn't quite a need. He'd allowed nothing in his life to grip him that intensely. But wanting . . . Christ, whenever he looked at her he knew a wanting of physical intimacy so violent it left him shaken. "Uh—no—I—oh, hell, here." He grabbed the silk-fringed shawl still draped over the foot of her bed and whisked it around her shoulders before she could stop him. He drew the edges together tightly at the base of her throat, took her hand, and anchored it there. "In case you get cold."

"That rather defeats the purpose, doesn't it?"

"That depends on your purpose." He turned and offered her his arm. "I'll take you to Frances Trainer. And if you need me, I'll be in the private quarterdeck saloon for the rest of the day."

To celebrate the enthusiastic response she received to her "Free the Bosom from Paris Couturiers" crusade, Savannah indulged in two desserts after a late luncheon of roast beef and potatoes, one a lemon tart smothered in cream, the other chocolates. Along with several other women who were traveling alone, she lingered at the table sipping tea and discussing plans for a National Women's Convention in New York with Frances Trainer until early evening when dinner was served. Afterward, the group took to the promenade for their nightly brisk turn about the ship.

She glimpsed Dominic several times throughout the day when he passed by the saloon windows. Her eyes had lingered on the pink feathered hat bobbing merrily along beside him. She waited for him to look inside the saloon windows for her, but he didn't, his attention obviously held by his buoyant companion.

Not that she cared. After all, Frances Trainer had spent the afternoon deploring men in general and in particular their mistaken belief that women were incapable of engaging in the sustained and analytical thought required by philosophy, the sciences, or literary criticism. Men were narrow-minded brutes intent on squashing all life from the female sex. What should Savannah care if one of them spent his days sketching beautiful young, pink-feathered women in a private saloon?

He passed by their table before dinner, politely inquired how she was and in general of the health of the other ladies, then retired to a corner table with three couples and two unescorted young ladies. Savannah spent the remainder of dinner feeling strangely distracted . . . and rather wishing he'd asked her to join him.

"I congratulate you, Savannah, in finding so obliging a husband," Frances Trainer commented later as they rounded the bow of the ship for the third time. "Every woman in New York will be green with envy."

Sea spray hit them with the force of a violent rainstorm but Savannah didn't dare break stride for fear of disappointing the stalwart females of the world. If Frances Trainer could plow along like a ship under full sail against the wind, then so could she. "Thank you, Miss Trainer."

"Indeed, you should be thankful," Frances advised in her grave tones. "Most men who are bored with their wives still find it necessary to police them and cage them and repress them from all outside interests. I suppose their thinking is that if we women are off indulging our interests, who will be taking care of the men, eh?"

"Yes," Savannah said, contemplating a sudden unease. Did she bore Dominic Dare? The idea struck her more deeply than a bone-cold wind. Even more troublesome was the idea that this should bother her at all.

"The earl might have little interest in you, but at least he has the decency to let you alone with your pursuits. A man like that won't make a bit of fuss when you fully explore your freedoms and take a lover or two."

"Two?"

"Or more. Just as he will. Even more than a man, a woman has to know some passion in her life."

"Of course," Savannah replied, though she didn't know precisely what that sort of passion might be or how to find it.

"Few women find it in a husband. You obviously haven't found yours."

Savannah puzzled and plowed along, head bent to the wind. How could this be so damned obvious to a woman she barely knew?

"The earl is quite something to look at," Frances said. "Fiercely foreign in a Mediterranean sort of way, but obviously lacking in that fire of the soul that we women must have to find fulfillment."

Fire of the soul.

The words haunted Savannah when she returned to the cabin and found it dark and unwelcoming. She undressed, put on her nightgown and her robe for good measure, and climbed into bed. For having so grandly successful a day—after all, she'd had lemon tarts _and_ chocolate—she felt oddly dissatisfied and troubled. She felt a bit like a ship chugging deliberately along through a fog, destination firmly in mind, yet missing everything she passed by.

Fire of the soul.

Frances Trainer was quite mistaken about that. Whenever Savannah had looked at him, Dominic Dare's fire burned so hot his eyes smoldered.

His subject's name was Daphne. She was the daughter of a New York Four Hundred couple who'd made their millions following after Getty in oil. This had been over fifteen years before, which made her, in a relative sense, of very old money. Just turned twenty-three, chestnut-haired, square-shaped, and not unpleasant-looking, she made an immediate point of telling him three things: that her family lived on Fifth Avenue not one block from the Astors, that the family's livery color was a rich, deep crimson that put the Astor peacock blue to shame, and that she was traveling from London—alone.

Her eye color deepened every time he shifted in his chair or lifted his pencil from the pad, however subtle the movement. Dominic could almost smell the spinster's desperation oozing out of her white skin.

"Do you know much art?" he asked in his bored English drawl, inclining his head and studying her. An instant later his pencil returned to the pad. "Is your father a collector?"

"All rich men are in New York, your lordship," she replied, squirming a bit under his scrutiny. "A private art gallery is as essential as a yacht in Newport or a private railroad car at Union Station. Should I sit forward a bit?"

"You're quite good where you are," he said, but she

wriggled some more. He kept his voice bored and his eyes lowered to his sketch as if his questions were of little import to him save for their use as idle conversation. "I'd wager the American elite are the greatest art patrons since the Renaissance. All the best in European artwork is never seen in European homes anymore. It all goes to New York."

"Oh, yes, my father must have anything that's painted by a French or Italian artist. Those paintings have been quite the rage for years now. At an auction just last month my father paid eighty thousand dollars for a Meissonier oil, the *Friedland—1807,* which depicts a Napoleonic battle scene. Pictures that tell stories are quite popular, your lordship."

"Please, call me Castellane. He has a dealer, does he?"

"Yes. He's had several. Only the very best, of course. Samuel Avery, at Fifth Avenue and Fourteenth Street. That's where all the dealers are. Bernard Melton. James Atwood. They all specialize in French and Italian imports and sell only to the Four Hundred. Most are imported from overseas. They've practically made French and Italian art the rage that they are today. Among my father's immediate friends, owning what a top-drawer art agent considers the best products means that you have the best possible collection of art. It's their eye, you see."

"Their eye."

"To find the jewellike picture. Of course, they also have an extraordinary ability to find large canvases."

Dominic had to pause and glance up at her. In his surprise he almost forgot to add the right amount of nasal accent to his tone. "And what does the size of the canvas have to do with it?"

She frowned. "Why, everything. As a rule, the more generous in size the canvases, the more satisfied my father is that he's getting his money's worth."

Daphne was obviously unaware that this would make no sense even to a mildly educated art lover.

"Art to most people means buying by the square foot."
Daphne beamed. "My father has the most square footage
of canvas of any collection I've seen, and I've seen many."

Dominic's interest focused. "The private collections?"

"Oh, yes. Whenever anyone has a caller they throw
open their art galleries to show everyone else what they
have. It's an extremely competitive arena. Men bid against
one another at auctions for a painting an agent has recommended. The prices can become extraordinary."

"These agents live exceedingly well, I take it—" He
arched a brow at her. "And justifiably so?"

"Oh, yes! Most have homes in Paris." When this didn't
rouse the anticipated awe in him, she added, "They know
all the French artists, and of course the Italians as well.
But there aren't as many of them. I suppose that makes
their paintings even more precious, doesn't it?"

And even more difficult to locate, particularly when the
canvases were of a size that would fit easily into a traveling
bag. Dominic wondered how many houses the New York
Four Hundred occupied. A hundred? Maybe more. In six
months he'd have to visit one every other day to view all
their galleries, a monumental proposition at best.

There had to be a way to narrow his search.

"Your father has the Italian art as well?" he asked, un-
caring that she might find his interest even remotely odd.
In six months he doubted that the squirming spinster
Daphne would be able to remember the particulars of
their conversation, even under duress from the police.
And they were sure to ask.

"I believe he has several."

Dominic forced his eyes back to the sketch. It looked
well enough for a consciously mediocre sketch, his tech-
nique broad and quick, indicating form and structure
through accents of darker and lighter tones. A single
patch of light indicated her hand on her lap. A few patch-
like strokes of light and shadow sufficed to define the

squarish features of her face. It looked like the preliminary sketches his father had made before he painted.

She gasped with delight when he handed it to her and clutched it to her bosom. "Would you like to see my father's collection?" she said with the kind of breathless wonderment that made him want to twitch. "I believe I could arrange an invitation."

"I would be honored," he murmured, drawing her trembling hand to his lips. "And I look forward to it. Good day, madam."

By the time Dominic finished the last of the day's sketches and returned to their cabin, he'd managed to secure invitations to visit the private art collections of several New York families. Each of these galleries, he was assured, contained "something Italian."

If the rest of the voyage and its multitude of sketch subjects went as well, he could be done with the charade before six months was up. And the sooner the better.

After all, he was descended of a family that was notorious for breaking rules, political or otherwise, no matter the punishment. He could hardly trust himself to rise above his ancestry for any great length of time. As it was, he intended to endure the next ten days by judiciously avoiding Savannah.

He was certain that he would prevail, over her as well as over himself.

Chapter 9

"You've quite outdone yourself," Savannah said to Dominic after lunch on their seventh day at sea. As had become routine during the voyage, they'd dined separately with their respective circles but took a tour together around the promenade deck after every meal. Savannah tried to smile at the people they passed but felt her fingers dig into his arm. "Mrs. Trapp came up to our table in the middle of dessert and made a point of telling me that she overheard some woman in the stateroom next to hers saying that the Earl of Castellane is making fast and loose with at least two of the single women aboard this vessel *and*," she added pointedly, "which is most distressing, he was caught with his hands in some woman's bodice."

"That would be Miss Drew."

Savannah clamped one hand on top of her hat against the stiff breeze that set her dress snapping like a ship's sails. "*Miss Drew?* You mean to say you admit it?"

"She lost an earring."

"A fine excuse."

He glanced down at her and a corner of his mouth

twitched upward. "Is that what it was? You're speaking from experience, I take it."

"Hardly. I can only assume some women will do anything to get a man's hands on their—" She swallowed the word and looked pointedly out to sea when he looked long and hard at her. "And then there was that incident yesterday with the French woman. She told positively everyone about it."

"She fell when the ship pitched in a rough swell. Someone had to help her up. She wasn't going to do it on her own."

Savannah felt her lips tighten and fidgeted with her shawl at her shoulder. "Poor dear. All twenty years and hundred pounds of her would be agony to set aright."

He didn't say anything for a moment. "I thought our arrangement was working out quite well. Don't you?"

"Oh, it is," Savannah quickly replied. "Exceedingly well. You're as authentic an Englishman as I've ever seen. I feel as if I'm alone in the stateroom. All the privacy I could want, and it's just wonderful." She glanced up at him. "Isn't it?"

He frowned at something farther ahead of them, not meeting her eyes. "Yes, yes. Wonderful."

The wind ruffled through his hair, making him look like a young girl's romantic vision of a dashing sea captain. Savannah forced her gaze away, aware that a mantle of disappointment seemed to have settled over her. She wished she could shake it and sought a good reason for it. "I just don't like being cast in the role of the spurned wife. People are beginning to look at me like I'm some orphan."

"I hardly believe that. For the record, I've done nothing for the last week but sketch and scowl and throw my aristocratic nose at the sky. I've done the English peerage proud and because of it people will talk. Let them. Few can look at you and feel sympathy. Take Mr. Wimpole, for instance."

Savannah felt herself pale. "Please, I'd rather not. Is he still following us?"

"I believe we lost him in the quarterdeck bridge game."

Savannah sighed with relief. "He wants to be my lover."

"Ah. Would you like me to step in and play the cuckolded husband?"

Savannah gripped his arm. "No, good heavens, don't do that. He'll want to fight you and then you'll squash him."

"And we don't want that kind of talk circulating."

"He's not a villain. I'm sure he's a very nice man. But I believe I have to get firmer with him. Of course, Hattie O'Neal—one of my fellow suffragists on board—said I should consider him. He's well off—for a shoe tradesman—although I don't like his checkered jackets and plaid pants, or his cigar, and he has no hair on his head, which means he has a godawful amount all over his back."

His look was quick and keen. "Is this a proven theory?"

"Hattie told me that too."

"A veritable font of information, isn't she, for a woman who spouts man-hating theories like a bubbling teapot? What else does Hattie say?"

"She says I should have two lovers, one older, one younger, preferably married, which now that I think about it, excludes Mr. Wimpole. I'd better tell him that. She also says that I'll have no difficulty meeting all these married men at all the parties we'll attend. We've already received several invitations, it seems, thanks to your artistic talents, so it shouldn't take me too long. 'Make sure he can afford to buy you Tiffany jewels,' Hattie says."

"And where will you wear your lover's jewels?" Dominic asked, his face darkening several shades. Perhaps the effects of too much afternoon sun.

"Whenever I'm alone with my lover. Hattie says that's all I'll be wearing. Isn't she wicked to say such things, and she must be close to forty years old?" Savannah smiled up at Dominic, but he wasn't smiling or looking at her. She watched his Adam's apple work in his thick throat and thought his face looked almost savage in intensity. So many sharp angles, so many deeply embedded lines, she felt that if she watched him closely enough, long enough, his face would reveal his multitude of secrets.

"I've an appointment," he said briskly, as if he couldn't wait to be rid of her.

"Yes, of course." Again, the cloud of disappointment hovered over her.

Dominic stepped up his pace and said nothing until they reached the entrance to the main saloon where Frances Trainer and fellow suffragists awaited Savannah inside. Mr. Wimpole, stout and undaunted in his ill-fitting suit, stood his post just outside the door like an obedient and eager puppy. His eyes lit up like beacons when he spotted Savannah, and he yanked the cigar from his mouth.

Determined to set him properly straight as to her intentions with him, Savannah gathered her thoughts and took a calming breath. But instead of continuing past, Dominic stopped directly in front of Mr. Wimpole. Perhaps it was her imagination, but Dominic's chest puffed out, blocking all the sunlight with height and breadth and savage magnificence.

"Stay the hell away from my wife," Dominic said with a snarl, "or you'll have me to deal with."

Mr. Wimpole went white as alabaster, gulped several times, then flushed crimson but didn't speak. Savannah almost said something, the poor man looked so distraught, and rightly so for just being threatened and by a member of the British peerage at that, but Dominic gave her no opportunity. With a strong hand at her back, he pushed her along ahead of him into the saloon.

"If he so much as breathes next to you I want to know about it," he said, very low and close to her ear. "I'll be damned if I play the cuckolded idiot." And then he turned and she watched him stride from the saloon. She stood in perplexed contemplation for a moment, trying to decide whether to be angry or not. Oddly enough, she felt unusually buoyant, a veritable gushing font of snap and vigor.

All traces of her prior disappointment had vanished in a whiff of ocean breeze. How odd. With no easy explanation for it, she hurried to join her friends and within minutes was swallowed up in plans for the New York convention.

"I cabled my parents when we left London," Savannah said, gripping the ship's rail with a pink-gloved hand and bobbing up and down on her toes. A line of black carriages crammed the dock, most bearing scrolled crests on their gleaming black doors. "Surely they've come to greet us—ah! I see Papa's coachman, Ernst!" She smiled, waved enthusiastically, then yelled, "Ernst! Look here!" She flung out an arm directly in front of the woman next to her, pointed at the dock, and tugged at Dominic's sleeve. "See, it's the coach without a crest. Mother hasn't chosen one yet."

"Ah. And here I believed them descended from prior generations." Dominic gently touched her arm and she lowered it, still oblivious to the shocked woman beside her. A hot breeze tossed the pink feathers of Savannah's hat into Dominic's nose. She bobbed again and stepped squarely on his foot. He winced a smile, caught the eye of the woman next to Savannah, and smiled harder. "My wife is delighted to be home," he offered over Savannah's head.

"Would that we could all be left in peace to enjoy the moment," the woman replied with a chilling look at Savannah's profile. "We're all anxious to set foot on something that doesn't pitch and roll, your lordship."

"Indeed, most anxious." As if to further remind Dominic of his anticipation to be off the ship, Savannah squeezed herself deeper between the rail and his shoulder, fitting her unbustled backside cozily up against his thigh. Dominic stared over her head and with a certain affable resignation felt his blood begin its daily heat.

A trickle of perspiration wove down his temple. His collar felt like a noose in the springtime warmth.

Their ten days of pretense as husband and wife aboard ship had gone swimmingly on every score except one: At about the midpoint of the voyage, Savannah had decided that whenever they were about the business of being the Earl and Countess Castellane they should be touching somewhere. Odd, since most of the married couples aboard made a determined effort to avoid one another.

And yet still Savannah was forever clinging to his arm, touching his hand, or sitting so near as to guarantee that some part of her touched him. Just last evening her thigh had wandered over beneath the dining table to rest against his.

That perplexed him. None of their fellow travelers could see under the table, so what purpose did thigh touching serve, precisely, other than to distract him? But she couldn't know that. She knew nothing beyond the need to put on a very good show. And like any passionate creature, she'd taken her part a little too seriously.

He'd obviously become habit for her, the touching something she did without even thinking about what it might be doing to him. After all, she was still suffering under the misconception that he was one of *those* kind of men. And he was most certain that she'd yet to hear one word of explanation of the true nature and function of the reproductive organs, despite her trip to Paris.

She'd simply grown used to him, like a well-worn pair of slippers. Or a faithful old dog. Yes, something about the way she patted his sleeve and smiled at him made him feel positively canine.

She shifted against his arm, as if it hindered her, and he had no choice but to curve it around her. Her dress was fuchsia pink silk and fit so snugly he could see the indentation of her spine through the fabric.

She wore no undergarments beneath the silk. His hand groped for the rail and covered hers. Lilac scent swirled around him. It was, he realized, an odd public display of closeness, even for a husband and wife who'd known true intimacy.

And certainly for an impostor who spent his nights fantasizing about it.

"He's not here." Her tone rang with hollow disappointment.

"Who?" He lowered his head beside hers and felt the soft brush of her cheek against his much rougher one. He watched the early-afternoon sun set aglow the pearl buttons that marked the swell of her bosom, then forced his gaze to the coach she'd pointed out. A pudgy coachman stood beside it wearing a dour expression. It was the first time in his life Dominic had been waited upon by a servant. The idea was an unexpectedly disturbing one for him.

"I thought at least Papa would come."

"Perhaps he's in the coach."

To Savannah's dismay, he wasn't. Ernst brusquely informed them that Mr. Merriweather was tending to business at his club and would join them for dinner later that evening. Mrs. Merriweather awaited them at the family town house and was tending to final details concerning their new accommodations.

"I hope it's not some vast, gloomy pile of granite," Savannah grumbled, situating herself opposite Dominic as the coach lurched forward. "They're all monsters of shingle, every one of them, bristling with bay windows and tower cupolas and crammed with French this and Belgian that and enough velvet to outfit the city. I could never feel at home in one of them. You'll have to speak to Papa about buying us something cozy and charming. He'll be able to find one."

Dominic shifted and worked his neck against his collar, but his discomfort had nothing to do with the heat. He scowled at the passing streets of New York and wished they were headed for his Tenth Street apartment. At this time of the afternoon most of his neighbors were rousing themselves from a midday snooze to set about capturing the mellowing hues of daylight on canvas.

"This matter of money," he said, drawing even less comfort from discussing it. "When our arrangement is over, I intend to even up on every score. I'm more than capable of—"

"That's kind of you."

Dominic looked at her and deepened his scowl. "Hardly kind. Posing as Castellane might serve my higher purposes at the moment, but I don't have to like all that comes with it."

"Ah. You were raised working class."

Her astuteness jarred him. "Yes. Very much working class."

"There's nothing wrong with that."

He felt his chin jut a notch and his jaw tighten. "I don't believe I said there was."

"Ah. I thought you did. You seemed—" She narrowed her eyes and he could almost hear her thoughts bubbling along. He felt himself tense in grim anticipation. "Yes, you seemed rather resentful in telling me. No, you didn't like being working class. You worked awfully hard to get above it. You're running away from it, aren't you?"

He stared at her and realized she expected an answer. His tone was dismissing. "You know nothing about any of it."

"No, but I wasn't raised on Fifth Avenue."

"You're comfortable there now."

"Really? I'd rather be the simple girl I was, born to a former hotel chambermaid and her husband pork farmer who'd never seen the world beyond Dogberg, Ohio. I'd rather live in a cozy little house with a swing on the porch and no pictures on the walls and three big dogs instead of ladies' maids and stewards. I'd rather help my mother in the kitchen and my papa in the barn.

"I sometimes wish my papa had never gone to Chicago with his pigs all packed in a railroad car. Two weeks after he came back, three men from Chicago came to visit him. And then suddenly we were moving to New York City and my mother was buying new dresses from Paris and keeping the *Social Register* right on her bedside table. My papa was going to clubs and talking about millions the way he'd spoken before of hundreds. The people we had to know were named Astor and Vanderbilt and Morgan and Getty, not Brown and Miller and Jones. They became the people-we-don't-know—" She flushed slightly and quirked her lips. "I still write to my best friend, Molly Flannery. Mother doesn't know."

Dominic watched her lift her chin and turn to the window, proud and stubborn and true as a young oak. But it wasn't the embodiment of pampered purity that captured his fascination. It was, as it had always been with her, the undauntable spirit that kept her struggling to stay afloat against a surging tide of expectation, repression, and duty.

And in the sun-kissed depths of her eyes he glimpsed a longing that seemed to strike the chord of a kindred longing in him.

"I don't take the food on my father's table for granted, Mr. Dare."

"I believe you just might. You've never been without."

"And you have?"

Her look was so forthright, her curiosity so compelling to him in a way he'd never experienced, he replied before he could remind himself that opening the doors to his past had never been wise. "These Astors you need to know own five square blocks of tenement buildings. While they dine on Fifth Avenue over champagne and French linen, immigrant families crowd four and five together on one floor in buildings crowded against one an-

other in an airless, sunless huddle. While servants ladle
heavy cream over cookies for fat, spoiled Astor children,
in those same tenements consumptive children cough out
their lives in living rooms where parents bend over piece-
work from sweatshops. Vermin are everywhere. Everyone
lives in fear of sickness and fire. And no, there isn't
enough food for even one family for a day, much less five
families for a month."

Her face seemed to have lost all color. "Surely the Astors must know—"

"The Astors have spacious ambitions, large appetites,
and very small consciences. Like the general populace,
they believe the immigrants to be the cause of their mis-
eries, not the victims of a hypocritical society."

Her voice was very low, her eyes unblinkingly focused
on him. "Surely you weren't a victim long."

"Ten years is a lifetime to many there. I was one of the
lucky few. I found pick-and-shovel work making roads in
Virginia and Philadelphia." Memory crept over him. "I
made very little money. I got tired of being treated like an
animal so I escaped. I walked back to New York and
turned to crime, picking pockets and paying my padrone
everything I stole so he wouldn't kill me. At fifteen I discovered cheap liquor."

"And your parents?"

He looked at her with hard eyes. "My parents, my sister, and my grandparents were killed in Florence in a pop-
ulist uprising my father led for Italian unification."

"You were spared," she whispered.

His laugh was cold. "I was at the stream swimming
when I should have been helping my father. The soldiers
came from out of the hills with their guns and their
knives, looking for him. I floated on my back in cool water
while they cut my mother down in the kitchen. There was
blood—my mother's, my father's—it splashed on some of
my father's canvases." He stared at a block of sunlight
sizzling in the fuchsia silk threads of her skirt and saw it

all as he had that morning he'd entered his home for the last time. "There were six of those canvases, leaning against a wall. They were his best works. He planned to take them to Paris with him. They would have made him an international sensation—had they ever made it to Paris. The blood almost looked a part of the paintings."

She reached and curled her fingers around and through his. It was a strangely provoking gesture. He stared at their entwined fingers, felt her pulse pumping along, and wondered why the hell he couldn't let go.

"My friend told me there were streets of gold awaiting me in America," he said. "He came on the ship from Florence with me, but he died in Philadelphia after he was beaten by a padrone. The streets in New York are made of immigrant blood and sweat, Savannah, not of gold." His breath came slowly through his teeth. "And now I'm to be one of the hypocrites. The irony of it sticks like a fist in my throat. I warn you, I won't suffer these Four Hundred fools as easily as I expected I would."

"No Englishman would. Not even one as awful as Castellane. You won't be out of order. I don't particularly like any of them either. We will be a shocking couple."

His thumb rubbed slowly over hers. "I knew a man once—a cold man but a brilliant lawyer—and a master with money."

"How did you know him?"

He glanced up. "I picked his pocket and got caught."

"You didn't run fast enough."

"I couldn't. I'd been beaten for trying to steal from my padrone."

"Dominic—"

"Don't pity me, Savannah. I was lucky. To save myself from jail I sketched some charcoal pictures for him. He liked them enough to commission a collection of oils, and in payment he invested some money for me in the stock market. Actually, I owe him a great deal. The money I made took me away from the tenement. But knowing him taught me about those rich businessmen who sleep in the Fifth Avenue brownstones I walked past every day when I was a boy. This man shocked the pious everywhere with his lectures espousing agnosticism. He was a known heretic. And yet in spite of his beliefs, which went vilely against most people's, he remained an honored and respected lawyer. And you want to know why?"

Savannah narrowed her eyes. "Let me guess. He was a Union veteran and belonged to the Knickerbocker Club."

His lips spread in a grim smile. "Very good. He was also a Republican and a good family man. He was known to eat heartily at dinner parties and he spoke fluently. Hell, what more could be required of him to deserve such an outpouring of respect?"

"And yet look what he did for you."

"That's the trouble of it. No matter how easy it would be for me to hate his kind with a singular purpose, I can't."

"You seek your vengeance against the Astors of the world elsewhere."

Her voice was so low, feminine and gently coaxing, he almost missed the curious edge. The turn of her thoughts was almost palpable in a way that made him sit stiffly upright. Memory and guilt washed away like sand beneath a tide. He moved her hand to her knee and covered it momentarily with his own. "Very good try, Savannah."

She blinked and looked abominably guilty and brimming with guile. "What? What are you accusing me of precisely?"

Dominic settled back against his seat and regarded her through lowered lids. "Female treachery."

"I'm not wicked. I don't know the first thing about being treacherous."

"Didn't your mother ever tell you that curiosity is going to get you into trouble one day?"

She sniffed and looked put upon. "I'm very good with

secrets, you know. I keep at least a dozen of my own concurrently."

"And if I threaten to take away your chocolate and your breakfast you'd spew them all out for me, wouldn't you?"

"Chocolates *and* breakfast?" Her teeth sank into her lower lip as if she pondered this calamity. "It would be a bit tempting, I'll admit, but this is different. M. Harrigan was murdered for what he knew. His killer could be jaunting about New York City just waiting for you to catch him."

"Wouldn't that be convenient?"

"You might not know it, but you're going to need my help in this. And catching a killer is a bit more important than meeting Charles at a bookshop or writing letters to Molly Flannery. Yes, I believe I would forgo chocolate and breakfast for months to keep your secrets and find M. Harrigan's killer."

She looked at him, cheeks rosy, lips petal soft and virgin pink, hair on fire with afternoon sunlight, pink feathers swaying with the coach, silk straining at the seams. No matter how decidedly she'd beguile and befuddle them, she'd be mincemeat for New York City police. In record time, they'd prod every last one of her secrets out of her.

And they wouldn't stop until they'd gotten them all.

"You'll know nothing about it," he said, grimly certain that his decision had more to do with protecting her than it did with protecting him. The idea was not a particularly comforting one.

Her mouth pinched, twisted, and she huffed a few times and pouted. She glanced out the window, then back at him, her eyes dancing with sparks. "You underestimate me. I can be quite determined, Mr. Dare."

"Darling," he corrected her, warming to her challenge in spite of himself.

"I swear I'm calling you Winny. You'll be the laughing-stock of New York. No one has a name like that."

"I still won't tell you anything. I'm rather used to being an outcast."

She shrugged, clearly self-satisfied. "Winny it is then."

Dominic gave a loud sigh. "And just when I was getting fond of 'darling.' I suppose I'll have to launch some sort of counteroffensive—" He narrowed his eyes and could almost feel her beginning to squirm from the inside out. "It's only fair."

"This isn't a war."

"Oh? Hell, but I feel as if my arm is being twisted to make me do something I'd rather not do. You're trying awfully hard to make me feel guilty for doing something that is clearly for your benefit though for some damnable reason you refuse to see it. Can I help myself if I try my own bit of arm-twisting?"

She stared at him, then swallowed noisily. "You're not going to call me some awful pet name, are you?"

"I'm considering it." With a pointed appreciation, he swept his eyes over her from the top of her feathered hat to the tips of her fuchsia pink shoes and back again. Her cheeks blossomed as pink as her dress. She looked as sweet as a gooey gumdrop. *Rosy* . . . the word drifted like a woman's soft whisper through his mind.

After a moment, she drew up stiff and prim as a spinster schoolmarm. "Fine. Call me Hortense. Call me Augusta. Call me Bunny or Tookie or Sissy or Mim. I don't care. Humiliation has never squashed an ounce of my curiosity. But be forewarned, my determination rises with every challenge."

Dominic fingered his chin and spoke in a soft rumble. "Of course, there are other methods of persuasion."

She blinked several times as if she mentally leafed through those methods, then waved a careless hand. "Well, I can tell you torture of any kind will get you nowhere, and if you're thinking of denying me food—"

"Ways to get a woman to close her mouth and forget about all those secrets she's itching to find out."

"—you should know that I can always get anything I want from my mother's cook. She's never been able to deny me anything when I—"

Dominic surged toward her, braced his hands on either side of her hips, and leaned so close to her their noses almost touched.

Savannah pressed so far back against her seat her hat slid over her forehead. Her lips remained parted but no sound came out.

"See there," Dominic murmured, nudging her hat back with his thumb. But his eyes were on the tender fullness of her lower lip. It occurred to him that he'd exercised a lion's share of self-control during the last ten days. He congratulated himself on his wisdom in avoiding sharing small spaces with her. Because whenever he was near her, as he was now, the desire to touch her, to taste those lips, washed everything else from his mind. Including good sense.

"Mr. Dare, are you ill?"

Dominic eased gently forward—or did the coach lurch at that precise moment?—and his lips touched hers. It was meant to be a chaste instruction, or so he'd convinced himself, a brief little lesson that he held the absolute power to silence her. But when her lips parted with a surprised gasp, unwittingly inviting him to take more, he suddenly forgot chasteness and the wisdom of forbearance. He was suddenly a starving man offered his first taste of forbidden fruit. He was a man without will.

At the first gentle thrust of his tongue she made a low sound in the back of her throat and stiffened. He slipped one arm around her waist and fit his mouth deeper against hers. That a woman so divinely made for sex should deny herself physical pleasure out of fear and ignorance was a heinous injustice Dominic wasn't about to let any other man remedy or further propagate, much less some simpering French writer or the likes of a bumbling Charles Fairleigh.

It was a job only he was fit for.

She made another soft sound and her tongue gently touched his. An instant later she retreated. She seemed to want to turn her head away, refuse him, deny herself.

One lesson, he told himself. All he had to do was somehow garner that lion's share of restraint and stop at some point.

"No," he rumbled. He cupped her jaw, eased her head back and her mouth fuller beneath his, and pressed her body up to his. The result was instantaneously, ominously combustive. Silk and broadcloth sizzled between them, searing skin, setting blood afire and passions on galloping rampages. Dominic crushed her against him in an onslaught of lust so startling he shook with it.

He fell to his knees with her in his arms. He tore his mouth from hers. "Ah, God, Savannah—" He pressed his open mouth to her cheek, her temple, her hair, the softness of her neck, her chin, and again her mouth. And then suddenly she was kissing him back, offering those succulent sweet lips, arching her heaven-made young body into his with an abandon that would have made a monk weep. Soft arms entwined around his neck, soft breasts pressed into his chest, soft loins fit against hard.

"Mr. Dare," she breathed, gasping for breath.

"Dominic—" He could hardly think. No, he didn't want to think. What mortal man could function with her plump thighs spread and clamped around his, warm soft womanhood pulsing into his loins? He slid his hand over her silk-stockinged knee, fingers stretching up under the bunched-up hem of her gown. He touched lace and garters digging into a creamy soft, bare thigh, lowered his gaze to the feast of bosom, and closed his eyes in speechless wonderment. He drew a ragged breath and thought he'd never been so painfully full and hard and distended in his life.

No, the lesson couldn't end just yet. A minute longer . . . and then he'd summon the power of God and stop.

"I can't breathe—" Her fingers tugged at the top few buttons of her dress. It was all the invitation Dominic needed.

The first few buttons just below her collar bone popped apart at the gentle nudge of his fingers. The next several seemed to sing with delight as they sprang open.

"Yes, that's better," she breathed. "Much better—yes, keep going—if you wouldn't mind—" Her small hands were braced on his shoulders, gloved fingers squeezing as the row of buttons continued to part over the upper slopes of her breasts, then squeezing harder when two more sprang free. Her sigh was like music to his ears. His manhood pulsed with almost frenetic need.

"You're wearing nothing under this dress," Dominic rasped, pressing his lips for the first time to the surging upper curve of one breast. Her skin was dewy moist and tasted womanly warm. His fingers flicked over the buttons, lower, quicker, trembling in their haste.

"It was too hot for anything but stockings—" She sucked in a breath and wriggled in his lap, unconsciously fitting herself deeper against him. It was all he could do to keep his hand from snaking up between her thighs and finding the aching center of her. He could almost feel her moistness seeping through his trousers. His fingers curled around her thigh and squeezed pliant flesh. So much softness, so much perfumed plumpness. His mind spun.

Her décolletage went on forever. It was a descent he would never forget.

"Mr. Dare, I'm still so hot—"

"I'll paint you this way," he rumbled, kissing mounds of sweet softness as the dress parted at the nudge of his fingers. An acreage of white breasts sprang free of fuchsia silk, firm and breathlessly full with nipples the color of sun-ripened peaches. "God almighty—"

"Nothing like this happened to me in France—" she breathed.

"I know."

"It's—almost painful—your shirt—rubbing against my—"

He slid both hands inside her dress and around her rib cage. Her skin was as smooth as fine white French silk. "Let me help you—"

"Are you certain—can you?"

A groan surged up from his dry throat. "Quite."

"Please do." There was no hesitation. "That is—only if you think it might help. It won't hurt, will it?"

"Not a bit." He moved his hand up under one breast, lifted the nipple to his mouth, and drew the rigid bud tenderly against his tongue. Ten fingers slowly sank into his hair. She sighed his name and the world began to spin for him.

His need gathered a tempest's strength, more frenzied than he'd ever experienced. And then her hips rocked with a courtesan's skill against his loins.

"Sweet Jesus," he rasped, grazing her nipple with his teeth. "If you do that again, I'll take you now, God help me, I will—"

Again she lurched against him, but the movement was a jerky one, almost unnatural in motion, and he realized that the coach had careened to an abrupt stop. A chill washed over him.

"Shit. How the hell did this happen?"

"Y-you kissed me, that's how. What is it?"

He glanced up at her and knew he'd never forget the way she looked at that moment. It was one of those defining moments of his life and would in seconds become even more of one. Passion burned in her eyes. It was unmistakable.

"Sit up," he said. "Quick. We're here."

"Where?"

"Fix your hat." With an inordinate amount of force he lifted her back onto her seat and knelt before her. He glanced out the coach window and saw an imposing set of double wooden doors inlaid with cut glass. An instant later the doors swept wide and a fashionably dressed blond woman lurched into the sunlight, hands folded beneath her ponderous bosom, face pinched with motherly anxiety.

The coach swayed sideways as the driver leapt from his seat.

"Shit," Dominic said again, and set his fingers to the endless row of very tiny, very resistant pearl buttons.

Chapter 10

Savannah stared at her mother descending the front steps, then looked at Dominic Dare. With a face set in grim concentration, he knelt before her and tended to the miles of parted buttons. He was only at the midpoint. And her mother had just reached the foot of the steps. She waved an impatient hand at Ernst. In another instant the coach door would fly open.

It all seemed a rather ominous way to introduce Penelope Bell Merriweather to her son-in-law, the impoverished but nevertheless well-titled earl.

Savannah tried to help but Dominic pushed her fingers aside. She closed her eyes when he swore again and tugged on the fabric. "It's like trying to stuff a sausage into a small casing," she said.

"Nothing like it." His voice was unmistakable in its appreciation despite the scowl he wore.

Savannah gulped. "Hurry."

"I am."

"That's my mother."

"Fix your hat."

"Oh. Of course."

"Dammit, hold your breath."

"I'm trying to. I honestly don't know what she'll think."

"Do you care?" He was looking up at her, hair ruffled from her impassioned fingers, full mouth set in a firm line. That same mouth had spread hot kisses all over her bosom. Savannah's heart did a somersault in her chest. She wanted to feel those lips again, the graze of his teeth right where the tingles had tingled most painfully.

He was right. The tingling had stopped. But what should she do about the pulsing high between her thighs?

"No," she said honestly. "I don't suppose I care."

"I didn't think so." His lips quirked faintly but the scowl remained in place. "Christ, we'll never get them all buttoned. Play along with me then. Can you?"

"I can do anything, don't you realize that?"

"I'm beginning to believe it. As for what happened here—we'll discuss it later—then again, maybe we shouldn't. It can't—you know—happen again."

"No, I didn't know."

"Well, you do now. There's a hell of a lot a woman your age ought to know."

"I'm feeling a bit better. You know—"

His look was ominous. "I'm glad to hear it."

"Yes, but I've another ailment now, right between my—" She looked at the impressive swell of his groin, remembered what it felt like pulsing up between her thighs. She swallowed and looked back at her mother.

"Christ, but I deserve this," he muttered, lurching onto the seat beside her. "So much for playing the detached Brit."

"She'd forgive you anything, you know. She needs your title too much."

"It's obvious what went on here, and it's not the kind of thing that happens between average married people."

"Thank heavens. I've never wished to be average."

"Passion doesn't enter marriage beds, Savannah." He

looked like he clenched his jaw and wished he could swear very violently. "Christ, what kind of precedent am I setting for myself? She'll have you taking cold baths for the next month and telling you not to enjoy any of it. Don't listen to her. Here—sit forward. Good—"

His arm swooped around her and then she was in his lap, and his face was half in her neck, half in her bosom, and his big hand was curved around her ribs.

Savannah closed her eyes and felt the caress of his warm lips on her throat. She reached up and curled her hand around his neck where the stiff collar met with the coarse fall of his hair. It seemed too deliciously comfortable to be an act.

The coach door burst open and her mother's voice rang like the clamor of a broken bell.

"Welcome, your lordship, to our humble brownstone and our even humbler family!" Penelope gave what sounded like a nervous titter of a laugh. "How delighted I am that you've come to visit us, and so soon—good God! Savannah, is that you under there? Ernst, quick, close the door! No! Go make sure Mr. Merriweather isn't looking out the window. Good grief—" Her mother sounded suddenly winded, as if she'd taken too much heat. "I must say, your lordship, I've never felt such heat in May! How dreadful for you to come in such weather."

Dominic lifted his head and gave a roguish grin that made stars dance in his eyes. He looked like the most affable man in the world. Even the most rigidly trussed up mother-in-law would forgive him anything, especially when her social future in New York rested squarely in his lusty lap. And they all knew it.

"Ah, finally, Madam Merriweather." His shrug was a study in self-effacement and befuddlement. "A man can hardly help himself when the bounty of heaven itself wouldn't compare with the charms of your daughter."

"Yes, yes, it most certainly wouldn't of late. And why look! Those—er—blessings seem to have grown measurably since she's been away. As has all of her. But I suppose that's a good deal of her charm for you, your lordship."

His face seemed to darken a shade. "Not even a fraction, madam." The air seemed to momentarily crackle and then he said, "And do call me Castellane, will you?"

"Ooh! Why, of course, Castellane. How poetic. My, but now that I see you, you're quite young."

"Thirty-five isn't young, madam."

"Yes, but—I thought—I don't know quite what I thought when we read your advertisement, but I can say I didn't envision you."

"I thank you, madam." He set Savannah straight, tipped her chin up with one finger, and looked deeply into her eyes as she gathered her dress together. His smile would have charmed Colonel Sharpe himself. His transformation was mind-boggling. Everything about him suddenly seemed to offer reassurances. "My darling Rosy," he said with hushed intimacy. "What you do to me."

She blinked up at him and felt warm all over. "Rosy?"

"A most fitting pet name."

He said this so softly Savannah wasn't sure her mother could have heard him. And surely he meant for her to.

"Good heavens, Savannah, look at you. A wife now! And in that striking shade of bright pink." Her mother laughed shrilly and seemed to flutter more agitatedly at the door. "Savannah, do get out of this vehicle, and quickly, before anyone sees you."

"Hello, Mother. Have you missed me?" Her throat felt dry, her cheeks so hot they pulsed, and she couldn't have met her mother's eyes for all the chocolates in France. She turned her cheek against Dominic's coat and found reassurance in his warmth. She wanted to curl up against him and go back to the ship.

"I say, a bounding good day to you, madam," Dominic boomed, lurching from his seat and into the open doorway, forcing her mother back with one swing of his walking stick. He lingered half bent through the door, exchanging mindless pleasantries that her mother seemed to lap up eagerly. Then again, the arrival of one's titled son-in-law was certainly occasion enough for anyone to trip all over herself.

Savannah seized on the opportunity to reassemble herself when Dominic started to regale her mother with many of the exchanges they'd received from their fellow travelers on the ship. While she'd strolled the promenade wishing people had something more or different to say than commentary on the weather and the latest in stock market news or Paris fashion, Dominic had been neatly cataloging and memorizing every nuance of the people around him, down to the precise turn of phrase. She imagined he could very easily assume the air of any social class. Little wonder he donned his guise as effortlessly as he hefted his walking stick.

But who was he really? Her glimpse into his past only made her hungry to know more. As for all those kisses—

She glanced up at his muscled backside and her fingers fumbled on her buttons. The wool of his trousers clung as if the skin beneath was damp from the heat.

Hungry—that's what she was. Only her need had nothing to do with chocolate.

She'd just righted her hat when he turned and offered her his hand. "Come, Rosy."

He preceded her out of the carriage, handed her down, and stood behind her as she faced her mother. Savannah wished the sun wasn't slamming out of the west directly into her face. She felt shoved beneath a magnifying glass, like some odd biological specimen. She sucked in a breath and hoped she didn't wear her duplicity today as flagrantly as she did her love of food.

It would be awful if she gave the ruse away right off the bat, and with Dominic doing so well at it.

She wished she could see more than the stark outline of

her mother's head, fringed with thin wisps of gray. How strange her mother should suddenly look so old to her.

"Savannah." Her mother bent and touched her powdered cheek briefly to hers. Savannah didn't realize she withdrew until her back pressed up against Dominic's chest. But her mother seemed not to notice.

"Is Papa well?"

"Well enough now, of course." Again her laugh seemed forced as she angled her head back to give Dominic a good look. "Good heavens, but you're exceptionally tall for an Englishman, sir. So broad and fit. My, my." Was that a blush staining her mother's cheeks?

Savannah squinted to get a better look.

"No," Penelope breathed. "I didn't quite envision you. Now, come. You both must be famished. Well, I know Savannah always is. Ernst, get the door—oh, and their bags."

"We've—er—only one," Savannah blurted.

Her mother stopped short and leveled a fiercely disapproving look at Savannah. "Only one? What did you do, take two minutes to stuff it full and dash?"

"Well, as a matter of fact—"

"Good heavens, girl, didn't I teach you to pack properly? Surely one of the servants could have helped you!"

"Madam, blame me," Dominic interrupted, his smile deepening when Penelope's brows shot up. "I'm a pitiful poor packer myself. Somehow came upon this damnable habit of buying whatever I need once I get where I'm going. Gives me a flavor of the cities I visit, you see. Scarves from Paris, silk from the Orient, wool from Istanbul, and carpets—I adore the Persian carpets."

"Indeed." Penelope looked as if she were sucking on a lemon and trying very hard not to show it. "That can add up to quite an expense, your lordship."

"Castellane can be impetuous." Savannah hastened to jump in before Dominic's leonine pride became unduly piqued at the reminder that every bit of money he would spend was indeed her father's. "But he's obligingly frugal—" She touched his arm and smiled up at him, at once seeing the tenseness around his mouth. His eyes seemed to darken the longer she looked at him. "He's especially frugal with himself. We'll make certain my allowance more than suffices to outfit us both for our stay."

"Indeed, you know him well, my dear," Penelope said slowly, "and in such short order." Her eyes flicked over Savannah's fuchsia flounces and ruffles and sweeping neckline. "I can see you chose carefully from among your Paris-made gowns."

"Oh, I made the selections myself, madam."

Penelope seemed to force a little smile. "Indeed. You have an eye for furious color, your lordship."

"Thank you, madam. I pride myself on it. Shall we?" He tucked Savannah's hand under his arm and strode jauntily onward, forcing Penelope to huff up the steps after them.

"You should be aware that Mr. Merriweather came home early from his club to join us. He's most anxious to meet you. I must say, we were surprised to learn of your visit. For six months! And so very soon, Savannah."

"Yes, well, it couldn't be helped. Surely you didn't expect me to be happy away from home and friends in sullen domesticity amid hostile servants in the English fogs. Or did you?"

Penelope looked momentarily taken aback. Then very stern. "Well, you've arrived even before the news of your marriage had a chance to hit *Town Topics*."

"I assume that's bad."

"It's dreadful. If you're seen before the news breaks, it will take all the drama out of it."

"For whom, Mother?"

"Why, for all of us! Until Colonel Sharpe announces your marriage to the Earl of Castellane, you must keep yourselves all locked away in your town house so you won't be seen *anywhere*. It's on Fifty-eighth, right off of

Fifth. A charming little place. It's furnished but needs a bit of decorating. I've already seen to hiring on a decorator for you—a French fellow my dear widowed friend Mrs. Gobin recommended highly. He's talented and discreet, a rarity in decorators."

"A rarity all the way around," Savannah put in, drawing her mother's pointed stare.

"He won't tell a soul he's seen you, and you can be thankful for that. When he's worked his magic, you'll be more than comfortable there. Er—why don't you just—excuse me, your lordship—" Penelope squeezed past Dominic into the foyer, turned around, flashed a smile, and clasped her hands together in a nervous gesture. "Yes, I think you should wait right over here in the parlor while I go fetch Mr. Merriweather. Savannah, pour your—er—Castellane a glass of whatever's in that decanter over there. Sherry. Yes, yes, I was sure to get some of that. The English do love a bit of sherry. I'll just—" Penelope waved a hand over her shoulder, smiled again, and bustled away.

"Good heavens, I've never seen her like this," Savannah said, moving to an elaborate gilt-edged sideboard. She splashed sherry into two lead-crystal glasses and handed one to Dominic. She all but smacked her lips in anticipation. "I've never had sherry."

"Sip slowly," he reminded her as she lifted her glass.

"Nutty," she said, licking her lips. She drank again, deeper, and glanced quickly around the overstuffed, overdecorated parlor. Not even a hint of sunlight filtered in through the triple draperies, but the room sweltered. "It makes me hungry for chocolate."

"Not surprising. It's usually an after-dinner drink."

Savannah looked at him curiously. "Don't tell my mother that."

"She's from Dogberg, Ohio, Savannah. How would she know what the English drink and when?"

Savannah shrugged and waved her glass. "She's expected to know. She's rich now. That's the rule if you want to belong. But those of us who don't particularly care to be in favor—" She narrowed her eyes at a sudden thought. A smile crept mischievously over her face. "—those of us who will be in favor simply by virtue of our title, not our behavior, why, I would think we can make our own rules—behave as we wish, eh?"

He was looking at her strangely. "Yes, we certainly could."

She sipped again and frowned. "Thank heavens we've fallen out of favor, or Mother would have been serving sherry at the wrong time to everyone in New York and then Colonel Sharpe would have been writing nasty things about her in his paper."

"Ah. Most people make a point of staying on Sharpe's better side."

"He's more powerful than the New York City police. I've heard that he can run an entire family out of town in shame."

"I see. You—uh—" Dominic angled his chin at her chest.

"What?" Savannah glanced down and lifted her glass aside. "Where? I can't see past all these ruffles. Did I spill? Good heavens, I always spill when I drink wine."

"You spilled on the ruffle. Here—" He drew his handkerchief from his breast pocket and frowned at her. "I told you to sip slowly. Would you like me to . . . ?"

"If you would, Castellane. I can't see down there."

"Ah, hell." With mouth grimly set, he bent and pressed the linen to a spot along the ruffled edge of her neckline. A scowl descended like a thunderstorm over his brow. "This *Town Topics*—is it a daily?"

"No. Once a week." Savannah turned her head, gulped her glass dry, as Dominic's fingers pressed linen gently against silk. She felt deliciously warm. She regarded his tousled hair, admiring the blue-black highlights, then frowned and lifted her fingers to pluck a bit of lint from

just above his temple. At the touch of her fingers he
jerked back and glowered at her as if she'd burned him.

"What? You have a tiny piece of one of my pink feathers in your hair. I was getting it out."

He shoved a hand through his hair, over one temple,
then the other, then through the rest of it.

She pursed her lips. "You certainly got it. Good grief,
you're suddenly awfully sensitive for a man who had me
half naked in his lap not fifteen minutes ago. I had every
one of my fingers in your hair, you know."

He shook a strong finger at her. "That won't happen
again. It never should have happened. When's the next
paper?"

"Wednesday. So . . . I don't know . . . what is today?"

He closed his eyes and almost looked in pain. "Saturday."

"Well, then, three days. Good heavens, whatever will
we do all holed up like rabbits until then? And you so
grumpy—"

"My thoughts exactly." He turned his back on her with
an abruptness that made Savannah feel oddly abandoned.
He moved to a window, shoved the drapery aside, and
scowled into the street. His fingers curled around his glass
as if he thought about crushing it in his fist.

Savannah turned again to the sideboard. "Three days of
waiting is hardly reason to mope."

"I'm not moping."

"No? Your jaw is poking out and I'll bet you're grinding your teeth. You do it in your sleep, you know."

"That doesn't surprise me." He drank long and deep.
"Frustrated men do a lot of teeth-grinding."

"Consider all that time as an opportunity to solidify our
plans."

"I know my plans."

"Oh, I believe they can be improved upon. Most things
can."

"Dammit, Savannah, you're not getting involved."

"Don't swear at me. I'm only trying to help."

"Help?" He looked at her, eyes hard and strangely cold. "You want to help? Stay the hell away from me."

Savannah blinked and felt something start to burn her eyes, and she didn't know why. She swallowed and poked out her chin. "Why are you angry at me?"

"I'm not angry."

"You look angry to me."

"And what do you know about it? Not a damned thing, or you wouldn't have to ask. You'd know—and you'd know why—and for your own sake you'd stay away because three days in a small town house together is not something I'm looking forward to."

"Fine." Savannah gulped her sherry and lifted her nose at him. "Don't believe for a minute that I'm looking forward to your company either. I'd prefer Frances Trainer."

"At this point, so would I." He swung his scowl back to the window.

"Good." Savannah drained her glass and turned her back to him.

"Savannah, get the hell over here and kiss your father."

His voice boomed over the room like cannon fire. Savannah spun, gave an exclamation of delight, and ran into her father's welcoming embrace.

"I've missed you, Papa," she said against his shoulder, arms squeezing tight around him. He felt huge and cushy and safe, and he smelled of tobacco and liquor, leather and broadcloth. His chuckle tremored up through his barrel girth and roused a chest-tightening warmth in Savannah. She pushed back and smiled at him, regretting at once the weariness in his eyes, the deepening lines around his mouth, the ravages of working too hard, too many hours, and for what?

"Look at you." His mouth was set with concern. "What the hell did I let your mother talk me into?"

Savannah swallowed and forced a smile, her heart trembling at the thought that he wasn't pleased that she'd returned so soon with husband in tow, or that she'd gotten herself a titled husband at all. He had to be pleased or she didn't know what she'd do.

Her voice sounded forcibly cheery. "I did a very good thing, Papa. I found myself an English earl of very old title and suitably dour disposition. That's him, over there, by the window. The tall one. He's trying very hard not to frown."

"I can see that."

Savannah met Dominic's unreadable dark stare, thought he looked exceptionally ominous standing there, and suddenly realized she wanted very much for her father and Dominic to like one another. Some part of her sensed that they could. They were both very strong, good-hearted men. They both made her feel very safe. The thought startled her.

She squeezed her father's arm. "He's come home with me, Papa. We're going to fix it all for you and Mother so she can have lunch with Mrs. Astor and you can build yourself a great cottage at Newport."

"Never liked sailing," her father mumbled. "Fix it, you say?" Her father lifted his chin, glowered at Dominic, and barked, "Castellane, is it? Winthrop something or other?"

"Twombley, sir." Dominic started toward them, face pleasantly set, one hand extended. "It's a pleasure—"

"Think so, eh? That's all you bastards over there think about is pleasure. I know all about you, Winthrop. Know all about you aristocrats and your gambling and your whores—"

"Papa—"

"Found out all I need to know from an acquaintance I made at my club. Seems Winthrop here rocked all of Britain several years back. Cheated at cards and had to be thrown out of society, debts so far up the ass he had to lock himself away in some old castle. I heard two of his wives poisoned themselves to get away from him. Some even suspected he killed his first wife and both their babies."

"*Papa—*"

"Has this strange preoccupation with birds. Did you know that, Savannah?"

"Why, yes, but—"

"Not in any house I pay for, you won't, bastard."

"Papa, please—"

"Worthless damned nobility. Everyone so damned impressed with a title. Well, I can tell you that I'm not and I don't give a damn if you think you're doing me any favors because I paid for every breath you take. Christ, the wife had the servants looking everywhere for that English sherry you're drinking. I'll bet you never worked a day in your lazy life, have you, Winthrop?"

Savannah spun toward Dominic, took two steps, and froze. Her heart pounded in her chest. She felt as if she'd run up four flights of stairs. Her eyes met Dominic's and her insides twisted in a knot. His face was bleak and cold as a snow-swept plain.

He'd stopped in his tracks, stiff and unbending as an ancient oak tree. And yet his voice languished in its lazy drawl. "Not a day, sir."

Only then did Savannah realize how difficult it was for a man as cursed with pride as Dominic to play the role of a wastrel. The reward must indeed be well worth the price he paid. Few men she'd ever known would sacrifice their pride for anything.

"Good grief, Stuyvesant, you're yelling." Penelope appeared in the doorway, wringing her hands, but the look she gave her husband would have turned any man less brash into pudding. "The neighbors will hear you. Your lordship—" She took two steps toward Dominic.

"Don't tell me what to do in my own house, woman!" Stuyvesant roared back, face mottled crimson, veins popping along his throat. With one thick arm he blocked her path into the parlor. "And don't you dare apologize for me. I'm setting Winthrop here straight." He wagged a finger at Dominic. "I'm watching you, Winthrop. Every step. One false move with my daughter—you make her cry, you make her pout—and my lawyers will make sure you spend the rest of your sorry life in a New York jail without one penny of Merriweather money stuffed in your pillow."

"Stuyvesant!"

"There's got to be more where he came from, dammit. You could find another one if you had to." With a satisfied nod of his head, Stuyvesant glanced at his wife. "Where the hell's dinner?"

Penelope's face pinched tight as a well-laced corset. "Dinner's in the dining room."

"Good. Let's eat." And with that, Stuyvesant Merriweather marched belly first out of the parlor.

Chapter 11

"Your breakfast, sir."

"What?" Dominic surged up from the bed and groped for the bedside table. Only there was no knife within reach in a sumptuous bedroom in a monstrous town house nestled on East Fifty-eighth. In a cramped loft on lower Tenth, where the lowest of New York rabble mingled with the artists and oftentimes robbed or murdered them for the money they thought they kept, yes, there he kept a weapon always at his bedside.

He'd only had to use it a few times. It was no great price to pay to live among the vagabond artists and immigrants, in the only place that had ever felt close to home for him.

"Breakfast, sir." The man standing beside his bed was a stranger, white-haired and liveried in black, peering down a thin nose. In one hand he held a linen-draped tray covered with plates of food he obviously expected to be eaten. Over the other arm he'd draped a sapphire silk dressing gown with long tasseled sash.

"Thanks, but coffee is all I ever need in the morning." Dominic lurched out of his pillow-piled bed, uncomfortably aware that he wore nothing at all. The man looked completely unfazed. Dominic paused to take the cup of coffee from the tray, offered the man a quirk of his lips, and quickly moved toward the chair where he'd left his clothes last evening. Only they weren't there.

"Your clothes are being laundered, sir," the servant told him, handing him the robe. "You'll find what you need in the wardrobe. Mrs. Merriweather had some articles delivered very early this morning. Shall I choose for you while you shave, sir?"

Dominic gulped his coffee and found it satisfyingly strong. But it did nothing for the festering unease in his gut. How did a man grow comfortable with being bought? he wondered as he shrugged into the robe. Against his skin the silk felt slippery and cool and very expensive.

"No, dammit, I'll do it my—" He caught himself, aware that the servant's odd look was warranted. Aristocrats, he remembered grimly, could do nothing by themselves, and that included bathing and dressing. He waved an agitated hand. "If you would, er—"

"Jarvis, sir." The servant moved to the wardrobe and drew the doors wide over enough topcoats, frock coats, waistcoats, vests, shirts, and trousers to outfit three men for several years. "I'm to be your steward."

"Good. Choose something." Dominic slammed his empty coffee cup on the tray, then moved to the wash basin, where an ivory-inlaid set of shaving brushes and hair combs awaited him on a gold-edged tray. After picking up a brush, he flicked the fine horsehair over his palm and rifled through his memory. "Did we—uh—meet last evening, Jarvis?"

"Yes, sir. You'd both taken a bit too much wine at dinner, I believe, sir. The Countess Castellane required a bit of assistance. Perhaps you don't remember."

It was a night he'd not likely soon forget. For the duration of the nine-course meal, Stuyvesant Merriweather had said nothing while he wolfed down his food and half a bottle of wine, then excused himself and disappeared. A fidgety Penelope Merriweather filled the dead air with the gossip and goings-on of the Four Hundred and made an obvious but strained effort to be as charming as her husband was rude. Savannah, seated opposite Dominic, pushed her food around on her plate, attempted little conversation, and devoted herself to drinking too much wine and eating too many chocolates. Halfway through the meal, her lids had fallen half over her eyes, her cheeks burned as brightly as her dress, and she yawned at thirty-second intervals.

Dominic had done the Castellane legacy proud and consumed his share of the wine.

By the time their Merriweather-bought coach and driver delivered them to their Merriweather-bought town house, Savannah was holding her head, clutching her belly, and looking ominously green. She stumbled up the steps, lurched three paces into the gargantuan foyer, and vomited all over the gleaming white marble floor at the feet of the three servants awaiting them.

One of the servants, a square, cherry-cheeked young woman named Brunnie, promptly whisked her up the steps and disappeared into what Dominic was told was the countess's wing.

"The countess is well this morning?" Dominic asked, slathering cream all over his face. The blade scraped without a whisper of sound over his jaw, so sizzling sharp he could have split a fine hair with it.

"Well as can be expected, sir. She's being roused at the moment."

Jarvis handed him a towel for his face and followed with a white shirt of paper-thin linen with a stiff celluloid wing collar that fit far too tightly for so early in the day.

Dominic jerked the black cravat into a knot high at his throat and felt trussed up as a Christmas package. "You should have let her sleep."

"Indeed, sir." Jarvis handed him a pair of striped trousers of fine worsted wool. "But you and the countess have an appointment this morning."

"With whom?"

"The decorator, sir."

"Oh, right. The decorator." Dominic shrugged into a double-breasted vest of charcoal gray, began to button it snugly over his chest, then shook his head at the knee-length frock coat Jarvis held.

The servant raised his brows.

"Too hot," Dominic muttered, shoving a hand through his hair in deliberate disdain of any ivory comb or brush. He contemplated a day spent in agonizing decision over drapery and upholstery.

No, not one day. Three days.

Three days of playing zealous husband to Savannah's stammering bride.

If the coach hadn't jerked to a stop when it had, what would have kept him from taking everything she had to give him?

He didn't trust himself alone with her. The thought was a sobering one.

Three days meant three nights.

The time stretched like a death sentence, and he envisioned dusky evenings over candlelit dinner tables, the air heavy with lilac, his bride dangling herself like a ripe cherry in front of his nose.

His eyes shot to Jarvis's. "Is there a back entrance?"

"Sir?"

"To the town house. A back entrance."

"Er—yes, sir, there is. The servants' entrance. It leads around the side of the house."

Dominic nodded. How many times in his youth had he found escape in the shadows between the town houses? The irony of it wasn't lost on him.

"We're going to need more coffee, Jarvis," he said, heading out the bedroom door and into a hall wide enough to accommodate seven men standing abreast. "Where's the kitchen?"

"The kitchen, sir? Cook can prepare—"

"No, this is something I have to do. The kitchen, Jarvis."

"Yes, sir. As you wish. This way."

When Dominic entered the front parlor some time later, he found Savannah perched stiff and pale on the only furniture in the room, a high-backed side chair. Her eyes were closed and her colorless lips were parted as if breathing was a great effort. He wondered who'd coerced her into the pale-blue, high-stand collar dress with long, leg-of-mutton sleeves, a cinched waist, and a gently flaring skirt. She looked dutifully repressed, corset-caged and wing-clipped, a shadow of the fuchsia-flounced, bosom-bared, wine-gulping chocolate lover from the prior evening.

A fissure of regret whispered through him, but he dismissed it and moved toward her.

"You're gloating," she croaked without opening her eyes.

"You knew it was me," he said, hesitating, then kneeling beside her chair. His eyes moved over the severely upswept blond curls and followed one where it dangled rebelliously at the back of her neck alongside a ribbon of the same pale blue as her gown.

"You move with a distinctive purpose," she said. "Besides, no man has legs as long as yours. What's this?" She opened her eyes and regarded the glass he handed her with suspicion.

"Drink it. I made it myself."

Her eyes slanted up at him, and the room suddenly seemed to flood with sunshine. "You obviously know all there is to know about making a person feel better at times like this."

"I know my share."

"Very good, Castellane." She lifted the glass, sniffed,

winced, and then she drank the glass dry as if she had all the trust in the world in him. "Aaugh—" She handed him the glass and made a vile face. "That was awful. I suppose that means it will work that much faster. You know, I was thinking about blue."

"Blue." He watched her glance around the room, her eyes flicking this way and that, her mouth twisting one way, pursing, then twisting the other. He'd anticipated some rehashing of the prior night's tension, at the very least some lingering antagonism from her. All the women he'd ever known lived and breathed for stirring up old antagonisms. But from her there was none.

And his? He was suddenly having a hell of a time remembering what they'd argued about in Stuyvesant Merriweather's parlor.

"You know—this color." Her hand made an agitated fluttering motion over her chest, luring Dominic's eye where it had no business going. To his way of thinking, the narrow pleats running from her throat to her waist only accentuated the full curves of her breasts. "Everyone's house is purple and brown and green and deep, dark, somber colors that are supposed to make it look like they've lived in their house for centuries when everyone already knows they moved in just last week. The scent of new money lingers, you know. What about blue—cool blue—the kind of blue that makes you feel like you're somewhere surrounded by sky? And yellow. Not golden yellow but pale lemon yellow. Imagine pale-yellow velvet pillows with wonderful big tassels and a pouf, you know, a big round cushion, with tassels. And blue curtains, with fringe, but they'll be draped back from the windows so the sun can come in and we can look out. Oh, and pale-blue walls."

She looked straight into his eyes and smiled.

"Blue," he said again. She had tiny freckles on her nose and lashes thick and dark as the horsehair shaving brush he'd lathered his face with. She looked too godalmighty young to have turned him inside out.

"Why, look at you, Castellane." Her eyes flickered over his chest and shoulders, then lifted to his hair, and God help him but he searched those emerald depths for a glimpse of appreciation. He swayed a fraction of an inch closer and wanted very much to feel her fingers brushing lint from his hair, smoothing a wrinkle from his collar, touching him. He felt dry-throated and young and green as a youth.

What the hell was wrong with him? Only a fool would fly too close to the flame after he'd been scorched by it.

But he didn't get up and he didn't move away. And the idea of discussing room color and poufs and tassels—no, it wasn't as dreadful as he'd imagined it would be. In fact, he imagined he could kneel there for an eternity watching her, listening to her, feeling her eyes on him.

He forgot his escape out the back door. He forgot the women he'd planned to find at the Seven Sisters' bordello, the experienced ones who'd free him of his lusty preoccupation with Savannah, mind and body.

She cocked her head and looked at him as if he stirred warmth and fondness in her. He ached everywhere to feel her lips parting in heavenly welcome beneath his.

"Come here, Castellane." She swept out of her chair and to a far corner of the room.

He followed as if he had no other choice. Surely she was thinking thoughts like his . . .

"Over here, in the corner here, right next to the window. But not too far into the corner—" She grabbed his hand, tugged, braced her other hand around his arm, and backed him up against the wall. "There," she said, looking up at him and smiling with such satisfaction he couldn't help but swell with pride.

"Coffee, madam." Jarvis entered the parlor, a tray balanced in his hands, and eyed Dominic with face set expressionlessly. "Sir, as you requested."

"Thank you, Jarvis," Dominic said.

"He's a Dutch clock," Savannah explained to Jarvis, stepping back and inclining her head. "He's exactly the right height, perhaps a bit too wide at the shoulders, but I think he looks good there. What do you think, Jarvis?"

"As fine a clock as I've seen, madam."

"Did you hear that, Castellane? And Jarvis has seen many impressive clocks. He used to be a butler for a very wealthy widow who died just last month. Have you ever seen a Dutch clock, Jarvis? I must have a Dutch clock. The French manor houses are full of them. I suppose that's why Mother hates them. She hates all things French."

"Yes, madam."

A bell sounded from the foyer.

"That would be the decorator, madam. Your mother sent him."

"Yes, of course, get it—" Savannah waved a hand and spun to Dominic, eyes dancing animatedly, hand reaching to his. "Tell me you think it will be fine."

Dominic couldn't help tightening his fingers over hers. "What?"

She gave an exasperated sigh. "The colors. The clock. Tell me you'll like it. Tell me you'll want to come and sit in this room and talk to me and you'll feel comfortable. Tell me it won't look like a gaudy Turkish bath."

Dominic's throat felt strangely tight. "Six months, Savannah—it's hardly any time at all to warrant my opinion."

"Six months can be an eternity if you're miserable. But still, this will be your home—" Her expression became suddenly serious. "What am I saying? Of course you have a home somewhere. Is it anything like this?"

"Nothing like it. It's a loft on lower Tenth. Very small. No curtains. Lots of windows. I can see the sun from the moment it rises until it sets."

Her lips curved. "It sounds wonderful. I'd like to see it sometime."

"I'd like to show you." Christ, but he meant it.

She looked up at him and every resolution he'd ever made to himself about her evaporated. The air around and between them suddenly charged with anticipation. His fingers splayed up her arm, gripped her elbow, and pulled her closer until he felt the soft breasts beneath crisp pleats brush his chest.

He looked down at her, then lowered his lips to her forehead. Her hair smelled like roses. "What the hell am I doing?"

"I don't know—" she breathed, "but it feels wonderful—"

"Bonjour, madame! Ah! Monsieur! Enchanté! Enchanté!"

Dominic lifted his head and regarded the man sweeping into the parlor with a mixture of disdain and fully felt hatred. Savannah spun around and blurted out a fluttering string of French phrases and greetings as she hurried toward him. She curtsied and giggled, and the decorator—an enormous, deeply tanned blond man named François—showed a muscled leg, tossed back his long black cape with a flick of his shoulder-length locks, swung his eyes around the room, and winced.

"Awful," he announced in what to Dominic's ear sounded like a Brooklyn-born meat-packer's accent.

Dominic moved to stand behind Savannah and glowered over her head at the decorator in a manner more suited to a protective bear. The man might be a flagrant fraud, but Dominic understood all too well Savannah's weakness for anything that even pretended to be French. Particularly a would-be decorator who wore his shirts open to midchest, his trousers far too close to the flank, and his intent as obvious as the gold hoop dangling from one ear. And none of it had to do with decorating. He looked more like a frustrated wife's pirate fantasy.

To hell with the Seven Sisters. At the moment, there was nowhere else Dominic wished to be, a feeling that increased exponentially when François devoured Savannah from head to toe with his eyes as she swept past him to point out a particular problem with mirror placement in the foyer.

François's eyes jerked up as Dominic planted himself between the decorator and Savannah's backside. There was no guilt on his chiseled rock features, just a ridiculous pomposity that screamed to be smashed off by Dominic's fist.

"You have business, *monsieur, non*? I would not keep you—"

"Business?" Dominic's snort would have done the English peerage proud. Lids slung over his eyes, hands clasped behind his back, he announced, "My dear fellow, noblemen do not engage in *trade*. Leisure is my business. In your country it's much the same with the peerage, is it not?"

François's brows shot up in an instant of undisguised surprise. "Oh, *oui, oui*. I only meant to say—men have clubs. Always their clubs. They are never home, especially during the daytime when I do my best work, *comprenez*?"

"Yes, I '*comprenez*.' "

"Most husbands—they are so bored with this. So many hours with fabric swatches, so much changing of the mind. A woman always knows what she doesn't want, *monsieur*, but rarely does she know what she wants. Until I help her, yes? Sometimes this takes weeks. It depends on the woman, no?"

Dominic's blood temperature began an ominously fast climb as François's eyes shifted over his shoulder and narrowed with unmistakable appreciation on Savannah. She was saying something about her pouf and the number of chairs she wanted, then appeared beside Dominic, all eyes for the blond decorator.

"I must have a Dutch clock, François. Say you can get me one."

"Dutch, you say?" François narrowed his eyes, cupped his marble-block chin, and seemed to be contemplating in which corner of the earth he would locate such a treasure. "I don't know, *madame*. This is difficult."

"Oh, but you've got to find me one." In her zeal, Savannah touched the decorator on his mahogany-basted arm, slender fingers pressing urgently, eyes full of hope, a tender, sweet little morsel of luscious womanhood eager to be pleased. "Oh, François, I would be so grateful."

François's turquoise eyes darkened a shade and Dominic was nearly certain he saw a lascivious glimmer of lust in them. "For you, *madame*—nothing would be too difficult." Then he lifted her fingers to his lips, and Savannah gave a soft giggle and those knife pleats over her breasts began to squirm.

It was then that Dominic decided he'd had more than enough. "Get out."

He registered Savannah's gasp of surprise but ignored it.

François looked outraged. *"Monsieur?"*

"You heard me, Frank. Get your phony ass out of my parlor."

François braced his solid legs as if he stood on a ship's pitching decks. *"Your* parlor? Stuyvesant Merriweather paid you a fortune for the privilege of wiping your ass with his French toilet paper. You don't even own the clothes on your back."

"Don't make me hit you," Dominic said. He realized he'd let the British accent slip a notch simply by the suspicious narrowing of François's eyes. And in that instant it came to him how completely he'd lost control of himself to the jaws of a demon's jealousy.

"He's Mrs. Gobin's decorator," Savannah hissed, anger bubbling in her voice. She gripped his arm, refusing to be shrugged off. "You can't throw Mrs. Gobin's decorator out of the parlor. I don't know any others."

"Watch me." Dominic had never been an overtly violent man. Using the full measure of his physical force didn't come as naturally to him as it did to most other men. He was a peaceful man, an artist by nature. For all his innate passion, he'd never known the curse of a jealous nature. But when he twisted his fists into François's silk shirt front a savage's energy unleashed through his body.

"I'll make you sorry, bastard," François hissed as Dominic roughly escorted him to the door.

"I look forward to it. Jarvis—get the door. Frank's leaving."

"As you wish, sir."

"No one will know you in this town!" François bellowed. He tripped on his cape, hurtled backward down the steps, and his gold earring fell to the pavement and rolled under the carriage parked at the curb. "I'll make certain of it! There won't be an invitation open to you from here to—"

The slam of the door rattled every window on the block.

"What the hell?" Dominic caught Savannah's arm just as she bolted past him and threw the door wide open.

"François!" she bleated after him. "Please forgive my doltish husband and come back—" She yelped as Dominic pounded the door closed with his fist.

Yanking at her arm, she spun around, met with the wall of Dominic's chest, and jarred back against the front door. Hot green eyes steamed up at him when he refused to let go of her arm or give her an inch of breathing space. She spoke through bared teeth, her voice bubbling with rage. "What the devil is wrong with you? I have to go get him. I want my Dutch clock."

Dominic fought for control of his anger and felt it pulsing at his temples, behind his eyes, swelling his manhood, clouding all his reason. He loomed over her, his blood on fire, and snarled, "That man is no decorator and you damned well know it."

She scoffed and tossed back her head to glare up at him. "I damned well don't know that. He comes highly recommended."

"For what? His prowess in a widow's cold bed?"

"Well, good for Mrs. Gobin if that's the case. And I can tell you, if I were Mrs. Gobin I'd be sure to let my friends in on that secret, especially the frustrated ones."

He was staring at her lips and trying not to remember what they felt like gasping open beneath his. "Christ, I don't doubt that you would."

"Oh, Dominic, you're too precious." Her voice was coldly patronizing. "You're one of those men who has to be the best-looking man in the room or else you feel threatened."

Something exploded in Dominic's mind, like a firecracker. He knew she was baiting him, and he couldn't keep himself from gobbling up the lure. "That man was not good-looking."

"He's a Nordic god."

"He can't even tell time. He wouldn't know where to find a damned Dutch clock. But he'd sure as hell know how to find you. His nostrils flared every time he looked at you."

"You're jealous." Her tone was mildly surprised.

His scowl was ferocious. "No more than any other husband would be."

"But you're not my husband."

"Tell me something I don't know. I'm reminded of it every damned minute of every day that I spend with you."

Her chin set stubbornly. "I'll get my clock and my yellow velvet pouf in spite of you."

"I know you will. But don't expect me to make it convenient for you to find your lovers."

"Then plan on being a very busy man. A woman needs at least two to be happy."

"You only need one good one, sweetheart." With the force of his chest, he pressed her deeper against the door, spanned her rib cage with his hands, and lifted those lush breasts full against him. He felt the plump cushion of her thighs, looked deep into her eyes, and saw a festering need that answered his own. His voice came out husky with lust. "And the only thing French about him will be his underwear."

Lashes suddenly veiled her eyes but he knew she stared at his mouth. Her breaths came shorter. Desire blasted through him.

Her tongue passed over her lower lip, wetting it. "You've been to Paris then?"

"Never. I got the underwear from a woman I knew once in London."

"Were you her lover?"

"I briefly considered it."

"And?"

"She was married. There are some things even I won't do."

"But you seduced Bertrice Hyde-Gilbert and she was married."

"I didn't bed her, Savannah."

She lifted her eyes. "Perhaps she wasn't the right woman."

Her words crept through the red haze of his lust and struck a discordant tone in his mind, but he ignored it. He thumbed through the knife pleats beneath her breasts. And then he looked into her eyes and touched the peaks with the pads of his thumbs. Beneath the cotton he felt the nipples pebble and push hard into his thumbs. His trousers pulled obscenely tight across his loins.

Her eyes fluttered closed. "I will let you be my lover."

He lowered his mouth and touched her soft lips with his. "You make it sound like you'll have a choice."

"Why, of course I will. Every woman does." She turned her head slightly and sighed when he pressed his open mouth to her throat. "After our six-month charade is over and I think of a way to be rid of Castellane without causing some awful scandal, I'll be a good virgin and marry someone like Charles, do my wifely duty and bear him an heir, and then I'll take my own bedchamber and every night you can climb up a flower trellis and into my window and into my bed—no, please, don't stop—"

He lifted his head and stared down at her, feeling as if someone had dropped a bucket of frigid water on him and hell if he knew why. "What?"

"Don't stop," she said huskily.

"Christ." For all that it felt unnatural, he dropped his hands to his sides and jerked back. Something about all of this was wrong—but in a way he hadn't expected. He glared at her, glared at her swollen lips, glared at the magnificent nipples thrusting through knife pleats at him, and snarled. "Goddammit."

And then he swung around and marched straight for the kitchen and the back door, and the escape he needed. Not from her. But from the man he was fast becoming.

Chapter 12

"Are ye finished?"

Dominic scowled into his empty glass, reached for the bottle on the floor beside his chair, and poured himself what was left. Slumping in his chair, thighs spread, legs outstretched, cravat hanging loose from his open collar, he tried and failed to cock a brow at the red-haired giant straddling a stool at his feet and lifted the empty whiskey bottle. "Not if you've got more, Bonnie."

The Irishman's green eyes regarded him from a face that had been smashed to near pulp less than three hours before in a bare-knuckles boxing match. Swollen, bruised, and blood-smeared, Bonnie looked like a medieval warrior just returned from battle. But Bonnie's prize wasn't freedom for his country or the claiming of new lands for his king. For using the only talents he possessed and ruthlessly pummeling his opponent into the floor, he'd pocketed twenty dollars in bills and coin, enough to pay his rent and feed himself and his orphans until the next fight in three days. He kept his winnings in a leather pouch that hung from his waistband so that the children could hear the tinkle of coins when he moved.

He got to his feet with a silent wince and moved to a corner cupboard tucked into the apartment's shadows. "Christ. I dinna know ye were such a fool, an' I've known ye now nigh te twenty years. How many bottles do ye need, Nino?"

"How many do you have?"

"Is that all ye've got te tell me, or have ye got yerself another wife somewhere?"

Dominic swallowed a hiccup and tried to focus on the pointed toe of one of his English-made shoes. He saw no less than five. Tipping his head back, he stared at the gray murk of early evening beyond a rain-splashed window. "There's only one wife. She's more than enough for one man."

A cupboard slammed. "Then we'll only need one more bottle. I don' 'ave much te say."

"And here I'd thought my luck had run out. Thanks— no, forget the glass. I'll take the bottle." He cradled it close for a moment, then tipped it to his lips and drank deeply. "God almighty."

Bonnie settled himself on the stool and looked grave. "Ye know I'd do anythin' for ye, Nino. Twenty years ago ye saved me life an' I'll never forget it. But with this—" Bonnie scratched his head. "This is the only advice I can give ye: Ye need te get yerself a woman."

Dominic hiccuped again. "I tried."

"Ye what?"

"I said I tried. It didn't work."

"What is it that dinna work for ye, Nino?"

The undercurrent of amusement in Bonnie's voice set Dominic's jaw. "All the parts were working, dammit. The problem wasn't down there, it was here—" He tapped a finger to his temple. "It just wouldn't all come together. I kept having this damned thought that she would find out where I was or someone would tell that damned Colonel Sharpe and she'd have to face people who knew I was an ass—shit. That's why I came here to get drunk. You've always known where to get the finest Irish whiskey."

Bonnie blinked at him. "Was it one of yer models?"

"Swore off the models a year ago. I want experience and finesse in a lover. A brain might also help."

"So ye were at the Seven Sisters."

Dominic rolled the bottle neck between his fingers and nodded. "I finally met Lola."

Bonnie exhaled almost reverently. "Jesus Mary, man, ye had the bonnie lass Lola beneath yer ruttin' loins an' ye stopped?"

"Let's say my loins were never quite rutting."

Bonnie looked stupefied. "Maybe 'tweren't the same Lola. Was she blond? Tits like mountains? God in heaven, tell me there's two o' her."

"Only one. She was quite something." Then why had she left him cold when she'd stepped out of her dress and pressed her naked body up against his?

He lifted the bottle and gulped, once, twice.

"Yer gonna kill yerself with that."

"Better this than going out of my mind. Tell me why the hell nothing has worked like I planned since the moment I met her?"

"I dinna think ye want te hear it."

"She cursed me, that's what she did, the minute I was fool enough to lay eyes on her in that stable. Nothing's made sense ever since. And I have a feeling things are only going to get more tangled up."

"She dinna kill Harrigan. Ye played yer own hand in that."

Dominic shot his friend a dark look, feeling the stab of guilt in his gut. "The enemy's not too big, Bonnie. The prize is worth it. The man who killed Harrigan—he's here, somewhere in New York. Harrigan's last letter to me was very specific on that point. I tell you, Harrigan was killed because he knew the name of the man I've been searching for for years. And that man killed him. I can feel it"—he touched a fist to his stomach—"right here."

"Aye, ye be gettin' closer."

"And very soon close enough to get my revenge on him and to recover all of it. At least that's my plan. God knows what she'll do to it."

"And then what? Ye get what yer after an' then ye go off an' live the rest of yer life alone. A man on the run. That it?"

Dominic shrugged. "There's an old Sicilian maxim that I live by, Bonnie: *Chi gioca solo non perde mai.* The man who plays a lone hand—"

"Aye, I know it. He never loses."

Dominic stared out the window and let his breath hiss through his teeth. "Three days of sequestration. What man could endure it?"

"Ye've been waitin' a lifetime for this, Nino. Best endure what ye must te finish it."

"She's bound by some ridiculous good-daughter code to please her father, and yet she doesn't know a damned thing about life or men. But when I look at her all I want to do is—" He caught himself and stared at his white-knuckled grip on the bottle, feeling the faint trembling in his limbs. "Today she was telling me about the lovers she's going to take after she marries some idiot and how I'm going to be one of them."

"The idiots?"

"No, dammit, the lovers."

Bonnie stared at him as if he'd sprouted horns. "An' ye believe ye've got a problem? So ye wait yer six months 'til ye've done what ye set out te do. Let her marry her idiot. Then take her to yer bed and teach her those things her husband can't. Ye know damned well it happens every day."

The snarl started somewhere deep inside Dominic's gut and erupted like a blast from a volcano. "I can't."

Bonnie's mammoth shoulders shrugged. "Ye made the

girl a promise te keep yerself from her an' ye've got te keep it. 'Tis the only way for a man o' his word, Nino."

"I'm beginning to question the wisdom of that."

"Aye. Yer wonderin' how ye can have what ye want now an' still live with yerself. Ye were raised te be an honorable man."

"Then tell me what kind of sense honor makes if I'd do anything to avenge my family and Harrigan, no matter what it takes, legal or otherwise?"

"Aye, it still makes sense—at least to me. Yer own father killed men for what he believed in, but he never would 'ave dishonored yer mother. Like it or not, yer the very same." Bonnie's keen eyes narrowed. "I know ye've always sworn off the married lasses, but Jesus Mary, man, 'til ye have her ye won't get her from yer blood."

"My blood," Dominic repeated, drinking again.

"Aye, 'twould be a different story altogether if ye were in love with the lassie."

Dominic's head jerked up. He tried to focus and scowled instead. "What was that? I'm not in love with her, if that's what you're saying."

"I dinna say a thing."

"Good. I didn't think so." He shoved out his jaw, rubbed a smudge from one of the brass buttons on his vest, then glanced up. "Thank God I'm not."

"Aye. Ye'd 'ave a tangle on yer hands, ye would."

"Yes, yes, I would." He contemplated the bottle. "How so?"

"When a man loves a woman, he wants her fer himself, all te himself, and it's all he thinks about. Hell, he'd ferget about all his other plans. He might even ferget about the men who'd died for the same cause."

Dominic's look was fierce. "Only momentarily."

"He'd not be content 'less he was the first fer her. An' the last."

"The only, dammit"—Dominic's fist thumped on the chair arm—"no matter what her frustrated suffragist spinsters tell her. Two lovers, my ass. I'd chain her to my bedpost."

"He'd be thinkin' he needed te marry the lassie."

"And why not? Hell, she needs someone to keep her in line. She's a woman of excess. Her father won't do it. Her mother can't do it. Charles Fairleigh wouldn't know how to be a husband to her. As for that French aunt of hers and her idiotic ideas of sex education, if I ever meet that woman and those French bastards—"

"Aye, 'tis a good thing ye don' fancy yerself in love with her."

"Never crossed my mind."

"Aye. Nor mine." Bonnie examined a gash in his hand.

"No more foolproof way to foul up all my plans."

"Aye."

"Hell, I would be asking for failure. Not to mention what her father would do when he found out about our charade."

"Aye. If it were my daughter I'd hit ye. Then I'd kill ye."

"He'd have damned good reason. She'll be lucky she doesn't end up in jail with me." Dominic tipped the bottle again and gave a satisfied grunt. "In love with her. I'm not that stupid."

"Aye."

"Guess I should find myself a woman."

"Try the Seven Sisters."

"Right." Dominic set the bottle down on the floor and lurched to his feet. The room tilted, righted, tilted again. "Shit, I'm drunk."

"Best ye go home, eh? Wouldn't want all the parts not workin' like they should at the Seven Sisters."

"Right. Another time." They left the apartment but Dominic paused abruptly at the top of the stairs. "How do I get home? Oh—my man is waiting for me. Did you hear me, Bonnie?"

"I heard ye, Nino."

They started down the narrow flight of steep steps.

"I have a man. I actually have several. A rich man's life is a study in making certain he has nothing of significance to do. I'm a bought husband. And I don't like it."

"No, ye wouldn't. 'Ave ye been by te see young Sam?"

"I stopped by the studio. He likes it there."

" 'e misses ye fierce, though 'e won' say it. More o' you in 'im than ought te be fer an orphaned boy."

"He reminds me of myself at that age. Always feeling like I needed to run. I want to get that out of him somehow, Bonnie."

"I think ye've done it. Ye need te paint again, Nino."

"Been too long. I wouldn't know how."

"Have ye thought about paintin' her?"

"Every God-damned day."

They stepped into a cool evening. Dominic's Merriweather-bought coach and footman stood curbside awaiting him in the gently falling rain.

"Maybe 'tis what's troublin' ye so. Paint her. 'Twill do ye worlds of good."

"Only as a last resort," Dominic replied, lurching into the coach after the footman held the door wide. He bid his friend good night and the coach rolled off into the darkness.

Maxine Beaupre, widowed French countess and reported millionairess, had been most recently banned from New York society due to the dinner party she'd hosted featuring her black poodle, Nippy, whom she'd seated at the head of the table and dressed as Queen Victoria. Even though her guest favors, chunky sterling silver poodles with rubies in their jaws, had been an undiluted rage among her guests and far outdid the gilded chocolate roses Mrs. Astor had given her guests at her most recent ball, Maxine had been accused by Colonel Sharpe in *Town Topics* of being the very thing that gives the rich a bad name.

Maxine was bored with New York, bored with the rules, bored with being heinously rich. She was intent on trying a little reform from within.

"I came as soon as I heard," Maxine announced as she swept into Savannah's bedchamber without knocking, a feat that would have left Savannah's severe gray-haired dressmaker slack-jawed if not for the pins clamped between her teeth.

"You may go now," Maxine told the dressmaker with a wave of one peacock-blue glove that seemed to give the woman no alternative. "I need to speak with my niece alone. Come back tomorrow."

As the dressmaker gathered her things and scurried from the room, Maxine stalked around, glancing behind chairs and into corners, the peacock feathers on her hat swaying this way and that as she moved. She was strikingly turned out in a walking dress of deep-blue satin with a circular-cut peplum jacket trimmed in gold braid and sporting huge sleeves. Her dark hair was swept up high beneath her hat, pearl bobs dangled at her ears. Not a stitch was out of place on her willowy silhouette. Banned or not, Maxine Beaupre was exquisite enough to turn men's heads all the way around. She paused in front of Savannah and braced her silk umbrella on the floorboards. "He's not here."

"Who?" Savannah asked, kissing the perfumed air beside each of Maxine's powdered cheeks. She stood in the center of the room, in a puddle of multicolored gowns wearing nothing but black silk stockings, lace garters, and a chemise and corset that was half laced up her back. She was always delighted to see her aunt, but even more so this morning. She'd spent the last two hours quarreling viciously with the dressmaker over corsets and bustles and confining gowns. The discarded pile at her feet was seven dresses deep. If a dress didn't fit without the corset tightly cinched, she wanted nothing to do with it. The dress she'd so far chosen to keep consisted of a dramatic white taffeta evening dress with tiny sleeves, shallow-cut bodice, and an overlay of intricate black lace. Savannah had envisioned black gloves and garters to complete the ensemble and had snatched it right up despite the dressmaker's protests that she would look like a cheap Flamenco dancer in it.

"Your husband. This Castellane fellow. Where is he? I didn't see anybody downstairs but very sour-looking servants your mother must have hired."

"I haven't seen him since yesterday morning." Savannah toyed with a stray thread at the top of her corset and couldn't help the slight thrust of her jaw. "He's out, I suppose."

"You suppose?" Maxine tipped Savannah's chin up and looked at her in a way that made her want to squirm. "A man who has a wife who looks like you goes out until midday? I see no signs of him even being in this room. Good God, but it's worse than I thought. And Stuyvesant made it sound dreadful. Gambling and whores and dead wives. What's this I hear about a peculiar fetish for birds?"

"Papa doesn't like him."

"He said he's too tall for a wastrel rogue. A pitiful poor reason to dislike any man as far as I'm concerned."

"Oh, but he's quite tall."

"Handsome, I hope? Better rich than handsome, I always say, but once he has your money, who will know the difference?"

Savannah gave a casual shrug that brought her breasts arching out of her corset. Her cheeks suddenly felt unnaturally hot. "If you like his type, yes, he's handsome—in a dark, hard way."

"Dark and hard. I see. And as a lover?"

Savannah snapped her head up, swallowed, and felt herself pale. Fooling a shipload of easily impressed passengers and a society-climbing mother was one thing, but how had she ever thought to keep up her charade with her Aunt Maxine? A full confession bubbled up into her throat, curled around her tongue, then suddenly stuck there.

Even her aunt would find it impossible to accept that Savannah was in cahoots with a dangerous man who dabbled in illegalities and was wanted for thievery and seduction. Or would she?

Of course, there was also the ticklishly unsettled mystery of M. Harrigan's murder. Having discovered his body and stepped in his blood, Savannah believed she had a duty to find his killer.

She clamped her jaw and looked woeful.

Maxine closed her eyes as if suddenly struck by acute pain. "Good heavens. I'm not going to ask you why you didn't consult me before you ran off and did this. I know why you did. I also know exactly what kind of man you've married. England is full of them. Oh, my dear niece. Something has to be done about this."

Savannah blinked. "About what?"

"About getting you bedded and quickly."

"Bedded? Why would I want to do that?"

"Good God. You didn't learn a blasted thing in France."

"Was I supposed to?"

Maxine sighed. "Perhaps you were too young. Perhaps they weren't right for you."

"The Jeans? Oh, they were wonderful. They taught me to kiss on the mouth."

"And then?"

"They stopped, of course, when I told them to. You know, when they wanted to put their tongues in my mouth and their hands on my bare legs."

"And well they should have stopped when you asked. My question, dear niece, is why tell them to stop at all?"

"Why not?"

Maxine stared at her. Gloved hands rubbed briskly over Savannah's upper arms. "I see what I'm dealing with here. I should have seen it before, but you have a look about you, Savannah, that is deceiving." She shook her head. "It's easy to assume you were born knowing how to use it all. Listen to me. You can't take a lover and experience everything you must until you've done your duty to your husband. Certain husbands are very particular about being the first. And, unpleasant as it might sound, you can't do your duty with some men —apparently yours— unless you apply a bit of seduction."

"I don't think that would be wise."

"No, you wouldn't, because you're a woman with her own mind and you want to play by your own rules. But I assure you, in the end you will know the rules were yours, though at times it might not feel that way. I know best in these matters. Trust me, you simply need to submit. You won't even need to act like you're enjoying it. Duty. It's a dreadful word."

"I've never liked the sound of it."

"And when it's finally over, then we can have our fun and he'll leave you alone for months on end until he drinks too much or his lover throws him out and then you can tell him to go to hell and there won't be a damned thing he can do about it."

"Aunt Maxine, I'm almost certain that would work with some men, but Castellane—"

A door slammed from below followed by the barking shout of a deep male voice.

Maxine looked sharply at Savannah. "The lord and master?"

"It certainly sounds like him."

"Such a strong set of lungs on such a weak-willed man. Odd, I don't believe I've ever heard of an aristocrat who shouts like a savage."

"He must have gone riding in the park."

"Ah. Yes, the English do love their horses. Stand right there—that's it—good—" Maxine reached around Savannah's back, grabbed the laces of her corset, and yanked them loose. White breasts spilled over the gaping lace edge of her chemise.

Savannah closed her eyes. "I don't think—"

"Don't, dear. I'll do the thinking." Maxine plucked off her gloves, tossed them on a chair, then snatched up the white-and-black lace dress on the bed. She held it up, smiled, and shoved it at Savannah. "Here—start putting this on—" Maxine moved briskly to the bedchamber door, stuck out her head, and called, "Your lordship, sir? Is that you?"

A moment later a servant's thin voice warbled, "Madam, is there a problem?"

"Get Castellane, if you could. He's needed in the countess's bedchamber. Faster," Maxine said, rushing back to Savannah. "But not too fast. Here—let me help."

Footsteps sounded on the marble foyer floor, then became muffled on the stairs.

"Quite tall," Maxine murmured, drawing the cap sleeves up Savannah's arms to perch at the edge of her shoulders. "Very long legs."

"Quite long," Savannah said breathlessly, fidgeting with the sleeves, but they didn't want to stay put. Her heart was thumping so fast in her chest she was certain Maxine could hear it. What the devil was she doing? Playing the blushing bride at balls and dinners was one thing. But seducing Dominic Dare wasn't a wise strategy on any day, and even more foolish given his almost violent rejection of her just yesterday.

She bit her lip. He was a dangerous man. A man she still knew very little about. She ought to be terrified.

So why wasn't her stomach filled with dread instead of this giddy anticipation?

"Here. Good. Suck in—" Maxine's fingers flew over the buttons along the front of the gown. "Good, good, good. God, what I wouldn't have given in my youth for bosoms like yours. I could have ruled a kingdom. Do something with your hair."

Savannah bit her lip again. The thumps on the staircase drew closer.

"Come on, dear," Maxine urged impatiently. "You want to set him afire, don't you?"

Yes. She realized a very wicked part of her wanted to see Dominic Dare go up in flames.

Savannah yanked a few pins from the high knot and shook her head. One curl fell and disappeared between her breasts. Another plopped right over her forehead, between her eyes, and touched the outer corner of her lips. She licked them.

"There." Maxine stepped back and beamed with satisfaction. "Wait. Let's leave one more button open—" She fussed with the buttons, inclined her head, tugged on the bodice, then stepped back again. "Perfect. Just a hint of nipple showing."

Savannah was struck with horror. "What?"

"It's not too much. We don't want the man to expire before he even gets started. How old did you say he was?"

"Thirty-five."

"Odd. I got the impression he was much older. Take your stockings off. Leave the garters hanging loose. Let yourself breathe, dear. It's healthful."

Savannah tried to draw a breath and failed. "The dress is too tight all over. I can't bend over."

"Sure you can. I'll help you. Darling—" With a tender smile, Maxine moved close and cupped Savannah's face in her hands. "Why, you're trembling, dear. There's nothing to be afraid of. Trust me. Women don't expire from wifely duty, though I'm certain some wish they could. There's nothing that can walk through that door that would surprise me, do you understand? Now relax. I'll be here for you if you need me. And I won't leave unless I'm absolutely certain you can manage just fine. Now, lift the dress from your waist, that's it, put your foot on this stool, good girl, now unsnap the garter and roll the stocking—" Maxine's breath seemed to suddenly snag.

Savannah's fingers froze on the lace. She looked sharply at the door. Her belly did a complete somersault when her eyes met Dominic's.

"My, my," Maxine murmured. "And I'd thought the world had lost all its surprises."

Chapter 13

Hard beds, cold baths, and religion. No, Dominic knew that nothing on God's earth—including gallons of Irish whiskey and miles of hard riding—could have fortified him against Savannah.

Except retreat.

But that had never been a viable option for any occasion.

His riding quirt still clenched in his fist, he strode into the sun-splashed bedchamber like a soldier claiming every inch of enemy territory as his own. His eyes touched on a plump curve of legs and black lace garters. Her fingers were tripping over the garter hooks, freeing the black stockings, pushing the silk over milky white thighs so long he knew they would feel like heaven clamped around his waist.

She jerked up, skirts swished back in place, and one silk stocking slipped from her fingers and drifted to the floor. She angled her eyes at him from behind a curl that touched her lips, shimmied her skirts up with a little jimmy and bob, and propped her other foot on the stool.

She bent over, sleeves slid from her shoulders, the gown gave, and her breasts leapt out of her bodice.

The room's temperature suddenly soared twenty degrees. Dominic was suddenly grateful he'd ridden Central Park sans the requisite coat, cravat, silk topper, and vest. His Merriweather-bought mount had done his frustration proud, kicking up clods of dirt in the faces of the elegant nabobs from Murray Hill and Gramercy Park driving their broughams four-in-hand, a skill required of any man of social stature determined to become a good "whip." Dominic preferred hard riding in a hard saddle, gloveless, coatless. Like a man.

A trickle of perspiration wove from his open collar and down his chest. He felt as if he were internally combusting.

"Your lordship." The woman moving toward him was a stunning brunette whose easy smile and laughing eyes made it extremely difficult for Dominic to remember that she was, quite obviously, the enemy at the moment. The scene looked far too professionally orchestrated to be any of Savannah's doing. Dominic took in the woman's clothes, her air of understated gentility, her easy manner with Savannah—most notably Savannah's quiet acquiescence—and made an instantaneous assessment.

"Maxine Beaupre." He lifted her outstretched fingers to his lips.

Her surprise registered in a subtle quirk of her brows. "How astute of you, Castellane." Her eyes were so keenly appraising he knew at once he had to be in perfect aristocratic form with her. She was not a woman to be fooled easily. He wondered how Savannah had managed to accomplish it. Or had she?

"Your niece has often spoken of her trip to Paris with you," he said lightly.

"We had an exceptionally good time, didn't we, dear?"

"Marvelous." Savannah's voice sounded breathless, as

if she'd just been ravished . . . or just confessed every
last one of her precious secrets.

"I'm afraid it left her with a passion for all things
French." Dominic angled his eyes at Savannah. She'd
made quick work of her other stocking and was staring
out the window as if she feared meeting his eyes.

Christ, he was getting soft-headed. There was no fear in
a woman who could parade before him in a gown three
sizes too small. She knew exactly what she was doing. Her
hunger for mischief and mayhem and making his life hell
was insatiable.

His eyes fastened on the pale pink semicircle peeping
above the scoop of shallow bodice and his blood began an
ominous galloping in his veins. The quirt slipped from his
fingers and smacked against his thigh.

"You live near Plymouth, sir?"

"An hour northeast if your horse is in top form," he
replied, forcing his eyes away from Savannah.

But Maxine Beaupre was a determined woman. With
very little effort, she swung her attention and therefore
Dominic's back to Savannah. "Arms up, dear," she said,
her hands tugging up on the bodice fabric as if she could
somehow make more of it to do its job. Savannah com-
plied, lifted her arms up, and both nipples popped out of
the gown with an eagerness that was staggering.

Dominic swung to the windows and concentrated on a
bird soaring above the treetops. With an almost helpless
fury he felt his trousers pull snug across his loins. And the
blood began pumping there hard and demanding.

"Then you must know the Viscount Highcote. He has
an enormous estate in that region. Goodness, Savannah
darling, there's so very much of you. How can we make it
all fit?"

Highcote. Dominic listened to women's hands fussing
with lace and overabundant flesh, thought he heard satin
give a surrendering tear, and had to force himself to rifle
through his memory. He'd earned himself a cushy enough

position in polite London society last year to meet more than his share of aristocrats. The experience had given him ample fodder for use in impersonating a member of the peerage. But he didn't specifically remember Highcote from among the pale, pinched, and passive.

If Maxine Beaupre was putting him to some sort of test, he didn't necessarily have to oblige her.

"I've been in seclusion for some time, madam," he said. "I see nothing of even my closest neighbors."

"How very fortunate you are, sir. Lady Highcote visited me in Paris several times without her viscount, of course. A lovely woman. So gay and spirited. She hated London."

"The gay and spirited don't often last long there, madam."

"I would have thought it quite the opposite, sir."

"It's much like New York, I suspect," Dominic said. "A woman, for instance, can't be too spirited, intelligent, or beautiful to belong. And if she holds an opinion, I doubt she'd be allowed past Mrs. Nesbit's dining room no matter how many times she'd been abroad. Indeed, the city can be a lonely place for those who don't quite fit with any part of it."

"You sound as if you know what it's like to be on the outside looking in."

"Madam, I've spent a lifetime there." He felt both women's gazes for several moments and wondered what the hell had made him say that, in such a heartfelt tone.

Maxine said, "Blast it, look at this open seam. And it won't stay unless it gets a stitch. Hold this, Savannah. No, no—you can't reach properly. And I have to go get a needle and thread. Your lordship, if you would, sir. We need your help here with a minor catastrophe."

With a certain resignation, Dominic released his breath and turned. "Yes, of course, madam. Whatever I can do."

Maxine beamed. "Very good. I knew you would. Some husbands can be such ogres about this kind of thing. Refuse to lift a finger to help. Here, come sit here, on this stool. It will be easier than stooping and I wouldn't want you to be uncomfortable. You're quite tall, sir."

"No taller than my father was, madam."

"You're quite proud of him then."

Her intuitive skills astonished him. "Yes, very proud. He was a great man."

"And he was the second?"

"The second?"

She was looking at him strangely. "The second earl, sir."

"Oh, yes, yes, the second." Dominic sat on the stool, mentally thrashing himself for his oversight.

"Spread your legs, sir—that's it. Right here, Savannah, between his legs. Up close. No, closer. He has to be able to keep hold of the seam, dear. You promise not to bite her, your lordship?"

"Without warning, madam, never." Actually, the thought had occurred to him given that his mouth was perhaps only three level inches away from the primest flesh in all of New York City. He directed his eyes to the length of Savannah's neck. Her skin was covered with a fine sheen and emitted the fragrance of a summer meadow bursting into bloom.

And beneath those skirts she wore no knickers, no stockings, just loose garters swishing against her bare thighs.

"You're quite amusing, sir." Maxine gave a husky giggle and anchored his fingers around the seam that ran over Savannah's right rib cage and disappeared beneath a spray of black lace that trimmed the neckline. The fabric was slippery against his fingertips, and beneath it, beneath whalebone stays, the flesh was soft and very warm. Her rib cage was doing little fluttering spasms, as if she was breathing irregularly.

Heat climbed up his chest, his throat, flooded into his face. Silk skirting rubbed against his erection. "Precisely why am I holding this together, madam?"

"So she doesn't burst out of it, of course."

"Ah."

"You do like it, sir?"

"What?"

"The dress, sir. Is it to your liking?"

"It's—very nice, madam."

"I thought you'd think so. Savannah's the kind of girl who requires clothes that make a statement. Stay right there. It will only take me a minute to find a needle."

The door thumped closed behind her.

A clock on the fireplace mantel ticked a full fifteen times. Dominic watched a tiny pearl of perspiration pool at the base of Savannah's throat and knew that if he had to sit this close to her and not touch her breasts, he would go mad.

"I've told her nothing," Savannah finally said. She'd turned her face to the window, clamped her hands into fists, and pressed them against her sides.

"I gathered that."

"She's extremely smart. She'll know something's not quite right before we even say anything."

"Is that why you haven't spoken in the last ten minutes? Afraid of giving it all away?"

"If you must know—" The pearl trickled slowly into Savannah's décolletage and disappeared behind a spray of black lace. "I believe she's expecting us—actually, expecting you—to behave a certain way and if we don't—that is—if you don't—"

"Yes?"

"I'm quite certain she'll know we're up to no good."

"And we can't trust her with that, can we?"

She looked down at him and bit her lip. "I'm not sure it would be wise at this juncture. I've never been involved in anything this illegal."

"I wasn't aware there were varying degrees."

"Oh, but there are. Though at the moment, I can't think of any. I only know that if my father finds out that you're a fake and that I lied—" She blinked quickly and again looked away as if she was entirely uncomfortable with the situation.

His heart thawed another twenty degrees.

"What sort of behavior is she expecting of us, Savannah?"

"She was—" Bosom trembled with her breaths. "She was saying things like seduced and bedded and duty."

"Ah."

She chewed at her lip and looked away, dejection swarming all over her.

Silence swelled.

"Ah, hell, what harm would there be in putting on a bit of a show for her."

"What?"

"I don't mean—you know—hell, no, you don't know, do you?"

"You mean the bedding and the duty parts, of course. After all, we agreed not to—"

"Exactly. Let's stick with the seducing—or making it look like a well-done seduction."

"For her sake."

"Only a first-rate performance will do."

"Obviously. She's very astute."

"How difficult can it be? After all, you seem the sort of woman who possesses a boundless capacity for fantasy. Pretend I'm someone else. Some say women do it all the time. As for you, you're—" He heard the sudden ragged edges to his breath, the utter reverence invading his voice. He couldn't help lowering his eyes to her bosom, filling his lungs with the heady fragrance that was all hers. "You're magnificent, Savannah."

"Stop." Her hands gently touched his shoulders.

"I'm afraid I can't stop." He closed his eyes, dipped his head, and hoped to God she'd let him. Her fingers spread over his shoulders, gripped, and pulled closer. The depth of his relief was startling. Black lace touched his mouth.

His tongue reached, laved that cavernous valley of perfumed flesh, tasted the salt-pearl.

"But you swore to me this wouldn't happen again. Yesterday you left so angry with me—"

"That was before Maxine Beaupre threatened to throw our charade into jeopardy if she's not properly convinced that I am who I say I am. And you know I would do anything to ensure the success of my plan." He shifted right, nudged lace aside with his tongue, and found one pink crescent barely concealed. His restraint suffered a maddeningly swift surrender. He stretched his fingers up and around one breast and felt the breath leave his lungs. "Walk the plank. Swim the channel. Seduce a beautiful woman." A flick of his tongue exposed the turgid nipple. "Hell, wouldn't you?"

"Oh, yes, yes. I've a civic duty to help you find M. Harrigan's killer—yes—" Her fingers were carving ten paths through his hair. "I've always wanted to be more civic-minded."

"Then have mercy on me, Savannah—" The words of a dying man, wrenched from him as he groped behind her back. His fingers stretched up over silk, found bare back, slid between whalebone cloth and clinging silk, and hooked into loosened stays. He tugged, hard, and they gave. The seam gave. Sleeves slid to elbows, silk split, and warm female spilled from the gown like a bacchanalian feast.

He was off the stool, legs spread, thighs braced, arms crushing her into him with a fury that wiped everything else from his mind. His mouth took hers in an open-mouthed feast of carnal delight, leaving her no doubt what he wanted, what he'd wanted since the instant he saw her in the stable.

"Remember to pretend you're enjoying it," he rasped against her open mouth. "I am." Chests heaved. Breaths came swift, shallow, almost in unison.

"I'm trying." Savannah gasped, digging her fingers into

his biceps, arching her breasts and hips higher, wanting
something she realized she was tired of knowing next to
nothing about. "God, I'm tingling everywhere. Perhaps if
you kiss me again—"

She barely got the last word out before his lips were
parting hers again. The world tipped end over end in
heady delight. She clung to him and realized she never
wanted to let go. A firestorm could have been raging
around them and she would have felt safe in his arms.

He brought her hands low, and yanked the cap sleeves
over her fingertips. With a soulful groan, she reached up
and curled her arms around his thick neck. Starched linen
rubbed her nipples. They felt raw, as if every nerve tip was
exposed. If he kissed her there—and God, but she wanted
him to—she would go up in flames.

Cool air swept over her back, silk rustled, stays gave up,
slipped, caught, and the entire ensemble plunged to the
floor.

Broad hands cupped her bare buttocks, fingers gently
squeezed, lifted, and her tiptoes grazed the silk heap at
her feet. With a heady boldness he pressed her loins
against the irrefutable evidence of his arousal. She realized
almost as an afterthought that she was naked for the first
time in her life with a man.

Naked. In stark daylight with sunlight flooding into the
room and nothing to hide all the excess everywhere that
betrayed her wicked, indulgent nature. She went rigid
with terror.

She'd wanted darkness, muted candlelight, sheets and
pillows and blankets, a nightgown to her chin and a husband who was half asleep from drink to notice all the
flaws.

There was nothing half anything about Dominic Dare
at the moment.

She would have fled had he not been holding her.

"I have to look at you—" He lifted his head, abandoning her to the jaws of shame and humiliation.

She gulped and could hardly watch when his eyes riveted unabashedly between her round thighs for several excruciatingly long moments. His hands slid low over the dramatic indentation of her waist where it met with the plump jut of hips, thumbs brushed over the full curve of her belly and reached down to touch the first dark-golden curls. Fingers spread around the fullness of her hips, where every ounce of chocolate she'd ever consumed had eventually settled.

Oh, God, she thought.

"Beautiful," he murmured.

Savannah's knees buckled. The unbridled reverence in his voice would have wiped even the tiniest trace of self-consciousness from a confident woman's mind. What it did for Savannah's wallowing self-image was staggering. In that instant she adored him for it.

"This isn't fair—" she breathed, and she reached with both hands, gripped the open edges of his shirt, and yanked it wide. Buttons flew, hitting Savannah in the chest, dropping to the floor, rolling beneath the bed. She glimpsed a wild wolf look in his eyes. Reckless thrill rippled through her. She splayed her fingers through the dark hair blanketing his chest, reached up and pushed the shirt from his shoulders. He was lean and well muscled, a broad and towering hulk of enflamed man.

She should have been thinking about running for her life. Had she thought two seconds about her situation, she might have. But she didn't. Instead, she reached for the buttons at the top of his trousers and flicked one open.

"Wait." He caught her wrist.

"I've never seen French underwear."

"It's not the underwear that'll scare you, sweetheart."

She looked up, saw the dancing flames in his eyes, the predatory set to his mouth, and swallowed. She knew nothing about that thing he kept in his trousers. But she wanted to . . . she wanted to touch it, wrap her fingers around it, press against it . . .

"Dominic—" She swayed on her feet, pressed her face into his chest. Her lips tasted his skin, and then she was swallowed in a crushing tide of uncertainty. "There's so much I don't know—so much I want you to teach me." Her hand fumbled on the trouser buttons, then pressed flat against his erection. The shape and size was fully palpable through the worsted wool, huge, hard, and pulsing. She rubbed her palm slowly up and down.

"Ah, God, Savannah—" His hand flattened over hers, stilling it.

"I want to—"

"You want to what? Christ, you want to learn, is that it?" There was a hardness to his voice that sent titillating shivers racing through Savannah.

"Yes, Dominic, I want to learn. Everything. But only from you."

"Not everything. And it won't all be from me. But we'll come as damned close as we can." His voice sounded like a growl. He caught her nipples between his fingers.

She sucked in a breath. He was watching her, his mouth set almost grimly, his eyes blazing dark and dangerous fires.

He gently tugged with his fingers and a corner of his mouth lifted. "Try to enjoy it."

"Dominic."

"I'm getting you ready."

"For what? I don't need getting ready."

"You're not even half there, sweetheart." He dipped his head, suckled one breast, then the other, with long, slow strokes of his tongue that turned Savannah's insides to melted butter. She mumbled something into his hair, cradled his head closer, and wrapped her arms around him as if she wanted to enclose him within her. She sensed he wanted to take his time but couldn't. There was an impatience to his hot kisses on her bosom, a feverish, uncontrollable need in the way he cupped her breasts and squeezed them to fit his mouth, a boldly rutting intent in the jut of his loins into hers.

Rapture. Surrender. Passion. Words that had meant nothing to her before now. Now . . . now she could lecture convention halls full of suffragists on the merits of losing oneself to emotion.

"We haven't even begun down here—" he rasped. Broad palms smoothed over her buttocks, then delved between her thighs so tenderly Savannah parted her legs without a whisper of resistance. The stroke of his fingertips was feather light on the swollen, sensitized bud high between her thighs. Spasms rippled through her. She shuddered as his palm cupped her most intimately.

"Christ—you're like hot honey." He caught a nipple between his teeth. His fingers were doing crazy slow things to her between her thighs, things that made her squirm and fit herself deeper against those fingers. "I have to kiss you, Savannah." He sounded quite desperate. He sounded as if he was asking her permission.

"Yes," she breathed, licking her lips, aching for the firm possession of his mouth over hers. Maybe that would make the throbbing down there stop. "Oh, yes—" His fingers were touching her *right there,* and if she rocked her pelvis even the tiniest bit . . . "Please—" She heard the almost frenetic shrillness in her voice. She knew her fingers were digging into his shoulders, grasping at his chest, twisting into his shirt with an embarrassing, helpless need. She could do nothing about it. "If you stop, I swear I'll die."

"This isn't dying, sweet, this is living."

She was spinning, and inside, soaring up and up, tighter and higher. She was beyond herself. Certainly beyond stopping.

He dropped to his knees, caught her around the hips, and, with little tenderness, brought her swollen loins to his mouth.

Savannah's eyes snapped open, her head fell back, she

saw cherubs painted on the domed ceiling overhead, and knew she'd gone to heaven.

He was kissing her, just as he'd promised, open-mouthed, with his tongue and his hot breath and his sensuous lips, parting tender flesh, probing secret recesses where all that hot honey flowed.

"God almighty—" He growled when the first spasm rocked through her.

Another followed, this one clenching her womb. She cried out, loud, her legs buckled, and she fell forward, catching herself with one arm on the bedpost, half turning, and he turned with her . . . somehow . . . in the tangle of skirts and useless limbs. The dress was kicked aside, the stool tossed across the room where it rolled up hard against the wall. And then he lifted her half onto the bed, and she was clutching at sliding bed linens and pillows, and gasping at the frilled canopy above her, crying out for release when his mouth consumed her and took her to the very edge of a precipice for two—three—anguished moments of pleasure and then she fell. With shuddering, soulful cries, she tumbled and kept tumbling until the last of the spasms left her.

Chapter 14

Savannah opened her eyes. Dominic was braced above her watching her, his eyes furiously blue. She reached up, curled her hand around his neck, and brought his open mouth down to hers.

"You're a wanton."

"I want to do it again." Her lips curved as she looked up at him and rubbed her palms over the jut of his chest. "I didn't even once have to think about duty. Did you?"

"Oddly enough, no."

She realized that she and the coverlet she lay on had slid halfway off the foot of the bed. She lifted her feet from the floor and began to work each up Dominic's calves.

"You woke the dead," he murmured, his attention lowering to the swells that were pushed up clear to Savannah's collarbone.

Savannah sifted her fingers through his hair. "Good heavens, do you think Aunt Maxine knows what just happened?"

"Your neighbors three doors down know."

Savannah felt heat creep into her cheeks. "That means the servants—"

"Hell, the Astors' servants."

"Do you know what this means, Dominic?"

"I haven't a notion except that your nipples are the exact size, shape, and color of overripe peaches. And they taste"—he suckled, nipped, laved—"sweeter."

"God, I haven't even thought about food."

"Neither have I." And then his hand was between her legs, and he was braced over her, watching every sweet stroke register across her face. "Will everyone in the Four Hundred now know that the Earl and Countess Castellane made the walls shake one morning on East Fifty-eighth?"

"I'm afraid they just might—"

"Will *Town Topics* be recommending that the Countess Castellane take her mighty lungs to the Metropolitan Opera stage?"

"I certainly hope they do. I've always wanted to perform on stage."

"The city would be at your feet." He brushed his lips tenderly over hers and murmured, "Will the Earl of Castellane be touted as the grandest of lovers? A prince of passion, lord of all things lusty, a man to bring a woman weeping to her knees with desire?"

"Oh, yes." She sighed, her eyes sweeping closed.

"Will you wear your satisfaction?"

"All over me," she breathed.

Lips warm and gentle touched hers. "Will any lover come within a foot of you?"

"They wouldn't dare."

"You'll refuse them all?"

"What woman wouldn't?"

He seemed to hesitate a moment. Again, a whisper-soft kiss and then his voice, hoarse, bottomlessly deep. "Will you look every inch a woman deeply in love?"

"I won't be able to help myself." Her thighs trembled

open wider. She arched her back, thrusting her breasts up at him and into his chest until he couldn't refuse the swollen and distended nipples. He took one deep and hard into his mouth, then buried his face in the softness of her bosom.

"God, to be inside you—"

"Yes," she breathed, fingers tugging at his waistband. "That's what I need."

His fingers slid, slipped, delved, delved deeper. "Sweet virgin—"

She slid one hand inside his trousers and touched hot, hard flesh. *"Dominic."*

"Don't make this any more difficult."

"But I only want—" Her voice clogged in her throat. He was kissing her down there again, and in a moment she was again soaring.

"I want to do it again," she finally said between breaths when the last of the flooding spasms had left her.

"Damned fool's luck." His face was buried in the side of her neck. His voice sounded strained, his breaths ragged, as if he exerted the energy of ten men.

"But I want to see all of you. I want to touch you."

"That wouldn't be wise."

"Wise? I'm talking about need. Wisdom has nothing to do with it."

"You're right. I can't remember the last time I thought clearly."

"And we have all day. Two more, actually, and even then we don't necessarily have to leave the town house if we don't want to. We could turn down every invitation." She wriggled with delight, fit her hands on his backside, and squeezed. "Dominic, you're like a great rutting stud horse. All muscle and power and—"

"Oh, God, get up."

"But I don't want to get up. I want to do it again."

"It's well past lunch."

"Is it?"

He was looking down at her with a grim expression. "What the hell have I done?"

She stretched slow and languorously. "I don't know, Dominic. Is there a term for it? Perhaps that's something you ought to teach me."

He closed his eyes, pushed his hand through his hair with almost punishing briskness, then jerked up and turned away from her. She shoved up on her elbows and watched, confused, as he jerked his shirttails together.

"Why won't you look at me?" she asked.

"Get dressed." He was shoving his shirt tails into his trousers.

"Well, that won't do me any good, will it? If I'm dressed and tidy Aunt Maxine might not be altogether convinced that there was any sort of successful seduction here."

"For chrissake, one look at you and she'll know."

Savannah sat up with the coverlet up over her breasts and leaned right until she glimpsed herself in her dressing table mirror. She saw mussed hair, splotchy cheeks, swollen red lips, and limpid eyes. "Really?"

"Really." He turned, his face so stern and hard she could scarcely believe he was the same man who'd whispered tender words to her not moments before. His hands were on his hips, making them look very narrow and his shoulders look acres wide. She wanted to jump off the bed and run into his arms. But something about his cold hard stare made her brace herself. "Your aunt should be well satisfied by our performance for some time. My understanding is that married couples do this sort of thing maybe once every two weeks. If that."

"Good heavens, how do they bear it that long?"

His eyes shifted to the window, his jaw clenched, two moments passed, and he looked back at her. "No more. This is it, understand?"

"No, I don't. You keep saying that and I know you don't mean it."

"Trust me, at this moment, with all my being, I mean it."

"Tell me why." She crossed her arms, jutted her chin. "Oh, I know, I'm too fat for you."

"You're not fat anywhere. And even if you were—"

"See. That's the reason. You couldn't even lift me onto the bed. I weigh too much."

"I could lift you onto the chandelier up there with one arm if I wanted to—which now that I think about it—ah, hell, I didn't *want* you on the bed. I wanted your legs off the bed so I could easily reach—" He bared his teeth, swore like a devil, as if he thoroughly enjoyed it, then turned and marched to the door. He gripped the door handle and looked back at her as if he wanted to shake his finger at her but thought the better of it. "I'm going riding."

"You just went riding."

"No, my dear, I didn't. At least not the kind of hard and deep riding that I need. But a horse will have to do. What do you think? To Philadelphia and back. Far enough? Hard enough? Will it leave me then? Don't bet your lily-white virtue on it." He yanked the door open and strode out.

"Twice?"

"That's what I said. We did it twice." Savannah shook her head at the dress Maxine had just pulled from the wardrobe. "No, not that one. Something brighter. What good is going to a suffragist meeting if I'm not seen? Let me see the orange one again." She drew a sea sponge to her neck and sank up to her shoulders in the hot bathwater.

The tub was an enormous copper bowl on gilded clawed feet, rumored to have once sat in the palace of Napoleon Bonaparte himself. Both it and the lilac-fragranced toiletries had been delivered courtesy of Aunt

Maxine not thirty seconds after Dominic had made a door-banging departure from the town house.

"Make the water almost scalding," Maxine had instructed Savannah's maid, Brunnie. "You'll sit in it for an hour," she'd then told Savannah in rather severe tones as she peeled the coverlet from her niece's rosy and ravished body.

"Is this really necessary?" Savannah asked, licking the dots of perspiration from her upper lip. She blew at a wispy curl dangling over her eyes. "I've been in here for thirty minutes."

"And you'll sit there thirty more to properly recover." Maxine looked long and hard at her. "Twice."

"I wanted to again."

"Good God, but you enjoyed it. This is unheard of."

Savannah's eyes swept closed. "Yes. He was magnificent. He was a beast. A gentle savage. A—" Her eyes snapped open. "Wasn't I supposed to enjoy it?"

"Most married women pretend to know nothing about it."

"Then they're all fools."

"Perhaps they don't have a man like Castellane in their beds, hmm?"

"Oh, we weren't quite on the bed. We were sort of halfway between the floor and the bed."

"I see." Maxine's glittering blue eyes—the eyes that had fascinated an Austrian prince, a Belgian chef, and a thrice-divorced French count—those fabled eyes swept over the floor, the stool rolled against the wall, the mussed bed, the crumpled coverlet and discarded dress as if she envisioned it all. But what did it matter? However keen and astute Maxine Beaupre might be, she couldn't possibly know that what had taken place halfway between the floor and the bed was indeed only halfway.

The breaching had not occurred.

"No," Savannah piped up. "On second thought, maybe the red one. What do you think?"

"I think you don't want to go to the meeting. I think you'd rather wait here for Castellane."

Savannah pursed her lips with a good bit of wounded pride. "He went charging off—" She realized she'd given something away, though she wasn't quite sure what, when Maxine's eye narrowed a fraction. Savannah waved a hand, suddenly certain that a sated bridegroom would have no reason to barrel off for a long, hard ride on horseback. "He—uh—he has an old acquaintance from his boarding school who lives near here and he was quite anxious to see him."

"And he rides his horse everywhere he goes."

Savannah pasted on a smile. "Positively everywhere. Can't stand the carriages on most days."

"Topcoats, either?" Maxine was examining the red dress as if she looked for invisible wrinkles. Her voice held a distracted tone.

"Or hats. He hates the hats."

"Somewhat unusual."

"Oh, I think you'll find Castellane the most unusual aristocrat you're likely to meet."

"A rarity among husbands."

"Yes, I like that about him too."

Maxine looked right at her. "You seem to like him a bit more than you should."

"More than I should?"

"He is just a husband, after all. Not a lover."

Savannah opened her mouth in protest, then snapped it closed. Maxine was looking at her as if she knew she hid a very deep, dark secret. "You know, you're right, Aunt Maxine. I'm not in the mood for Frances Trainer tonight. I feel like doing something for the cause, of course, but something that's never been done." She pursed her lips and narrowed her eyes. "Something that will make a statement, but nothing too awfully naughty. But I'm so damned tired of being a bystander, even at Frances Trainer's meetings. I have a deeply compelling urge to participate in something that I'm not supposed to be participating in. And then I want to tell everyone all about it."

"Otherwise what's the point?" Maxine perched on the edge of the tub, a smile tweaking her lips. "My dear Savannah, the basic social graces are like dance figures to be learned and repeated without innovation. You learn them early and you go on repeating them, all the words and the acts, throughout your life. You're expected to keep time and not get out of step with your partner and the other dancers in your set. If you break rhythm, if you fail to do what others expect of you, and at the precise moment they expect it, you're to feel as if you failed both them and yourself. I lived half my life believing precisely the opposite and feeling awful about it. Then I tried a bit of reform, because I knew everyone was as bored as I was."

"And now?"

"Now?" Maxine leaned down and Savannah was certain stars danced in her blue eyes. "Now dullness is the one sin I can't forgive. I demand that anyone who sits at my table or takes up a moment of my time be funny, handsome, scintillating, or, like me, superbly arrogant. It makes no difference to me if their families came over on the *Mayflower* or in the last boat to unload from Europe. And you, my precious Savannah, are just like me."

Yes, she was. Savannah had never thought of Dominic as the immigrant Italian. He was a gentleman rogue. "I'm thinking wicked thoughts, Aunt Maxine. I'm thinking that my father needs to learn a lesson about me."

Maxine's brows shot up. "Ah. He doesn't much like your gentle savage, and that disturbs you."

"He was a brute to him. He didn't even give him a chance to speak. He has narrow, pig-headed ideas and brash ways of telling them."

"I've never heard you say a cross word about your father."

"Well, that was before I realized how badly his ideas

about the world and women need broadening. It's no wonder his opinions are so narrow. He spends his entire life, dawn to dusk, either working at his office or smoking at his club with other narrow-minded, backward-thinking, pig-headed men. God knows what they do in those clubs. Why, how will any of the men in this world broaden their thinking if they never allow free-thinking women into the place to show them the error of their ways? I'd bet you they don't think a woman would dare to breach their secret club haven. And if she did, why, what the devil would they do then?" She blinked. The idea burst through her brain like cannon shot. "Oh, God."

Maxine arched a brow. "That wicked, eh?"

"Will you help me?"

"Just tell me what you want me to do."

Dominic rode his horse at a demon's pace for precisely three blocks before he realized what a bounding ass he was making of himself. Had he not spotted the copper tub and guessed Maxine Beaupre's intent with it he might have turned back around and been content to listen to Savannah discuss poufs and velvet tassels while attempting in her own maddeningly guileless way to seduce him. But her naked in a hot bath at this juncture was not something his abused resolve was up to.

He rode down to his Tenth Street studio and spent the afternoon with his orphan pal Sam, doing what any typical eleven-year-old boy would want to do with his first opportunity to sample a piece of prime horseflesh. They'd gone to the park, pretended to be riding swells from Murray Hill, ate hot dogs, watched the parade of the powdered and privileged in their broughams and victorias, and returned to the studio around dusk. Sam fell asleep watching twilight creep into darkness beyond the windows. Bonnie arrived shortly afterward and took the boy to his apartment for the night.

It was well after dark, certainly well past dinner, when

Dominic returned to the town house. He shrugged off the groomsman and tended to his horse himself, taking his time unsaddling and cooling him. He could hardly help himself. The animal was a work of art, a flawless piece of mahogany muscle that slid beneath Dominic's admiring hands like a sculpture. It was then that he gained his first insight into what he'd thought was rich men's fascination with horses.

Until now he'd viewed horses only as a means to an end, a simple mode of travel, not as something capable of bringing profound pleasure. But even he, the great scorner of excess and overindulgence, could anticipate a summer afternoon spent at Saratoga, where the bluest of blue-blooded horseflesh raced. He could well imagine the emotion inspired by a charging brigade of sleek Thoroughbreds pumping savagely toward a finish line.

Perhaps he was gleaning some understanding into Stuyvesant Merriweather's set in spite of himself.

But he still couldn't shake the feeling that his life and fulfilling his dreams had somehow, inexplicably, stalled.

He left the horse in the common stable half a block from the town house, and by rote or simply out of the angst that continued to plague him about his "bought" condition, he entered the town house through the rear door from a garden path that led alongside.

It occurred to him as he pushed the door open that a thief would find the town house an uncommonly easy mark, especially since the door had been left unlatched and all the gaslights were out along the rear of the house. The hall he entered was dark, the kitchen to the left as well. Only one gaslight sputtered in the entry, casting a dim and insufficient glow.

Where was Savannah?

He softly closed the door, reminding himself to have the locks checked. He turned and froze. A bulky shadow moved silently across the splash of moonlight spilling into the kitchen. It was the shadow of a man, thickly made and stout, with short legs but a powerful ballooning girth.

Dominic knew immediately by his stealthy, creeping pace that he was not a servant.

An intruder. And Savannah was asleep upstairs, fresh from her bath, innocence left intact beneath her white cotton nightgown.

His mind exploded. In three charging strides he was across the kitchen floor. Clamping the intruder around the neck, he swung him around and shoved him up against the cupboards.

It occurred to him in a blinding flash that he was unarmed. He went cold.

And then the intruder cupped him by the buttocks and squeezed.

Chapter 15

Dominic jerked back and snarled.

"Really, Dominic, you must stop swearing all the time."

Dominic narrowed his eyes against the spray of moonlight filling his vision. "Savannah." Her name sounded like another angry curse.

"Nobody else puts their hands on your behind like that, do they?"

He ignored that, ignored the leap to attention that occurred in his groin, and muttered, "What the hell are you doing dressed up in all that padding? And this—" He braced one hand on the wall beside her head, reached out, and flicked a short-brimmed bowler from her head. Blond curls spilled to her waist where a gold watch and chain were pinned to what looked like a tailored waistcoat squeezed over a prosperous paunch. Her breasts were indistinguishable beneath her clothes. "You're dressed like a man."

"I'm glad you think so. I meant to look like one."

"Men don't smell like lilacs. Where the hell are you going? A suffragist meeting?"

"No. You weren't supposed to see me, you know. Nobody was, except Maxine."

"Of course."

"It was her idea to stuff the bed in case Brunnie looks in on me. I had to wait until Cook finished up and Jarvis and Brunnie disappeared before I could come down. I was halfway out the door when I smelled that bread over there under the napkin. You know, bread is irresistible to me when it's fresh-baked and slathered with butter. A girl needs something to sustain her through adventure so I went back for some. I'm still glad I did." She lifted her hand to her mouth and took an enormous bite of a chunk of bread. "Duwishush."

Dominic looked into her milky, moonlit eyes and felt his resistance crumbling with an inevitability that was becoming almost comfortable. "I don't suppose I can talk you out of this."

She swallowed. "Not a chance."

"Then I'm going with you."

"I rather wish you wouldn't. You'll get angry and start swearing at someone and then you'll shout and stomp around and throw some poor man out of the room."

"And if the situation warrants it, you'll be glad I did. You see, I've never completely trusted the men of the world."

"Hmm. And you're one of them." She took another bite, chewed a few moments, then sighed. "Fine. You'll need your topcoat and a hat. A nice black silk topper will do. Something befitting an earl. You have to be so well dressed that your dress won't be observed at all."

"Will the ironies never cease? Fine. Let's go." He grabbed her hand and tugged her along behind him, out of the kitchen and toward the stairs. His lips twitched when he heard the scrape of her planted boot soles on the wooden floor.

"I don't want to—" she hissed in a loud whisper.

"I'm not letting you get away from me that easily," he

replied. "I would have caught you before you got halfway down the block."

"I doubt that. I'm a very swift walker."

"Yes, avoid running. You'll give yourself away to anyone within a hundred yards." He started climbing the stairs two at a time, forcing her to do the same at a lumbering pace. "Don't worry. I'll be quick."

"But I don't want to—"

"Sir." A silhouette disengaged from the shadows at the top of the stairs.

"Jarvis," Dominic muttered, ignoring the servant's startled look as he charged past with stout young man in tow.

"He'll think you're one of those men who likes other men," Savannah said when Dominic slammed his bedchamber door closed behind her.

"Let him." Dominic turned up a wall sconce and, with fingers flying over his shirt buttons, moved to his armoire. "Better that than risk having your evening activities reported to your father." He glanced at her. "You want this all kept secret, I assume."

"For a short time."

"Ah. What good is adventure if no one knows about it?"

"Precisely. But I want to be the one to give it all away. I don't trust the servants to do it properly."

He shrugged out of his shirt, drew another from the wardrobe along with a cutaway topcoat of deep burgundy gabardine, a necktie of burgundy silk, and a double-breasted vest in black Chinese brocade. He tossed all but the shirt on a high-backed chair and slid one arm into the shirt. Starched linen unpeeled with a satisfying crispness at the shove of his fingers.

From underneath the shadow of her bowler, Savannah watched the shirt billow around his torso. She licked her lips. Desire pumped through Dominic. He buttoned several buttons, then lowered his hands and flicked his trousers open. Her lips parted. Beneath padding and vest and waistcoat her breasts did a feminine heave.

It occurred to Dominic that he hadn't felt this empowered since he'd first laid eyes on her. And by God he wasn't going to relinquish it just yet. He could almost hear her desires raging war inside her—for adventure outside or pleasure inside.

His manhood was straining like a rutting stallion against an unresisting bit. Another button flipped open. Her eyes riveted on his groin and he swelled another impossible degree.

He watched her gloved fingers twist into the fabric of her trousers, felt the hesitancy in her, and knew a sudden realization: She didn't know a thing about launching the first salvo of a seduction. With Savannah seduction was an accident. She oozed with a need to be gently taken in hand and tutored.

And he knew that if he walked toward her, took her in his arms, and kissed her, she would be his for the rest of the night, a sweet piece of heaven in a hellish world.

God almighty, but the idea of such a woman within ten feet of a bed would have brought most men to their knees weeping with thanks.

Deceive her, use her, endanger her, yes, he could do all these. And then he would, inevitably, have to leave her in her world.

A sour taste filled his mouth. He'd made the mistake once. He didn't plan to repeat it.

He turned his back, reached for his tie, and shoved his shirt tails into his trousers. There was a tightening around his neck. He was no great avenger whose every action could be shrugged off and justified. He had become a selfish, thoughtless man.

He grabbed his coat from the chair, a black silk top hat from a shelf in the armoire, scooped up a pair of white gloves and a black walking stick as an afterthought, and swung around with mouth grimly set. "I'll get the carriage."

She blinked and looked startled. "We'll hire one."

He put on his hat. "What aristocrat looks authentic in a hired brougham?"

"An aristocrat who wants to sneak around without anyone knowing where he's going, particularly his servants and his wife. I'd wager you'll be no different than any of the other bored husbands we'll meet tonight." She turned, pulled the door open an inch, and peeked out. "I don't see Jarvis," she whispered over her shoulder as Dominic tugged on his gloves.

He moved up behind her, touched her hand, and her gloved fingers curled into his. His chest squeezed a fraction tighter. "Not much of an adventuress, are you?"

Her head snapped around as if yanked by a string. "I beg your pardon. I was merely thinking of you, Castellane."

"Please do think of me, my dear."

Their eyes met in the dusky shadows. And then she yanked open the door and stalked out ahead of him. He hesitated long enough to admire her sprightly step, then, with walking stick smartly set, followed after her.

"I hate that name," Savannah grumbled, tugging her bowler over her eyes and her collar higher around her neck as a white-whiskered man in elegant clothes jostled past and glowered at her.

Clouds of cigar smoke billowed around them. She blanched and resisted the urge to wrinkle her nose and retch. Despite the thickness of the air, every tufted leather chair and green baize table at the Fifth Avenue Patriarch Club was occupied by a cigar-belching, barrel-chested man of wealth, stature, or connections. In their case, Savannah was certain that Dominic's aristocratic grace and exquisite delivery had gained them hallowed entrance into the place.

She smothered a cough and slanted her eyes up at him, feeling that familiar tug and twist that happened in her chest every time their eyes met. She spoke huskily out of the side of her mouth as she'd seen some men do. "Herman isn't too awful, but Shnable? That's not to be tolerated. Surely you could have chosen a more suitable name for the dear friend of the newly arrived Earl of Castellane. The man at the door would have still let me in had my name been Sutton or Leland or Houndstooth. He drooled when you introduced yourself."

"Herman Shnable is a butcher on lower Tenth and he's been a very good friend of mine for more than twenty years. He's quite proud of his German heritage."

Savannah blinked. "Do I look German?"

He gave her a critical look. "You look just a day shy of sixteen and quite able to appreciate a thick cut of beef." He eyed her well-stocked girth, then directed his gaze around the main room. He looked very leonine and aristocratic in his hat and gloves. She felt an unexpected surge of pride to be with him. "I don't see him," he said.

"Who?"

"Your father. That is who we came to see, isn't it?"

She experienced again the unsettling feeling that Dominic Dare always knew exponentially more than he ever let on. It was a defeating notion but a strangely comforting one. She tugged her vest down over her paunch and puffed up her chest with self-righteousness. "If you must know, he spends most of his time here and, yes, you're correct. I mean very much to teach him a lesson."

"In what?"

"Humility."

"Ah."

Something in his tone made Savannah want to frown. She resisted. "When he learns that his daughter snuck into his men's club perhaps I will throw some much-needed light into his narrow-minded opinions. Perhaps he will see me with new eyes."

"Then again, he might not."

"I won't be found out, if that's what you're suggesting."

"I wouldn't dare think of you as failing."

"Good. Neither would I. I also intend to let the women of the world know precisely what goes on in these establishments. Diffuse some of the mystery, you see."

"Women sit around wondering, do they?"

"Heavens, no. That is, at least *I* don't. A true suffragist never would. It's the idea of penetrating something that's assumed to be impenetrable that is so tantalizing."

"A person could obsess about such a thing—night upon night." He looked at her meaningfully and she went instantly hot from the inside out.

Huge guffaws erupted from a nearby table. Savannah was grateful for the diversion. Several of the men seated around it were red-faced and sweating. All had loosened their collars and abandoned their coats and ties. Cards lay scattered on the table beside half-filled glasses and piles of coins and bills.

"Odd, but it reminds me of a tavern in Dogberg," Savannah said. "I always imagined the New York men's clubs to be much stuffier, more . . . English. Thank heavens they're not. My father would prefer this sort of club."

"Especially if he's a poker player."

"Papa is not a gambler." Savannah sniffed.

"Really? I hope the men at his table don't know that."

Savannah's head jerked to his. "Where?"

Dominic's chin jutted a fraction. "The table closest to the far window. He's across from the man in the brown bowler and next to the . . . shit."

"What?" She peered up on tiptoes, squinted through smoke and over the heads of several men, and spotted her father the instant he threw back his head and drained his glass dry. His face looked swarthy and hot as if his tie was too tight. But he'd loosened it askew, his collar as well, and his hair fell over his forehead and into his eyes. His shirtsleeves were rolled to his elbows and his shirt front looked stained with spots of gravy. His face bore the look of a weary warrior.

A lump swelled in her throat. "That's not Papa."

Dominic's voice was low and close to her ear. "I wish it weren't. That's Tweed Black he's seated next to."

"The fat one with the black hair and the red velvet coat?"

Dominic nodded but his eyes never left Black. "Always wears that damned Prince Albert coat no matter the weather so everyone will know him when he enters a room. Most arrogant, crookedest politician in the city. Some say he's the king of the underworld. He makes friends by arm-twisting and using his lieutenants' fists. Owns the city administration. Some say he kills whoever he can't buy. He's originally from Florence."

"Good grief, you know him?"

"I had a misunderstanding with one of Black's lieutenants several years ago over a poker game."

"Did you hurt him badly?"

His eyes shifted to hers and narrowed. "Bad enough. Black asked me to work for him."

"You didn't."

"Are you asking me?"

Savannah lifted her chin. "No. I know very well you wouldn't work for that kind of man. Your demons are more personal."

"Are they? Or is it that I'm just too damned nice a fellow?" He was looking deep into her eyes. His voice was suddenly like the hungry purr of a lion.

Savannah's heart did a little stutter. She had to look away. "Black will recognize you."

"That's a distant possibility."

"I doubt he's refused anything very often. He's sure to remember you, and with Papa sitting there it would be a disaster. Let's go home. I've lost all appetite for adventure."

"Hold on." His fingers wrapped around her upper arm, keeping her where she was. "Your father just lost another hand and his pockets look empty."

Savannah's heart fell. "I wonder if Mother knows."

"Most women don't find out about this kind of thing until their husbands are found murdered somewhere for unpaid debts."

"Are you trying to scare me?"

He didn't answer. He was striding very purposefully toward her father's table, tall and regal, pompous as a bantam rooster with burgundy coattails snapping and walking stick extended. Watching him, she couldn't shake the feeling that he was sailing headlong into disaster. Or was he saving her father from certain disaster?

She jostled through the crowd after him, head bent, lower lip snagged between her teeth, heart slamming against her ribs with rising fear. Her father's voice reached her before she was ten feet from their table. It was loud and strident, the words ominously slurred. It was the voice of a man who knew he was trapped.

"Whaddya mean you don't take a marker, Black? What the hell kind of business is that? I'm good for it. Hell, I'm supposedly worth millions. Just didn't bring them all. I want in again, damn you. I'm going to win my two thousand back, same way as you took it."

Savannah bumped chest first into the back of a man who turned around quickly and gave her an agitated look. She glowered at him, collapsed her breasts into her chest, and squeezed around the table and between several other men so that she faced her father. She poked her head between two men's shoulders just as Dominic slid a chair up to the table, directly next to Tweed Black.

Her father gaped at Dominic. "What the hell?"

"Stakes are five hundred to get in," the man in the brown bowler said to Dominic without looking up. His hands were a blur as he continued shuffling the cards.

Dominic reached into a lower pocket of his coat, then

into the other, frowned, then reached into one upper inside pocket, the upper outside pocket, then inside again, smiled, and tossed a pile of bills into the center of the table. He cocked a brow at Stuyvesant Merriweather. "I'll take your marker, sir, and loan you a thousand."

"You're gonna *what?*" her father barked.

Savannah stared at the bills on the table, fifteen of them, all crisp hundreds. The man in the bowler glanced at Black. Black flicked his cigar back and forth in his mouth with angry sweeps of his tongue. One mammoth hand was clamped around a glass. Up close he looked like a dressed-up bulldog with small black eyes and hungry, loose jowls. He was staring at Dominic and Dominic was fidgeting and fussing with his gloves and his walking stick. Behind and on either side of Black stood thick men with wide flat noses and expressionless faces. His lieutenants. Savannah suddenly couldn't breathe.

"Who the hell are you?" Black snarled bulldoglike.

"Winthrop Twombley, Earl of Castellane." Dominic extended a slightly limp wrist and pristine white glove at Black and smiled as if apologizing for the obvious fact that the world was his playground and everyone in it there simply for his enjoyment. Somehow, miraculously, he'd transformed his features and entire character. He looked so foppish, so bumbling and harmless Black couldn't help but dismiss out of hand any similarity he bore to the man who'd dared to refuse his offer of employment.

"Chee-rist." Stuyvesant Merriweather snarled, rolling his eyes heavenward.

Black ignored Dominic's hand. His eyes narrowed, shifted to Stuyvesant Merriweather, and his head jerked at Dominic. "You know him?"

"I wouldn't own up to it," Stuyvesant muttered.

Black glanced at the man in the bowler and nodded with a jerk of his chin. Stuyvesant Merriweather lunged across the table, slapped a beefy hand over the bills, and jerked them in with a growled "God-damned English bastards think they own the God-damned world—"

A moment later play began. Turn moved several times around the table with each player tossing bills and coins into the center of the table until the booty shot well past two thousand. Dominic continued fidgeting as if he couldn't get comfortable on his chair or in his clothes. The man in the bowler swore and threw in his cards as play passed him a third time.

"Bloody fine weather for this time of year, eh?" Dominic said, grinning at Black, at Black's lieutenants, fussing with his cuff, then starting as if he hiccuped. "Oh, so sorry. My turn, eh? What did you just do, sir?"

Black's face measurably darkened. "I raised five hundred."

"Oh, yes, of course. Then I must meet that and raise—oh—another six hundred." The limp wrist sent the bills fluttering into the center of the table.

Stuyvesant stared at his cards so hard Savannah was certain he perspired from the effort. One hand wavered over the bills at his elbow, or was it trembling? Her heart twisted in her chest. She wanted to run to him, throw her arms around his neck, and beg him to take them all back to Dogberg, Ohio, before he got himself killed.

Stuyvesant's eyes darted to the pile in the center of the table, then to Black, then back to his own cards. "Your six and I raise another hundred."

"Bloody hell, look at the time." Dominic had snapped open the watch pinned to his coat and was frowning at it.

Black looked murderously at Dominic. "I meet and raise another five."

Stuyvesant Merriweather barked a curse and tossed in his cards.

Dominic clicked his watch closed, looked up expectantly, and smiled. "Oh, my turn again, eh? I'm in a bit of a hurry so I suppose I must call, sir."

Black stared at him, then showed a poisonous smile and

lowered his hand. "Four kings and an ace. Beat that, Mr. Earl."

"I'm afraid I have to. Straight flush is what we call it in England." He laid down his cards, then indicated the pile of bills in the middle of the table. "I take it all that is mine."

Savannah gasped with delight.

Stuyvesant Merriweather let out a victorious hoot.

One of Black's gorillas growled and would have lunged at Dominic had Black not lifted a hand to stop him. Black's face wore a look of deadly calm. Only the thick vein throbbing at his temple and the crimson cast of his skin gave away his rage. He lifted his glass and jerked a quick swallow. "Castellane," he said slowly, watching Dominic scoop up his winnings. "They teach you to cheat like that over in England?"

Dominic laughed low and easy, his eyes never lifting from the bills he neatly folded with his white-gloved fingers. "I beg your pardon, sir. This is a game of chance, not skill."

"Cheat, you say?" With a chuckle, Stuyvesant Merriweather leaned back in his chair, rubbed a hand over his paunch, and Savannah felt herself tense with dread. "Don't see why he can't win same way as you did, Black."

The air seemed to crackle for an instant. The hair on Savannah's neck stood on end. Her father had just publicly insulted one of the most dangerous men in New York.

And then suddenly a chair toppled, bodies moved in a blur, and Dominic was out of his chair, braced protectively in front of her father with one hand holding one of Black's gorillas right at the curve of his neck and shoulder, as if only he kept the man from charging at Stuyvesant Merriweather.

"We're peaceful men here," Dominic drawled with sugary calm. His eyes were fixed like hard diamonds on Black. "Call off your dogs, sir. I'm quite certain Mr. Merriweather meant no insult." As he spoke his fingers seemed to squeeze gently, and the Goliath wheezed and sank like falling bread dough to his knees.

Black stared at Dominic with an intensity that made Savannah's knees weak.

"Jesus—" Stuyvesant Merriweather looked at Dominic, then at the man kneeling on the floor, then at Tweed Black. He jerked out of his chair and fumbled on the back of it for his topcoat. Savannah pushed her way around the table toward him. She helped him draw the coat around his shoulders, but he didn't once look at her. She laid a hand on his arm and felt the trembling in him as if it came up from his bones.

"My good friend Mr. Shnable will see you out, Mr. Merriweather." Dominic released the gorilla, tugged his coat smooth over his chest, slid the folded bills into his pocket, and took up his walking stick. "A good evening to you, sir."

Touching his fingertips to his brim, he gave Tweed Black a brisk nod, turned on his heel, and strode through the silent crowd behind Savannah and her father.

Chapter 16

They emerged from the Patriarch Club into a rainstorm. Dominic hailed the nearest hansom cab and yanked the door open before the coachman could jump from his perch.

"Fifty-eighth and Fifth," Dominic barked, shoving Savannah in the backside to help her in. "And quickly, man." He lurched in and settled on the seat opposite her and Stuyvesant Merriweather just as the coach leapt into traffic.

"Know your way around awfully quick," Merriweather muttered, glaring at him from beneath shaggy brows, arms folded belligerently over his chest.

Savannah was looking at her father as if she was torn between weeping and scolding. Dominic looked out the window and silently started to count to ten.

At three Merriweather snorted. "Fine, dammit, if it's thanks you're looking for, Winthrop, you've got it. Satisfied?"

"Papa!"

Merriweather's eyes popped and he gaped at the young man beside him. "Good God almighty, Savannah!"

Savannah thrust out her jaw and glared like an angry puppy with cheeks rain-kissed and bright pink. "If you don't properly thank Castellane I swear I'll tell Mother you nearly got yourself killed tonight by insulting a crooked politician over a bad poker game."

"You'll do no such thing. Your mother has a bad heart."

Savannah snorted. "Bad hearts and rheumatism. How convenient that these ailments arise only when I need reining in. I don't believe a word of it anymore. I swear I'll tell her. She doesn't know about any of this, does she?"

Merriweather's hand slashed through the air. "Doesn't need to know, dammit. I was about to win it all back, every cent, even the five thousand from the other night."

"The other night." Savannah crossed her arms. "And if Castellane hadn't been there the police would have found you tomorrow lying in a gutter on some awful street beaten to a bloody pulp."

Merriweather looked sharply at Dominic and poked out his jaw. "How'd she know that? You teaching her things like that, Winthrop? Sounds like something you've done."

"I learned a great deal tonight, Papa, mostly from you, and I'm not proud to say it."

That garnered her a hot look from her father but he said nothing.

"Papa, if you don't stop being so nasty to Castellane I'm going to start thinking you're a hypocrite."

Merriweather's face mottled purple. He swung to Savannah and shoved a fist skyward. "Dammit, daughter, that's the limit of it. I've always been a man of highest honor, of moral conviction and fairness in my dealings with all men—"

"Indeed I know you have. You, Papa, in spite of yourself, are a gentleman." Savannah settled back on her seat, fiddled with the watch chain at her waist, then lifted a confident gaze. "You possess certain moral principles that are not learned or adopted but are an inborn part of a man and give him quality. Honor, integrity, and forbearance—that is, when your luck is with you—these are what make you who you are. And to my way of seeing it, you and Castellane have an extraordinary amount in common."

"What?"

"Oh, be graceful and thank him. He's quite likable, if you give him a chance. I think you owe him that at the very least."

"*Owe him?* I just handed him two hundred fifty thousand dollars and my daughter. I tell you I'll never have use for idle foreigners and no wish to support them in their slothful ways."

"Really? That particular idle foreigner quite possibly saved your life tonight. Is there a going rate for that service in New York City, Papa? I wonder what Tweed Black pays his thugs to protect him."

Merriweather's mouth snapped closed, then jerked open. He looked at Dominic but the sparks of rage began to sputter and in their place dawned that curious look of befuddlement that plagued men the world over when dealing with women. "How the hell did she learn so much?"

Dominic looked meaningfully at Savannah. "She came to me that way, sir."

"Did she now?" Merriweather's shoulders seemed to sink into their sockets. He looked at Savannah with a kind of resigned helplessness that Dominic knew and understood all too well. "God, look at you."

Savannah grinned. "I'm a German butcher, Papa. Castellane knows—" She caught herself, looked at Dominic with outright terror in her eyes, and his heart seemed to tangle in his chest. She was protecting him; even now, as she taught her father his lesson in humility, she was protecting him.

He was overcome with a mountainous urge to crush her in his arms with gratitude. It was then he realized how alone he'd felt in his quest.

"What was that?" Merriweather said.

"I said Castellane knows many Germans from his travels."

Merriweather frowned. "Didn't know earls bothered with the butchers. Curious fellow, aren't you?"

"So they say, sir."

"Quit calling me sir, dammit."

"He could call you 'Papa.'" Savannah met their sharp looks with a lift of innocent brows.

Dominic exchanged a frown with Merriweather.

"Stuyvesant," Merriweather said quickly. "Call me Stuyvesant."

"It would be a pleasure."

Merriweather shifted on his seat. "Ah, hell—" He thrust his hand at Dominic and clamped it in a grip that would have rivaled Bonnie's. "Thank you, Winthrop. I—I damn well don't know what came over me tonight. Thought I could get my luck back. Guess I thought for a minute there that I was back in Dogberg playing cards with my old friend Tom Flannery. Hell, I don't know what would have happened if you hadn't—"

"Forget it," Dominic said quickly. "Let's call it even."

Merriweather smiled and his eyes twinkled just as his daughter's did every time she laughed. "Even, then, Winthrop."

And from her corner of the coach, Savannah smiled. For a brief moment the world was a warm and sunny place for Dominic.

Merriweather Heiress Weds Britain's Third Earl of Castellane on Second Sojourn Abroad.

At noon the news whispered throughout the magic parallelogram between Fourteenth and Fifty-ninth streets and between Third and Sixth avenues, courtesy of *Town Top-*

ics. At precisely three o'clock, a gold-liveried footman employed by one of the reigning triumvirate of social lionesses, the venerable Mrs. Gabriel Nesbit, left Mrs. Nesbit's calling card in the lower hall table just inside the foyer of Savannah and Dominic's town house.

"You're now in," Maxine told Savannah with a good amount of sarcasm as they watched from an upper window Mrs. Nesbit's brougham pull away from the curb. "Congratulations."

"That's it? But I didn't even see the woman's face. She didn't even look out her carriage window."

"You had to stay up here. It would have been a horrendous social faux pas to be at home today."

"But I am at home. So is Castellane, sketching somewhere."

"That's well and good. But you're not at home to visitors. You don't want to look as if any of this *means* anything to you. Don't worry. Everyone who matters will soon know you're in."

"Fine. But when will Mrs. Astor invite Mother to lunch?"

"Within the week. A pity this is all for Penelope or I would have had such fun with it all."

Less than an hour later an invitation arrived via a red liveried footman:

Mr. and Mrs. Howard Sully

request the pleasure of

His Lordship the Earl and Countess Castellane

at a kettledrum party this evening,

seven o'clock.

Maxine lifted her meticulously penciled brows as she read the invitation a second time. She paced the length of the front parlor, her rose-pink foulard skirts swishing over the floor like a fancy mop. Savannah sat in a chair by the window. Dominic stood at the fireplace, one arm braced on the mantel, staring into the cold hearth.

"You're both assured a meteoric rise to social acceptance," Maxine said as gravely as if she sentenced them to death. "Mrs. Howard Sully is the second queen in the triumvirate behind Mrs. Astor. She's the third generation of a top-drawer family originally from Boston where I believe a great-grandfather chucked British tea into Boston Harbor. Speaking from a climber's point of view, you could do no better for your first time out. Let's see if I remember anything else—oh, yes. Mrs. Sully believes it next to impossible to wear too many jewels. And her daughter Margaret seems as stunned by her own willowy beauty as any of her admirers. She's managed to avoid any contact with an education for all of her nineteen years."

Savannah sighed. "We'll be unspeakably bored."

"Without question."

Savannah chewed at her lip. "Well, we can't have that, not when they seem so anxious to embrace us. Perhaps they'll excuse us for not having an ample supply of small talk at our tongues' ends, which gives me an idea—"

"Sully, Sully—" Dominic looked at Maxine. "Wall Street."

Maxine stopped in her tracks and seemed somewhat taken aback. "You're right, Castellane. Howard Sully and his ruthlessness are as legendary as his wife's lineage. Second to Jay Gould, he's the most merciless man on Wall Street. You know him?"

It was Dominic's turn to hesitate. A shrug worked its way through his shoulders. "I've a passing interest in the American stock market, is all."

Maxine continued to watch him. "I see. Any other passing interests, sir?"

He looked right at her. "Art, madam."

"Anything in particular?"

"Good art." His smile was bland.

"I told you Castellane sketches," Savannah offered, drawing Dominic's steady gaze. "He was quite the rage aboard ship. Everyone was sitting for a pencil portrait to help pass the time. We came away with at least a half-dozen invitations to dine at homes with galleries supposedly well stocked with the finest paintings. He wants to see them all."

"Ah." Maxine stared at Dominic for several seconds too long. "And now that you're in, you may."

Savannah found herself holding her breath and not knowing why. "He—uh—enjoys the Italian artists perhaps best, don't you, Castellane?"

Dominic looked at her in a way that made her go suddenly cold, as if he looked right through her. "I look for passion in the work. That's my only preference."

"You have the soul of an artist, sir," Maxine said. "A pity you were born an aristocrat."

Dominic swung back to the fireplace and gave them both a magnificent view of his coatless backside. "Men have overcome worse."

Maxine turned to Savannah and laid a hand on her arm. "If it's art you want, passionate art, or even art that everyone else will want, you'll need a consultant. Ask Templeton Snelling. He never misses a triumvirate party. He'll be sure to direct you. Oh, Castellane—do ask Mrs. Sully to show you her collection of Jean François Millet scenes of peasant life. The real beauty I see in the work is the emotion it calls out. Perhaps you will agree. Now, I must be off. Smile, Savannah."

"Smile?" Savannah grimaced prettily. "I've been invited to the home of a woman known to scheme, maneuver, plot, and engineer social coups with all the deadly guile of a Byzantine queen mother. Should I be smiling?"

"Yes, dear. After all, this is what you wanted all along."

Templeton Snelling, the self-appointed chief arbiter of social ranking, had made a career out of flitting around a ballroom in short red cape, matching velvet chapeau, fitted trousers, and three-inch silk high heels. He wallowed happily in a woman's realm, concerning himself with social precedence, guest lists, and directing the arch little niceties of a cotillion. While his main objective in life was to amuse the wives of rich men, he was known by all to be a lapdog, not a stud. At the commencement of each Four Hundred party, he stood his post just inside the front entrance. As the honorary invites arrived and swept past him, he commented on each *sotto voce* to anyone fortunate enough to find themselves standing near him.

"Old family. Good old stock.

"He's a new man.

"Here's one who intends to dance his way into society."

He conducted his weeding-out process with all the scientific specifications of a first-rate stud farm. After all, with enormous fortunes of an unprecedented volume being made every day by the most unlikely people, the fortunes had to be weighed and the social or financial taints detected. So adept had Snelling become at spotting the squirming social fraud, Colonel Sharpe at *Town Topics* paid him handsomely for his list of "Who's In," which was published monthly in the gossip column and read with rabid intensity by anyone with even a hint of aspiration to belong.

Colonel Sharpe had sizably augmented his publishing income with the bribes he received to remove an aspirant's name from the "Who Will Never Be In" column or to suppress information he'd received that would deal the fatal blow to a climber.

He'd accumulated a king's fortune suppressing information about the elite members of the Four Hundred. Anyone willing to subsidize Sharpe's extravagant tastes could barter his way out of any predicament that came to his attention through a pervasive network of backstairs spies coordinated by the irrepressible Templeton Snelling.

Savannah knew this. And with Dominic's interest taking a decidedly artistic and intriguing focus, who better to assist Savannah in honing in on the reason for his interest than Templeton Snelling himself?

"Poor Lady Ribblesdale, dumpy as a Dutch housewife," Snelling was musing to those within a five-foot earshot when Savannah edged near his cloistered circle. Dominic had gone off in search of champagne and canapés only after securing from her a promise to behave. She'd read so much about Snelling she'd instantly recognized him across the ballroom, his darkly oiled head topped with its red velvet chapeau and scarlet-draped shoulders poking out of the top of a circle of bobbing coiffures and frothy gowns.

Snelling indicated the object of his sympathies with a lift of his pointed chin, a narrowing of his basset hound eyes, and a sweep of his cigarette at the cream puff–like figure of a woman in a hideous white dress lumbering across the Sully ballroom. "She's called in a succession of masseurs to pound away at her aldermanic corpulence. She's tried diets that would have wrung tears from a Chinese peasant. And still look at her. What can a woman do with such a tidal sweep of bosom? Thank heavens her charm is even more potent than her husband's millions. Society can't help but take her to its heart."

"But what will you advise her?" a puffy woman in diamond tiara asked breathlessly. The circle of women seemed to stop breathing in unison. Not a rustle of silk or creak of straining whalebone could be heard above the bubbling of the trio of violins in one corner.

Snelling chortled and blew smoke in one woman's face. "Why, dear pet, I intend to tell her what I would tell any of you poor dears, with your older faces and your younger clothes. The sovereign remedy for everything from lumbago to a ruined family name is foreign travel. Shall we ask the Merriweather heiress? She's here with us, recently returned from London a countess, no less. Do come nearer, sweet pea. Yes, we know you're there. Who could miss you in your insufficient white silk and black Spanish lace? If it's from Worth I've never seen it. I spotted you the instant you entered and set the room on fire with your snapping eyes. Mark my words, one day you will be the sultana of New York society."

A gasp resounded from the ladies at such a proclamation. Savannah went cold with terror. An instant later a hand clamped around her wrist and tugged her into the circle of curious faces. She felt the women's eyes devouring her in the kind of shameless, humiliating assessment she'd received countless times from her mother. And for an awful, indecisive moment she wished she'd opted tonight for the tasteful gown over the daring, the elegance of understatement over the shamelessly overstated. But the feeling, as always, was fleeting. She swept the circle with a confident look and tested the shallowness of her bodice with a hugely satisfying breath that turned more than half the women on their heels in self-conscious defeat.

"No corset, dear, shame on you." Snelling giggled into her ear in a hot waft of smoky breath. "A good twenty-one inches at the waist but who can tell except those of us with the expert eye, eh? Ah, where's your dashing Castellane? Heard some nasty tales about him I'd rather not believe now that I've seen him. Fetching wine like a good fellow?"

Savannah gave Snelling a gooey smile. As in her mode of dress this evening, she opted for the direct salvo over innuendo. She waved a hand to indicate the paintings that hung on the dull red tapestries covering each of the four walls. Sufficient lighting was provided by gas jets attached to pipes that crisscrossed the ceiling. "I believe he's looking for Mrs. Sully to show him her Jean François Millet."

"Zounds!" Snelling gasped, his eyes popping so wide Savannah could see the black kohl rimming them. "We've an art lover extraordinaire in our midst. Perhaps he can appreciate what so many do not! Where is he? I must speak to him before he makes a ghastly error in choosing an agent. Only the best will do for him. And only I know the very best."

"That's why I'm talking to you," Savannah replied sweetly. But the glitter in her eyes was all devil. "I'm only looking for the best art to hang on my walls. Like all the good wives, I must be certain to spend the money just a little faster than it comes in."

Snelling stared at her a moment then gave a snorting guffaw. "My dear Countess, I fear you've become a student of my dear old friend, your aunt Maxine Beaupre."

"An apt pupil, sir."

His expression hardened. "Not too apt, I hope. She has been wrecked by scandal, sweet pea, whereas you appear to have been saved by it."

"She doesn't want to lead or belong to society, sir, she simply wants to keep it from expiring from boredom. Can you blame her? While outsiders break their necks for entry into these parties, the elite wander about aimlessly, saying nothing, and chafing at their fate. You cannot deny it."

"Zounds, you must stop listening to her."

"She never told me that, sir. I can see it plainly myself."

"So wise for so green a girl." Snelling moved a fraction closer and his voice dipped conspiratorially. "But humor me now, sweet. I'd thought you'd gone off and married to save your poor father. After seeing your Castellane, however, I'm beginning to believe you had very selfish reasons. Where *did* you unearth such a tall and handsome man?"

"Colonel Sharpe's column. Where all the indigent aristocrats are found. Such a service Colonel Sharpe provides, don't you agree, sir?" Savannah peered up on tiptoes to scan the room. She wasn't fooled by Snelling's light banter and feminine swagger. She sensed that there wasn't a moment that he wasn't fishing for a story, and the juicier the better.

"He looks something less than indigent, I'll give you

that. How awful must a man be if his wives have to kill themselves to be rid of him?"

Savannah laughed, throaty and deep and with gusto. "He grinds his teeth in his sleep, if you must know. Is that too awfully bad?"

"For some women, indeed, yes. But oddly enough not you."

"Quite the opposite, sir." She spotted Dominic, standing head and shoulders above the rest of the crowd. He wore the standard issue black dress coat and trousers, white waistcoat and cravat, white kid gloves and thin black patent leather boots. Even from across the room, he bore the arcane essences of upper class too subtle to be learned or noticed by an outsider. He, like every other man present, seemed to have learned from birth that manner of self-confidence fused with a genuine indifference to opinions and reactions. He moved with the easy assurance of a man born into money. He was, judging by the common eye, one of them, indistinguishable from the rest of the men. And yet Savannah's heart catapulted in her chest only when her eyes settled on him.

She'd nearly stumbled down the stairs when she'd first seen him this evening awaiting her in the foyer. In their brougham she'd found it impossible not to stare at him and blush every time he stared at her. He was now, as he'd been then, the only man in the room for her.

Her insides did their familiar quiver and tug. "Ah, there's Castellane now." She gave a little wave and felt a smile tug at her lips. "Good, he's spotted me. Oh, he looks a bit dour. Perhaps he got lost."

"Good God, but you're quite in love with him."

Savannah's head snapped around. She felt herself pale. "I'm what?"

"Look at you—" The glint in Snelling's eyes made Savannah suddenly wish she could run away and hide. Hide . . . from what? "You almost look as if it would be criminal to love him. How odd."

Savannah dug deep for her voice and a thread of an argument. "Not so odd. I don't know of any women who love their husbands."

"I can tell you of many who wish they could, sweet pea. A pity so few of the men are deserving of it. If you believe your Castellane is, then allow me to give you a piece of advice: Don't show it so damned eagerly. He'll take dreadful advantage of it. The men always do. They can't help themselves."

Savannah flushed hot and looked away. Chagrin washed over her in mountainous waves. *Love him?* How could she show it so brazenly to a complete stranger and not know it herself? How could she have allowed herself to love such a dangerous and mysterious man?

Indeed, knowing herself as she did, how could she not?

"Christ." Dominic snarled, as he pushed his way between two women wearing outrageous feathered hats. He shoved a flute into Savannah's hand, spit feathers from his tongue, swiped one from his nose, and gave the women a scowl that sent them both away with frightened yelps.

"I've never seen such a gaudy stream of bespangled, belaced, and beruffled barbarians in all my life," he muttered in his flawless aristocratic drawl, his nose lifted with pompous disgust. "There's plenty here who know how to get money but to be rich properly is quite another matter." He looked right at Savannah, then at Templeton Snelling, and offered his white-gloved hand with its flagrant limp wrist. "Castellane. And who are you, sir?"

Savannah offered quick introduction then said, "Mr. Snelling can advise you on an art consultant, Castellane."

"Indeed. And who might that be, sir?"

"Er—I—what is it that appeals, your lordship?"

"Pictures that tell stories. Do you know William Bouguereau's *Going to the Bath?* He's a contemporary French artist."

"Yes, yes, I know. Of course, those sorts of pictures are quite the rage now. So easily understood by the uneducated all around us. Little anecdotes of contemporary life. Like all the rest of us you prefer the French school, your lordship?"

Dominic shrugged and drank deeply from his glass. "Meissonier. Bonheur. Or the Italians."

"Lega?"

"Silvestro—" The name sounded almost like a groan. Or was it simply that he'd said it into his glass?

Savannah looked sharply at Dominic. She was almost certain that his entire manner softened like butter melting over a low fire when he spoke the name. Dark and mysterious fires danced in his eyes, fires that made Savannah itch all over to find out more. She felt suddenly as if she was trembling on the brink of a monumental discovery. If only she knew what she was looking for.

"You know Lega?" she asked.

His shoulders moved slightly beneath the black worsted wool. "I didn't know he was known here."

"Ah, all the rage in London, is he?" Snelling asked.

Dominic's Adam's apple worked once in his throat. "Yes, quite."

"Peculiar little Italian man. The only one of those notorious Italian Macchiaolli to stay alive and make it to Paris to be discovered. Atwood found him, of course. He has a nose for the very best. Lega has since made him a fortune commissioning work for the Four Hundred."

"Lega's here, in New York?"

"Good heavens, yes. Where the devil else should he be?"

Dominic blinked once. "Of course. And this Atwood fellow?"

Snelling flushed. "So sorry, James Atwood, art agent. I'll direct you to him, of course. He has an auction house at Fourteenth and Fifth. He's just recently returned from London. Tell the man at the door that I sent you and give him my card"—Snelling fished into his pocket and handed Dominic a card of fine ivory vellum—"or he won't let you in. Atwood can get you anything"—Snelling leaned nearer and muttered out of the side of his mouth— "without the enormous import tax fee attached."

"Ah," Dominic said.

Savannah frowned. "That sounds illegal."

Snelling gave a poisonous smile. "Is it? Well, don't tell Mr. Atwood that or his English connections. He'll start charging even higher prices."

"And people pay them?"

"My dear Countess, when James Atwood recommends something at auction, it inevitably brings many times what it was originally paid for. Few will buy anything else. J. P. Morgan is his client. Need I say more? But if you don't like him, I know of several Frenchmen who make exceedingly good art agents. Ah! There's Mrs. Nesbit. I promised to help her move about this evening. Poor dear, found out too late that if she bends too much in any direction her bodice with its encrusted pearls and beading will crack like an armadillo's carapace. Prithee, allow me to call upon you at your earliest convenience, my sweet pea Countess."

Savannah allowed Snelling to smear his lips over the top of her hand. An instant later he disappeared into the crowd.

"I don't think I like him," Savannah said, rubbing the back of her hand on her skirt. She glanced up at Dominic. His eyes were moving like darts around the room, above the faces of the people, up, up toward those gas jets that illuminated the Sully art collection. In a matter of seconds, Savannah was certain he'd memorized every piece of artwork hanging on display. She was also certain he hadn't heard a word she'd said.

"Let's go," he said, taking the empty glass from her fingers. He gave both glasses to a passing footman, then, with his hand at her lower back, pushed her ahead of him and out of the room.

Chapter 17

" 'For further instruction in the arcana of rank, turn to page four.' " Dominic jerked the pages of *Town Topics* closed, open, closed, open again, folded the paper and laid it on his knee. "Four . . . four. Ah, here. Listen to this. 'Dukes are the loftiest kind of nobleman in England.' And this is news? 'There are only twenty-seven of them available for matrimonial purposes. Several notables are the Dukes of Manchester and Roxburghe. The Duke of Hamilton is already spoken for, and the Duke of Norfolk is an old widower. The Duke of Leinster is only eleven years old.' "

He looked over the top of the paper at Savannah, bouncing along on the brougham seat opposite him. The sunlight blasting through the window set her salmon-pink, striped dress aflame and brought the pink birds and their tiny nest on the brim of her feathered hat into sharp focus. She looked as juicily delectable as the melon and whipped cream canapés he'd devoured whole at Mrs. Sully's several nights before.

His hands itched to feel her, his tongue burned to taste her, his loins heated whenever she was within sight or bombarding his thoughts. He was, for all practical purposes, in a state of constant, flagrant arousal. Only he had a small problem.

He liked her. Genuinely, to his bones and in spite of all her idiosyncrasies and his own better judgment, he liked Savannah Rose Merriweather far too much to take her any further down the path to dishonor and disgrace.

And so, as with most things, a man could get comfortable being uncomfortable so long as he busied himself with distraction. And found things to fill his itching hands and lust-driven mind, even things he might otherwise never have touched.

"You read this?" he asked, rattling the paper.

Savannah's pink gloves dipped into a pink satin reticule and withdrew something wrapped in tissue. "I try not to," she said, plucking a chocolate from the tissue and popping it into her mouth.

He watched her chew, her eyes half lidded with full-blown ecstasy. The woman oozed sexuality out of every pearly pink pore.

He felt himself stiffen, his gut clench. "Perhaps you should. There's something almost tongue-in-cheek about Sharpe's style, but you must listen closely. Here—'Mrs. Harriman is giving a tea party. Mrs. Fish will remove to Garrison-on-the-Hudson on Thursday. Mrs. Gabriel Nesbit will give a masked ball next Saturday.' It's almost as if Sharpe is trying to make society so deeply disgusted with itself to continue in its silly, empty way of life."

Dominic gave her a moment to digest that, somewhat astounded that he'd hit upon such a theory. But hell, he needed something to keep his mind from the sweep of her tongue over her lips or the rhythmic swell of her bosom up and out the modest neckline of her walking dress as the carriage sped along.

Sway-bounce-surge. Sway-bounce-surge.

He jerked his eyes to her face. "Have you considered that Sharpe considers himself the guardian of society's manner and morals? That this paper stands for moral purity, written by the gentlefolk, for the gentlefolk, on topics of interest to the gentlefolk?"

Savannah looked up and smiled in a way that made Dominic's insides churn like butter. "I'm thinking about Mrs. Nesbit's ball. It's the premier event of the season. If we don't receive an invitation soon, I'm to understand from Brunnic that several thousand dollars in the right hands can get me one. You do want to go, don't you?"

Another of her fishing expeditions. He chose deflection this time. "And if we don't?"

She sighed and pushed out her lower lip as if all this actually meant something more to her than just a bit of fun and adventure. "We might as well resign ourselves to social inferiority. We'll be left to take up philanthropy and spend all our time and money on racehorses and yachts somewhere in Florida."

"A fate not altogether unkind." He found himself watching her closely and not understanding why.

She looked straight at him, smiled again, and he saw honest and true affection on her face. Or had he simply imagined it? "Yes," she breathed. "I think it would be quite fabulous to be banished and talked about. With you, of course."

A lump materialized in Dominic's throat. A bigger lump was pressing into his chest, squeezing all the breath out of him. He felt twisted up into a knot, held captive and rendered impotent by a pair of sparkling emerald eyes, an innocent's smile, and a guileless statement.

"I—quite agree, my dear." There, he'd said it, whatever it was. His voice sounded raw and husky and choked with emotion. "Christ." Another raw sound, like an animal in agony. He frowned at the window, then banged a fist on the coach roof. "This is it. Fourteenth."

They departed in front of a modest building with plain glass front and a squeaky sign hanging over the door that read ATWOOD AUCTIONEERS. From the outside, the place looked like nothing more than a quiet little warehouse, its contents indistinguishable through the glass. But as they stepped inside, a large and imposing man in an ill-fitting suit coat and plaid trousers presented himself in their path with legs braced and hamlike hands braced on his thighs. The bowler sitting on his enormous square head looked almost infantile.

"The Earl of Castellane for James Atwood," Dominic said, withdrawing Snelling's card from his pocket and handing it to the man. He stared at it, looked Dominic over from head to toe, then without a word turned and disappeared to the rear of the place.

"So tidy but musty," Savannah said, rubbing a finger under her nose and moving off a few paces to run her fingertips over the rim of a large porcelain vase sitting on the floor.

"He must get it all from haunted English castles when the resident destitute aristocrat needs money for food." Dominic studied an oil on canvas leaning sideways against the wall. There were canvases stacked against the wall beneath that one, even more next to it.

Dominic flicked through each and drew the smell of the place deep into his lungs. He thought about the years he'd spent peering through the glass windows of such places, unable to step foot inside because of who he was or, better yet, who he wasn't. In more recent years he'd scoured the public auction houses and accessible art galleries without success. The wealth he'd accumulated in the stock market had conferred upon him the privilege of attending the more private auctions. But he'd somehow sensed even then that he wasn't going to find his prize at any ordinary auction or in any ordinary home.

"I like that one." Savannah had moved beside him and was angling her head severely sideways to get a better look at the canvas he'd just uncovered.

"What do you like about it?"

She narrowed her eyes, pursed her lips. "It looks—

unfinished. Very raw. All light and dark patches. Hardly any color. I don't even know what it's supposed to be."

"A woman's face."

"Poor thing."

Dominic couldn't help but smile. He reached out with both hands, cupped her head, and tipped her face upright. "There. Now do you see it?"

She instantly smiled. "Oh, yes. She's quite lovely when you don't look at her sideways. He loved her."

"Who?"

"The painter, of course."

"Really?" Dominic looked at the painting and frowned.

"Her face has no detail, just all those formless patches of light and dark, and yet he made her exquisitely beautiful. He must have painted her outdoors."

"The style is based on the evocative patterns of nature's light. Sunlight filtering through the trees, for instance, or between clouds, casting shadows with buildings. Dawn and dusk are the best times to paint. The light is purest then. I've always believed an artist should first look to nature as his teacher."

"I want you to paint me."

He looked down at her and knew an ache so pervasive, so deep and profound his breath came out in a strangled groan. "I—don't—"

His voice snagged when she blinked up at him and laid a hand as gentle as a bird's wing beat on his lapel. "I want something to remember you by, Dominic Dare."

Oh, right. He was planning to leave her at some point. Damned strange that he couldn't seem to remember that.

She lowered her eyes and seemed to be staring right at the diamond-headed stick pin in his cravat. "If you don't paint me, I'll have to sit for some French artist to have my portrait done, and you know he'll want me to take off my clothes."

"And you don't think I would?"

"But with you I would want to take them off." Her eyes

lifted to his, vibrant, welcoming pools of deep green so intoxicating he felt as if he were suddenly drowning. He lowered his head, she lifted hers.

"We both know this isn't wise," he rumbled.

"Dangerous too," she whispered.

Their lips touched, parted, breaths mingled, tongues danced. Savannah sighed and Dominic groaned with the staggering depths of his defeat. He slipped one arm around her waist and drew her so deep against him he knew she wore only a thin chemise beneath her pink silk stripes.

"Say you'll paint me," she whispered against his mouth, cupping his head between her small gloved hands.

"I will." He turned his head, pressed his open mouth to her palm, and caught sight of a man watching them. Again he'd forgotten who he was, his reasons for being here, his sole damned purpose for living the past twenty years . . .

He clamped Savannah's hand in his and turned her close beside him.

"Oh, my," she whispered.

"Castellane?" the man asked, moving toward them. "James Atwood at your service. You come highly recommended by my good friend Templeton Snelling." Atwood extended a hand. He was utterly common-looking, his suit fine enough for his station, his frame tall, narrow, and slight. His look of complete boredom must have served him exceedingly well with the customers who appreciated hauteur in their agents. His narrow face was accentuated by short, slicked dark hair and a large hooked nose with nostrils that flared as he spoke. He shook hands with Dominic, looked at Savannah, and spoke in a hushed and grave tone. "I know of your father, Countess."

"Thank you." Savannah beamed, impervious to Atwood's startled frown. She thrust out her hand and smiled when he had no other choice but to bow over it. "We're looking for good art."

"Aren't we all, Countess?"

Savannah peered around as if she looked for something she couldn't find. "I like the French or Italian paintings best. I hope you have some somewhere."

Atwood looked as if he exercised great patience with his smile. "I . . . can certainly try to find you some. These are the rage at the moment, madam, and therefore quite difficult to find."

"Did you find any when you were in London recently? I do so worry that I will not like them when you find them, sir."

Atwood blinked and looked deeply affronted. "Indeed you will, madam."

"Hmm." She tapped a finger to her lips and angled her eyes at Dominic. "My dear Castellane here is particularly fussy about his art, aren't you, Castellane?"

"Most fussy," Dominic said gravely, his curiosity burgeoning. Whatever her game she obviously thought she knew precisely what he was after from Atwood. But could she be that clever?

She sighed and looked truly pained. "And we've so much money to spend. An entire four-thousand-square-foot mausoleum to decorate. Do you have any idea how much wall space that is, sir?"

"I can only imagine, madam."

"It's hellishly intimidating. How does one go about choosing?" Again she tapped her finger and looked around, finally settling her gaze with some intensity on Atwood, who'd measurably perked up and looked somewhat like a drooling Belgian sheep dog. "I believe I would like to see some examples of your work, sir."

Atwood blinked again. "I beg your pardon, madam?"

"Clients." Savannah smiled. "More particularly the ones you've sold the most French and Italian paintings. I want to see if I like what you've done for them, sir."

"Madam, I—"

"Well, very good, then. If you're going to be that difficult. Come along, Castellane. I recall Mr. Snelling saying something about several French agents. I'm quite certain they will be more accommodating—"

"Wait!" Atwood splayed his arms and blocked Savannah's path to the door. "My dear Countess, forgive me. It's just that I've never met a client who expresses such a need to—that is—to—"

"Be informed?"

"Indeed."

"How surprising, sir. You mean to say that people come in here and give their tens of thousands to a stranger simply because someone tells them they should?"

"Why, yes, madam."

"And they like what you get them because you tell them to like it, is that also correct?"

"Indeed, madam."

Savannah chewed at her lip. "I see. You could tell someone to pay twenty thousand dollars for something worth five hundred and they would do it, wouldn't they?"

Dominic tensed.

Atwood went stiff as a stone block. "Madam, I would never—"

"Why, of course you wouldn't." Savannah laughed and laid a hand on Atwood's arm, which seemed to make him stiffen even more. "I've this awful imagination, sir. Don't I, Castellane?"

"Quite awful," Dominic said.

"Well, sir?" Savannah was looking expectantly at Atwood.

"Madam?"

"The list, sir."

"What?" Atwood seemed to shake himself. "Yes, yes, of course, the list of clients." He fumbled in one pocket, then another, drew out a card, mumbled something, located a pen atop a desk in the corner, and scribbled on the back of the card.

"Thank you, sir," Savannah said with a huge smile as he handed her the card. "Oh, look here. Mrs. Gabriel Nesbit is right at the top. She called on me just yesterday. I will be certain to visit her now."

Atwood looked sharply at her. "Be sure to visit her anyway or you'll be out before you're even in."

"I'll remember that, sir." Savannah turned to leave but Dominic caught her arm.

"What do you want for that one?" he asked, indicating the portrait of the lady.

Atwood seemed momentarily stunned. "That work is by an unknown, sir." Atwood's nostrils jerked as he sniffed, "Looks to be local. I picked it up at the estate sale of a very rich Wall Street financier who left no wife or children."

"I'll give you fifty dollars for it." Dominic counted off the bills from his pocket, handed them to Atwood, and retrieved the canvas. He tucked it under his arm and escorted Savannah to the door.

"Thank you, Castellane," she said when they were again in the brougham. She held up the canvas, admired it, then her eyes widened. "Oh, the artist did sign it. See here, in the lower corner just above the frame. 'Nino.' How romantic, don't you think?"

Dominic grunted and watched her look at the canvas with eyes full of warm appreciation.

Without glancing up she said, "Odd that you didn't ask about your friend Silvestro Lega. He knew your father in Italy, didn't he? He knew you."

Dominic resisted the urge to shift his shoulders. "I find it odd that you didn't ask about him. Hell, you acted like you knew exactly why we were there."

"Of course I did. You want to see Italian art, don't you?"

"Do I?"

"A bit intriguing that our friend Mr. Atwood recently returned from London. Perhaps he was there when M. Harrigan was killed."

"And so were thousands of other people."

She looked at him with outright exasperation. "Really, Dominic, when are you going to give up all this secrecy? I would make a formidable ally."

"Without question. But can I trust you?"

She blinked with disbelief. "Of course."

He snorted and looked out the window. "I buy you a cheap oil on canvas and the next minute you pledge your loyalty."

"You think I'm fickle."

"Fickle as they come, sweetheart."

"Oh, really? Dangle a box of bonbons in Savannah's face and you've got her, is that it?"

"Something like that."

"You must not sleep at night."

"What?"

"Well, if all my most secret plans hinged on a fickle, immature woman, who also happens to be somewhat curious and a wee bit clever, I know *I* wouldn't be able to sleep. It's a wonder you don't flee for your life, or at least for some other unsuspecting little heiress who knows her place better than I do. I've given you social standing in New York. Why not go elsewhere to get what you want?"

Why, indeed. The thought that he couldn't or, better yet, didn't want to, stabbed like a sharp stick right into his gut. He had utterly no explanation for it. "No time," he muttered.

"I beg your pardon?"

"You heard me, dammit." He watched the city speed by and listened to his teeth grind. Time, yes. The sooner this was over, the better for all involved. He'd finally get on with the rest of his life and lay the past to rest. But why the hell did he feel such a yawning emptiness inside, as if he'd suddenly stepped into a cold, dark cave, whenever he thought about saying good-bye to Savannah? It was unexplainable. It was terrifying. It was, he suddenly realized, an unpardonable weakness. He would, of course, conquer it . . . somehow.

"Shall we call on Mrs. Nesbit tomorrow afternoon?"

Dominic glanced at the card she held. "How many did Atwood list?"

"Five. Oh, I recognize one of the names from the ship. You must have painted her."

"Good. We'll call on three tomorrow. Two the following day."

"You *are* getting impatient. Well, don't work too quickly or you'll have to leave before everything's ready. Did I tell you my new decorator is coming later this evening? He's bringing swatches."

"If he's French he won't step foot in the place."

She gave him an exasperated look. "Maxine recommended him and promised he won't make you want to hit him. He likes big patterns and bold color and doing what no one else does. That means no Turkish parlors and lace doilies, thank heavens. He can get me my Dutch clock. Oh, and tomorrow night is the suffragist meeting, very late, ten o'clock. There's something deliciously covert about that, don't you think?"

"I'll take you there."

"That's not necessary. The coachman can wait for me—"

His level look silenced her. "I said I'll take you."

She blinked at him in a way that made him feel as if he'd bruised her tender sensibilities and owed her an enormous apology. To his chagrin, his tongue itched to spew one out for her.

She shrugged. "As you wish."

"I do." He swung his attention back to the street and fiddled with a gold cuff link. Did she honestly believe he'd let her gallivant about without him?

"I plan to tell the suffragists all about my escapade at the Patriarch Club. Frances Trainer won't be able to help herself she'll be so impressed. Do you think they might make me an honorary member?"

She sounded buoyant, not a spirited hair out of place.

Life for Savannah was always so damned rosy, infectious, on most days. So why the hell was he restless and grumpy as a curmudgeon today? He needed something . . . something to exorcise her from his thoughts . . . to free him up to think clearly and objectively as he could about his next step . . .

He watched the sun dapple the sidewalks through leafy trees in formless patches of light and dark. He saw the face of a corner fruit vendor, weathered and beaten, a splash of emotion in a blur of passing streets. He glimpsed the mischievous smile of a child holding his mother's hand on a street corner. Something tugged like tiny hands in his chest.

"When is he coming?" he asked her.

"When is who coming?"

"The decorator."

"I—" She frowned. "I believe seven."

"Good. We should have enough time. Damned light is too good to miss." He pounded his fist on the coach roof and shoved the door open when the brougham lurched to a halt. "Tenth Street at the docks," he told the driver.

"Sir?"

"You heard me, dammit. Go now. Before it decides to storm." He settled back in his seat, met her quizzical look, and smiled his most heartfelt smile of the day.

Chapter 18

Dominic jammed the key in the lock, twisted it, shoved, swore, twisted it again, then threw his shoulder against the massive door. It didn't budge. "God damned son of a—"

"Give me that." Savannah jabbed him aside with her elbow, took the key, and gently slid it in the lock. She wiggled it until she could hear it catch, then angled her eyes up at him. "Why are you being a bully?"

"I could pick the damned thing faster."

"Interesting. You seem too nervous to do that well."

"Nervous? Why the hell would I be nervous?"

"Oh, I don't know. On the off chance that I might discover something about you here that you don't want me to know."

"No chance of that. You're my model. You do as I say in my studio."

"Oh, really?" A shiver of anticipation whispered up her spine.

"Push." He laid his big palm flat on the door above her head. The door squeaked open.

Savannah didn't realize she held her breath until the door swung wide. "Oh, Dominic."

"Disappointed?"

"Oh, God, no—" At the nudge of his hand on her back, she stepped into his realm. With one greedy sweep of her eyes she took in the small room. Beneath her feet lay a fine-weave rug of vibrant reds and black. But it was the enormous four-posted wrought-iron bed that drew her eye. It loomed out of the corner, its tangled white bedding almost blinding in the direct sunlight. A dilapidated trunk rested at the foot of the bed, the lid thrown open. There were stacks of starched white shirts inside. On one wall sat a large armoire. One door had swung half open. A dark suit coat hung over its edge, a shirt draped over that. She saw a pair of expensive Hessian boots lying half beneath the bed, a pair of diamond-studded cuff links on a table next to jars of vinegary-smelling liquid and a plate eaten clean of everything but crumbs.

White canvases were stacked in piles against the walls. Empty frames were stacked in one corner next to several easels. One held a canvas that was splashed with angry shades of deep blue and black. Brushes lay in neat rows beside glass jars of murky liquid and tubes of powdered pigment. A palette lay on a small table nearby, caked with globs of gooey paint that looked dried hard. Next to that lay fat wedges of chalk in an array of colors. Savannah counted four empty liquor bottles upended beside a lead crystal goblet on the floor. Candle holders sat everywhere, some four feet high, all with tapers completely burned and wax spilling over their edges and caked on the floor. There was no hiss of gas sconces on the walls, no lamps to be seen anywhere. But artificial light was hardly necessary when two walls and half the ceiling were made entirely of glass.

The city was spread like a sun-splashed feast before her.

She walked into the middle of the room where the sun seemed to converge into one fat ray that beat down through the ceiling. She closed her eyes and felt her skin beneath its thin silk covering heat twenty degrees.

"This is wine," Dominic said as he pressed a glass into her hand. "Sip slowly. I want your eyes open for the portrait."

"I'm capable of exercising control, you know," she said. She sipped once, then sipped again, deeper. "Even if I haven't shown it. Please—don't clean up on my account. I've forgotten what a home that's lived in looks like. And feels like. It's wonderful. And the smell—"

"Oil of turpentine. To seal the paintings."

"I like it." She sipped and watched him move about, accumulating a pile of discarded clothing over one arm and exposing an array of upholstered furniture in his wake. Even at a glance Savannah guessed the pieces were very old and very fine, almost incongruous in such a raw, unfinished place. And yet it all was so pleasing to her senses.

"I haven't been here for quite a while." He disappeared behind a dark screen in the corner, then emerged and moved to a crimson velvet chaise longue that had been hidden beneath clothing. "Here." He angled it out of direct sunlight. He glanced at her. "Nervous?"

"A bit."

His lips quirked in a fleeting smile. "Good. Then you'll sit very still for me. Come." He lifted the reticule from her wrist, peeked inside, and took out another chocolate wrapped in tissue. He tossed the reticule aside and eyed the chocolate. "Good. Another prop."

"It's a cherry. Tends to be gooey."

"Better still." He pocketed the chocolate and took the glass from her fingers. "Sit. No, not facing the windows, face me. Pretend I'm there, behind that easel there. Not that the idea of painting you from behind is a bad one, but . . ." His words trailed off. Savannah looked up at him and started to turn in the proper direction but he caught her arm. "No, no. I've had a thought. Hell, why not? Sit as you were. Face the windows. Stay still now." He moved away. The easel legs slid on the floor. Something fell over. Savannah glanced sideways and saw the blue-and-black canvas lying on its back. And in the lower corner, in small crimson letters, she read Nino. She saw another oil leaning against the wall, and another behind it. The scenes were all landscapes done in fiery sunset tones but were marred with angry crisscrossing splotches of dark paint that obliterated the works. Each bore the crimson insignia Nino in the lower corner.

She gasped. "Nino—"

"Yes, that's good. Keep your head turned in profile and your lips parted."

"But you're the—you're Nino."

"Models aren't allowed to talk and distract the artist."

"But you bought your own painting from Atwood."

"Did I? Yes, I suppose I did."

"But why didn't you tell me it was one of yours—ah, but you couldn't. Mr. James Atwood would have been very curious about that."

"Wouldn't you?"

"Indeed. The Earl of Castellane has been banished to seclusion in the South of England, not painting portraits in New York. I'm very curious about that woman. Was she . . . ?" Her voice evaporated in a swift intake of air. His fingers were moving down the row of buttons along the back of her gown. Each brush of fingertips made her back arch like a purring kitten's, but the flutter in her belly felt cold, like terror. "Stop, Dominic. I don't think you should—"

"You're in my studio, remember?" His voice could have coaxed a rattler from its den. But a woman from a lifelong accumulation of anxieties . . .

She bit her lip. "I know where I am but I don't want to—"

His hands went still. "You said you'd take off your clothes for me to paint you."

"I did? Yes, but that was a weak moment. You understand, of course."

"Better than I'd care to admit."

"I just didn't think it would be—you know—" Savannah swallowed and felt herself blanch. "Why does there have to be so much light?"

"So I can see every inch of you the way you were meant to be seen in nature's light." His hands cupped her upper arms. "I must have you this way, Savannah."

She closed her eyes and seemed to curl around his words from the inside out. He spoke with such passionate appeal surely angels were weeping. "You must?" she whispered.

His hands slid down her arms. She felt the pressure of his chest into her back, his ragged breath in her ear. His fingers twined through hers, gripped, and she saw the landscapes defaced with black, the sullying, defiling splashes of anger. The dissatisfaction oozing all over his work. Something melted like butter inside Savannah.

"Let me capture the essence of who you are, the spirit of the woman within." His voice rasped like a lonely winter's wind in prairie trees. She barely felt his fingers on the buttons of her gown. "It would be a sacrilege to have you fully clothed. All the times I've pictured you here—and there must have been hundreds—it was like this—"

The dress was open clear to her buttocks. Through the thin layer of chemise Savannah felt the pulsing warmth of his body. He tugged the dress wide, slipped his palms up, and eased the gown over her shoulders. It sagged to her elbows. "The woman was my mother." His voice was warm in her ear. "I painted her the way I last remembered her."

Savannah felt dizzy and breathless. "You captured her magnificently."

His finger flicked over the ribbon binding her chemise. "Loosen this."

She touched the ribbon with trembling fingers. "I—"

He eased her hat from her head and moved away again. She heard shuffling. She bit her lip and felt as if her body had begun humming. Her fingers tugged the ribbon loose. Swallowing, she turned her head in profile. She licked her lips. "Is this how you paint all of your models?"

"I'm not painting today. I'll do a pastel. And no—" Again his breath caressed the nape of her neck. He'd moved as stealthily as a mountain lion. "I've never painted any model as I intend to paint you." His fingers slipped inside the back edge of the chemise, knuckles rubbed against her skin, and then he tugged. The chemise ribbon slipped free, the garment slid off her shoulders, sagged halfway down her back, and clung to the peaks of her breasts like the last bits of unmelted snow to a mountain. She jerked a hand to keep it in its tenuous perch.

A dewy sweat sprang to her skin.

"Yes. Just like that." He was at the easel again. "Turn your head again. Yes, right there. Perfect. Don't move."

The room swelled with the sound of chalk working over linen canvas. Hot sunlight blasted through the ceiling. Savannah could feel the temperature steadily climbing, the air growing thick with the smell of baking lilac-scented skin.

"Beautiful," he said. "God—but the lighting couldn't be better."

"I'm hot."

"I want you flushed." His hand seemed to be working in a blinding frenzy over the canvas. He muttered something, groaned with a breath, and after that his breathing came shorter, faster. "Damned heat—"

"Open a window."

"No, no. Not now. I can't stop yet—not when I'm working like this—" No artist ever welcomed interruption, but the depths of his intensity astonished her. Perhaps even more astonishing was her utter absence of self-consciousness.

She felt his eyes on every inch of exposed skin, and there was much for him to behold. The flaws were all there for him to capture, the curves that curved a bit too full and the hollows that weren't nearly hollow enough, the profile that was more pixie than lofty, the chin her mother had labeled as too strongly clefted for an unmarried woman.

"Beautiful." His voice rumbled unmistakably with reverence. The sound washed over Savannah like a welcoming rain on a parched prairie. She bloomed like a new flower with vibrant shades of rosiness unfurling from deep in her soul. The heat of the sun was nothing to the warmth suddenly coursing from within her. It filled her bloodstream, poured into her limbs, shot out of her fingers, and burst from every pore. She licked perspiration from her lips, drew trembling breaths, and knew with a staggering certainty that her entire life had been one stumble after another along a tangled, twisted road that had been leading—she knew now—to this tiny room of utter happiness. For the first time in her life she felt at peace within herself.

It was a newborn joy, vulnerable and pure, too new to be tainted with a consciousness of reality and the impossibilities of their situation. She had to express it now or she would burst. She might never have another opportunity.

"Dominic—"

"No, don't move just yet."

"I have to. Dominic, please—" She swung around.

He was looking at her from behind his easel with a fierce and intense expression, one hand frozen over the canvas midstroke. He looked hot and wild and untamed and clearly possessed by what he was doing.

Savannah suddenly felt herself go up in flames of desire.

His shirt was unbuttoned to midchest, plastered to his skin and transparent. His hair hung over his forehead, clear to the ominous downward slant of his brows. His chest heaved as if he was as breathless as she. And his voice was as raw and cutting as a jagged-edged knife. "What is it? I'm not showing it to you yet, not until it's finished."

"No—it's not that—I—please, come here."

"Is it the chocolate you want?" He reached into his pocket and looked as if he dealt with a petulant child.

She bit her lip. "Well, if you must know, yes, bring it here—if you could. My dress is all bunched down there, I can hardly be expected to move and—"

"Fine. Fine. Damned impatient woman." He stepped from behind the easel and moved toward her with a foreboding look that might have daunted any other woman. But not Savannah.

She held out her palm, lifted cat's eyes as he placed the chocolate into her hand. "Thank you. Oh, look, I dropped it—right there—" He hunkered down on one knee, she bent forward, their heads bumped.

"Sorry—"

"No, I'm sorry—"

They both reached for the chocolate. She waited for Dominic to scoop it up and turn back to her before she decided to ease back up.

A chaste pressing of her hand to chemise would have kept it in place. But Savannah was feeling far from chaste, especially with him so near, smelling hot and male and musky, thighs spread wide, loins within a hand's reach.

The man she loved, emanating sex and passion and a lust for life she'd believed only she felt . . . he'd made her feel as glorious as a woman could imagine feeling. And Savannah had probed the depths of her own imagination many times.

She eased up another inch and felt the lace cling to the turgid tips of her nipples. She drew a breath, her chest lifted, trembled, and the chemise spilled to her waist, accompanied by a tremendous roaring sound in her ears.

The longing in his eyes as he looked at her made her want to weep with joy. Every woman should be looked at that way by a man, every day of her life.

"Dominic—" Was her hand shaking as she reached to

touch his cheek? Even her voice was shaky, all stopped up and thick with emotion.

"What are you trying to do to me?"

She opened her mouth. Tears formed in her eyes. Tears? She blinked to dispel them and felt her throat thicken. "I—I don't know—I—something's happened to me here—I feel like I should tell you that I—"

His fingers pressed to her lips. The look in his eyes was almost compassionate. "It happens to models."

"It what?"

"This feeling of intimacy. It's as common as an artist falling in love with his model."

She swallowed. "You have? H-how many times?"

He reached out and tugged pins from her low chignon. His eyes followed the tumble of her hair over her shoulders and breasts. "That's better."

Savannah jerked her chemise up. "Who was she?"

"Who was who? No, sweetheart, it's too late for that—" His smile was lopsided, heavy-lidded, and irresistible. At the nudge of his fingers the chemise fell away again. "Yes—like this—"

Savannah felt breathless and angry, lusty and confused. She dug her fingernails into sumptuous crimson velvet upholstery and wondered how many other women had happily shed their clothing in this precise spot, with him kneeling at their feet and his eyes all hot and devouring on their bosoms. "You're thinking about painting."

He inclined his head, narrowed his eyes, and glanced at the roof. "What the hell else should I be?" He gripped her shoulders and shifted her an inch right. "Yes, there— God almighty, Savannah, you look like Venus coming down from heaven."

Savannah licked her lips. "Then kiss me."

He glanced up and looked deep into her eyes. His face suddenly looked worn, slightly haggard. "Then what?"

She blinked. "I kiss you back, of course."

"And where are my hands?"

"Where do they want to be?"

"My point exactly. I'm not going down that path half-way with you any more, Savannah."

"What path?"

"I've never meant it more. It will kill me."

"What will? You seem to be managing just fine right now. No outward distress of any kind—"

"You're not looking close enough, in the right place."

"—and here I sit, within a hand's reach and wearing no drawers—"

"Enough, Savannah. You're my subject. At the moment it's a considerable help for me to think of you merely as a subject."

"And not as a woman. To you I'm a potted plant."

"Exactly."

"Or an apple."

"Better still."

"Sweet or tart?"

He didn't hesitate. "Both. Everything anyone could want."

"In an apple."

"Or a woman."

Savannah closed her eyes and sighed. "Oh, Dominic, you make me want to kiss you so desperately."

"Here." He took her hand, palm up, and set the chocolate cherry in the center. "Sink your teeth into this. Maybe it will help."

"It won't. I know it won't." She scowled at the chocolate, tossed it aside, then reached up when he seemed about to rise. She caught him around the neck with one arm, then the other, and hung on despite the look of warning in his eyes.

"Listen—" His teeth were bared. His eyes were flashing warnings. But his hands were telling a different story. One was tangled in her hair, the other pressed against the tender side of her breast.

"One kiss," she whispered, "and then I'll sit here and

be quiet for as long as you wish—at least until the decorator is supposed to come. That's at least several hours. You could paint ten women in that time."

"You're bribing me."

"Is that what I'm doing?"

"In Tweed Black's circles they call it extortion. You could find yourself in jail."

"I think—" She hooded her eyes on the sensuous curve of his mouth. "I think it would be worth going to jail."

A subtle arch of her back sent the chemise spilling past her hips to pool around her knees. He registered this with a growl that sounded like it came from a hungry lion. Broad hands spanned her waist, squeezed, and pulled her closer.

"One kiss," he said in a low and menacing voice that turned Savannah into heavy cream. "Understand?"

"Perfectly."

"It's a pact. A God-damned promise. A contract."

"A pact. I understand."

His face was getting closer. "One kiss. Nothing more."

"Nothing." She closed her eyes, tilted her lips, and murmured, "Make me look ravished in the portrait. I want to look like I was just made love to by the most marvelous lover in all the world and—"

His mouth crushed over hers, wiping out words, smashing through thoughts, obliterating intentions, making mincemeat out of promises. He didn't kiss her. He consumed her. Like a force of nature he lifted her up out of herself and threw her heavenward in a spiral of intoxicating sensation. Unintelligible murmurs filled her ears, sounding wicked and lusty. When he bent to her breasts, Savannah went liquid with desire. She gasped, arched, and saw the brilliant lapis blue sky overhead. And then his fingers touched her thighs, touched her right where she felt most hot and swollen and pulsing, stroked once, twice, again, and the sky exploded with shooting stars and quivering spasms. And her outcry of delight echoed like the peals of a bell.

"The most godalmighty responsive woman—" Dominic was breathing heavily against her breasts.

Savannah licked her parched lips. "I'm sorry—I couldn't help myself—"

"No, no. If anyone apologizes it should be—"

"No." Savannah pressed her lips to his hair and slid her palms down his back. "Please, don't."

"Damned useless promises. I shouldn't come within ten feet of you. When I touch you, it's like I've been without food for a month. I can't get enough—it's—" He rose up, his mouth slack, his face pulled taut, his body like a spring wound too tight. His shirt stretched with his heavy breaths. He looked as if he were about to explode. "—damned obsession. It's that cursed wanting what you know you can't have."

"It is?"

"Hell, yes. What else could it be?"

"I hadn't thought of that."

"No? Then what did you think this is?"

"I—" Savannah swallowed. He looked so anguished, so in need of something, like an animal with raw and savage desires. Her heart swelled to three times its size in her chest. "I—I thought perhaps it was—you know—"

"No, I don't know."

Savannah licked her lips again. "You know—love." There, she'd said it. Only the instant she did she wished for some reason that she hadn't. The magic in the air seemed to vanish.

"Love." The word sounded like a curse, especially since he was scowling. She could almost see him withdrawing inside himself, physically inching away from her as if he couldn't bear to be near her.

She curled her fingers as they slipped over his shoulders and let her arms fall to her sides. It took every ounce of will to dredge up a cavalier tone. "Silly, isn't it?"

"Ridiculous."

"I mean, I hardly know you."

"And you never will." Abruptly he rose and returned to his easel.

Savannah felt as if he'd dealt her a physical blow. Everywhere. She couldn't seem to catch her breath.

"No, leave it," he growled when her fingers touched the chemise. "I want you as you are —exactly as you look."

Savannah lifted her chin and wondered if any mix of colors or level of artistic skill could capture the depths of her unhappiness at that moment.

Chapter 19

"His name is Bernard Wilton."

Savannah glanced at her aunt Maxine over her teacup. They sat side by side on a velvet settee in Mrs. Frances Cushing's overfurnished brownstone on East Fifty-first. Maxine wouldn't have been found at such an address had she and Frances Cushing not gone back far enough to forgive her most scandalous sins. She'd insisted on accompanying Savannah and Dominic on this particular call.

"Who are you talking about?" Savannah asked.

"That gentleman over there, standing by the fireplace. The beautiful one in the green cutaway. The one with the complexion of a sixteen-year-old Swedish girl. The only man in the room smart enough to be looking at you."

Savannah looked at Bernard Wilton. He instantly stood up straighter and gave her a charming smile that sent her heart to her toes. She angled her eyes at Dominic. It was bad enough that he was ignoring her. But how vexing that Aunt Maxine should notice he found more interest in the walls than in her . . . or the man staring at her.

And why shouldn't he? Their hostess was near the top of James Atwood's list of French and Italian art collectors, and rightly so. Every inch of wall space in the foyer and parlor was covered with framed oils, watercolors, and pastels. Dominic hadn't spared Savannah a glance since they'd stepped foot in the place. True, he'd sat beside her on the settee, elegant in afternoon calling wear, walking stick in hand, one leg crossed over the other, his shoes gleaming with high polish. He gave all the proper responses and exuded the suitable amount of interest in whatever meaningless topic was being bandied about. But Savannah knew better. His mind was elsewhere.

He'd been staring at something for several moments now. She followed his gaze to an upper corner of the room where a group of smaller oils hung. Instinct tweaked at her. She deepened her gaze. Something about the splashes of color on one of the paintings seemed to speak to her. Or was it the rendering of light filtering from the background? Or the face of the child playing in the foreground among splatters of black? Something about that child . . .

"He just had a house built on Park Avenue in the style of the Chateau of Francis I," Maxine said in a hushed tone. "It's of Caen stone imported from France and is rumored to be much larger than the house his father built. On purpose, you see."

Savannah toyed with the frills and furbelows decorating the bodice of her yellow gown. "Then he has too much money."

"And he'll tell you no one could make as superlative use of it as he can. He inherited everything his father made in the Civil War selling the Union Army outmoded and defective rifles acquired from European armories. The awful scheme was revealed when soldiers firing the rifles all had their thumbs blown off."

"And this is how the upper classes enriched themselves."

Maxine's hand stilled Savannah's fidgeting fingers. She leaned closer and continued in a hushed whisper. "Don't blame poor Bernard, dear. Like many of his contemporaries, he was born the son of a very corrupt man. His chief vices are polo, riding in Central Park, and amusing himself with actresses."

"Then why should he be looking at me? I'm a married woman."

"And like any married woman, you're in desperate need of a lover or two."

"You can't be serious?"

"You deserve to be fulfilled, not ignored."

Savannah felt her back stiffen. "I am fulfilled—in my own right. Why, don't I look like I am? Surely I don't require a man to do it for me. Besides"—Savannah attempted flippancy—"Castellane likes art."

"A bit too zealously for my taste. Look at him sitting there, as if he's brooding about the end of the world, and you looking like a delicious little lemon tart. Every time he looks at you he scowls."

"I know. He's full of dark passion."

"Passion? You keep separate bedrooms."

Savannah took a long sip of tea and felt suddenly as if she were skating on very thin ice. "I—yes, we do. So?"

Maxine's voice seemed to purr. "Quite surprising, you know. It almost makes me think your ravishment the other day was merely a show put on for my benefit and that the enjoyment of it—twice over, if I remember—was simply incidental. But then why would you go to such trouble to convince me that all was well between you? And why, if it was so enjoyable, would you then keep to separate rooms? You *are* married. It makes no sense to me. Does it perhaps to you, dear?"

Savannah felt as if she'd been poked in the behind. "Brunnie should know better than to spy."

"God help me if you've committed the unforgivable and become your mother."

"What did you say?"

"Blaming the servants to cover up for her wretched unhappiness. Listen to me. I know what's best for you."

Savannah reached for her aunt's hand and squeezed. Another squeeze pulled her chest tight inside. "Yes, I know you do. You always have."

"There's something about Castellane that's not quite right, Savannah, and I'm not talking about the rumors. Don't fall in love with him."

Savannah stared at her aunt, then laughed as fake a laugh as she'd ever heard. "What a ridiculous notion."

Maxine arched a brow. "Ridiculous, you say? You ooze with a need to be properly loved, and yet the mention of another man's attention makes you look like you want to vomit."

"Indigestion. Too much chocolate."

"Now I know you're lying."

"In order to prove to you that I'm not in love with Castellane I have to take a lover, is that it?" Savannah's strident whisper drew the sudden regard of several other women seated in the parlor. But Dominic remained distracted. An instant later he and several other gentlemen rose from their chairs and followed Mrs. Cushing from the room.

"I have several more in the upstairs hall, your lordship," Mrs. Cushing said to Dominic. "I make sure to show them to everyone who visits. Would the countess be interested?"

"Not at the moment," Dominic cut in.

"She's taking him somewhere," Savannah said, swiveling her head around to look after them. "And he doesn't want me following them. Now why—"

Something pinched Savannah's arm. "Here he comes," Maxine whispered.

"Here who?" Another pinch. This one forced a pained smile to Savannah's face. Bernard Wilton stood before her, the beautiful wastrel, devouring her with his child's blue eyes. His hair was a golden halo of curls in the soft candlelight. He was tall, well built, a beautifully handsome and desirable man in every respect except one: He wasn't Dominic.

He might as well have been a potted plant for all the interest he stirred in Savannah.

Maxine stood and smiled at Savannah in a way that made her almost jerk to her feet.

"Countess." Wilton bowed over her hand, looking long and appreciatively at her bosom until Savannah blocked his view with a fluttering of her hand. His eyes jerked to hers. "My dearest lady, do me the honor and take a turn with me around the room."

"Sir, the room is a bit small for walking."

"And so it is. Perhaps a walk in the hall, then? The Four Hundred hasn't stopped talking about you, Countess, ever since the Sully affair."

"Then they've far too little to talk about."

"On the contrary. They've finally found something worth discussing." Wilton stared at her in uncomfortable silence for several moments, then offered his arm. "Countess?"

Savannah almost refused, caught Maxine's eye, and smiled at Wilton. "Do you perhaps know anything about Mrs. Cushing's art collection? I'm a great admirer of art."

"Imagine that," Maxine muttered before turning away.

Wilton seemed momentarily stunned. "I—why, yes, Countess, I believe I do know a little something. I've been to Paris once. And Mrs. Cushing and I are great friends."

"Very good then." When she laid a hand on his arm he turned her toward the wall. "No. Not here." Savannah met his look with a tilt of her lips. "In the foyer. I believe I saw something interesting there."

He stared at her a moment. "Then of course, the foyer."

"Is there anything Italian?" Savannah asked as they swept out of the parlor. The foyer was deserted, cloaked in the dusky half-light of late afternoon that dared creep beyond the thick drapery. Several gas wall sconces hissed and sputtered. "I'm interested in the Italian art."

"Italian—" Wilton studied the walls, turning around and around. "I see some French. See there? Yes, a few of those. But I don't see any—oh, I believe there's an Italian in the parlor, a smaller work in the corner—"

"I thought so. Very good. Let's try upstairs." Savannah climbed two steps before Wilton tugged on her hand.

"My dear Countess, this simply isn't done."

"Says who?" Savannah perched on the step above him. "The upper hall, sir, is hardly considered trespassing, even in Chicago." She became aware that he was precisely eye level with the large bow at the center of the upper flounce of her bodice. It was designed to conceal a great deal of décolletage but not all of it. More tease than taming, Dominic had brusquely observed when she'd bent to get out of their brougham earlier that afternoon.

"Don't call me sir," Wilton said softly.

"Bernard it is, then." She bent, looked him directly in the eyes, and smiled. "This way, Bernard." He followed her up the stairs, pausing when she did at the very top. She glanced right, then left, chewing at her lip. "I can't see anything. It's awfully dark. Where the devil did they go?"

His chest pressed into her back. "Countess—"

Savannah felt hot breath at the back of her neck and twitched. "Which way do you think, Bernard?"

He took her hand and tugged her left. "This way." He seemed to know where he was going in his quick and determined pace. It occurred to Savannah that an upper hall in a house the size of Mrs. Cushing's could indeed be miles long.

She squinted at the walls. "I wish I could see better. Someone should remove this awful drapery so a person can see to walk and wait! There's a picture here—" She stopped below a very large framed picture. "Blast, it looks like flowers to me. What does it look like to you, Bernard?"

He moved beside her but he didn't look at the picture. "Does he beat you?"

Savannah looked sharply at him. "What?"

"Your husband. Does he beat you?"

"Castellane?" Savannah's laugh echoed down the hall, throaty, deep, and heartfelt. "Beat me? Good heavens, no."

"I was with my mother in England years ago. I was too young to remember much. But I do recall the tales she told about him. The scandal was all over London. It's followed him here, you know."

"They're all tales, Bernard. Tell everyone you know that."

Wilton moved a step nearer. "How charming you are to defend him. It's not necessary."

"Of course it's necessary. None of it is true."

"Odd, but I thought he would be much older. He looks quite nothing like a reclusive madman."

"That's because Castellane is a gentleman."

"And a fool."

"No, I believe he's quite intelligent."

Wilton's voice plunged deep. "He will never know."

"Oh, but I believe he does know he's intelligent, though you might be on to something there. He doesn't see his own talent, that's very clear—" Savannah froze.

Wilton had taken her gloved hand and was stroking it. He lifted it to his lips. "Countess, you're an innocent delight."

"Mr. Wilton—"

"I could make love to you right here—now—"

"That's impossible."

His chuckle made Savannah's hair stand straight up. "My darling, my discretion knows no bounds. And my talents—why, standing up against a wall, in a closet, in your armoire, whatever suits—"

"Good heavens—in a closet? One would have to be an acrobat—sir!" Her voice tangled in her throat when Wilton pushed her back against the wall and anchored her arms to her sides.

He dove straight for her bosom and began spreading hot, wet kisses on the skin surging above the frilled neckline. "Such sweetness! I could gobble you up."

Savannah jerked against him. "Good God—"

"Sweet, luscious morsel, since the Sully affair every man I know has been intent on having you—loving you, the way you were meant to be loved."

"As if they know what that is—*Mr. Wilton,* please—"

"I must be the first one to do it."

"Who says anything needs doing?"

"Darling, husbands can't love wives like you. They put you on a pedestal as a model of decorum, respectability, and motherhood and there they are content to leave you while they satisfy their lusts elsewhere. Let me satisfy yours, Countess! Don't deny yourself the delights of heaven itself!"

Savannah gulped back her shock and disgust, and felt a sliver of fear pierce through her when he refused to release her arms. To hell with finding Dominic. She had to escape Wilton. Her voice became shrill. "Bernard, please—"

He slurped hungrily. "I saw you and knew I had to have you."

"You should have controlled yourself." She shoved harder with her arms, struck out and up with her knee, but he'd anticipated her and blocked it with his thigh. "Mr. Wilton—"

He lifted his head and looked at her with eyes shining eerily in the dim light. Against hers his chest heaved as if he exerted great effort. His hands were like iron clamps on her arms. To Savannah he looked possessed. "Perhaps I should mention that I'm the most sought-after lover this season. I come highly recommended by Mrs. Stewart Taft.

Just over a year ago, she was so ignored by her husband
and children, so self-denied, she'd developed extreme
neuroses, took to her bed, and had nearly become a permanent invalid. The doctors had all given up."

Savannah fought for a controlled tone of voice. Perhaps
she could talk him out of this . . . and at the same time
make herself undesirable. "Well, that's what happens
when women allow themselves to take second place to
men. They become swallowed up in the rhythm of their
lives, happy or not, insulated from the world in their
overfurnished homes, glimpsing little reality. They pretend to lose their minds."

His teeth flashed in a satisfied smile. "Unless they have
lovers like me to save them."

"On the contrary. I believe they can save themselves
very well without you and your peculiar talents." There,
that should do it. Insult his abilities. Get him good and
angry and—

He looked down at her breasts again and wheezed.
"Sweet Mother of God, let me save you—"

Savannah groped for a strategy, something that would
penetrate the man's astonishing ego before he decided to
start slurping at her bosoms again. "My husband will call
you out."

"I've won my share of duels." He pressed his mouth to
her throat. "I have to touch you—"

"Bernard—" She grabbed his hand as it zoomed in on
her breast. "I swear to you, Castellane can be quite vi-
cious. He's an expert marksman. He won't kill you. He'll
leave you a cripple, without use of your—you know—and
your reign as lover extraordinaire will end. What will you
do in your big Caen stone house then?"

"Darling, as I said, he'll never know. The husbands
never do. One touch, just one. I must be the first one—"

"Oh, but he will know. You see, I'll have to tell him."

Wilton went still. "You'll *what?*"

"I'll have to tell him. I cannot tell a lie, especially to a

man with his temper. Indeed, it will be written all over
me."

His head jerked up. "What will?"

"What happened here. He'll know simply by looking at
me that another man kissed me right on my bosoms."

His eyes narrowed as he drew back. "How will he
know that?"

Savannah swallowed. "The Merriweather flush, sir. It
plagues all the Merriweather women whenever we lie. You
can imagine how inconvenient that can be. I've been
forced to resort to complete and brutal honesty at all
times because of it. It starts right here"—she patted the
deepest point of her décolletage—"and goes straight up
to my hairline. I turn fiery red with big white splotches. If
you were a woman and that happened to you, would you
ever lie?"

He frowned and drew back farther, releasing her arms,
but he looked skeptical. "I don't believe I would. Odd,
but I've never heard of such a thing."

Savannah rubbed one arm where he'd gripped her hard
and pasted on a charming smile. "Then you've never met
a Merriweather woman before, have you? Of course, since
what happened here wasn't too, too awful, and if you
promise not to try this kind of thing ever again, perhaps
he need never know about any of this—"

He leaned slowly toward her, eyes narrow and piercing.
"Are you toying with me, Countess? Because if you are, I
can tell you I've never stood for that from anyone without
exacting some kind of—"

"Oh, look there—" At a muffled thud of footsteps, Savannah looked down the hall. She almost sagged against
the wall with relief. Two shadows moved toward them,
one short, plump, and round with skirting, plowing along
like a cumbersome vessel, the other very tall and broad-
shouldered, moving with the casual grace that only he was
capable of. Her voice was breathless. "There's Castellane
now."

Wilton's head jerked sideways. "He's taller than I thought."

"Stronger too," Savannah added, chomping on to the slight quiver of indecision in his voice. "A devil of a temper."

"Expert marksman, you say?"

"The very best England has to offer." She could almost hear Wilton weighing the odds. Through the dusky lighting her eyes met Dominic's. His face tight and grim, he looked pointedly at her bosom, and God help her but she flushed hot over every inch of her skin.

Wilton glanced at her. "Perhaps it would be best if I— God, but you look red of a sudden, and, yes, I believe I should be—"

"Going?"

"Yes."

"Another engagement?"

"Several. Yes, yes—a busy day of calling." Wilton jerked a bow at her, then hightailed it back down the hall, green coattails snapping behind him.

"Ah, I see you've met young Wilton," Mrs. Cushing said when they drew up, her smile sweet, her powdered face pleasant. "Charming fellow. All the women like him."

"Yes. I can see why." Savannah glanced at Dominic.

He was staring after Wilton. And then he looked down at her, his face a mask of cold indifference. "If you're quite ready."

Ah. He'd found what he was looking for. He'd seen enough—somewhere down that shadowy hall. If only she knew what that was. Damn Wilton for sidetracking her. There certainly wouldn't be any prying anything out of Dominic.

After leaving Mrs. Cushing's, they dropped off Maxine at her brownstone in Gramercy Park and continued on to make two more calls. Without Maxine's chatter to lighten the mood, the coach ride was stilted; Dominic silent, brooding, and stormy-browed, Savannah still nursing the pride that had taken such a beating in his studio. Well, it wasn't exactly her pride that hurt; it was somewhere very deep in her heart. If Dominic was determined to sulk for the next six months, by God, she'd let him.

Each call proceeded much the same, with Dominic's manner civil and coolly arrogant in a way that endears aristocrats to the common man everywhere. Having been made uncomfortably aware of her sought-after status, Savannah spent the afternoon dodging ambitious would-be lovers and wishing she hadn't worn such a low-cut dress. Had she been the least amenable to the idea she was certain she could have bagged herself a half-dozen lovers that afternoon. On the whole, they were a handsome, engaging lot, daring almost to a fault in their persistence, being that Dominic's black scowl followed her wherever she went. A pity, really, that none of them stood out for her. She gave it a good try, engaging in lighthearted conversation about nothing, smiling a great deal, nodding a great deal, sipping an inordinate amount of tea.

At their hosts' insistence, they toured ballrooms that had been transformed into art galleries. The amount of artwork they viewed would have filled several museums. When they finally headed home, Savannah's mind swam not with the faces of her would-be lovers but with the images of all the paintings she'd seen.

If she'd thought to find some clue to Dominic's obsession in those vast collections, she would have been better off pounding sand. The man sitting across from her in the brougham, staring out the window into gathering dusk, was more mystery today than he'd been when she'd first met him.

And she was even more determined to unravel the mystery, no matter what it took. Deceiving everyone she knew and loved was a price she'd have to pay. After all, what option did a woman have when she was desperately in love?

* * *

The night was perfect. Dominic had known such nights in his youth, when the air hung thick with the promise of summer and the clouds seemed to hover just above the gas lamps. Fog threaded between the brownstones, stealthy as a man cloaked from head to toe in black, a man with a clandestine purpose.

He knew these streets. He felt as if he'd always known them, perhaps better at night than at any other time. The smell of damp cobblestones, the dew falling on his face, the clatter of passing carriage wheels—every bombardment to his senses roused memory, and none of it was particularly pleasant.

Odd that he should have to return to his best-forgotten youth in order to recapture it. He'd never thought he'd be thankful for the skills he'd learned in his days as a common thief.

Thief.

Normally, he could shrug off the disquiet. The strength of his convictions was as unbending as tempered steel. But tonight, of all nights, the agitation seemed to have taken root in his gut. No reasoning could dispel it. When he'd looked at Savannah tonight sitting cozy and snug in the parlor with a book and a glass of sherry at her fingertips, his disquiet had festered like an infected wound, and he'd felt suddenly and unexplainably more alone in his life than ever before.

Why did the course he'd chosen in this suddenly feel conspicuously wrong, the rationale, after nearly twenty years, sound hollow?

He tugged his coat collar higher around his neck, his hat lower over his eyes, wound his gloved fingers tighter around the valise handle, and lengthened his stride. There was, he knew, only one other option, which he'd dismissed as an option long ago, and that was forgetting. Letting it go, a lifetime of struggle. The thought made his mouth taste sour.

There was even less honor in that.

He was getting soft. Too much parlor decorating and chocolate eating; too much listening to a woman's chatter and smelling her perfume. He'd been hypnotized silly by hips and breasts, garters and bows, blond curls and cat-green eyes. That's why an evening spent with her sounded infinitely more appealing than the job he'd set for himself.

Damned pitiful since he wasn't even enjoying himself with Savannah. It was hell to be anywhere near her without an easel in front of him and chalk in his hands to distract him.

It was torture to remember the heartwrenching appeal in her voice when she'd said that word: *love*. Every time he looked at her, his mind reverberated with the sound and he broke into a sweat. Every time she tilted her eyes up at another man, curved her full lips, laughed that low, husky laugh, exchanged a few words he wished he could hear, he felt as if his chest were swelling beyond the limits of his clothes and his fists were clenching and that if she didn't look at him quickly he'd do something savage— something he'd likely regret.

This was the sort of thing that happened to idiotic child-men with no control over their lives or their lusts. Only those kinds of men boxed themselves into impossible, no-win situations and expected to prevail. Not men like him. Men in control. Men who knew what they wanted and even better how to get it.

He turned off of Fifty-fifth onto Fifth for three blocks, then found Fifty-first. Third brownstone on the right, if he remembered correctly. The street was deserted. All the brownstone windows were dark. It was just past two.

There was a second-story window on the west side of the house with a trellis of thick ivy winding through the brick below it. He might not even have to pick a lock tonight.

He hesitated, concealed in the shadows between the brownstones. Dampness pressed in around him. His chest seemed to push against the confines of his coat with every hammer of his heart. He could go back to her, feed her chocolate, read her poetry, wallow in all her delightful excesses. He didn't have to take this one critically defining step that would start him down a path from which there was no return.

Chapter 20

Savannah reread the last line of the speech she'd written out loud. She tried very hard not to hate it, failed miserably, and balled up the paper. It landed beside a dozen other little paper balls scattered around her wastebasket.

With agitated movements, she straightened the stack of blank paper, lifted her pen, and glared at the top page. She blew stray wisps from her eyes. "What does a woman say to a convention of women about freeing the bosoms and waging war on the corset? Why can't I think of anything meaningful? Because I'm not a suffragist at heart, that's why. I'm a fraud. No, I'm even worse. I'm an adventuress looking for distraction, pretending to believe in the cause because I have nothing else in my life to claim as my own—"

A tap sounded on the door. Brunnie's white cap and cherry cheeks appeared in the doorway. She got out "Pardon me, madam, but your—" before the door was shoved open hard enough to slam against the opposite wall.

Penelope Merriweather swept into the sunny bedchamber, fringe swaying on her hat, jacket, and skirt, a newspaper tucked under one arm. Over all of it she wore her typical agitated air that announced that she had more to do than anyone in the world, and all of it important. Today she seemed particularly overwrought.

"Hullo, Mother." Savannah stood to give her mother an obligatory kiss on each cheek, but her mother swept past without pause or notice. Savannah quickly sat and refocused on her blank page. "Brunnie tells me you had your lunch with Mrs. Astor yesterday. Congratulations."

Penelope swished to an abrupt halt, spun around, and marched to Savannah's secretary. Her parasol tip thumped on the floor in a demand of attention. "What the devil is the matter with you?"

"Ah, it wasn't successful. Did you spill gravy on your lap and now no one will want to know you?"

Penelope grimaced impatiently. "Of course it was successful. I'm in now. In fact, I'm pleased to say I received just this morning an invitation to the event of the season: the Nesbit masked ball. Have you?"

"Not yet. Should I be weeping in my pillow?"

"Not just yet. I brought your mail." She slapped the *New York Morning Journal* and several letters on top of the desk, then glanced at the oil painting hanging on the wall just to Savannah's right. "Good God, but that's awful."

Savannah glanced up. "It's Italian, Mother. I like it very much."

Penelope's brows shot up. "Italian, you say? Why, now that I look a bit closer, I could have told you that. Yes, yes indeed. It's a picture of a beautiful woman. Nino. Odd, but I've never heard of him."

"No?" Savannah thumbed through the letters.

"I'm not here to discuss art, Savannah."

"Is Papa pleased that you're now in?"

"If he were not he'd not dare show it. I've engaged Templeton Snelling himself to find us some property in Newport. We're going to build ourselves a house there."

"But Papa doesn't like sailing. He never has."

"He needn't *sail* the boat, Savannah. He simply needs to buy one and be seen on the deck so I can be properly in Newport for the nine-week summer season. If you want to be fashionable, Savannah, you must be always in the company of fashionable people. Now, quit distracting me. I'm very angry at you."

"I'm not distracting you. I'm worried about Papa. He's not happy."

"The devil take you. You did your job. And as usual you've done it a bit too zealously. Wait—there! That envelope there. That's the Nesbit invitation. I recognize the handwriting."

"Thank heavens," Savannah said, tossing the invitation aside and focusing again on her speech.

"Look at me, Savannah. I came as soon as Brunnie called me. There's a pile of rugs and drapery and furniture in your foyer and very little of anything left in this house."

"Oh, that. I'm having it taken away."

"Taken away?"

"That's what I said. Well, not all of it. I'm keeping a few things in the parlor, in Castellane's room, this secretary—oh, and my bed." She glanced at the four-poster, then up at the cherubs frolicking on the ceiling overhead, and her heart stuttered just as it did every time she remembered clutching at the coverlet and gasping at the ceiling and begging for more from Dominic. She glanced at her mother. "I'm opting for the sparse look, none of that overdecorating which to me is done by so many to symbolically cram content into the empty places of their spirit."

"I think you just insulted me."

"I'll be getting a few new pieces. Oh, and a lovely Dutch clock. Don't worry, it's not all going."

"Going? Going where, pray?"

"To Mrs. Astor's tenement."

Penelope's face pinched tight. "Her what?"

Savannah sat up with a jolt of self-righteousness. "Your

Mrs. Astor's husband owns acres of tenement real estate in this city. It's little better than a slum, Mother. He charges high rents and evicts widows and invalids the instant they're delinquent in rent. Families live in one room with no furniture or food. Children die of consumption while the Astor children grow spoiled and fat in their mausoleums and—"

Penelope's gloved hand slammed flat on the table in front of Savannah. "Listen to me," she hissed.

"I know all of this to be fact."

"And like a good little heiress you'll look the other way and not embarrass one of your own."

"My own? You mean Mr. Astor? I say it would be better for him to die suddenly than to live a hundred years longer as he is now."

"Good heavens, don't let anyone ever hear you say that." Penelope frowned. "Don't get all tender-hearted, Savannah. There's far too many in our circle who feel we're surrendering our nation to the immigrant rabble outcasts of other countries."

A knot in Savannah's throat thickened her voice. "You know nothing of them."

"And you do? My dear, we all see them wearing their queer and shabby clothes."

"Not all of them are shabby."

"Perhaps not. But no elite woman empties her home for them. We assuage our consciences by performing little acts of charity while our husbands give money, and lots of it. It's the speediest way to advance socially."

"Particularly when it's done very visibly for the people-we-know and everyone has tea afterward."

"Precisely."

Savannah stood up. With her fists she twisted her satin skirting. Anger pounded in her cheeks. "I will not be one of those women who addresses envelopes and rolls bandages whenever Mrs. Oldname might need me to."

"You will or you'll disgrace us all. If Mrs. Astor finds out where all that furniture came from—"

"I'm afraid this is yet another time when my heart refuses to respond feebly."

"I'm not surprised." Penelope's cold gaze raked over Savannah's uncorseted bodice, from the surge of bosom to the twenty-two-inch waist. "You've recently abandoned all your restraint. You look positively plump and out of fashion. Good heavens, you're not with child already, are you?"

This stopped Savannah cold. She could almost feel the fire sputtering out of her. "I—"

"You don't have the body to carry it off with any grace or elegance. You'll be fat and cumbersome as a beached whale. If you find you can't control your maternal needs, whelp the earl one child. After that he won't touch you. He won't be able to bear it. The English women are very thin and elegant, aren't they?"

Savannah had to look away. That niggling, hateful feeling of inadequacy started her belly squirming. Her eyes burned. Horrified, she looked down at the paper spread on her secretary. The headlines were a blur. She groped for memory, for those moments she'd sat for Dominic in his studio, feeling the reverent warmth of his eyes caressing her bare skin, making her blush from the inside. He'd made her feel beautiful. A man as passionate as he wouldn't turn aside his pregnant wife. Savannah imagined he would find her a blossoming miracle, a wonder worthy of oils and pastels . . .

A new ache spread through her, this one raw and vulnerable and needful.

She blinked, focused. The headline jumped out of the page:

VALUABLE OIL PAINTINGS STOLEN:

DARING MIDNIGHT THIEF TERRORIZES THREE BROWN-

STONES IN EXCLUSIVE FIFTH AVENUE NEIGHBORHOOD, BAF-
FLES POLICE.

Savannah dropped into her chair. The room suddenly
got very cold.

"But I suppose children are a necessary evil to an earl.
Just as they were to your father. Lineage and all that."

Savannah's eyes flew over the print.

**French and Italian oil paintings stolen . . . Mrs.
Frances Cushing said to be in a state of shock over
her loss . . . Police begin investigation . . . No
suspects named.**

"Savannah, did you hear me?"

Savannah's head snapped up. "What? Oh, yes, yes, that
would be fine. Thank you, Mother."

Penelope poked her face closer. "What did you say?"

Savannah left her chair and looked quickly around. "I
have to—oh, there's a hat." She slapped the hat on her
head and shoved a pin in as she searched for her shoes.
Under the bed she found the red silk pumps with the
three-inch heels.

"Good God, those don't match. You're wearing yellow."

"Yes, very good," Savannah said, hopping into one
shoe, then the other. "Thank you, Mother. I'll show you
out. Castellane isn't here, you know, so no use trying to
see him. He's been gone since breakfast."

Penelope grabbed Savannah by the arm as she started
past. "Are you ill? You look positively glassy-eyed."

"I do? Yes, yes, well, too much chocolate. Shall we?"

"I can take you wherever it is you're going," Penelope
said when they stepped from the town house into glorious
late-spring warmth.

"Yes, that would be—oh, no, no. I'll just—" Savannah

waved a vague hand over her shoulder. "Wrong direction. Completely out of your way, Mother. But thank you."

Penelope stared at her very strangely. "Rethink this matter of the furniture, will you?"

Savannah nodded as she swept down the steps. "I'll try. Good-bye, Mother. Tell Papa I love him."

"I believe he knows that."

Savannah jerked around and met her mother's penetrating look. "He does? Why, of course he does."

She knew her mother watched her hurry down the entire length of the block. The instant she turned the corner and was out of sight, she hailed a cab. Thirty minutes later she paid the driver and stepped from the carriage onto Tenth Street in what was widely known as the Artists' District. She moved quickly down the narrow street, avoiding the stares of the shabby bums loitering in the doorways of buildings that rose up three stories on either side. She recognized the studio building, made a quick dash up the stairs, and let out a sigh of relief when she reached the third floor and Dominic's door. She paused, listened to silence, then tested the door handle. It turned easily. Gently she pushed and the door swung open. Ignoring a stab of conscience, she poked her head inside and froze.

The boy looked to be all of ten. He was small and thin, his coat three sizes too large, hanging past his fingertips. A red cap fell over his ears and forehead and flattened his dark hair to his shoulders. But his eyes were enormous and bright blue and his toothy smile seemed to light up the studio. He was sitting cross-legged on the floor beneath the glass ceiling in a spray of sunlight, and held a loaf of crusty bread in one grimy-looking hand.

"Funny name," he said, looking toward the corner of the room that was hidden by the door. He took a huge bite of the bread and chomped away, oblivious to Savannah.

"No funner than Sam." Dominic's voice boomed through the studio.

Savannah's first instinct was to jerk out of sight behind the door. She gently pulled on the handle. The door inched closed, then suddenly gave a quiet squeak. She went still instantly. Her heart slammed around wildly in her chest.

Footsteps made by long legs sounded on the floor, then stopped. "Herman Shnable got me some lamb. Try it. But take off your hat when you eat. Even cowboys do."

Something about Dominic's tone made Savannah press close against the door. He sounded positively paternal.

Paternal?

Her eyes snapped wide. God, but she hadn't even considered he might have a family . . . a child . . . a mistress . . . a wife?

A sumptuous aroma twitched at her nose. Lamb . . . with warm crusty bread. Her mouth started to water. She pressed a hand to her belly and it rumbled.

"Funny-sounding name," the boy said. "What country is she from?"

"Ohio. She grew up on a farm. With cows. You ever see a cow on these streets, Sam? I never did. I'll show you a cow someday."

"But I still don't like her name."

"If you meet her, call her Rosy."

Rosy? Dominic and this little person were discussing her. Savannah strained her ears.

"I don' wanna meet her. She's just a girl."

"That she is." Dominic sounded like he was talking with his mouth full. Several moments passed. "Here— have more. I think you'd like her."

The boy made a satisfying sound like the groan of a hibernating bear. "Uh-uh. I don't like girls. Why do you?"

"Good question. Here—" Something thumped on the floor. "Read this."

"I don' wanna."

"Don't want to. Three *t*s. Say it."

"I say it all morning with that lady at Bonnie's. The teacher."

"Miss Myrtle. She's an old friend of mine, Sam."

"I still don' like her. She makes me read all the time and talk right and do numbers."

"That's her job, Sam. She did the same thing to me. Tell me what you read today."

The sound of smacking lips made Savannah's belly gurgle. "Some man named Horsho."

"Horatio. Horatio Alger."

"Yeah. That's him."

"I used to read him all the time when I was younger. Miss Myrtle made me." There was a buoyant tone in Dominic's voice Savannah had never heard before. He sounded . . . young. "But I had one problem with the stories."

"Mmmm." More lips smacked. "This is better than Bonnie's cooking. What problem?"

"It always troubled me that none of the stories tells how the hero fares after he achieves what he wants and finds success. No one in his life questions the worthiness of his goals or dares to suggest that his goals might be a snare and a delusion. No one considers that other goals might be more admirable. Thinking about it now—I don't know—Alger teaches honesty and frugality and piety and duty not for their own sake, but only as a means to success."

"What?"

"The paths he chooses all lead to one end—affluence."

"Oh, like you, Nino."

"Right. Just like me." The wistfulness in his voice tugged at Savannah. He was speaking to this child in a way that made her eyes feel hot and watery and her heart twist around itself. Gone were the invisible barricades and steel traps and clever sidesteps. For once she could see through a window he'd let slide open on himself. Finally she could glimpse the tortured man within. And she wanted more . . . so much more her chest hurt with the frustration caged there.

She knocked softly.

Feet scuffled on the floor. Something fell over.

"Christ, Sam—" Dominic barked. "What the hell's the matter—"

"It's the padrones!" Sam cried. "I told you they'd find me and take me back. Don't let them, Nino. Please, don't—"

"No one's going to take you back to the streets. You know Bonnie and I won't let them—Christ, come in—"

Savannah shoved the door wide, stepped inside, and smiled. "Oh, hullo."

Dominic's face darkened instantly. But for all his efforts at looking ominous, he failed. Savannah wondered if he realized his hair fell over his brow and his shirt was wrinkled and askew. He needed a shave, quite desperately. He looked as if he'd been wrestling with a puppy on the floor. He looked as if he'd been up all night.

The sight of him made her heart soar with relief.

He hadn't left her yet.

"You know you could have been killed out there," he muttered, moving toward her with eyes narrow and hips jutting. "I don't suppose the rabble came near you, did they? Hell, they've never seen anything quite like you. Sam, say hullo to Savannah Rose Merriweather."

A muffled, mangled "hullo" came from Sam. Savannah glanced around Dominic and found Sam on the floor again, stuffing lamb and bread into his mouth. He seemed to be trying very hard not to look at her.

"A pleasure to meet you, Sam." Savannah looked at Dominic. "Is he your son?"

His brows quirked almost imperceptibly. For an instant his mouth softened, parted, then drew tight. "No. No, he's an orphan. He just kind of—" He shrugged and

looked so self-effacing Savannah almost threw her arms
around his thick neck and sobbed. "—he thinks he lives
here."

"I *do* live here," Sam muttered.

Dominic glanced over his shoulder. "When I'm here,
you do. Otherwise it's too dangerous." He looked at Savannah. "He's staying with my friend Bonnie."

"Bonnie."

"He's—" His scowl deepened. "He's a he, dammit."

"I see."

"We have this—" Dominic's hand slashed through the
air, then jabbed into his hair. "—it's an orphanage."

"For immigrant orphans."

"Children of the streets."

"Like you."

His eyes met hers. "Like Sam."

"Funded by all your Wall Street profits."

His eyes flicked around the room. "I didn't sink it into
a damned mausoleum or a private railroad car."

Savannah lifted her brows and lowered her voice. "Ah.
And here I'd thought you were keeping a mistress somewhere, and very well at that."

"You know I have no woman."

Savannah blinked. "I do?"

"You should." His gaze swept down past her throat
and darkened with obvious appreciation. "Hungry?"

"I—as a matter of fact—"

He grasped her by the upper arm and led her toward
Sam. "We're having a picnic," he murmured close to her
ear. "We'll eat and then you can tell me why you've
come."

"I missed you," she replied, meeting his gaze, trying a
coy smile, but she failed. He made her bones positively
quiver.

"Move over, Sam," he said without taking his eyes from
Savannah.

The boy rolled his eyes, mumbled something, and slid

himself and the white paper heaped with lamb and bread
several feet over. Dominic grabbed the back of a tall chair.

"No—" Savannah laid her hand on his arm. "I'll sit on
the floor with you."

"Not in that you won't," Sam muttered, glancing dis-
dainfully at Savannah's dress as if her being "just a girl"
was about the most awful thing that could happen to a
person.

"Is that so?" Savannah kicked off her red shoes,
reached low to grip a flounce that ringed her dress, and
tugged up, hard. She glanced at Dominic, smiled, and
shimmied just a bit to get the narrowest part of the dress
over her hips. He watched it all with a cheek-twitching
concentration.

"They're bloomers," she said to Sam when the hem of
the dress slipped up past her pantalooned knees. "From
France."

Sam chomped and looked bored. "They look like
pants, except for the ruffles. I hate ruffles."

"At times, so do I. There—" Savannah settled herself
on the floor, feet tucked under, dress pooled around her
hips. "Can I have some of that?"

"Share," Dominic muttered, squeezing Sam on the
shoulder until the boy slid the heaped paper in front of
Savannah. "I'll get wine," Dominic said, moving away
again.

Savannah tore off a chunk of bread, scooped up a por-
tion of lamb with it, and sank her teeth into it. "God."
She groaned, chewing slowly, savoringly, licking her lips
of every juicy drop. "I want to meet Herman Shnable."

Sam grunted, she assumed in agreement, and continued
eating, half turned away from her. She glanced quickly
around the studio, her eyes darting into the far corners,
along the walls where the canvases were stacked and leaning.

Nothing there. She'd know it when she saw it.

She lifted her eyes to an easel and saw the pastel of a

naked blond woman sitting on a scarlet divan in full sunlight—

She stopped chewing and stared. Dominic had added
excruciating detail to the portrait since she'd seen it last,
detail to the face that made her look fresh and young and
as serenely beautiful as a porcelain doll . . . lush detail
to the body that was seductive and captivating, all long
lines and slender curves. Lovely, not repelling. Her hair
was an enchanting swirl of myriad blond, gold, and white,
her skin the palest of peachy pinks, the peaks of her
breasts a lush rose.

When she'd last left the studio, he'd captured only
shape and vague color on the canvas. The rest he'd since
rendered from memory.

"Here." He was hunkered down beside her, holding
out a glass of red wine, looking at the pastel. "Do you like
it?"

She swallowed the last of the lamb. "I—it's—"

He looked at her and his mouth seemed to soften. "It's
not finished."

"I'm going now." Sam surged to his feet, swiped his
sleeve over his mouth, glanced at Savannah, opened his
mouth. "Umm—good-bye."

"Good-bye, Sam."

Dominic jerked his head to the door. "I'll get him a
cab."

"I don' wanna—"

"Don't want," Dominic barked, marching after the boy.
"Two *t*s."

The door thudded closed behind them. For an instant,
Savannah listened to footsteps on the stairs, then struggled to her feet. Pushing her skirts back in place, she
headed straight for the canvases stacked against a far wall.

She thumbed through them speedily. "Where the devil
would he put them? Not here—" She found several paintings she liked, all done in very violent shades of deep
color. Dominic Dare was an angry man.

When she thumbed through all the canvases she paused, looking around the room and worrying her lower lip. "Oh, hell—" She flew to the armoire, threw open the doors, and was assailed by a scent that was so masculine, so Dominic, her knees went weak. She glanced on a top shelf, then below the neatly hung row of topcoats. She spun to the trunk, dropped to her knees, threw up the lid, and found neatly pressed shirts that smelled like starch. The top one begged to be touched, so she laid her fingers on the fine linen, imagining she could feel Dominic's heat through the cloth. Guilt washed over her. Panic tore at her frayed nerves. The article screamed through her brain: "Several Italian and French oils were taken from Mrs. Cushing's brownstone, one from a hall just outside Mrs. Cushing's bedchamber . . ."

She pressed trembling fingers to her temple. What was she doing? What was she thinking? Just because he'd admired Mrs. Cushing's art, just because he'd visited that upper hall just that afternoon didn't mean he'd—

Was she in love with a thief?

But if he'd found what he was looking for, was their masquerade up? Was Dominic Dare planning to disappear from her life . . . perhaps as soon as today? Could she stop him?

She looked up and went cold. There, secreted behind the bed and half draped with a piece of duck sailcloth, was the small framed Italian oil she'd seen hanging in the upper corner of Mrs. Cushing's parlor. The boy seemed to be looking right at her with eyes as black and intense as Dominic's. Numb, she got to her feet and walked slowly to the oil. When she lifted the sailcloth she found a larger oil that on quick inspection bore no relation to the others in either style or subject. There were two small oils beside the smaller one, all three obviously done by the same artist, all depicting a dark-haired boy playing between humble-looking dwellings. In one oil, the boy was alone. In another, women in peasant garb worked beside him. In another, he stood beside a young girl with a horse while a man worked the fields just behind him. Considered altogether, the oils seemed to be telling a story . . . a story of a family.

In the background mountains rose majestically and sunlight dappled the scenes. In the foreground black flecks marred each canvas in haphazard patterns, as if indiscriminately splashed there. Savannah flicked at one fleck with her fingernail. It disintegrated, leaving a fine powdery substance on her fingertip.

Like pigment. Or dried blood.

Chapter 21

For a man who'd awakened that morning with a single-minded determination to keep Savannah Rose Merri-weather in a proper, business perspective, Dominic faced a disturbing sense of emptiness when he entered the studio and found her gone. He took the depth of his response as he might have a fist in the gut, especially when she appeared from a dark corner and in an instant flooded the lonely recesses of his life with promise. He stopped in his tracks, dry-mouthed in a second.

She walked toward him, a full glass of wine in one hand, eyes limpid, mouth gently curved, wearing nothing but a transparent white chemise. She was a feast of such womanly splendor he swore he could hear angels singing.

She stopped close in front of him, looked up at him, and handed him the wine. "I want to finish the portrait."

No sane man could argue with her. Dominic managed a shrug, as casual as he could, then gulped his glass dry when she turned and walked toward the scarlet divan. He followed two paces behind her, watching bare legs swish-ing against linen. Her backside looked like a plump peach. She lifted her arms and blond curls spilled to her

waist. She fiddled with something at the front of the chemise and a strap slid off one shoulder, then the other.

Dominic's blood started to percolate.

Abruptly she turned and looked startled to find him so
close behind her. Her smile seemed to tremble. "Where
do you want me?"

He had the presence of mind to glance at the sky. Puffy
white clouds with ominous gray underbellies scudded
across the glass. Christ, as if the light mattered at this
point.

"Uh—" he said. She smelled like a hothouse full of
lilacs. He nudged past her, grasped her wrist, and scooted
the divan one way, then the other, as if positioning was
critical.

The only thing critical at this point was getting himself
behind the easel with chalk in his sweating hands. He was
drowning in lilacs and damned near to self-combusting.
His trousers felt as if they were splitting at his groin.
"Here," he said gruffly. "On the divan."

"Perhaps you should show me precisely where."

There was an underlying tone in her voice that made
him look into her virgin's eyes and wonder, just for an
instant, if she wasn't trying very hard to seduce him. It
wouldn't be comfortable for her. She was trembling very
slightly.

The idea, oddly enough, made his arms ache to crush
her close and whisper the sweet, soothing words bride-
grooms murmured in the darkest moments of a wedding
night.

"Fine." Taking both her hands, he drew her in front of
the divan—perilously close, too close, he soon realized.
He knew she could feel the heat pulsing out of him. He
could feel hers.

She looked up at him, her eyes enormous and shining.
Something twisted in his chest.

"Like this?" With a subtle shrug of her shoulders she
sent the chemise plunging to the floor.

Yes, he was certain this was seduction, chock full of guile. The kind of seduction he'd avoided all his life because it screamed of some sort of wily, wicked female trap.

The instinct for self-preservation demanded he extricate himself before the trap's steely jaws clamped around him.

"Rosy—" He sounded like a dying man. He couldn't move.

She laid her palms on his chest and slowly sat on the divan. Her hands smoothed down over his belly and stopped, cupping his manhood between them. He heard her intake of breath and swelled another impossible inch. Her fingers tugged his shirt out of his pants, flicked his trousers open, releasing the binding pressure a fraction, then another fraction. She gasped again, her fingers fumbled over themselves, his erection bucked for release. And then buttons slid free and he sprang into her hands and his mind screamed . . .

With both hands he hauled her up against him, his voice a low, menacing snarl. "What the hell is this?"

She gasped his name, closed her eyes, and gripped his forearms with a desperation that fired his blood. "Please—"

"And now you're begging for it—" Teeth bared, chest heaving, he stared at her lush mouth, at the breasts flattened high against his chest, felt the moist warmth of her loins pressed against his own, and his mind went red with lust. "Is this what you want?" Roughly he grasped one breast, lifted the distended nipple, and flicked at it with his tongue. She cried out, as if every nerve tip over every inch of her lovely body was on fire.

He knew what that felt like. He'd been living it since he'd met her.

Her fingers tore at the buttons of his shirt. "Please—"

"Whatever you say, sweetheart." With one hand he snapped the shirt open from neck to waist. Buttons spilled to the floor. She shoved it wide over his shoulders, splayed her hands over his chest, and arched her breasts into him.

"More . . . you want more? What about this?" He looked into her tortured eyes and slid his hand between their bodies, over the soft mound of her belly, and deep into the lush curls between her thighs. Heat flowed from her over his fingertips like a river of honey. He gripped her hips, slid his manhood against the sweet wetness, and she sagged against him. "Jesus-God almighty—"

And then she was beneath him, on the divan, her lips parting beneath the punishing force of his mouth, her thighs spread in welcome. He was there, right there, so easily fitting there, as if she'd been born for him. He was nudging open the gates of heaven itself.

"Say no," he rasped, bracing himself above her on his elbows. He cupped her head in his hands and looked deep into her eyes. "Just say it and I'll stop. I can touch you there and you'll explode and it will be over. Remember our pact—God damn if I'm not trying—"

"Dominic—" Her fingertips pressed to his lips. She wriggled her hips, arched them, and he slid a precious microinch inside of her. She breathed in with a shudder.

He broke into a sweat. He felt every vein in his neck popping. "Say no, dammit."

"Yes." She lifted her mouth to his, brushed her lips back and forth, slid her tongue over his teeth. "Make love to me, Dominic."

"That's not what you want to say."

"I do." Another wriggle. Another microinch. She was a mercilessly tight sheath of hot velvet. "You're so big, Dominic."

"No—" The sound of a man on the brink of insanity. "That's not good either."

Another wriggle. Her legs clamped around his waist, fitting the tip of his manhood against the barrier.

"Yes," she breathed against his mouth. "Make me a woman, Dominic. I'll go mad wanting you like this—"

This wasn't some virgin's wicked scheme. Passion drove her, a passion he shared and now knew and understood was as inevitable as the rising of the sun. His resistance fell with the roar of an avalanche. It filled his ears, drowning out her gasp of pain and any clamoring of his conscience, as he drove himself deep inside of her.

He lay there, fully embedded, breathing as hard as if he'd dug ten miles of road in August heat. "God, Savannah—"

"Y-you sound like something's wrong . . ."

"God no—" He lifted his head, bracing himself on one arm. She looked angelic beneath him. "I just can't move. You're"—he gave a ragged breath of defeat and lowered his mouth to her breasts—"sweet heaven." He drew a nipple against his tongue and sucked until she writhed and he withdrew and drove deep, once, twice was all it took and she gave that kittenish outcry of release that brought his own climax crashing down on him with a staggering fury. He spilled himself deep into her womb with great, wrenching spasms.

Perspiration trickled into Dominic's mouth. He tasted it and realized his throat was thick and dry as old wood, as if he'd spent the last ten minutes in a state of slack-jawed amazement. He also realized that he was wrapped around Savannah, legs and arms wound tight, face buried against her neck, as if he had no intention of ever letting her go.

As if consuming her was all that mattered to him.

"I—" Her rib cage spasmed beneath him. "You're—I can't breathe—"

He pushed up. "God—I'm—I was crushing you." He didn't sound like himself. Hell if he felt like himself either. The sating of his passion usually demanded sleep and that he be left alone. He felt the need for neither, only to look into her eyes and know that all was right in her world.

Except she wouldn't look at him, even when he jerked up off the divan and straightened his trousers. And hell if he knew what to say to her.

He didn't know what any of it meant, except that for so enormous a mistake, it had felt so God-damned right. She'd turned his life inside out. None of it made sense anymore. Not the tangle of convoluted feelings, not even the canvases leaning against the wall behind his bed.

She scooted from the divan, reached for her chemise, and would have slipped past him if he hadn't caught her arm. He might not know how to fix it but he couldn't let her go, not like this, with them behaving like strangers.

At first the knot in his throat clogged his words. "Listen—"

She was gripping the chemise to her breasts and looking down and away. He swore under his breath and spotted the dark splotch soaking the scarlet velvet divan. This time he swore good and loud.

"Listen, Savannah—what happened here—"

She looked right at him. "I won't apologize."

"What?"

Her chin poked out a fraction. "I'm glad it happened."

"Christ, I'd be lying if I said I wasn't, but—"

She pressed her fingers to his lips. "No. I don't want to hear any of it. You owe me no explanations, Dominic. You owe me nothing."

Anger stabbed at him from out of nowhere. "That's a damned fine attitude."

"Thank you." Another jaunty lift of her chin that looked almost too pronounced. "I learned it in France."

"You didn't learn anything in France, not even enough to mangle one French verb. And you can tell Maxine that."

When she shrugged away from him he let her go. "I learned enough," she tossed over her shoulder, slinging the chemise over her head and slipping her arms through.

"Is that right?" He stuffed his shirttails into his trousers and watched her walk to the yellow dress she'd left lying on his bed. Every wriggle of her hips was like tinder heaped on his simmering anger. "You want to explain to me how babies are made, madam?"

She picked up the dress and slowly looked at him. Her lips parted. "Babies," she said, blinking once, twice, as if only now registering precisely what had transpired on that divan. At the exact moment of realization her cheeks burst into vivid scarlet.

"I'm supposed to believe you didn't consider that, eh?"

Her brows dove straight down in a petulant frown. "Did *you?*"

"I've always believed a man should."

"And?"

"He takes precautions."

"Like?"

He shifted his feet, jabbed his hands into his trouser pockets, and scowled. "Withdrawl."

"I see. And did you?"

"Christ, Savannah—"

"Well, why didn't you?" She shook out her dress and bent to step into it.

Her backside went one way, her breasts arched another, she shimmied, wiggled, everything jiggled, and Dominic closed his eyes. The depths of his fascination with her defied imagination. The power it gave her over him . . .

What the hell *was* this?

"I wasn't thinking," he muttered, shoving a hand through his hair. He saw the canvases behind the bed, felt the responsibility pressing down and in around him like walls—or a gravestone. Suddenly a life's passion had become a burden. "Listen—"

"Oh, you needn't fret."

"Dammit, men don't fret."

"How convenient for the men of the world." Her fingers flew over the pearl buttons at the front of her gown. "My mother tells me this sort of thing happens all the time."

"Not to me, it doesn't."

"Well, that's a comfort." Her delivery was pure jaunt, but when she looked at him he swore her eyes darkened with appreciation and some kind of heartfelt emotion. That he lapped it up like a salivating puppy only augmented his frustration.

She tugged down on her bodice to smooth it, almost came out the top in the process, and gave a satisfied smile. "We'll simply have to speed things up a bit."

"Speed things up."

She waved a hand as she scooped up her hat from the bed. "You know, your business." She plunked the hat on her head and angled her eyes at him. "Is all going as planned in that regard?"

"Er—yes—as a matter of fact, better than planned."

"Better? I see." She looked long and hard at him. "Are you perhaps close to finished?"

"Finished?" He scoffed, jabbed a hand through his hair, and felt a great need to pace. He opted for marching to his easel and fiddling with chalk. "No, not quite."

"I see." Shoes followed. She bent and hopped into one, then the other. "Well, I still plan to hold up my end of our bargain until it's complete. After all, you did. My mother had lunch with Mrs. Astor this week."

"How very nice for your mother."

"Of course, it is. Papa's another story. Being *in* means he's to have a yacht and a house in Newport or he must hang his head in shame. I know for certain he hates boats."

"No men's clubs in Newport?"

"Oh, I'm sure there are several. Men don't go where there are no clubs to escape to."

"Then he'll be fine."

"You make a man's happiness sound pathetically simple."

"In most cases, I think it is. A man must be financially comfortable. His wife needs to be marginally content. A miserable wife makes for a miserable man. He needs children, even defiant ones. And last, he needs those moments of escape. Yes, I believe most men want little else."

"And you?"

"Not everyone requires as much as you and I for happiness, Savannah. When you realize that you'll stop worrying so much about your father. I think he's far happier than you might wish to think he is."

Her chin jabbed at him so sharply the tendons on her neck stood out. "I might wish? As if I have nothing else to fret over?"

"Every woman needs at least three things to keep her in constant turmoil. And in your case all three happen to be your father."

She blinked furiously. "As if you know all there is to know about what females need, particularly me."

"I'm beginning to think the only thing you need is a husband."

She paled three shades. "A what?"

"You heard me. And babies. A dozen at least."

Savannah gasped. "A dozen? Childbearing and house-wifery are the purest forms of bondage to a woman's spirit—"

"Save it for Frances Trainer." Dominic narrowed his eyes on her. "You were made for it. I think you know it. You just won't admit it."

She blushed, then looked hotly away, swished up her skirts in one hand, and marched toward the door. "Enough of this. We have work to do, Dominic. Calls to make. Art to see. A murderer to catch."

"Is that all?"

"Move quickly now."

He caught her arm just as she reached for the door

handle. "And if there's a child?" He stared at the squashed cabbage leaves on her hat and felt as if a vise were squeezing his chest.

"Oh, I won't expect you to do right by it, Dominic. You may feel free to take your leave from me just as you please. And as the woman played false by a scoundrel, I'll have little trouble finding myself a husband. He'll believe the child his own. You'll have no responsibility in the matter. Simple enough."

She tugged the door open two inches but he smashed it closed with his fist. "The hell you will."

She looked up at him with fire in her eyes. "No? Who's going to stop me? I say that's small penance to pay."

"It didn't feel like sin, Savannah, not to either one of us."

"Then why do you look like you want to smash your fist into this door again? Because it was a mistake. Because you have far more pressing matters in your life, matters of life and death."

"And if I do?"

"It's torn you apart for so many years it's become the fabric of who you are. It's some sort of revenge, I know it is, and it must be dealt with and resolved or you won't have a fool's chance at any kind of happiness. You can hardly afford distraction. And after all, in the end, I'll be just another model who couldn't keep her clothes on for you."

"Goddammit—" He gripped her by her upper arms and couldn't decide whether to kiss her or shake her. Christ, but he couldn't tell if she was baiting him or truly believed what she said. All he knew was that she stoked a squirming kind of frustration in him that he knew he'd never understand. "Damned harebrained woman, you're the only woman I've—the only virgin—the only—"

She blinked up at him. "Why, Dominic, you look positively beside yourself and very ominous. If you go around like that this afternoon people will think you've something to do with the art thefts."

Dominic narrowed his eyes against the dash of cold that pierced him. Could cunning be so adroitly disguised? Had she been conducting slick little maneuvers while he grappled with conscience and his heart thrashed about like a harpooned fish?

She lifted her brows. "The paper says everyone in top-drawer New York society is suspect. I mean, who can honestly say they're not as fascinated by French and Italian art, say, as you are? Everyone is. Everyone's throwing open their doors to their art galleries. It was a crime just asking to be committed. You want my theory? I think the thief was after one piece in particular and stole several other pieces to camouflage what he was after. What do you think?"

"I haven't read the papers."

She was looking up at him, eyes wide and expectant. "Ah."

Tell her. The thought exploded into his mind as if she'd shot it there from a cannon. *Tell her?*

And then what? Steal her away from the family she loved with nothing to offer but a life that was no life at all for a woman?

Dominic had suffered the loss of his family too acutely to deliver her into that fate.

He drew himself up with a shrug of his shoulders and a jut of his chin. "The Nesbit ball. Have we received the invitation?"

He heard her swallow. "It came just this morning."

"Very good." He reached out and straightened a sagging cabbage feather. She looked up at him and he couldn't resist brushing his knuckles under her chin. His thumb touched the cleft, fingers tilted her face up, and his lips brushed hers. They trembled open with an eagerness that made the floor tilt. He lifted his head. "Savannah—"

She laid a palm on his chest. He covered it with his

hand and they stood there for several moments. He felt his heart swelling, aching, close to bursting . . .

"Let's go," she said, reaching for the door handle. This time he let her.

Chapter 22

"Ah, Chicago, that legendary center of social savagery, where the rich have bowling alleys instead of art galleries installed in their mansions." Templeton Snelling's gaze swept the group assembled in front of the blazing fireplace. Satisfied that he'd commanded everyone's attention with this dramatic turn of conversation, he settled his gaze pointedly upon Savannah and gulped his tumbler dry, the better to prolong the moment.

It was, thankfully, their last event of a busy day. As with all their afternoon calls over the last week, this impromptu early-evening kettledrum was so well attended the guests barely made it past the foyer before they were met with the crush. At the last town house visited, a settee had collapsed beneath the weight of the four women who'd crammed themselves onto it. One of the women had refused to be treated by a doctor, claiming that she had to stay for the rest of the conversation.

It was obvious everyone was eager to be one of the first to hear the latest gossip on the art thefts, a feat requiring a good deal of cunning, coercion, and patience since no one could go so far as to come right out and ask. And of course no one had been forthcoming about anything they might know. But to the last, everyone seemed to be looking at one another an instant longer than was typical, as if they suspected the thief lurked in the very same parlor, right beneath their noses.

Savannah was squeezed so tight onto a settee between two puffy spinsters she feared their hostess would have to pry them all apart with greased tongs. The problem was growing exponentially with each of the tea cakes the spinsters devoured. The air in the room was wickedly hot and stale. Perspiration trickled down Savannah's back. She felt wilted, bored to tears, and emotionally wrung out.

Something about Snelling's look made her yearn to execute a smooth escape. Even a clumsy one would do. She spotted Dominic at the sideboard, bent in conversation with their hostess. What was her name again? She was quite young and very beautiful in an elegant willowy fashion so completely opposite to Savannah. When she spoke she touched Dominic on his sleeve in a way that made Savannah's nostrils flare.

"Didn't your father make his money in Chicago, Countess?"

"Yes, slaughtering pigs," Savannah replied into her teacup, distinctly not in the mood to play the tell-me-where-I-actually-stand-in-the-social-hierarchy-so-I-can-try-harder game with Snelling. The spinster on her right hiccuped and looked at her, horrified. Powdered sugar clung to the fringe of dark hair marking the woman's upper lip. Savannah looked at her with mock sympathy. "Oh, but nobody cares *how* you make your money there so long as you've got plenty of it. And to get any higher socially, you simply make more of it." Savannah smiled sweetly at Snelling. "Slaughtering more pigs."

The spinster on her left made a gurgling sound in her throat.

Savannah patted her arm. "There, now, they only

squeal for a moment and then it's over. By the end of the day, bacon."

The spinster lurched forward, gurgled again, fell back, lurched forward again, like a ship rocking with ocean swells, and finally with some assistance from several gentlemen managed to get to her feet. One hand clamped over her mouth, she fled the room. Dominic glanced up as she lurched past, then looked at Savannah.

Her heart did its somersault and stutter when he lifted a curious brow as if he knew she was responsible for the woman's sudden malady and in his own way appreciated it. Lips quirking, she glanced at Snelling. At once she realized she skated perilously close to making an enemy of him by not playing by society's unspoken rules.

After all, at their first meeting he'd been more than gracious and complimentary. Indeed, it was he who'd "made" her a heated topic of conversation throughout the Four Hundred. Wasn't he, therefore, accorded every right to remind her of who she was at their second meeting? Even insult her, if he so chose? She should be grateful for such attention.

Her spine prickled at the notion. So, she'd gone two steps too far in making it clear she cared very little for the games these people played. But she could hardly resist exploiting her "in" status in the face of all the droll drudgery and empty conversation and dancing around the subject that was forever going on at these affairs.

After all, being a product of Chicago, need anyone expect anything more of her?

She lifted her brows at Snelling. "Any news on the thefts?" She couldn't resist a sly smile and glanced around the assemblage. "Do tell me, are we all suspects?" To the last they averted their eyes, glanced at one another in horror, then bent their heads together to whisper. The spinster on her right wheezed, lurched off the settee, and took refuge in the corner of the room.

Undaunted, Savannah pressed on. "Mr. Snelling, surely Colonel Sharpe has his theories. I know you do."

With a flick of his hip-length cape, Snelling moved with the grace of a dancer around the perimeter of the chairs, pausing to refill his glass at the sideboard, glance at Dominic, and move on. He stopped when his arm draped over the back of Savannah's settee. His voice had dropped to a level that was inaudible to anyone but her, particularly since he spoke into his glass. "I've read the papers, Countess."

"Oh, but haven't we all? I must say there's something very telling about the pieces that were stolen and the people they were stolen from."

Snelling glanced up sharply at her. "Indeed, now there's a notion. And what might that be?"

"Something links them together. Perhaps the artist. I believe that link is a clue. Our thief was discriminating."

"Ah, you're a romantic, dear Countess."

"My theory bears scrutiny. Why would a thief go to Mrs. Cushing's second floor and risk being caught if there's a parlor full of art on the first floor—all of which, save for one, he decides to leave behind?"

"Because he's a reckless devil."

"Oh, yes, I'll give you that. But he also knew precisely what he wanted and it was on the second floor. I also believe the mystery goes beyond the actual paintings themselves. There is a deeper intrigue here." Savannah frowned. "I wonder if the police know that."

"You are singularly brave, Countess," Snelling replied, eyes glittering from beneath the rim of his chapeau. "Spouting theories to the police could make you a target."

"Target?" Savannah laughed. "Of what, pray?"

"Reputations in New York are guarded with fanatical determination, Countess. Some pay exorbitant sums to squash even the untrue rumors that could mark them."

"So you too believe the thief lurks somewhere in the Four Hundred."

"Imagine the murderous intent roused in men's breasts when they discover they've been branded a thief by one of their own."

"Murderous? Good heavens, if I didn't know better I might think you were trying to get me to stop asking questions."

Snelling smiled. "Why would I do that to you? Warn you, yes, I might do that. You see, I find that I like you, Countess. I want very much to be your friend."

"And I yours, Mr. Snelling. After all, you were so very kind to recommend James Atwood to my husband."

Snelling's chest jerked with a hiccup. "Known the man for years. Don't particularly like him but I help him . . . he helps me . . . businessmen helping each other, you see. I hope he can be of service to you, Countess."

"Castellane demands a level of exclusivity that can only be found by a man of Atwood's obvious connections. International, of course—"

"Yes, yes, nothing but the most exclusive there."

"Sotheby's, Christie's, Boothby's—"

"As I said, he deals with the most discreet."

"Discreet. Odd that you would use that word. Discriminating, perhaps—"

"Yes, that too."

"Hmm. And yet I can't help but wonder—being as curious as I am—how does one go about acquiring the very best in French and Italian art when the market is so hungry for it and the quantity, even in Europe, so scarce?"

Snelling leaned a fraction closer, scanned the room, and licked his lips as if savoring a delicious treat he wished to share only with her. "I will tell you a secret, Countess."

Savannah tried her very best to look demure. "Isn't that the reason everyone comes to these things? To hear all the secrets?"

"How delightfully naughty you are, Countess. I think you are far too clever a girl for us."

"Curious is all. I do love a good secret."

"Perhaps a bit more than you should, eh?" Snelling narrowed his eyes on her for a moment. "My dear Countess, if you were an art agent, a clever one, of course, because you must be very clever to be successful, wouldn't you make what you can find appear to be the very best in quality?"

Savannah's heart rate jumped. "You mean forgeries?"

Snelling snorted. "Do you think Atwood would risk dealing with anything but originals? The masses know how to detect an original Renoir from a fake. Entire four-set volumes have been written about detecting the fraudulent piece."

"Yes, of course." Savannah slanted her eyes at Snelling, noticing that he had again drained his glass. "Mr. Atwood only exploits the rich for what they don't know."

"I've seen great art agents commit professional suicide dealing in forgeries." Snelling's voice plunged deeper. "But consider this: It's the quality of the work that the eye isn't trained to see."

"Quality." Savannah repeated the word slowly. "What makes the art good or bad. And the Mrs. Cushings of the world want very much to be told what is good. They know no better."

"Pitiful, isn't it?" Snelling shoved his glass at a passing footman. "If you're pouring—another glass would be marvelous."

Savannah declined and waited for the footman to move past before continuing. "Someone could be sold an amateurish piece, believing it to be of the highest quality."

Snelling gulped his drink, closed his eyes a moment, then seemed to take an instant longer to focus on her. "My dear Countess, I know firsthand of entire collections of worthless oils painted by unknowns that were sold for fortunes simply because Atwood decreed them to be of the finest quality." Snelling glanced about, then leaned nearer and dropped his voice another octave. "Many of these pictures are among the most coveted in New York and hang in the most exclusive art galleries in Manhattan. I've seen one hanging in the great art gallery of Mr. J. P. Morgan himself. I almost peed my pants the first time I saw it hanging there right beside a da Vinci. I mean, good God, the thing had been in the bilgey bowels of an immigrant ship not two days before, a worthless piece of canvas."

"Immigrant ship," Savannah repeated, feeling a strange squirming sensation in her belly.

Snelling's grin twisted. "Do you have any idea of the collections the greasy rabble fill their little valises with, the pottery and sculpture and oil canvases they bring with them from their homelands? No clothes, no money, just this godawful junk."

"I'd imagine for many it's all they've left of their heritage . . ." Her voice trailed off. "Or their families."

Snelling waved his empty glass and leered at her. "It's a fortune begging to be made, a veritable import business all its own, what with the right connections in ports like Liverpool and London, the possibilities are endless."

Savannah blinked. "But immigrants would never sell their priceless mementos, no matter how desperate they might be."

Snelling looked at her over the rim of his glass. "Don't you think men like Atwood know that?"

Savannah frowned. "Do you mean to say he steals them?"

Snelling lifted innocent brows, then turned to the woman who'd appeared beside him. "Ah, our fair hostess, Mrs. Rush. With the brandy this evening, madam, you have quite outdone yourself. I do hope the thief is getting his share of it, eh, Countess?"

"Come with me." Dominic's voice shook the settee Savannah sat on like thunder rolling through the countryside.

She could hardly ignore or refuse the arm he held out to her.

"Looking well tonight, Castellane," Snelling observed, giving Dominic a head-to-toes sweep of his eyes. "So fashionably turned out for a man who's been moldering on his estates for a decade—oh!" Snelling plucked at Dominic's sleeve and preened. "I know someone you know."

For some reason this proclamation made Savannah's blood cool dramatically.

Dominic seemed disinclined to pause. "Is that so?"

Snelling tapped his lower lip. "But damned if I can remember who. They told me they'd met you in London several years ago. *Before* the scandal with the Prince of Wales."

"Ah," Dominic said, looking at Savannah for a brief but strangely compelling moment.

"I'll remember," Snelling said, as they turned to the door. "I always do."

"You're the talk of the party," Dominic murmured, steering Savannah by the elbow through the throng filling the foyer. He directed her behind a very broad woman in a tall feathered hat who was clearing a path toward what looked to be a ballroom. That room seemed as packed as all the others. "One of your victims got only so far as the potted palm in the foyer before she retched. She was shrieking something about Merriweather bacon."

"Poor thing. I hope she recovers."

"You should have told me you were suffocating in boredom, Savannah, before you resorted to torturing poor spinsters."

Savannah slanted her eyes at him. "Weren't you bored? Oh, but of course, you had Mrs. Rush to occupy you. I do hope she picked every little piece of lint from your sleeve before she turned you loose. There's nothing worse than a linty aristocrat."

"She's trying very hard not to be a frightened woman."

Savannah lifted her nose a notch. "Trying a bit too hard, don't you think?"

"This kettledrum was designed to show how unconcerned she is."

"About what? Ah, yes. Our thief. You don't suppose he's here, do you?"

"Mrs. Rush certainly hopes he is." Dominic jerked his chin at the uniformed policeman standing guard at the entrance to the ballroom.

Savannah raised her brows as they passed. "Imposing-looking fellow, isn't he?"

"There's another inside. By the windows on the far wall there."

Savannah looked above the throng of heads, spotted the policeman, then lifted her eyes. The walls were covered with artwork. "Stationed round the clock, I presume?"

"It's certainly meant to look that way." Dominic eased in front of her and moved deliberately through the room, his eyes scanning the paintings.

Savannah did her best to try to memorize what she saw. "If our thief is here, he won't be able to resist all this."

Dominic paused but didn't glance at her. "Resist what?"

"The lure. And I don't mean the paintings. To my way of seeing it, Mrs. Rush has virtually guaranteed that she'll be our thief's next victim."

"Is that so?" Dominic moved on.

"Oh, yes. He's a rascally fellow. If there's something here that he wants, these two policemen are only making him want it more. You know, Castellane, the lure to possess what has been made unobtainable."

"Ah."

"Of course, I could be wrong."

"Say that again."

"It certainly heightens the suspense. Why, it fairly dances on the air. And did you notice? It's past ten and everyone's still here. More are coming in the door. I think our thief has done the hostesses of this town a favor."

"Try telling Mrs. Rush that. Just this morning she was thinking about packing up and fleeing early for Newport."

"I hope she doesn't. This is just getting fun—" Savannah's voice caught a fraction. There, in the middle of the wall, was a small framed oil depicting the dark-haired boy, a peasant woman holding a basket of flowers, and a cow. Everything about the work was familiar to her, the colors, the lighting, the rendering, the splattering of dark spots. It was part of the continuing story . . .

Dominic moved on so decisively Savannah was certain he didn't see it.

When they'd reached the opposite side of the room, he paused and stared at the wall. Savannah stared with him. But try as she might, she could find no relation between any of the works here and the oils of the boy. Still, he lingered. She glanced right, fidgeted with a bow at the top of her dress, then caught sight of herself in a large mirror on the wall right in front of her. It struck her immediately that she was standing very close to Dominic and that he towered over her and looked very leonine, darkly fierce. Oddly intense, his eyes like steely pinpoints piercing through anything in their path . . .

Like her, he was looking into the mirror, but not at himself. And not at her. He was looking at the reflection of the oil of the boy on the opposite wall.

"Hungry?"

Savannah almost jumped. "I—well, you know—"

"Yes. I do. Let's go."

Savannah jerked awake. She lay on her back bathed in sweat, her nightgown plastered to her chest, her hair wrapped like a wet rope around her neck. Every sense was suddenly, brilliantly attuned. The house echoed with cavernous silence.

What had awakened her?

Damn. She hadn't meant to go to sleep at all, but they'd

had beef and wine and an entire box of French chocolates when they'd returned home and she'd indulged in more than her share of all three. Dominic had dismissed the servants, which had left them feeling very much alone at the big dining-room table with its lone candelabra. He'd poured and served and charmed her with lazy smiles and black-velvet looks and humorous anecdotes about the people he'd met that evening.

She'd forgotten all about the art thefts, all about coercing things out of Dominic, all about seduction, all about the injustice of loving a man who was quite possibly the last man on earth she should ever consider loving.

He was, after all, a sly, wicked man. She had a vague recollection of him carrying her up to her bedroom, undressing her, putting her to bed. He'd kissed her. They were long, lingering kisses, and she'd lain in her bed with the coverlet up to her chin and he'd leaned over her. She remembered looking up at him, murmuring his name, feeling warm and fuzzy with sleep and . . .

Oh, God. Had she told him she loved him?

She would have groaned but her throat was cottony dry and thick as pea soup.

The cherubs on the ceiling over her bed flashed with blue-white spasms of light. Savannah sat straight up. An instant later a low menacing growl of thunder rumbled in the distance. Perspiration trickled onto her lips. Her heart slammed around in her chest. Another spasm of lightning. This time the thunder shook the floor like the approach of an army of black-cloaked demons spiraling out of the sky.

She was suddenly cold, a quivering, bone-deep kind of cold. Her teeth chattered. No—she wasn't going to give in to this. She was a woman now. Women weren't trapped in childish fears. They didn't cower. They were pillars of strength in the face of all danger.

Lightning exploded through the room. Her scream was obliterated by the answering roar of thunder. She threw off her bedcovers. The floor was cold under her feet. She ran for the door. Lightning flashed and the floors seemed to tilt. She froze, squeezing her eyes tight, clutching her arms around her.

"No—no—*no!*" The roar was deafening. Wind howled. Rain pounded at the windows like furious ice pellets. The house started to shake. The spiraling demons were coming closer. She bolted for the door, yanked it wide, and stood paralyzed with terror. The foyer walls burst with ghostly light. Windows rattled as if shaken by an inhuman force, the demon trying to get in. Her terror was like cold steely jaws closing in around her.

She saw Dominic's bedroom door at the end of the upper hall. It was closed. He was there. He had to be there, not out, not creeping through Mrs. Rush's ballroom, hitting policemen on the head with gilded candelabras.

She started to run toward his door. She tripped on her nightgown and caught herself on the upper stair rail, half falling to her knees. A flash blinded her. The world exploded with thunder. Her legs, like thick blocks of ice, refused to move. And then she saw a man . . . silhouetted in lightning, standing at the window beside the front door, looking in, looking up at her.

Dominic. No. This man was too slight. Something about him . . .

Lightning flashed again. He lifted his face and smiled. Cecil Hyde-Gilbert.

Chapter 23

Dominic caught her up in his arms just as she slumped to the floor. "Easy," he said, rising to his feet.

"He's here—there—down there—"

There was a limpness in her, an almost eerie lack of fire and life in the way she felt in his arms. He might well have been carrying a sack of bones.

Thunder blasted through the house. She made a mewling noise, like a kitten's whimper.

"There's a cow in the attic"—she turned her face against his bare chest—"check on the cows, Dominic. They have no place to go."

Her nightdress was wet and cold, her skin strangely clammy through the cotton. Shivers wracked her in jerky spasms. He felt the dig of fingernails into his shoulder where she gripped with all her might. The whimpering continued, low and singsong.

Like an animal in a trap. A woman paralyzed with terror.

"The dust—I can't see through the dust—I can't see Papa—"

The change in her was almost incomprehensible. The

raw twist of feeling it stung him with was as foreign as it was consuming.

He turned toward her room, took a step, and she stiffened and cried out. "No—please—Dominic—not in there. Cecil will get me there—"

Cecil? Now he was certain she'd sunk into delusion. What the hell kind of madness had gripped her?

"Dominic—Cecil—Hyde-Gilbert—he's here—"

"And the cows are in the attic. Shh." With one hand he cradled her head close, felt the smallness of it, the rose-petal fragility of her, and turned to his own room. He drew up suddenly when a shadow blocked his path. Lightning lit up the hall. "Brunnie."

The maid blinked at him from beneath her nightcap. With both hands she gripped a robe closed over a bulbous chest. Worry tangled her brows. "Yer, lordship, I heard the countess screamin'. Is she all right?"

"I'll tend to her, Brunnie. But thank you. She would appreciate your concern." He took a step but the maid didn't move. She looked at Savannah. The faint singsong seemed to echo in the gap of silence left by the retreating storm. And between the whimpers came a muffled "Dominic."

" 'Tis the storm what woke me, sir," Brunnie said. "That an' the back door bangin'. Did ye not close it when ye come in tonight?"

Dominic had never been fooled by a blanker-than-blank look from a woman, especially one who could creep around upper halls and back stairs like this one. She knew he'd been out. No doubt she'd seen him come in. Unease began to fester in his stomach. "I closed it. Maybe the wind jarred it loose. Check the latch now when you go back to your room."

Brunnie bobbed her head. "Aye, sir, I'll do that."

Dominic watched her shuffle down the hall and disappear down the back stairs. The door banging open and Savannah muttering things about Cecil Hyde-Gilbert. He shrugged it off and continued to his room, shoving the door closed behind him. He didn't pause by a chair or his settee. He strode right to the bed, jerked back the coverlet, and tried to lower Savannah. She resisted, wouldn't let go of him, clung and twisted her body, wrapped her legs around him until he had to contort himself and stretch out on his side with her attached like a baby monkey, curled up in a ball against his chest.

"We f-found the cow in the attic." She blubbered. "It was my cow."

"I know. In the attic." He reached low, jerked the coverlet up over his feet, over the shoes he still wore, the trousers that were damp from rain and clinging, up and around Savannah. He flattened his palm against her back. Tremors still vibrated through her. His fingers touched her skin above the low back scoop of neckline.

"So cold, sweetheart." He pressed his mouth to the top of her head, smoothed that clammy band of skin on her back with the pads of his fingertips until it warmed. The eerie singsong continued.

"Go get the cows in the north pasture before it comes."

"I'll get them." He listened to rain pattering the roof and realized that he'd begun humming. It took him a moment to realize it was a song his mother had sung to him when she'd put him to bed as a child. He'd forgotten the words decades ago. He thought he'd forgotten the melody with all the other memories.

He couldn't remember ever singing or humming before in his life.

His voice snagged. Silence.

Her head tilted. Soft lips grazed his stubbled throat. Her arm slipped around his neck. Like butter warming, her body melted a fraction closer to his. "Don't stop, Dominic. Make it all go away."

What was a bit of sophomoric humming when he'd fell mountains to drive the demons from her mind and bring her blissful peace?

* * *

He thought she was sleeping. Moonlight spilled through
the sheer linen draping the bedside window and flooded
the pillow where blond curls lay like a tangle of damp
rope. The storm had cleared as suddenly as it had arrived.
The room was a quiet, moon-splashed corner of heaven.

"Sing something else." Her voice sounded small.

Dominic threaded his fingers through her hair in slow,
gentle strokes, nudging the tangles apart. "I don't remember anything else. I'm surprised I remember this."

"Then talk to me."

"Can't you sleep?"

"You're not."

No. Sleep was the very last thing Dominic wanted at the
moment. His mission of mercy was taking a dramatic turn.

She nuzzled his neck. "You smell like rain—and you
taste—" Teeth nibbled at his throat, tongue touched, lips
smoothed, soft body wriggled up closer, and Dominic's
body temperature began to inch up. "Horse." She tilted
her face up full into moonlight to look at him. Her brows
quivered. "You taste like horse."

"You've tasted horse, have you? Some delicacy in
France, no doubt." He pushed the heavy mantle of hair
from her brow. Her hairline sparkled with perspiration—
like dewdrops sprinkled from heaven. He pressed his
mouth there and tasted salt and lilac and warm woman.

"I can imagine what horse would taste like, yes." Her
toes wiggled down the length of his calf to his ankle. "You
still have your shoes on."

"Couldn't sleep—went out—" He brushed her lips
with his thumb, nudged them open, slipped his thumb
inside the rim of her mouth where warmth and sweetness
waited for him. He ached to pull her beneath him, crush
her into his mattress, bury himself in her velvety haven.
She felt like a gift he didn't deserve, or one that would be
yanked away from him long before he'd had his fill of her.

His lips brushed her nose, her cheeks. "Are the demons gone?"

"Are you telling me you want me to go back to my bed?"

His arm tightened around her before he could think to command it. Their bodies were hot, damp and steamy, pressed together from breast to thighs, cocooned under coverlet. "Just try to leave," he rumbled, cradling her head nearer. They lay still, hearts pounding out staccato rhythms, breaths coming uneven. He could almost have sworn there was magic in the moonlight tonight.

"I saw Cecil Hyde-Gilbert outside the front door."

"You also saw cows in the attic."

"But the cow *was* in the attic. The storm cloud blew it straight up from the north pasture and drove it headfirst into the attic. It's back feet were hanging out the side of the house. It died, Dominic. It was my cow."

"Just a dream."

Her head jerked back and she looked at him with fists braced against his chest. "It happened. And Papa was in the north pasture with the cows. I was running to the storm cellar with Mama. I heard the windows rattling and popping and then they started breaking. I saw three pigs go by. Glass went everywhere and Mama was screaming . . ."

"Shh."

"You don't believe me. It happened in Dogberg. The storm cloud flattened half the town. Molly Flannery saw the cloud and told me it was like a swarm of black devils spinning out of the sky. Big black devils with wings—I—I saw the cow and I didn't know where Papa was. I ran to the north pasture and I didn't see—I couldn't find—" Her eyes filled with tears.

"Christ." He cupped her face and kissed her eyes closed, kissed the tears that slid to her cheeks, kissed her lips. They felt hot and swollen. "Sweet Rosy, you found your father in that pasture."

"B-but not right away. It seemed like forever that I couldn't. I screamed and screamed—and out on the prairie no one hears you scream, Dominic. No one. The wind and sky just gobble it up. And now every time the thunder comes and the wind throws the rain around like tiny stones I think about that cow—I think about Papa in the pasture, rolled up in a ball in a ditch, crying like a madman when I found him. He told me he looked death in the eyes that day."

"Facing mortality will certainly change a man—make him do things he might not otherwise do."

"Soon after that he took the pigs to the railroad and went to Chicago. He came back home and said he was a millionaire. He said he could give Mama the things she'd always wanted."

"And he has."

"Yes—maybe he has." She paused, looked up at him. "Do you think I imagined Cecil? He was looking up at me and grinning his queer grin as if he conjured up the storm all on his own. Did you check the doors? All the windows? Are they secured?"

"If you want me to check them—"

"I—if you could—"

Refusing her anything would always rub instinct the wrong way. He slipped from the bed.

"Take this." She scrambled over to the far side of the bed, reached for something, turned, and held out a small table lamp to him with an earnestness that tore through him. "You might need it."

He hefted it as he might have a saber. "Right. Better to be armed."

When he returned she was sitting in the middle of his bed, a milky, moon-washed Aphrodite. Her hair looked like a riotous white cloud, her skin ivory as the finest porcelain. Embroidered red rosebuds dotted her nightgown and covered the row of buttons that ran straight up to her throat. The blue-white cotton billowed and clung as she moved, sat up straighter, eager. Through the sheer cloth he could see the outline of her nipples, the promising curve of full breast, plump hips, round thighs.

He suddenly felt as if he'd been gone for months.

"Well? Are we all battened down, safe, and secure?"

He put the lamp on the bedside table, slipped off his shoes. "Secure as we'll ever be."

"No sign of an intruder then?" Her smile was a slow, sweet promise. She looked up at him, touched the buttons at her throat with a hesitancy that screamed to be wiped away. No, he wouldn't tell her about the muddy footprints outside the front door.

Not yet. When she was frightened he couldn't think straight.

"I don't want to go back to my bed, Dominic."

"Then stay with me." He lifted a knee to the bed. The mattress dipped, he leaned over, crawled the short four feet toward her until he felt her warm breath on his mouth. "Stay, sweet Rosy—" He touched the top rosebud button, nudged it open, then another. He lowered his head, nudged aside damp cotton until his lips touched warm skin where a pulse fluttered like a trapped moth.

This changes nothing . . .

Oh, but if he could only believe that.

His fingers fumbled over the next button. His breath came in rasps. She murmured something soft and tender in his ear, threaded her fingers into his hair, the sweetest, warmest, loveliest thing he'd ever known. He could hardly believe the wonder of her.

Christ, why hadn't her aunt taught her anything? Why wasn't she playing the woman soon to be wronged, throwing tantrums and demanding marriage in exchange for her sullied virtue and carrying on with spoiled petulance?

He'd like it even better if she'd stomp around and throw things at him.

But hell if she wasn't making it torture to think about waking and not knowing she was beneath the same roof as he—even if she was in another bed. She asked nothing, demanded nothing, accepted him as he was, the impossibility of their circumstances as he'd laid them out for her and in doing so gave him the world.

His fingers trembled, fumbled again. "Christ—I can't— Maybe we shouldn't—"

She took his inept hand in hers. With a subtle shift of her weight, she reached low and lifted the nightgown over her head. It billowed to the floor beside the bed.

His breath drained out of his lungs. She drew his hand to one breast, pulled his head down to hers, and offered the sweetness of her mouth and body and unfettered spirit with wholesome honesty and goodness.

Like a wife . . .

She lay back upon the pillows, angelic in the moonlight, and he was breathless with the wonder of it. Had he spoken the endearment or merely thought it—wished it?

For this sliver of time she made him believe anything was possible. Anything . . . even abandoning a life's quest for a gossamer dream of love.

He gathered her in his arms and, with little preamble, slipped inside her. They soared to heaven and finally slept when dawn began to creep along the eastern edges of darkness.

"This just come fer ye, mum."

Savannah tried to open her eyes but thought the better of it. "What time is it?"

"Near te twelve noon, mum. Ye nigh te slept the day away, ye did."

"Noon?" Savannah blinked, focused on a secretary that was not hers, on the Prince Albert topcoat draped over the back of a wing chair, looked at the ceiling and saw no cherubs. She closed her eyes. "Where is my—Castellane?"

"Out, mum. Sit up, mum, if yer te eat. An' ye should."

"Yes. Yes, of course." Savannah shoved herself up,

clutching the sheet, but God knew why she bothered when Brunnie knew exactly what had gone on in this bed. What Brunnie didn't know was that Castellane was not hers and she not his and—damn, but she'd promised herself not to think about all that until she'd thought of a way to fix it. "What exactly did he say?"

"He didn't, 'cept that ye shouldn't be goin' out teday." Brunnie laid a tray over Savannah's lap and tapped the envelope beside a teacup. "Messenger just brought it fer ye, mum. Oh, an' here's the paper. Late teday."

Savannah gulped hot tea and wrestled with getting the paper open. "Shouldn't go out, is it? Curious request, don't you think, Brunnie? Why, if I were a man I would never think to tell my wife on a sunny spring day not to— oh, God."

The headline jumped out at her and instantly blurred. But she would remember what it said until the day she died!

ART THIEF STRIKES AGAIN.
KNOCKS OUT POLICE GUARDS IN DARING MIDNIGHT HEIST AT HOME OF KNICKERBOCKER CLUB PRESIDENT ARNOLD RUSH. MRS. RUSH TAKES TO HER CHAISE LONGUE FOR THE SEASON. FOUR HUNDRED IN PANIC.

"Mum? Is it the tea?"

Savannah looked blankly at Brunnie. "The tea? No, no. It's—the news. It always unnerves me."

"Aye, mum." Brunnie was looking at the headline until Savannah snapped the paper over on itself and reached for the envelope. Her fingers trembled. She avoided Brunnie's stare and said, "I'll call you if I need anything else, Brunnie."

"Aye, mum."

Savannah stared at the door when Brunnie closed it behind her. Reality was so damned painful to take after a night spent jettisoning through the heavens. Especially when one's jettisoning partner was a petty—

No. Everything about Dominic was noble and good. She wouldn't believe the worst of him even if it was shoved into her face. His cause was a worthy one. It had to be—or she'd never believe in anything again.

She tore into the envelope and flipped open the note. It was unsigned but there was a gnawing familiarity to the script, something about it that made her mind flit and fly.

> *Mortimer's Bookshop*
>
> *1 P.M. sharp*
>
> *if you want help with*
>
> *your predicament.*

Her heart lurched. Predicament? Did someone suspect Dominic? No, they couldn't—how could they?

But if they did, were they considering exposing him before he could complete what he'd set out to do? Was he to be thrown in jail, or worse, hanged for—?

"Oh, this is awful." She threw back the covers, found her nightgown under the bed, and slipped it over her head. She almost ran into Brunnie in the hall.

"I need a carriage," she said over her shoulder.

"Aye, mum—but, mum! His lordship said—"

"A carriage, Brunnie. And quickly."

"But—"

Fists tight with frustration, Savannah paused in her doorway and swung on the servant with teeth slightly bared. "Your situation and all you have, Brunnie, are because of me and my inheritance. Not Castellane. You'd do well to remember that."

Brunnie blinked and took a step back. "Aye, mum. I'll hire the carriage."

Savannah smiled and closed the door. It was indeed time she exploited her situation to its full advantage.

At five minutes past one, Savannah pushed open the door to Mortimer's Bookshop on East Forty-ninth. She nodded to the elderly shopkeeper behind his counter and proceeded down the first aisle, making an effort to swing her bustled skirts with more than her usual amount of shimmy. The rustle echoed so clearly off the walls even a passerby on the street would have known the sound had been made by a dress bought at Worth.

At the end of the aisle, she paused and glanced over her shoulder at the shopkeeper. He was watching her over the top edge of a book. She smiled at him, turned, and angled her cabbage leaf hat around the corner of the tall shelves. A well-dressed woman was standing at the end of another aisle ten feet away, reading. Savannah inched around the corner shelves and peered down the next aisle. Nobody.

Again she swished her way down the aisle. At the end, she encountered the shopkeeper again. She smiled, coughed into her glove, and quickly rounded the shelf corner. The woman was walking toward her. Savannah stared hard at her and knew she'd never met her. And yet the closer the woman came the louder Savannah's heart pounded. She paused to let her past, met her eyes, and smiled so hard her face hurt.

The woman scowled at Savannah's fuchsia and feathers ensemble and brushed quickly by without once meeting her gaze. Savannah lingered, thumbing through the volumes on one shelf as the woman paid the shopkeeper. The bell over the door tinkled as she left.

Savannah bit her lip. Was she too late? Had traffic done her in? Who the devil would save Dominic now?

Footsteps sounded, slow, measured, the tread too heavy to be a woman. A man. Savannah turned. The footsteps were from one—no, two aisles over. Should she wait? Should she run for help?

God, but she felt ill. Funny, how adventure wasn't so deliciously exciting when a man's life was at stake.

She turned and started down the aisle. Her heels clicked, bustle swished, heart slammed around in her chest. She turned the corner and ran smack into a man.

She jarred back, slammed a hand on top of her hat to keep it on her head, and gasped. "Good heavens, Charles!"

He looked at her as if he couldn't believe his eyes. "You came."

"Why, of course, I came. I thought—oh, no."

"You didn't know the note was from me?"

"I—" Her smile felt completely fake. "Why, yes, yes, of course, I knew it was from you. I recognized your handwriting immediately."

"We met here once. You remember, don't you?"

"Yes, of course, I remember. How could I forget? Are you—that is, you look older, Charles. Thinner. You've come back home to stay?"

"I couldn't remain in England. My father's business, indeed, my future is here. And you left me, Savannah."

"Yes—yes, I believe I did but you see that was—that was part of the plan."

"Whose plan? Dominic Dare's?"

Savannah breathed openmouthed for exactly two seconds. "Dominic who?"

Charles Fairleigh grabbed hold of her arm. His pleasant-featured face went cold as hundred-year-old gravestone. "Dare. The man who shares your bed. Do you remember him now?"

Savannah swallowed and attempted a lighthearted laugh. "Someone's been telling you tales, Charles. I'm a married woman now. A countess, if you can believe that."

"I don't believe it. You married an impostor—a brigand jewel thief and seducer of married women. He's wanted in England on those charges and one other."

"Another?"

Charles's face was grim. "Murder. He was seen leaving the Boothby offices of a man named Harrigan. Harrigan was found in his offices, stabbed. They found shoe prints. They saw a man who looks like Dare leaving quickly from Boothby's. With a woman. She had blood on her shoes."

"A woman?" Savannah's voice sounded breathless.

Charles's gloved fingers pressed hard into her upper arms. His chest heaved with every breath. Perspiration wove down his temples.

Savannah almost choked on dread. She felt the blood drain from her face and knew her eyes were huge. *He knew.* The fine, upstanding, people-we-don't-know Charles Fairleigh was holding her charade by the neck and he was damned angry. Thrown over. Jilted and left to rot in England. How was she going to right this? Good God, did that mean she was wanted for murder in England? *Pork Heiress Hanged as Murder Accomplice.* She could see the headlines now.

And then Charles yanked her against him and sobbed into her hair. "My darling, my dearest darling—"

Savannah blinked with disbelief as another sob wracked his slender frame. "Good heavens, Charles—"

"No, don't try to talk, love. I knew you didn't know you'd been duped. I told Hyde-Gilbert you couldn't possibly have been party to a masquerade of such gargantuan proportions. He's a man driven by hatred and revenge. I—I don't have a vengeful bone in my body."

"Thank heavens—"

"He told me to ruin you. I told him I couldn't—and why should I?" Charles drew back and cupped her face in his shaking hands. "You—my sweet innocent love, my bride, unsullied, virtuous in body and thought—this—this devil's spawn Dare played upon your naïveté, exploited your sweetness, your goodness, your desires to always do what is right, and somehow made you believe he was Castellane. He's using you in some wretched scheme, using your good name, your money, God knows what else. How easy you must have been to trick—"

"No—" Savannah pushed back so hard her hat slid half over her eyes. She shoved it back impatiently and stared hard at Charles, knowing she was about to destroy the illusion for him but unable to do anything else. "You're wrong, Charles. I did know. And I played willing party to it. I still do. It's not fair that I lie to you. I can't anymore."

Charles drew back against a shelf of books so suddenly he looked as if he'd been hit in the stomach with a lead ball. His face twisted out of proportion. He groped at the shelves and knocked three books to the floor. "No—don't tell me this—I can't bear to look upon you and think—" His eyes flew wide. "The murder—you're wanted along with him—"

She gave a swift and dismissing shake of her head. "He didn't kill Harrigan. Harrigan was his partner, Charles. Together they were going to expose someone very powerful, someone who was willing to kill to protect himself. Someone who was doing some very bad, very illegal things. I—" Savannah bit her lip. "I'm not quite sure yet what those bad things were except that I think—no—I'm almost sure it has something to do with stealing art from unsuspecting immigrants and reselling it—"

Charles closed his eyes as if hearing such a tale brought him torturous pain.

Savannah grabbed his arm and squeezed. "—No, listen to me, Charles. I know how this sounds—at least I can imagine how it must sound to you. Quite impossible and far-fetched, but you must know that I wouldn't be party to something if I didn't believe deep in my heart in the goodness of it."

He stared at the floor. "What goodness comes of deceiving everyone who loves you?"

Savannah felt her heart twist. "Don't think I'm not burdened by that."

"I hope they forgive you—for your sake. Because when

he's finished using you, this Dare will leave you with nothing, Savannah—nothing but scandal and disgrace. I hope then you'll have your family beside you. You'll need them."

"He's not—he's not like that."

"You know him that well, eh?" Charles swiped the back of his sleeve over his mouth. "You love him, don't you?"

Savannah looked down at her fingers twisting in the bow at her waist. "I believe I do."

Charles's laugh was cutting. "So did Bertrice Hyde-Gilbert and he used her for her jewels, for all her knowledge, and to escape his prison. The women in London society loved him, and you want to know what he did with them? Used them good and well, to the last. According to the people I spoke with in London at the *Times,* he left a half-dozen women on the verge of suicide when he vanished. One claimed he'd fathered her babe."

Savannah shrugged. "Mere exaggeration. It happens here in the papers all the time."

"Exaggeration? It seems while in London for a brief several months he got himself invited to all the right parties, attended all the season's events on the arms of the most sought-after young women, became a regular at Boothby's auctions, at all art events, became a great patron of artists and art connoisseurs, and in general insinuated himself so deeply into the fabric of English society that to this day they speak of him as if he were one of them."

"Yes, he does that remarkably well."

"He stole Bertrice Hyde-Gilbert's necklace."

"I'll never believe that. Good grief, Charles, everything you're saying—it all fits. Dominic Dare has devoted his life to this. Everything he does, everything he is, is for one purpose and one alone."

"Nothing can justify criminal acts."

"I've yet to be convinced he's done anything illegal. But

you want justification for a life's obsession? What about family, Charles? What about avenging the loss of your family and retrieving the only thing that remained of them? And if someone exploited that loss—in a vile, criminal manner—wouldn't you do anything you could to make it right?"

Charles looked up at her. His face looked weary, haggard. "I would never hurt you, Savannah, not for anything on God's earth. I could never do that. And Dare will. Mark my words—if he's not stopped first."

"What?"

He tugged his suit coat together, jerked his neck up from his collar, and straightened his tie. "Be careful, Savannah. I would ask you to come away with me—from all this—the inevitable scandal. I could provide for you— give you a home, a good name, forgive you your—your indiscretions."

"Charles—"

He closed his eyes, slowly opened them. "No, I know you wouldn't. You were always much—much stronger than I was. Perhaps you still are. Indeed, I do hope that you are."

"Is—" Savannah swallowed. "Cecil Hyde-Gilbert has come to New York, hasn't he?"

"I wouldn't be surprised."

"He's come to ruin Dominic, hasn't he?"

"No. I believe he's come to kill him. And I'm not inclined to disagree with him. Good day, Savannah." Charles touched the brim of his hat and left her.

Chapter 24

The building was like every other artist's studio on Tenth Avenue. Rickety and badly lit, it reeked of oil paint, pigments, and turpentine as if it had been steeped in a mixture of all three. Dominic climbed up two flights of stairs, two at a time, and proceeded down a long hall to the last door. He checked the scrawl on the note he carried against the number on the door. He knocked. Waited. Silence. He knocked again and listened to his teeth start to grind. He'd spent the better part of the day trying to find this studio and its occupant. It had required scouring the Artists' District and a good deal of bribery.

Against his better judgment he'd left Savannah at the town house. But what he had to do had to be done, and done alone. Besides, he suspected Hyde-Gilbert's intention for now was merely to scare them, if indeed he had arrived in New York. He wasn't a real threat, at least not yet. But time was the enemy now.

Answer the goddamn door.

A sudden hail of Italian curses sounded from behind the door. Dominic closed his eyes and felt an overpowering sense of relief. His smile felt odd on his face. He rapped again with his gloved knuckle.

"Open the door," he barked with mock severity. "Open it now, dammit. I don't have all day."

Something thumped. A curse vile enough to curl hair sang on a deep vibrato and then the door burst open. A man faced him square. Bare toes poked from beneath clothes that were paint-splotched and sloppy. His white hair flew every which way. His face was worn and whiskey ruddy beneath its five days' growth of grizzle. In one hand he carried a half-empty liquor bottle by the neck. With the other he was pointing a very large rifle at Dominic and looking crazy enough to use it without a whisper of provocation.

He was exactly how Dominic remembered him.

They'd all been like him, Dominic's father perhaps more than the rest, too eager to take up their weapons against insurmountable odds, too willing to die for their causes. They'd been rebels, every last one of them. And here stood the last of those great, foolish men.

Dominic's voice snagged. Memory overcame him. For an instant he was back in Florence, at the Café Michelangelo, crawling beneath tables and between easel legs, nestling himself against the knees of the most gifted Italian artists of the century, the Macchiaolli. He'd been naive enough to believe he'd one day be good enough to be one of them. "Silvestro—"

The man jerked the bottle to his lips, poked out his gun a little harder, and frowned at Dominic as he would have a stranger. He saw everything with a sweep of his eyes, no matter how bleary and bloodshot they looked.

Silvestro Lega, Italian painter extraordinaire, sole survivor of the political upstart Macchiaollis, his father's best friend and compatriot. He snorted at Dominic as if he'd labeled him a worthless rich man. "What the hell is this?" he snarled in heavy accent. He jerked his head. "*Va via!* Get lost!"

Dominic shoved his hand in the door to keep it from closing in his face. He pulled his top hat from his head, pressed it to his chest, and looked deep into the tortured eyes of memory. *"Sono Domenico Darinello."*

Lega went absolutely still. His lips repeated the name silently. Bleary eyes pulsed a fraction wider, narrowed, and memorized as only a master's could. His mouth fell slack. The bottle crashed to the floor. Whiskey splashed Dominic's trousers. Glass splintered in all directions. The nose of the rifle tipped down as if the arm that held it suddenly lost all strength to lift it. "Nino?"

"Sì."

"Not my little godson—" Lega's chin wavered. He swiped his forearm over his mouth and blinked. "Y-you look like your father did when I first met him. But you are a ghost."

"I'm no ghost, Silvestro."

"You disappeared. We thought you were dead."

"They didn't kill me, Silvestro."

A moment passed. "Y-you ran away, eh? Like me? After all the killing, after you found your mama, your papa—"

"Yes. I came here."

"You are lucky to be alive after so many years in New York. It was not easy."

"I didn't expect it to be."

Lega stepped aside and swept a hand with great flourish. "Come. You must come in. You will excuse. I have no woman to clean for me."

Dominic moved into the small studio. Canvases littered the floor, cluttered easels, and lay in heaping piles. He paused before one, a brilliant rendering of a beautiful black-haired woman in her bath. Lega's wife. Dominic remembered her sitting at his mother's table, drinking red wine and laughing deep and husky and vibrant. She'd died the same way his own mother had, in a hail of gunfire and swipes of banditti blades.

"I went to Paris," Lega said, closing the door. He scooted past Dominic, tossed the rifle on a chair, and slanted his eyes at Dominic. "Was not loaded." He pushed rags from another chair onto the floor. "You were a boy running to a new life. Me? I was a coward. I hid in Paris, afraid the banditti's men would come for me. I painted in closets for fifteen years, afraid to show my face to anyone until the American came and promised to make me a rich man in New York. You see how rich I am." The words were almost spat. One fist shoved toward the ceiling. "I do not require much. But this man—he is *mascalzóne*."

"*Sì*. New York is full of scoundrels."

"Sit. I will get more whiskey. And you will tell me why you've come here."

Dominic waited until Lega returned and handed him a smudged glass. He swirled the whiskey around. "I need your help, Silvestro."

"*Sì*." You know I will do anything for you."

"I was hoping you'd say that. James Atwood. He commissions all your works. He was the man who found you in Paris."

Lega's wiry brows shot up. "The American *bastardo*? You know him, eh? Did he cheat you too?"

Dominic snorted into his glass. "He stole from me."

"You know this?" Lega puffed up his chest. "Then like a good soldier you must kill him."

The whiskey lit fires in Dominic's chest. "It's not enough anymore that I know he cheated me. I thought it would be enough. I was wrong. I have to convince others. I need proof. Something tangible—something more than instinct—something—" He clenched his fist with frustration, then shoved it into his outer hip pocket and withdrew a folded paper.

Lega watched Dominic unfold it. "That's blood," Lega said softly.

"Yes." The stains were deep purple, soaked through

half the crumpled page, obliterating all but the first letter
of the customer's last name, a scribbled, illegible signature
and the city of destination: New York. The bill was a
carbon copy of an original. "My friend Harrigan worked
for Boothby's in London. He was murdered for what he
knew about an international black market art ring. He was
holding this bill of shipping in his fist when I found him.
With a knife in his chest, he dragged a file full of them on
top of himself to find this one. I think I know why. You
see this letter here? 'A.' The signature? It's a clue, Silvestro. Harrigan was telling me who murdered him."

Lega began to shake his head slowly. His eyes filled
with doubt. "You have a woman, Nino? A woman helps a
man keep his mind."

Dominic's lips softened as he lifted his glass. "I have a
woman, Silvestro. A beautiful woman."

"The only kind to have. You love her, yes?"

"*Si.* So maybe I am a little crazy. Hell, I wish I didn't
have any of this hanging over me. I almost wish I'd never
walked down Fifth Avenue that day—hell—it must have
been fifteen years ago, but it feels like a lifetime ago. I saw
one of Papa's paintings hanging on the wall in some rich
man's parlor. Right there—I could see it—through the
window of his brownstone. My fingers burned to touch it.
It was raining. I remember the rain on my face and I knew
what had happened to all his paintings. They were stolen
from me, Silvestro, before I even arrived in New York, the
satchel full of them, all taken from me. They were all I had
left of my parents, the only things I took with me from
Italy. They were Papa's masterpieces. I vowed to spend
the rest of my life trying to get them back and finding the
man who stole them from me. Harrigan was helping me."

Lega let out a ragged breath and shook his head with
disbelief. "Your papa would have been a rage in Paris
with them. He would have been internationally famous."

"Oh, but he is." Dominic snorted. "He's as famous in
New York now as da Vinci." Dominic stared out the win-

dows at a wall of brick on the building next door. "There are times when I wish to God I'd never started this, never felt it was my duty to recover what belonged to my family. I've become what I said I would never become again. I never should have involved Harrigan in London—but then I never would have found her." He shook his head, stared at the floor. "Christ, but I wish I could be with her with peace in my soul, not this rot—I choke on it—" He closed his eyes and forced the breath from his lungs. "I'm sorry—"

"No." Lega's hand was firm on Dominic's shoulder. "You must never be sorry for feeling anything. Some men live without feeling anything for anybody and they die empty men. Do not worry. I will kill him for you."

Dominic laughed softly and covered Lega's hand with his. "No, Silvestro. *I* want to get the man. I want him to know I got him. I want him to see my face in his mind every day when he wakes up in a jail cell. Do you understand?"

"*Sì.* But you will still need a soldier's help if they try to put you in jail first, eh? Come. Your beautiful woman, she will not wait forever for you."

"Thank you, Jarvis," Savannah said to the servant as she entered the town house. With a frayed sigh, she pulled her hat from her head, paused, and glanced from the door's side windows. It was hell to feel as if someone followed you. Her eyes hurt from probing behind the glass of every passing carriage. Hyde-Gilbert lurked out there somewhere, plotting his next move. It made her want to be held in strong arms, against a warm, hard male body where comfort was just a heartbeat away. "Has Castellane returned?"

"No, madam."

Her eyes suddenly felt hot. Despair was harder to put off when she felt so tired. "I'll be upstairs in my—"

"Madam. The Countess Beaupre awaits you in—"

"Savannah." Maxine appeared in the parlor door. She looked as elegant, cool, and unruffled as a duchess in tall feathered hat and a narrow sheath of a dress that made her look seven feet tall. Perhaps a bit too cool. The arm she extended to hold her parasol tip to the floor seemed too straight, too strained. Her rouged lips looked a bit less full, a bit too pinched. She glanced at the servant. "Thank you, Jarvis. The countess and I will be in her bedroom." She swished past Savannah and headed straight up the stairs.

"I feel as if I'm about to be scolded," Savannah murmured when she closed the bedroom door behind her.

"Scolded? Hardly." Maxine tossed her parasol one way, her hat the other, and swung around so hard her skirts swished back and forth for several moments. "If I'd flown I wouldn't have come quicker. You look tired. Here." Maxine thrust a folded paper at Savannah. "What do you make of this?"

Savannah glanced at the scrolled *Town Topics* above the headlines and worked the buttons of her gown loose. "Ah, the venerable Colonel Sharpe is sinking his editorial fangs into some poor unsuspecting soul today, hmm? Who is the wretch?"

"Your husband."

Savannah grabbed the paper. "Oh, no. Where is it?"

"Top middle column. In bold letters. Even the blind couldn't miss it."

Savannah's heart felt as if it would rip through her chest. She could hardly breathe. And then she saw it. And closed her eyes.

"Read it."

"I don't want to read it."

"What are you so afraid of? You used to harbor nothing but contempt for Colonel Sharpe."

A bilious lump of dread and grief almost choked her. The end. That's what she was afraid of. The end of a love affair. The shattering of a dream. Paradise cut into ribbons by the hatchet pen of a mean-spirited editor. "All lies—" she whispered.

"It says the Countess Castellane has stolen the very heart of the Four Hundred. That's quite true. You can hardly deny it. It also suggests—though it doesn't say precisely how—that the Earl of Castellane seems to have undergone a most dramatic transformation in the past few years. While the rest of us have grayed and spread and wrinkled, has he perhaps grown less in years but more in stature, and hair? Odd, don't you think?"

Savannah dropped the paper and swung around so that her aunt wouldn't see the tears forming in her eyes. The fingers tugging at her buttons blurred. "Lies, I tell you. Someone hates Castellane."

"Quite obviously. They're suggesting, my dear, that he's not who he says he is."

"Does Colonel Sharpe say that?"

"He doesn't need to. The power of suggestion is legendary in the Four Hundred. It's almost better not to come right out and say anything. Although Sharpe does promise that more will be forthcoming."

Savannah stared at the oil painting on her wall. Her chest heaved. "Who would do this?"

"You want my guess? It could be anyone. But to name a few? Why not the jilted would-be lover—what was his name?—Bernard Wilton? With Castellane ruined, you would be ripe to fall into his arms. Then there's the decorator, François, the one Castellane threw out of the house. I have it from Mrs. Cushing that he can scarcely breathe at the mention of Castellane's name. He's lost half his clients because of his ill humor. Of course, Templeton Snelling thinks it's his duty to slander the upstarts. And then, if I remember correctly, your very own father wasn't all that enamored of Castellane—until that incident at the Patriarch Club. He told me very little about it except to say that Castellane saved his life."

"Yes, he did," Savannah murmured, remembering all

too well the chilling look on Tweed Black's face when he realized he'd been outwitted by Dominic. Had he later recognized Dominic as the one young man arrogant enough to refuse his offer of employment? He would have known then he was an impostor earl.

"It seems he's made few friends," Maxine mused. "Of course, this could merely be sport for some bored socialite with nothing better to do. God, but don't I know there are women like that out there."

A knock sounded on the door. Brunnie poked her head and a tray of tea around the door, then blinked at Maxine. "So sorry, mum, I dinna mean to disturb ye."

"Set it on the secretary, Brunnie." Savannah watched the servant with a gnawing suspicion. Cherry cheeks and a starched apron had concealed many a twisted, conniving, traitorous spirit. Had Savannah been conscious of guises when she'd soared to the heavens in Dominic's embrace? Had she cried out his name once, twice, a dozen times? She'd never know. A servant listening at the door, lurking in the hall, would have much to report to the malicious Colonel Sharpe for even a small token of thanks.

Or had she merely been listening too long to her mother?

The door closed behind Brunnie. Savannah felt as if she might vomit. She swallowed and began to rebutton her gown, quickly. "He has to be stopped. I need—" She turned, paused, her mind flying, and then she ran to her secretary. There, in a small gilded box, she found the watch pin her father had given her, the same watch pin Dominic had run into a burning stable to save for her. She curled her fingers around it and reached for her hat.

"What the hell are you doing?"

"Don't tell me no, Aunt Maxine."

Maxine grabbed her by the shoulders just as she was about to head for the door. "Look at me, Savannah. Tell me. You're in love with him, aren't you?"

Savannah pushed out her chin. "Quite desperately, if

you must know. I'd sell my soul to Colonel Sharpe for him. I'm going to find him and bribe him not to print another word."

Maxine looked stern, then let out a swift breath. "Well, I'm not going to let you do that. And I'm certainly not going to let you pawn this watch off for nothing so that Sharpe can laugh at you."

"You can't stop me. I won't let you."

"Stop you? My dear, I'm going to help you. I'm going to get you some money."

"What?"

"And lots of it. Sharpe's silence won't be bought for mere pennies, you know." Maxine scooped up her hat and parasol, then arched a brow at Savannah. "Good God, don't cry. This is fun—a bit crazy—particularly since I think there's a good deal of truth behind all this—but hell. What good are two dead husband's fortunes if a woman can't do anything adventurous with it?"

"I adore you," Savannah said, grabbing her aunt's hand.

"And I adore you, my dearest niece. Let's hurry. Luncheon at Delmonico's lasts only until three and I'm certain Colonel Sharpe is there. We don't want to miss him."

Silvestro was doing his rousing best to champion rebellious artists' spirits everywhere. Shouting curses in a voice that echoed to the second floor of the building, he stalked around Atwood's gallery consumed in a temperamental fit. When he threatened never to paint again, Atwood's voice leapt two octaves. When he started for the door, Atwood commanded his guard to block the way and stay there. When Lega then suggested he might make far more under a competitor's commission, Atwood roused into a pleading frenzy that would have been the humiliation of him had any outsider paid witness to it. But his anxiety was understandable. Judging by the ledger Dominic held up to the light of a small window, Silvestro Lega had been responsible for making James Atwood a very rich man over the past several years.

That and the sizable import business he did beneath the very noses of the New York customs officials. Atwood was as meticulous with his records as he was with his studio. It was all there, every shipment from London and Liverpool that had been snuck past customs, every inventory item catalogued by description and with no value assessed to any of them.

Stolen? Without question.

Liverpool. Dominic lifted his head and watched dust dance in a shaft of late afternoon sunlight. The ship he'd fled Italy on had docked in Liverpool before continuing on to New York. He'd discovered his satchel missing somewhere in the middle of the Atlantic.

He looked again at the inventory lists. Each shipment was authorized by one particular agent at Boothby's, a name Dominic recognized from his discussions with Harrigan.

So Atwood had an international conspirator in thievery and customs evasion. Illegal though it was, it certainly wasn't enough to get Atwood imprisoned for murder.

A confession would be nice. But how to do it? Only desperate men confessed. Only desperate men acted guilty.

He tore several pages from the ledger and folded them into his inner topcoat pocket. He turned to the wall of file drawers and began rummaging. In a small drawer he found bills of lading, filed in numerical order. In moments he located what he'd come for: the original to match the carbon that Harrigan had been holding when he'd been stabbed. The customer name was clear: James Atwood. The signature matched. Dominic stared at it for a moment, then a host of doubts flooded his mind.

What if he was wrong? What if Atwood was the wrong man?

He tucked the page into his pocket and moved quickly

to the back stairs. Here the voices from below echoed clearer. Lega was still swearing and Atwood was promising to increase his commission by five percent. Yes, Atwood was desperate to keep Lega to himself, desperate to hold on to his reputation. Without it, who was he?

Lega snorted another curse. "I will think about that. And I leave now. Move your man from the door."

Dominic snuck down the steps, his boots barely whispering a sound on the wooden treads. Before the bell over the front door quit tinkling, he'd disappeared out the rear door and around the side of the building. He found Lega awaiting him half a block north, standing in front of the brougham.

"I do good job, eh?" Lega preened, tugging his broad-brimmed feathered hat lower over one eye and showing a leg in a jaunty bow.

Dominic touched his fingers to the brim of his hat. "I am in your debt, Silvestro."

"Bah. I am thanking you. I get five more percent. Maybe I will have enough to get a good woman. What you do now?"

"Force his hand. If he's my man, he'll take the bait."

"You go talk to him, then? I come with you."

"No, Silvestro. Anonymity would serve me best at this point."

Lega smiled, white teeth dazzling in the sunlight. "You write him letter, *sì*?"

"I'm thinking about it."

"You tell him he is going to jail for cheating everybody he meet—" Lega paused midsentence, his attention, like Dominic's drawn to the black hansom cab pulling strangely close alongside their brougham. The windows were draped in black. Odd for a cab, almost as if its occupants wished to travel in secret.

Dominic watched the door start to open before the carriage had slowed to a stop. Something struck him very strange a millisecond before the muzzle of a pistol slid through the door.

He shouted and dove toward Lega. And then the world exploded with gunfire.

Chapter 25

Colonel Sharpe's hangdog eyes, droopy mustache, and gentlemanly accoutrements could easily mislead the naive and unsuspecting. The educated knew better.

Exuding buoyant animalism from every pore, he conducted his daily business at his table at Delmonico's. His appetite was not at all diminished by the suffering and penance in which he dealt, and his customary lunch included six mutton chops, two heads of lettuce drenched in dressing, a basket of biscuits, a quarter of a chocolate cake, two bottles of vintage champagne, and a dollar cigar. He always carried a Scotch fir walking stick, a weapon that would have floored a mule, and claimed that his ambition as editor of *Town Topics* was to become the guardian of society's manners and morals. Spreading scurrilous gossip, and employing all manner of backstairs spies to dredge it up, was for the sake of the country, by God.

After all, only that sort of bloat could convince the charming but penniless young cousin to sell out his rich relatives down the block. With the common good at stake, and a few dollars for their efforts, the footman, steward, and scullery maid could easily find themselves peering from behind the hedges of formal gardens by moonlight, the better to catch the illicit, the scandalous, the stuff that makes for increased circulation, titillation, desperation.

"So, our most recently landed aristocrat sends his woman, eh?" Sharpe puffed up his mustache with jerks of his mouth. "Damned English are all cowards." He looked like a fat walrus as his pudgy fingers turned the beaded purse over and over again on the table. He hadn't opened it since Savannah had put it there. But those droopy eyes would judge from years of experience and know that the bills stuffed inside were many.

"Castellane doesn't know that I'm here." Savannah sat on the edge of a chair, spine rigid, feet tight together, reticule empty now, Maxine waiting for her outside. She'd insisted on doing this part of it alone. She wanted to look into the eyes of the man who threatened to ruin her for the second time. She only wished she trusted herself not to lose control and spit on his white linen tablecloth.

"What is it you wish to buy, Countess? It *is* Countess now, isn't it? Lady Castellane. And how handily that was done. I remember it took over two hundred thousand to forgive your father's sin. What will it take now?" Sharpe tipped the purse upside down. Bills spilled to the table. He sifted through them, brows registering faint appreciation.

"That's enough to buy me an invitation to Mrs. Astor's annual ball," Savannah said through her teeth.

"Fifteen thousand? Perhaps. But silence, Countess, does not come so cheap, particularly with society's interest so keen. I've never seen the Four Hundred so taken with a couple. It's the title, of course. Castellane's peculiar reputation. You. The fool your father made of himself. You see, Countess, anything that beguiling is just begging to be ruined."

Savannah thought she would vomit when Sharpe showed long yellow teeth in a grin. "Mr. Sharpe, take this money and forget whatever stories you've been told."

"I'm afraid that's impossible."

Savannah gripped the corded lacings of her reticule so tight the muscles in her arms strained. The words stuck in her throat like thick glue until she choked them out. Bargaining with this man went against every instinct and conviction, against the fiber of who she believed herself to be, against everything except the one defining ray of hope inside her: her love for Dominic. "How much more will it take?"

Sharpe chuckled and leaned back in his chair with a look of undiluted pleasure. He motioned a waiter, ordered another bottle of champagne, and looked at Savannah with hands folded over his belly. "Typically—" He shrugged as if he'd shrugged like that, in this exact situation, at least five times a day. "A hundred thousand."

Savannah felt herself turn green.

"But for you—" Those lazy eyes traveled a slow and consuming path up the front of Savannah's dress and stopped where the fuchsia feathers crisscrossed over her décolletage.

Savannah slammed her hand down on top of the bills and started to get up. Sharpe slammed his hand on top of hers and shoved his face so close she could smell the stench of cigar on his breath.

"Let go of my hand," Savannah growled very softly.

A spark lit Sharpe's eyes. His voice was a thick snarl. "I've never been adverse to making a deal, Countess. If it's the right deal. Negotiation is the heart of my business. Ask any number of the women in your new circle. Ask them what they've done to keep their husband's illicit assignations—or, God help them, their own—out of my column and thus preserve their gilded reputations. Their husbands don't give them access to the kind of money it takes to silence the poison pen. And most of the men would refuse to pay it. It's the women who live and die by what I write, Countess. So for them I negotiate." He leaned a fraction of an inch closer. "Delmonico keeps a room for me here. You understand."

Spit congealed on Savannah's tongue. "Any negotiation I do involves only money."

Sharpe's eyes delved into the feathers. His tongue flicked at the corner of his mouth, like a salamander's, and Savannah's stomach heaved.

She jerked her hand. He clamped harder.

She bared her teeth. "You're quite mistaken about me. I don't give a damn about my standing in society, Colonel Sharpe. I've never lived and died by anyone's opinion of me."

"Then why the hell are you here?" Sharpe squinted at her. "Not some damned selflessness for the husband, is it? Never heard of such a thing. You intrigue me, Countess."

"Good. Then negotiate on my terms. Give me two weeks."

Sharpe smirked. "Two weeks. Then what?"

"Then you can print every piece of fact or fiction that you have in your hands involving me or Castellane."

Sharpe retreated slowly back into his chair, then laughed, a full, from the pit of his mutton-engorged belly kind of laugh. "Sorry, Countess, but that's just not good enough."

"No?" Savannah withdrew the final weapon from her empty arsenal. It was a hell of a gamble. It was her only option. "What if I promise to solve the mystery of the art thefts for you?"

"You'll what?"

"You heard me, Colonel. Think about what it would do for your circulation if you were to beat the police and every other daily in reporting it all."

"What the hell kind of mystery are you spinning, Countess, or do you play some game? An adventuress's game?"

"I wish it were a game, sir." Savannah clamped her hands on her purse and shoved up her chin. "Indeed, I've lost all taste for adventure. We have an arrangement then?"

"How can I resist?"

"Indeed. Why start now? Good day, sir."

She left the money lying on the table. Twenty minutes later Maxine's victoria pulled in front of the brownstone. Savannah alighted, bade her aunt good-bye, and hurried up the steps.

"There's a brougham parked in front, Jarvis," she said upon entering. "Do we have visitors?" She froze and stared at the servant. "Good heavens, I'm not supposed to be at home today, am I? What day is it—oh, hell, I really don't care, if you must know."

"Er—madam, you're not at home today to visitors."

"Thank heavens."

"It's the doctor, madam."

"The what?" She blinked at Jarvis, looked up the stairs, and felt as if the floor fell out from under her feet. Hyde-Gilbert was in New York, with every intention of killing Dominic. "Dominic—"

"I beg your pardon, madam—"

She ignored Jarvis and flew up the stairs, skirts hiked past her knees so she could run faster. Crimson spots dotted the stair treads. They continued through the upper hall in a zigzag path that ended at Dominic's closed bedroom door. The spots blurred before her eyes. Blood. Dominic's blood. She gripped the banister.

God, but she was so terrified of losing him before—before she told him—

She ran toward the door, tears flowing like water gushing from a spigot, words blubbering from her lips. "Dominic, please God—"

The door flew open. She saw a red shirt—or was it a white shirt soaked with blood?

"Savannah."

She ran toward his voice and then she was in his arms,

crushed against his bloodied shirt and the warm, vibrant body beneath it.

"Y-you're alive."

"What the hell? Yes, yes, I'm fine. Where the hell have you been? I was about to send Jarvis out looking for you. Damned Brunnie for letting you leave. Wouldn't tell me where you'd gone—refused to speak to me."

"I was—I was—out—"

"Why the hell don't you listen? Christ—you're crying."

Her fists pounded gently against his shoulders. "Of course I'm crying. I thought you were dead."

His hand smoothed the back of her head for several moments. "You would—" His voice seemed to catch. "You would miss me, Rosy?"

She looked up at him, face blotchy, eyes swollen, nose dripping. Her lips trembled open. "I believe I would—a little."

His eyes darkened. "Just a little?"

She drowned in the heady huskiness of his voice. His finger was tender beneath her chin, his mouth touching hers warm with comfort and promise, and she clung to him as if a wild wind raged around them, threatening to tear them apart.

"Er—your lordship—"

"Yes." Dominic lifted his head, looked at Savannah a moment, swallowed her hand with his and turned to the young man standing beside his bed. The man had Silvestro's blood on his shirt and a black bag in his hand. He didn't look seasoned enough to be saving lives and extracting bullets, especially when he glanced at Savannah, blinked, and smiled as if he'd never seen a beautiful woman in his life.

"My wife," Dominic said, hearing the sheepishness in his tone and wondering where the hell it had come from. He sounded like a—like a—

Did he sound like a man in love?

"Mr. Lega shouldn't be moved, sir."

Dominic looked at Silvestro lying on the bed, his eyes closed as if he slept peacefully. His muscled chest with its furring of white swelled above the wrapping of bandages and looked damned capable of taking an army of assassins' bullets. It was the chest of a soldier. "Yes, Doctor, of course."

"He'll need round-the-clock tending, particularly through this first night. If he lives 'til morning, I'll have a better chance at prognosis. The bullet carved a nice hole in his chest, just missed his heart. He was a lucky man."

"Damned lucky," Dominic said softly.

"I gave him a dose of morphine that should last him the night. But he shouldn't be left untended."

"No. Absolutely not. I intend to stay with him. And if he begins to stir, if there's a fever, I'll send for you."

"Yes, please, you must. I'll return in the morning to change his bandages and give him medication." The young doctor closed his bag, shrugged into his coat, took up his top hat and bag, and stepped past them. He paused at the door and looked at Dominic. "I assume you intend to notify the police."

"I—yes, yes, of course."

"Whoever it was who shot him wanted to kill Mr. Lega. I'm certain of that. Good day to you, sir. Madam." With a tip of his hat, he left the room.

"Dominic—"

Dominic moved to the bedside. "He's my godfather. And I nearly got him killed."

She moved up behind him, took his hands in hers, and laid her head against his back. He didn't know how long they stood like that, him looking at Silvestro, hating himself for throwing this man into it all. She said nothing, did nothing but warm his back, and somehow, in some magical way, it seeped through his skin and touched the pain.

A short loud knock came on the door an instant before it banged open.

"I'm here fer ye, Nino," the brawny Irishman yodeled. "Came as soon as I got yer message."

Dominic barely glanced over his shoulder. "Bonnie."

"Here."

Dominic turned in time to catch the rifle Bonnie tossed at him. Savannah registered it all with a gasp and a shrill "Those are guns."

"Indeed, madam." Dominic hefted the rifle to his other hand and caught the pistol that was tossed to him. "Bonnie O'Fallon, my w—er—my—this is Savannah."

Bonnie slapped a paw on his cap and slid it off his head. A red eyebrow quirked up with blatant admiration, and he seemed to shift the rifle slung over his shoulder a little higher. "I couldna be more pleased te meet the lady what sent the clothes an' furniture te the tenements. Yer an angel o' mercy, Countess. Barnabas O'Fallon is me name. But I give ye leave te call me Bonnie, Countess."

"Countess, my arse." Savannah folded her arms over her breasts, pursed her lips, and looked at each of them as if she knew instantly that they'd been friends for a lifetime and that no secrets could exist between them. Finally she lifted a stern brow at Dominic. "What the devil is going on?"

Despite all his reasons not to, Dominic had to smile. Anger did fabulous things to her eyes, the color of all that skin, and made him want to yank those ridiculous feathers from her dress.

"I've come te protect ye," Bonnie boomed with a grin. He reached inside his secondhand, ill-fitting Prince Albert coat and withdrew a bottle. "Brought us some Irish whiskey, Nino." He handed Dominic the bottle and smiled wolfishly at Savannah. "Had a devil of a time with yer man downstairs when he saw me."

"And little wonder," Savannah said, brows still low, arms still folded. "Poor Jarvis. You look like you're ready to defend a fortress."

"If need be, my dear." Dominic moved to the window

overlooking the street and nudged aside the sheer drapery.

"He's not out there," Bonnie muttered, fiddling with his rifle. "No coaches anywhere on the block."

"Who?" Savannah moved beside Dominic. "It's Hyde-Gilbert, isn't it? He shot Mr. Lega. He meant to shoot you."

Dominic looked down at her. Fear seemed to have pulled her skin tauter over her cheekbones and taken the bloom of roses from her cheeks. Her teeth were caught in her lower lip. Like a child's. His blood fired with a need to protect her, to take every ounce of fear from her, to take her to places so far from here. He brushed his thumb over her brow and murmured, "You're so very certain, are you?"

She swallowed and hugged her arms closer around herself. "I am. I saw Charles Fairleigh today. He warned me that Cecil had come to New York."

"Charles, eh? Begged you to run away with him, did he?"

She gave him a look of such swift and complete exasperation he was convinced beyond a doubt that Charles didn't own an inch of her heart. God help him, but he felt as if he grew in his shoes.

"Listen to me, Dominic. He said Hyde-Gilbert didn't come to ruin you. Dominic—" She laid a hand on his chest where Silvestro's blood had already dried. "Charles said Hyde-Gilbert means to kill you."

"Ah." Dominic frowned from the window.

"That bullet was meant for you, wasn't it? You knew it when it happened. You knew I saw him last night."

"I did."

"Don't you know that I'm never scared when I'm with you? You could have told me."

"Where I come from, a man is a man with his woman. He protects her from everything that could harm her."

"Damned backward thinking," she muttered, angling

her chin down, her eyes coyly up. Burnished lashes curled clear to her eyebrows. A corner of her mouth twitched upward and warmed him to the tips of his toes. "It's that kind of attitude that keeps women in subservient roles, Dominic."

He tipped up her chin and looked stern. "It also keeps them alive. Sorry, my dear, that kind of thinking is in my blood. I can't change it."

Her expression softened dramatically. "No," she murmured in husky tones. "I wouldn't want you to change a thing."

A crisp knock sounded on the door.

"There are too many people in this house," Dominic muttered.

Bonnie yanked open the door.

"Madam!" Jarvis poked his head around the door. His face was white as the celluloid collar shackling his neck. "Good heavens, you're still alive. I thought he'd—he'd—" Jarvis shot Bonnie a look that would have wilted a hothouse full of flowers. "He looks every inch the savage, madam. And the guns—do forgive me."

Savannah gave the servant a smile that would have reassured the worst kind of cynic. "I understand, Jarvis. This is our good friend Mr. O'Fallon. He's to stay with us for—a while. As will Mr. Lega until he recovers."

Jarvis barely gave Bonnie's grin and bow a notice. "As you wish, madam, but I have another matter—" Jarvis jerked his hand and produced a scruffy, red-cheeked Sam from behind the door. "I found this in the kitchen, madam."

Savannah smiled. "Hullo, Sam."

Sam flushed red, looked down, into one corner, then the other, and mumbled something that sounded like "hullo."

Dominic nodded to the servant. "It's fine, Jarvis. He's with Mr. O'Fallon. If he's hungry—"

"Hungry?" Jarvis scowled. "Never seen a child eat like

this one. Well, then, if we must. But Cook will not be pleased, madam."

"Oh, Jarvis." Savannah walked slowly toward the servant. "I'd appreciate that you not speak of any of this to my parents." Her hand swept the room, encompassing Bonnie, Lega, the arsenal of guns.

"Madam?"

"I wouldn't want them to worry unnecessarily, as they surely would." Again she smiled.

"Of course, madam."

"And send Brunnie to my bedroom, if you will."

"Yes, madam. If I can find her." He slanted reproaching eyes at Dominic. "Scared the life out of her, sir, with your yelling."

"I'll be sure to apologize," Dominic replied, raising a brow at Bonnie.

The servant left and Bonnie followed after him, glancing between Savannah and Dominic and muttering "I'm a bit hungry meself."

"Watch the back," Dominic called after him. The door closed with a thud. From his post at the window, Dominic watched with hungry eyes as Savannah moved to Lega's bedside. She pressed a hand to his forehead. It was a gesture so female, so maternal Dominic was struck by the poignant yearning it roused in him. Yes, she had a way of bringing out all his base desires, particularly those he didn't know he had.

He watched her. So many things to say and yet he couldn't think where to begin. Perhaps because the time wasn't yet right. Not now. Not yet. The feelings going on between them were so new, so fragile, so easily destroyed or tainted beyond repair. He wouldn't risk anything so precious. One more thing to do and a lifetime quest could be put behind him. Then—then the future would be his to mold, the woman his.

He would do it right. The prize was well worth the wait.

"The Nesbit masked ball is tomorrow night." She didn't look at him. She was staring at the circular blood-stain in the middle of Lega's bandage. "With Silvestro here—I don't suppose we'll be going, of course."

"We're going. Silvestro won't die. I won't let him. Besides, Hyde-Gilbert poses no threat to either of us in a Four Hundred ballroom. It will be as impenetrable a fortress as we could hope for."

"When will you go after him?"

"After tomorrow night. And then the hunted will become the hunter."

"Tomorrow night." She paused. "I'll get you some tea."

He met her halfway to the door, blocking her path. "You know I don't drink tea."

"A glass then?" She looked up at him, eyes wide and shining unnaturally. "For your whiskey?"

"The bottle will do tonight." He tried to swallow and couldn't. The sound in his ears was his blood rushing through his veins. He'd never felt so alive, so tangled, so on the verge of self-destruction—or was it the destruction of his future that he could feel . . . even as he vanquished his past? "Listen, dammit—"

She twisted out of his reach. "I have to talk to Brunnie before she tells the whole world—"

"Since when have either of us cared about the rest of the world?" He tossed the rifle onto a chair, advanced two steps, and grabbed her by the upper arms. "Goddamn you, don't turn away from me!" He caught her by the jaw, forced her eyes to his, her mouth open. He yanked her against him and his body went up in flames. "You're all I want," he rasped, lowering his head, needing to feel the soft warmth of her mouth under his.

She went unnaturally stiff and averted her face. "Do you believe that, Dominic?"

Anger boiled in his blood. "Christ, but no other woman—nothing has existed for me since the day I met you. You've possessed me. I lie in that bed and smell you in my skin and I go out of my mind. You know I do. Dammit, you know—"

"Yes. Yes, I know. I know your obsessions only too well." Her mouth tightened. "Odd, but you sound rather unhappy about it. Muddling things for you, is it?"

"If I were to let it—yes."

"Plans all awry?"

"Hardly. I'm almost finished."

She looked at him with a forthrightness that screamed for a confession from him. A moment passed. His chest ached.

"Please finish," she whispered, gripping his arms with a strength that startled him. "Do whatever you must but finish it. Make it all go away—quickly—and then—" She swallowed. "And then you can."

"No." This time he didn't let her avoid him. He couldn't. His mouth crushed over hers, devouring, possessing, promising the world to her. His arms couldn't hold her close enough, tight enough. He mumbled incoherent promises, Italian love words, and sank to his knees, half dragging her with him. He tasted feathers, satin, warm skin scented with lilac water, and felt his world tip.

"You must be mine." He was powerless with her. "Mine." His breath fanned hot and fast on her breasts. His fingers trembled and touched the soft skin above low neckline, touched, rubbed, spread, squeezed. Great tremors shook his body. Perspiration trickled from his brow, onto his lips, her skin. He was consumed.

He would never leave her. He couldn't. He'd die in prison before he'd leave her to anyone else.

"My God, Dominic." She sounded as breathless as he. The hands at his shoulders weren't pushing, they were tugging, closer, harder.

Callused fingers twisted into feathers and yanked, hard, curled between satin and skin and tugged the fabric down to her navel.

"Dominic—"

"I have to—I can't help myself—" He twisted his fists into the plumage of her bustle and panted against the divine heaven of her bare bosom. Her skin was meant for his mouth alone. The pain engulfing him became exquisite. "Rosy—what in God's name have you done to me?"

"I know—I feel it too. I know—"

A groan sounded from the bed.

"God almighty!" Dominic looked up at the bed, then at Savannah. His mouth was dry, slack. His heart thundered like a charging brigade in his chest. He felt as if he'd walked ten miles, dragging his gaping soul along with him. "I'm sorry—"

She pressed shaking fingers to his lips. "No. Please don't. I've never felt such—such—" She seemed unable to catch her breath. "It was almost too much."

"Yes. Almost." He stood, helped tug up on her bodice, and shoved a hand through his hair. What the hell was wrong with him? Forgetting Silvestro. Christ. He'd have made love to her while the man struggled for his last breath five feet away.

"Here." He picked up the feathers and handed them to her as if there were any purpose to them now. His brows tangled. Another moan from the bed brought his scowl into a permanent spot. "I've Silvestro—"

"I know. You have to tend to him. Nobody else can do it for you." And then she cupped his face in her hands and lifted her mouth to his in a soft, openmouthed kiss. "I'll be downstairs." She left him then, closing the door gently behind her, and he drew a chair beside Silvestro's bed, intent on keeping this solitary soldier, the last vestige of memory, alive.

Chapter 26

At just after midnight, Savannah gave up the impossible fight to find sleep, grabbed her robe, and left her room. She went to the kitchen to boil water for tea. Bonnie sat alone at the table, rifle slung over his shoulder, eyes closed, snore buzzing softly.

"Don't worry," she said, touching his massive shoulder. "It's me."

His behemoth body jerked. One leg kicked the table. "Aye." He growled, blinking up at her. "Countess."

"Hardly a countess, Bonnie, and we both know it. Tea?" She moved to the stove.

The glass on the table slid. "Not with me whiskey."

Savannah lit the flames beneath the kettle, found a basket of crusty bread under a napkin, and took the chair facing Bonnie's. When her eyes met his he looked away and started to get up. "Best man me post."

"Please, talk to me. You know him so well, far better than I do."

"I—er—" His smile crinkled his eyes. He hesitated, then settled again in his chair. "Aye, miss, I've known Nino for over twenty years now. We shared a ship, miss.

From Liverpool. I taught him how te fight. He taught me how te pick locks an' pockets an' steal food. He saved me life. I'll never be able te repay the debt."

"I don't believe he wants repayment." Savannah tore off a bit of crust. "The friends he has—they're all from long ago."

"Like a family to him, miss. The only family he's had fer most of his life. An' he's always had an intense attachment to family. It's the reason behind everything he does, miss."

"But he refuses to embrace anything but his past. He's closed himself off to everything but that. It's consumed him. Not one of his close friends is a recent acquaintance."

"Savin' yerself, miss."

Savannah smiled wryly. "I feel very little like his friend, Bonnie." She sighed and looked at the candle burning low in a lamp on the table. "I know so little about him and yet it's enough. His spirit, what makes him who he is, it's so powerful, so strangely compelling I'd do anything to—to help him. I have this in-my-bones kind of belief in him, as I suspect you do."

"Aye. I'd put me life in his hands."

"Oh, yes. It's quite beyond anything I've ever known."

Bonnie's lips twisted up. "Aye, miss. I believe he feels the same about you."

Savannah went completely still. Their eyes met.

"Y-you're a loyal friend, Bonnie. Thank you for being here."

"Aye, miss. Ain't nobody gettin' past Bonnie O'Fallon. Now, if ye don' mind, miss—"

"Yes, of course." Moments later she left the kitchen, tray in hand, and climbed the stairs to Dominic's room. She touched the edge of the tray to the door and it swung open. A lamp burned on a bedside table, throwing soft light onto the bed and the hulking male frame sprawled in the chair beside it.

She stepped over Dominic's extended legs to place the tray on the bedside table and glanced at Silvestro. His face shone with a thin sheen of perspiration. Beneath her fingertips his forehead was cool. She lifted the sheet, checked the bandage, and let the sheet fall gently back. He had the seasoned face of a warrior, lined and rugged. She imagined he'd been devilishly handsome at one time. His hair was a wild white cloud fanned on the pillow. He looked more soldier than artist, headstrong and restless even as he slept.

She knew she would like him very much. She liked all the people in Dominic's circle, even the butcher she'd never met, Herman Shnable, the man with the delicious lamb. A man's friends said so much about him, their loyalty to him even more.

A broad hand curved around her waist, tugged gently, and she turned into Dominic's lap.

"Silvestro's sleeping peacefully," she murmured.

"You brought me something," he said. His voice was sleep-husky, his body warm almost to the point of being hot.

"Yes." She glanced at the tray but he was fiddling with the buttons on her nightgown, not the buttons at her throat. The buttons farther down, where the vee in her robe gaped open. "Warm milk," she said, threading her fingers into his hair as he tugged loose the belt knotted at her waist.

"Just the way I like it." Her bare breast was in his hand, the nipple in his mouth with startling ease. His passion hadn't suffered in her absence. There was every bit of the savage simmering in him now as there'd been earlier, when he'd unleashed himself on her, dropped to his knees, and begged her.

She'd do anything for this man. Her heart ached in her chest. But would she be given the chance? Hours of tossing in her bed had brought her to the same, frustrating conclusion: If she told Dominic what she knew, what she suspected of him, the paintings she'd seen in his studio, would he trust her with it? Or would he vanish, thinking to protect her, save her the pain and embarrassment, and all her dreams vanish with him?

"Dominic—"

"Mmm." He lifted his head. His finger traced up the remaining buttons he'd left buttoned, clear to her throat. "I don't like this. Too many buttons. Too much fabric. Not enough of you." He looked up at her. Candlelight played in angled shadows over his stubbled jaw and threw his eyes into darkness. And then he murmured something and rested his forehead against her chest.

Tears sprang into Savannah's eyes. His heart beat against hers in frantic, tragic rhythm. "Dominic—there's a way—I—" His fingers touched her lips, rubbed, parted, touched her teeth, her tongue, spread and engulfed her jaw then her throat, her neck, and down the row of buttons.

"There's a place in Florida," he murmured, looking up again at the buttons with a strangely compelling concentration. Slowly he began to push each button through its loop.

Savannah felt the lump in her chest move up into her throat. God, he didn't want to know anything. He didn't want her to spill any of those wild, reckless thoughts she'd had, and some of them had been of the two of them fleeing before the whole thing blew up in their faces.

But how could she ask him to forsake something that he'd devoted a lifetime to? It was as much a part of who he was as the artist within him.

She'd change none of him.

And no, perhaps just like him, she didn't want to face the horrible realities yet—not now, or this haven of warmth against the world would vanish.

She couldn't leave it yet—not yet.

"A friend of mine," he said, "an artist, went there. He's written to me about it. He has a studio in St. Augustine."

Savannah forced out her voice. "I've heard of it. The Four Hundred winter there at the Ponce de León Hotel."

"Yes. There's a group of artists that have studios at the Ponce de León. But it's not there that I'm interested in. It's north of there—up the St. Johns River. It flows for four hundred miles." He spread his palm against the base of her throat, fingers stretching along her collarbone.

A nudge of his hand and the nightgown whispered open, laying her bare to her waist. "I—" Savannah swallowed deeply as he pushed the gown off her shoulder and pressed his open mouth to her skin there. "Where does the St. Johns River go?"

"Nowhere. Everywhere." His voice breathed heat onto her skin. "A riverboat steamer can take you as far as you wish to go, deep into the swamps, beyond the towns and large estates of the rich, beyond the orange groves, deep into the tropical vegetation—as far as the ocean." He lifted his head and looked at her body with such unbridled reverence on his face Savannah had to close her eyes and gulp back a sob. "I would paint you on the sand, in the ocean, just as you are—my sweet beauty—"

"Dominic—"

"I will make love to you with my eyes if I can't any other way."

Savannah felt weak everywhere.

"I will make you mine, Savannah."

"I am yours." She held his face between her hands. "I want to see that river—I want you to take me there with you—I want—" The tears came again. She bit her lip, looked away, swiped a hand over her cheeks. "God." Again she closed her eyes. "You have to stop that."

"I told you." His voice was muffled against her neck, his tongue dancing gently over her skin. "I can't help myself. What else am I to do with my mouth? Ah—" He cupped a hand around her head and brought her mouth close to his. His eyes glittered with the light of an ocean full of stars. "I could kiss you until the sun comes up. Could you kiss me until then, sweet Rosy?"

"And do nothing else?" Savannah traced her thumb over the contours of his mouth. "Yes, my love, I could do anything with you, even the impossible."

"That sounds like a promise."

"It is."

A moment passed. Silvestro groaned. They both looked at the bed and froze. He mumbled something, twisted his head, opened his eyes, and looked right at them.

"Good heavens," Savannah whispered, gripping at her nightgown.

"Wait." Dominic covered her hand.

Silvestro frowned, blinked, and his eyes swept closed. An instant later the room filled with the sound of his deep even breathing.

"Damned old soldier."

"He'll be recuperating for some time, won't he?"

"Several weeks, I'd guess."

"Hmm." Savannah touched her fingertip to the base of his throat, where his shirt lay open over his skin. "He'll have much to say."

"Say? About what?"

"Oh, I don't know. He'd have much to tell me about you." She rubbed her finger into his skin, angled her eyes up at him through the curtain of her hair. "I can be extremely persuasive."

"Charm the vows from a priest," he rumbled, looking at her mouth.

"Yes, but from you?" She lifted a brow, a corner of her lips. "I don't ask much."

"No? Maybe not with words."

"And it will keep your mouth busy, unless you'd rather sleep."

"I want you here with me."

"I want to stay. I—I can't sleep without you."

"Good." He angled his chin at Silvestro. "What would you ask him?"

An almost childlike joy leapt in Savannah. It was the joy she remembered from early Christmas mornings. A new-found joy of discovery. With hands that seemed to tremble, she drew her nightgown together, snuggled deeper into his lap until her head rested on his shoulder. She wriggled her bottom against his thighs. "First, I have to get comfortable."

"I don't think I like this."

"You want me to move?"

"No, no. I want you right where you are."

"Tell me when your arm is asleep."

He grunted and drew her closer. One hand reached low, lifted the whiskey bottle from the floor, and tipped it to his lips. He drank long and deep.

Savannah watched the flame in the bedside lamp. "I want you to tell me about your life in Italy, when you were a boy."

"It will bore you."

"Never."

"I've forgotten most of it."

"No, you haven't. I want to know where you lived, who you lived with, who you loved." She glanced up at him. "The woman you first made love to."

"She was a prostitute. My uncle paid her to teach me. I was just thirteen. Enough?"

"See there? You're already remembering. Tell me what you did, how you met Silvestro. I want to know the home you had there. Will you tell me—even if it takes until morning?" She blinked at the candle and felt her breath catch with anticipation.

His breath came out in a long sigh. He pressed his mouth to the top of her head and murmured, "Yes, Rosy, for you, anything."

* * *

Savannah jumped when her bedroom door burst open. "Damn," she said.

"All right. I think it's high time you tell me what the devil is going on."

Yanking up on her skirt in one hand, Savannah tried to bend over and peer under her secretary. She threw a smile at her aunt that felt as if it tore through her face. Anxiety did awful things to a girl. "I dropped an earring and I can't bend over in this thing. Do you see it?"

"I'll get it." Maxine closed the door behind her, swished across the floor, and with an uncommon grace scooped up the pearl bob. "Ah," she said, drawing the earring just out of Savannah's reach. "Not so fast. I have a few questions that need answers. I just met a street urchin eating chocolate on your new sofa and a giant of an Irishman armed to every one of his big white teeth. He's below, you know."

"Yes, I know."

"Pacing holes into your parlor carpets. Bonnie. Is that his real name?"

"Barnabas O'Fallon. He's a boxer." Savannah gave another game smile and reached for her earring. Again it was lifted just beyond her fingertips. Savannah sighed. "If I start to tell you anything I'll be late for the Nesbit ball."

"Must be quite some story."

"You wouldn't believe half of it."

Maxine's smile oozed experience. "Don't bet on it."

Savannah tried to look grim. "Castellane will be furious with me if I'm late."

"Gobble you up, will he? Here." Maxine stepped close and inserted the bob in Savannah's ear. "My, but you look lovely. Gold—yes, we were right to think it suits you. You'll glow in that ballroom like a torch. And this mask is absolutely perfect."

While Maxine admired the gold sequined and feathered mask Savannah had chosen for the evening, Savannah glanced almost distractedly at her gown. It was a whimsical tulle-over-taffeta concoction, shimmering with a dotting of sequins over the outerskirt that bustled high and swept in a fan over the floor. The underskirt was so narrow she could scarcely take full steps. The whole thing fit like a gold glove, suitably insufficient through the bodice and held up by thin straps that dipped behind clear to the middle of her back, proving beyond even a Puritan's doubt that she wore nothing beneath the dress. Elbow-length gold gloves, the mask, and a gold lace fan completed her ensemble.

At the couturier's shop in Paris where they'd found the dress, Savannah had been tickled almost silly at the thought of wearing such a scandalous concoction. Maxine, ever eager to indulge scandal, hadn't been able to deny her. "I thought it would be appropriate, considering the rumors."

"An excellent choice. Give them a little more to talk about, eh? Particularly when I suspect they think they've scared you into hiding. That's my girl." Maxine cupped Savannah beneath her chin and lifted it. "You look as if you didn't sleep last night."

Oh, but she had. Sometime after darkness had begun to fade she'd fallen asleep listening to Dominic's deep voice, cradled in his arms. She'd awakened alone in her bed just after noon.

"Not lagging in spirit tonight, are you?"

"Uh—no, never that." Nerves drawn taut as string over a bow, but not lagging in spirit. Savannah's lips twitched her smile felt so fake. Her voice sounded a pitch too high. "I'd wager you wish you were going. It's the event of the season."

"And leave all this mystery behind? Never."

Feeling Maxine's unwavering stare, Savannah glanced in her mirror and began tugging up on her bodice. She didn't look golden, she looked as if her blood had been sucked out of her face and throat. She looked scared out of her mind. "It's a wonder the whole affair wasn't canceled. Mrs. Nesbit has one of the largest collections of artwork in New York, second only to J. P. Morgan. An irresistible lure for our thief."

"Perhaps, if he's reckless as the devil."

Oh, but he was that and more. Her eyes looked enormous, her lips white-pink. She sank her teeth into them, hard.

Maxine moved behind her, tucked a stray curl into place, cupped her shoulders, and donned the lofty air of a socialite with expert ease. "But, my dear Countess, a woman of the Four Hundred will risk her entire art collection to prove she can reign supreme as queen of party favors. I hear from Mrs. Cushing who heard from her maid who was told in greatest confidence by Mrs. Nesbit's steward that the favors are solid gold miniature oil paintings. Even I have to admit it's awfully clever, considering the recent thefts."

"Clever. Yes, very clever."

Maxine covered Savannah's trembling hand with her own and squeezed. "What did you need?" she asked softly. "You know, I can never resist one of your secretive little summonses."

Savannah made a great show of flapping open her fan. "We—uh—" She turned to her secretary, dabbed a bit of lilac water at her ears where the curls fell from high on her head. She spoke very quickly, as if that would help deaden the impact. "We have a patient here who needs tending while we're out. He was—he was shot."

A moment passed. Savannah fiddled with her fan.

"I see. Not by the Irishman."

"Good heavens, no. His name is Silvestro. He's in Castellane's room. He's an artist."

"Not another one. A friend of Castellane's, is he?"

"An old friend."

"Bonnie as well, I suspect."

"Yes." There was nothing more to fiddle with except her hair. She poked, tucked, smoothed, looking very concerned at her reflection in the mirror, feeling her aunt's stare like two hot pinpoints of light on her. "The doctor's been here. Changed his bandage, gave him some laudanum. He seems to be doing well—but someone needs to be here if he wakes or a fever—"

"I understand."

"We won't be late."

"It's a wonder you're going at all."

Savannah looked sharply at her aunt. "Castellane cares a great deal about Silvestro."

"That's obvious. He also cares a great deal about this ball. Why, I wonder—"

Savannah waved a hand and picked up her mask. "The rumors. We have to go."

"Of course. To defuse the rumors."

"Precisely. Besides, if we don't make an appearance we'll be off everyone's guest lists for the rest of the season."

"And we can't have that."

"That's exactly it." Savannah turned to brush past her aunt but Maxine grabbed her arm. Savannah looked at the corner, unable to meet her aunt's eyes, afraid that she'd start to cry out of guilt.

"Savannah, if you're in any danger you must tell me."

"Oh, God—not me—don't worry about me. Please—I know I'm asking a great deal of you—especially since you helped with Colonel Sharpe—and I'm so grateful but you must"—she looked at Maxine—"you have to trust me. I'll be safe."

"With Castellane?"

"Especially with him." This time when she tugged on her arm and turned to the door, her aunt let her go.

Chapter 27

The streets for three blocks surrounding the Nesbits' pa-
latial home at the corner of Fifth and Sixty-third were
jammed with arriving carriages and the gawkers who came
out on such occasions to gape at the arriving guests. Had
Dominic been alone in the carriage with Savannah, he
would have found the delay in traffic a welcome interlude,
the calm before the storm.

But they weren't alone. Stuyvesant and Penelope Merriweather had joined them for the short eight-block ride,
which was seeming endless. The brougham was stuffy,
Penelope's inane chatter well beyond annoying and her
perfume suffocating. She talked as if she didn't care who
listened, about other women mostly, and all of it snide
gossip. Beside her on the seat opposite Dominic, Stuyvesant had taken the easy way out and was pretending to
doze. His chin had sunk deep into his starched white cravat.

Savannah was staring out the window. She'd been doing a great deal of that since her mother had proclaimed
her dress an abomination and an insult to dressmaking
everywhere.

Dominic had quite the opposite opinion of the dress. His inability to show the depths of his appreciation was part of his problem. The rest of it had to do with his business tonight—and his festering need to be done with it.

He felt a trickle of sweat work down his temple, looked at Savannah, and found her hand buried under her skirt on the seat between them.

He took her fingers in his. Penelope's chatter droned into the distance. Impatience squirmed in his gut. Or was it unease, the kind that takes slow but infinitely deep and inextricable root? Again the questions poured into his mind. Was he tempting his good fortune? Why not end it now? Call it off before he buried himself so deep he'd never get out.

Because his prize was in reach, everything he'd sworn to recover—all of it—and it could be his. If he didn't see this through, Atwood wouldn't get his comeuppance. It would all have been for nothing. His vow of revenge to a dead father, worth nothing. His pride—

Savannah glanced over at him. Her lips curved and he saw faith there. Beneath her skirt, her fingers squeezed his.

Christ, but he had all the prize he could want in this woman and her belief in him. How the hell had he managed to accomplish that?

The brougham door burst open. A path lined with expectant faces of the want-to-bes led to the grand entrance. Dominic wondered if anyone else felt the sizzle in the air. He started to get up, hesitated, looked at Savannah, and felt his world tilt. He'd give it all up for her. All of it. He'd relinquish who he was, a lifetime of vengeance, the legacy of his family—his stupid pride—all of it.

The realization left him feeling as dry-mouthed and green as a thirteen-year-old boy.

"We won't stay long," Savannah said, looking up at him

and giving another trembling smile. "Will we, Castellane?"

Christ, but the power of a woman's faith and a smile was staggering. She made him believe he could vanquish the world's armies single-handed. When he looked at her, he began to think he could have it all—and that she'd be right there beside him while he did it—and after, when he paid the inevitable price.

She made him believe there was a way.

"Not long," he replied, taking her hand and slipping on his black mask.

They made their way through the inevitable process of presenting invitations to footmen and the energetic crush in the foyer to the grand ballroom with its gilt cornices and crystal chandeliers. An orchestra's music filtered through the din. A Viennese waltz. Dominic spotted the musicians on a floral-draped balcony overlooking the circular dance floor where couples spun past. At the front of the long room two women dripping enough diamonds to light up the city sat on a long divan scattered with red silk cushions, overseeing the festivities from behind elaborate diamond-studded masks. From there they dispatched gold-liveried footmen to pick out a guest honored with an invitation to join them on the Throne.

Mrs. Nesbit and Mrs. Astor, no doubt. The sultanas of society. To be invited to sit beside them was the reason most women attended such functions. It put a stamp of cast-iron approval on a woman.

Dominic glanced over their pompadoured heads where their tiaras glittered like lighthouses over the assembly. The walls were all lined with tapestry. No art.

As expected. Silvestro had said Mrs. Nesbit's art was in a private gallery on the second floor. Locked, if she was wise.

"There are more than four hundred people here," he said to Savannah.

"Four hundred is the capacity of Mrs. Astor's ballroom," Savannah replied. "Mrs. Nesbit obviously means to outdo every hostess this season even with attendance. Oh, yes, please." She took the champagne flute Dominic handed her and smiled again. Too much damned smiling going on, as if she were waiting for him to do something.

As if she knew damned well why they'd come and left Silvestro at home. As if the enormity of it didn't matter— just the accomplishing of it so that they could return to the town house and that chair by the bed where they'd shared a sunrise and his memories of childhood.

How easily it had all come back to him.

He gulped champagne and glanced quickly around. Damned masks. Made everyone look alike. Another gulp, a swing of his eyes to Savannah, and he marveled that he felt great need to do only one thing at the moment: take Savannah back to that carriage, alone, and drink her moist lips dry of champagne. They were uncommonly plump and red tonight, as if she'd been biting them out of nervousness. She didn't seem at all aware that she was the embodiment of feminine allure tonight and that every man in the place was staring at her in that incredible dress.

Even men of questionable masculinity.

"Countess!" Templeton Snelling suddenly hovered over her, red cape aswirl, chapeau drooping over the red velvet mask at his eyes. "Good God, but you've set the room aflame, my dear. The temperature soared ten degrees when you stepped through the door. Dress defies gravity, I'd say. And the earl! I would recognize you anywhere, your lordship, even with the mask. All that height and breadth and hair—oh, do remind me to find Mrs. Wilton. You remember her, yes?"

Dominic lifted his glass and looked away. "I'm afraid not." Beneath his fingertips he felt Savannah's spine go stiff.

"And why the devil should you? You're aristocracy and she's new American rich with a few well-placed English friends." Snelling laughed, the kind of laugh that insinuates at deep friendship when there is none. "I believe she told me she met you in London quite a long time ago at a party hosted by the Prince of Wales himself. But she remembers you very well and would like to see you again. As I said, you're quite difficult to forget."

Damned bothersome man. Dominic wished he'd go away.

"I want to dance." Savannah was looking up at him with that fake smile pasted on her face. She'd turned her back to Snelling quite suddenly.

Dominic wished he could see her face behind the mask.

Her lips parted slightly, trembled, and she whispered, "Y-you do dance a simple waltz, don't you?"

Dominic murmured an assurance, handed their glasses to an astonished-looking Snelling, and turned to the dance floor. As he took her in his arms, he pondered the irony of her question. So much faith from her and yet she didn't know some of the simplest things about him.

It was baffling. It was, he realized, the most heady feeling he'd ever experienced.

"Tell me why he upset you," he murmured, looking over her head at the faces of those watching them. Yes, they were being watched from behind all those faceless masks, and perhaps more than usual. But hell, Savannah had been born begging to be noticed. Damned strange that her heart wasn't in it tonight.

Too much damned looking at him with that heart-wrenching smile. It made him want to take her the hell out of here.

She shrugged. "I've decided I don't like him. He's taunting you with that Mrs. Wilton and what she thinks she knows. If he exposes you as an impostor—"

"Your family will be ruined."

She looked up at him. "Good heavens—I—yes—but I wasn't thinking about them. I've stopped thinking about them—about me. I was thinking about you, Dominic."

"I want to kiss you."

"Dominic—" She looked over his shoulder, off to the side, her lips compressing slightly.

Dominic pressed gently at her back and her breasts lifted up against his chest. His voice plunged very low. "Do you want to know what I'm thinking?"

"About a life's work and schemes of revenge?"

"Frankly, no."

"Oh, Dominic."

"You've bewitched me, you know. Why the hell did you wear this?" His thumb flicked at one strap along her back. "You know damned well I can't think straight when I look at you. I don't even know my God-damned name. Ask me. Just ask me. I've quite forgotten it."

"You're teasing me."

"I wish I were. I have a great need, Rosy."

"Yes, I know all about need—"

"Things I need to say to you."

"I need to hear them, Dominic, so very badly—I *need* to hear them."

He grabbed her hand and would have led her off the floor, through the sea of masks, into the foyer and up the stairs to some private little haven in a dark room where he could make love to her and make the rest of the world go away. And he would have been successful at it had he moved an instant sooner.

"Lady Castellane." A severe-looking footman in gold livery and white gloves suddenly blocked Dominic's path. He gave a short bow, inclined his head at Dominic, then turned to Savannah. "Mrs. Nesbit and Mrs. Astor request the honor of your presence with them, madam."

"What?" Savannah said, looking suddenly pale.

"Go on," Dominic said, flattening his palm at the lower curve of her back. He leaned close to her ear. "I'd say you have no choice. I'll try to amuse myself while you're gone, but it will be impossible. Don't stay away long."

She looked up at him. Her throat jerked as if she forced back a swallow. "I could decline."

"For that you'd be punished with all the cruelty of a wild dog pack against an offending bitch and her whelps. Go."

"But—"

"I won't leave without you." He looked deep into her eyes, wondering why the hell she looked almost afraid. She could bend anyone in this room around her finger with a slice of her tongue and she knew it. He couldn't resist brushing his knuckle under her chin. "I promise."

She stared at him another moment, then turned and followed the footman to the front of the room. A path seemed to clear for them through the crowd.

"Good heavens, that's Savannah going up there."

Dominic barely glanced at Penelope Merriweather, very much aware that a hush had fallen over the room when the music stopped. "Indeed, madam, I believe it is."

"Why the devil did they invite her up there?"

Dominic drew his brows together thoughtfully, clasped his gloved hands behind his back, and indulged himself in a bit more comeuppance. "If I were to guess, madam, I would say it's the dress."

Penelope gawked at him. "The dress, you say? To lambaste her for wearing it, I certainly hope. That girl deserves a scolding from someone."

Dominic watched Savannah settle on the divan between the two dowagers. She looked godalmighty young, a welcome breath of springtime in a jaded world. He understood the hush in the room. She had the ability to steal away thought, speech, breath, even dreams. "Er—hardly lambaste, madam. They wish to congratulate her, I believe the footman said, on her brilliant fashion statement this evening. She's about to make some French dressmaker extremely busy and very wealthy."

Penelope's mouth curved down in a grimace. "Do you

mean to tell me those two dumpy dowagers think they can
wear a dress of that design?"

Dominic looked at Penelope squarely. "But that's the
real beauty in your daughter, madam. She makes everyone
believe they can accomplish the impossible. A pity you've
never appreciated that part of her."

Penelope's mouth dropped open and she looked at him
in complete silence for several moments. Above her head,
Dominic spotted the inimitable Templeton Snelling by the
arched doorway. He was talking to a tall, angular man in
peacock blue, wearing a black mask and carrying a valise
in one hand. The conversation seemed to be heated.

Dominic narrowed his eyes on the man in blue. Something about him struck a familiar chord. Atwood? It could
be.

A tiny burst of satisfaction heated his chest.

An instant later the man in blue turned, Snelling barked
something at him, and they both disappeared out the
doorway into the foyer.

"Excuse me," Dominic muttered, brushing past Penelope Merriweather. Just as he entered the foyer he bumped
squarely into a man dressed in black who suddenly
blocked his path. The man paused, looked at Dominic a
moment from behind his black mask, then muttered an
apology as if realizing they were strangers, and shouldered
past.

Damned masks confused everyone. Though something
about the man's voice tweaked at a distant memory . . .

He shrugged it off, glanced up, and spotted Snelling's
crimson velvet cape sweeping up the steps and into the
second floor hall. Jerking off his mask, he followed, brushing past couples lingering on the stairs. All conversation
seemed to stop as he passed.

At the top of the stairs, he glanced below. The man
he'd bumped into stood at the foot of the stairs, watching
him. Abruptly he turned and disappeared through the
arched doorway into the ballroom.

Odd? Maybe not. At every event they'd attended over the last several weeks, Dominic had been the recipient of stares of heated animosity from young whips intent on becoming Savannah's lover. This man was no doubt one of many here tonight. Dominic had probably exchanged inanities with him at some soirée a few days ago. Little wonder he seemed familiar.

Dismissing it, Dominic proceeded down the upper hall with long strides, turning at the end of the hall into another long hall. This too was dotted with couples, some sitting on settees. Where the hell was Snelling?

At the end of this hall, he turned right again and stopped. The hall was very dark, insufficiently lit by hissing gas wall sconces. He didn't see anyone in the gloom. Something jangled. A key?

He spun around and heard Snelling's voice an instant before a set of large double doors at the end of the hall thudded closed. Quickly he moved to the doors and barely paused before them long enough to glance back down the hall. It was momentarily deserted. He tested both door handles. They lifted easily. Gently and very slowly, he pushed.

Chapter 28

"No image is more suggestive of high-class living than tooling down the avenue in Newport in a *demi-daumont*," Mrs. Nesbit said to Savannah with a pleasant smile. "It's a carriage, dear."

"Yes, from France," Savannah said, craning her neck to find Dominic. "I've heard of it."

Mrs. Astor added in a bored tone, eyes glazed from too many balls, "But to do it properly, one must have four horses to draw it and two postillions outfitted as jockeys to drive it." Her head turned the merest inch toward Savannah. "You are an exquisite young woman, Lady Castellane. Turning everyone's heads around. How easy it is to forgive you your sins."

"You must get the earl to buy you one, dear," Mrs. Nesbit interjected. "Newport is the only place to be on decent display in the summertime." An appropriate choice of words, display, coming from a woman whose diamond necklace was reported to contain no fewer than two hundred four stones.

"And a house," Mrs. Astor put in, weighted like an anchor in her twelve-row fall of diamonds over her bosom and a stomacher that was fashioned of a diamond-studded brooch. "You *are* going to build yourselves a Newport castle? We so look forward to seeing you there."

"It's the picnics we love most," Mrs. Nesbit said with her delightful trill. "*Fêtes champêtres,* Mr. Snelling calls his picnics. Incomparably more elegant-sounding than English, don't you agree? He rents a flock of Southdown sheep and a few yoke of cattle to give his Bayside Farm an animated look."

"We *will* see you there?" Mrs. Astor asked. "And the earl?"

" Newport." Savannah lifted her brows, drew a deep breath, and almost swore out loud when she spotted Dominic leaving the ballroom at an urgent pace. She had a mad desire to sprint after him. Or shout. She chose instead to say something inflammatory. "That seaside Valhalla of swaggerdom."

The ladies shot glances at each other over the swell of Savannah's bosom.

Savannah knew of only one way to get thrown off the divan so she could follow Dominic. She need only be herself. "How I look forward to the daily afternoon drive cum-exhibition, where the idea of it all is to appear as aloof and as haughtily uninterested in the spectacle as if you'd joined the procession quite by accident."

"I don't"—Mrs. Nesbit giggled nervously—"that is—I believe you're quite right about that."

Savannah pressed on. "Most horses in Newport fare better than many of the occupants of slum tenements, isn't that right? I've heard the ground floor at Belcourt is given over to the stables."

Mrs. Nesbit leaned very close and whispered, "The horses bed down on white linen sheets from France. Mr. Belmont insisted."

Savannah's brows quivered. "To lodge horses so and be content that men and women and children should lodge in the sheds and collars of your tenements. A bit strange, don't you think?"

"You are a willful young woman," Mrs. Astor said gravely.

Savannah scanned the room. "Perhaps a bit too frank. I'm afraid I can't help it. Things just have a way of slapping me in the face. Oh—I see that my husband has vanished. No doubt he'll get himself lost without me. The English have a perplexing sense of direction. Do you mind, ladies?"

"No," they said in unison.

"Do what you must," Mrs. Astor said.

"Thank you. I will." She walked quickly away from the divan toward the entrance to the ballroom and wondered if anyone had ever purposely drawn and quartered themselves as she just had with those ladies. She felt a twinge of regret that her parents might feel the repercussions a bit more than she would.

Where was Dominic?

Someone grabbed hold of her arm. "Lady Castellane, if you please—" It was a man, garbed in black, as indistinguishable behind his mask as the rest of the people in the ballroom.

She could have met him a half-dozen times already. She just didn't remember. She gave him a quick smile she didn't feel and tugged on her arm. "I'm sorry but I'm looking for my husband. If you would—"

He inclined his head. "Indeed, madam, I was sent by your husband, the earl."

"You were? But I don't know you—"

"We've met, Lady Castellane. This way."

Savannah locked her knees when he took her by the elbow and turned. "Wait just a minute. Where did we—?"

The man's lips were barely visible below the bottom of his mask. They curved up very slightly but he didn't smile as Savannah wished he would so that she might then recognize him. "Castellane awaits you. Through the foyer here—"

The foyer, where the invitations were put to a grueling test of authenticity. What reason did she have to doubt this man? None that she could think of offhand, and even less considering that she'd felt the tension in the air tonight so palpably she'd been shaking since they'd arrived. Something was going to happen. There was a gallery full of paintings somewhere in this house. She had to find Dominic.

He'd promised not to leave without her. And she believed him.

"Take me to him." She allowed the stranger to steer her into the foyer. She saw her parents with another couple, standing to one side, but no sign of Dominic.

"Savannah, dear, over here—" Her mother waved, looked expectantly at her, and she tried to pause, say something, even in her haste, but the hand on her elbow suddenly gripped so hard it sent a twang of pain down Savannah's arm.

Savannah grimaced. "What the devil are you—that's my mother over there—ow!"

"This way, madam." As if he hadn't heard her, he propelled her toward the double-doored entrance, flanked by liveried footmen. Beyond the open doors, a faint mist swirled in the darkness. He was taking her out there. Forcibly. Or so he thought.

She yanked on her arm. "Wait just a minute. Castellane didn't leave. He promised—wait—we've never met. You're English, aren't you? I can tell. Are you a servant? No—you're—" Savannah's voice snagged. She gulped, braced her legs, and felt her soles slide on the marble floor. "Oh, God."

Her arm was twisted up painfully against her back. "Move." He snarled close to her ear. "I'm holding a pistol in my coat which I'm not afraid to use. Shut up and move."

"Wait—I can't walk fast in this dress." She craned her neck back, spotted her mother watching them with a curious expression. She opened her mouth.

"Don't say anything or I'll kill you." He shoved something that felt like the muzzle of a pistol into her back.

Savannah snarled through gritted teeth. "Go ahead. Shoot me like you shot poor Silvestro. But then you'll have no lure for Dominic Dare, will you, Cecil?"

"Oh, he'll come for you, dead or alive. I saw him watching you. He's a man ruled by his passion. I know his kind. Pitifully weak man. He'll come." The pistol poked hard into her spine and she stumbled through the entrance.

One of the footmen looked at her as she passed. She closed her eyes with chagrin. "God—how could I be so stupid?"

"Indeed." Cecil steered her down the steps. "You made it almost too easy for me, but then again, you owe me. Over there—to the right—the hansom cab there. That's it. Smile for the spectators. They're watching you."

"It's a wonder they let you in."

"Invitations can be bought, Miss Merriweather."

"With my father's money."

Cecil snorted as the driver stepped from his perch and yanked open the cab door. "None of that is mine—just yet. No, I used something else. A pity I was robbed. Bloody pirate at the pawnshop gave me only fifteen thousand for the piece. It was appraised at four times that. Get in."

Again the poke of the pistol into her back. He'd already shot Silvestro. He obviously had no aversion to using the weapon. Damn. She'd think of some way to escape . . . soon . . . but getting into a vehicle with him seemed to rather limit her options. Hiking her skirts up, she lurched inside, and he followed, settling on the seat opposite.

"You pawned your wife's stolen necklace," she threw at him.

Hyde-Gilbert lifted his mask. "Very good."

Savannah's voice dripped contempt. "What kind of a man—"

"Desperate circumstances call for desperate measures. I'd gambled away my allowance. Debtors were lining up at my door and yet my wife went everywhere with a fortune in jewels hanging around her neck. What man wouldn't have done the same?"

"Dominic knows you stole it. So you falsely accused him and had him thrown in jail the first time. That's why you wanted him in jail again. You were going to kill him, weren't you?"

Hyde-Gilbert fingered the pistol lying against his thigh. "The man seduced my wife right under my nose and everyone in England knows it. She's left me. Ran back to her father and took her bloody living with her. I know she helped you escape. Just as everyone knows she helped Dare escape the first time. Tell me, how I am to live that down when I emerge back into society?"

"Killing Dominic won't bring Bertrice back."

"Bertrice?" Hyde-Gilbert's laugh sent a chill through Savannah. "Good God, you think I want her back? Too much damned trouble for what she was worth."

Savannah grasped the infinite coldness in him. "Oh, but of course, you're the beneficiary of Castellane's fortune now."

"Two hundred fifty thousand merely got my uncle out from under a mountain of debt. It was your yearly stipend that was key, Miss Merriweather, and still is, particularly since desperate and very rich little heiresses are pitifully difficult to find. You're coming back to England with me. You're going to live up to your end of the contract you signed."

"I'm afraid that's impossible."

Hyde-Gilbert's brows shot up. "Impossible, you say? With Dominic Dare dead and out of my way for good, who could possibly stop me?"

"My father—"

"Your father?" His snort was deeply felt. "My dear girl, if your father found out about this charade you've been putting on, I'd wager he'd put you on a ship himself and pay me to take you back where you belong before he becomes the laughingstock of New York and you smeared as a tart. And you wouldn't want that, would you?"

Savannah stared at him, chillingly certain she didn't know what her father would do. After all this time, she was still the desperate heiress, perhaps even more now. Protecting her father had been at the crux of her reasoning when she'd agreed to Dominic's scheme. It still was. And Hyde-Gilbert knew it.

"Sit there and think about it a moment. You'll realize I'm giving you an easy way out."

Easy? How she hated the patronizing tone in his voice. Savannah stared at the pistol, at the gloved fingers slipping over the trigger. She swallowed and looked out the window. "I'll go with you. I'll marry Castellane. Just don't kill Dominic."

Hyde-Gilbert's chortle made Savannah flinch. "You're in no position to negotiate, Miss Merriweather. You'll go with me, on my terms. And Dominic Dare will no longer be a threat to anyone. Relax. We've yet a ways to go. And I'm afraid it's going to be a dreadfully long night."

"If Mrs. Nesbit finds out I let anyone into her art gallery this evening, she'll never entrust me again with choreographing her quadrilles much less the keys to—"

"Shut up, Snelling. Turn up a lamp. I can't see a damned thing. It's black as pitch in here."

Heels clicked on the floor. A hiss echoed from behind the door and soft light spilled through the half-inch-wide opening into the hall where Dominic stood with his hand frozen on the door handle. His eyes darted back up the hall. Deserted. Christ, but if anyone came down that hall he'd—

"What the devil are you?" Snelling's voice jumped an octave. "James, you can't do that. Those are Mrs. Nesbit's paintings! You can't just take them off the wall—"

"Get the hell out of here, Snelling. Go rehearse quadrilles with the ladies."

Snelling gasped. "Good God! *You're* the thief!"

James Atwood laughed hollowly. "Snelling, you're a fool. But not me—I'm not going to let him get me—whoever the hell he is. Threatening to expose me in his damned letter. You've been talking too much, Snelling. Somebody knows things they shouldn't. But I'm not going to let them ruin me. That bastard at Boothby's tried but I shut him up for good."

"You're scaring me, James. You sound . . . delusional. Perhaps you should see a doctor. I know of an excellent one—"

"Turn it on him. That's what I'll do. I'll steal them before he can. Then I'll be the one to find the stolen paintings. I'll be a hero. He won't ruin me, the bastard. Lega won't leave me. Everything will be fine, I tell you!"

The distinct rustle of skirts came from somewhere down a side hall. Dominic closed his eyes. No . . . not now . . . not yet . . . Let whoever it was turn around and go back.

The rustle was getting closer . . . closer . . .

"Castellane?" A woman's high-pitched voice clamored like the tolling of a bell. Penelope Merriweather.

Dominic swore under his breath with as much savagery as he'd ever felt. Silently he pulled the doors closed and retreated quickly up the hall and around the corner. He met her ten paces farther.

She looked unusually flustered. "There you are! Good heavens—you have to come—it's Savannah."

Dominic slid his teeth together and groped for a tone that wouldn't reveal his utter frustration with her at the moment. No doubt some calamity with a dress was the cause for her distress. "Where is she?"

Penelope gripped her chest as if she couldn't catch her breath. "That's just it. She left."

"She *what?*"

"Not five minutes ago. She left with a man."

"Who?"

"Well, don't you know? I thought you'd arranged—" Her face went white. "He was dressed all in black."

Dominic felt his heart stutter. "I see."

"What were you doing up here all by yourself?"

"Nothing." He grasped her arm and turned her back up the hall. "Nothing of any importance. It's—quite forgotten."

"Something's happened to her!"

Dominic lengthened his stride and fought for control of his voice, the terrifying turn of his thoughts. "Calm yourself. It's nothing. I'm certain you've no cause for alarm."

"If you say so—but when he was taking her out the door she looked at me—I don't know—there was something on her face I've never seen before. Helplessness. That's it. She looked helpless."

Dominic looked at Penelope, recognizing deep concern when he saw it. His heart and his attitude toward her couldn't help but soften. "Perhaps she ate too much," he offered as they descended the stairs into the foyer.

"Quite the contrary. Brunnie's told me she's all but abandoned chocolate in the last week. Quite unlike her."

A footman met Dominic at the landing. "A message for you, your lordship."

"Thank you." Dominic took the envelope with an overwhelming sense of foreboding. He glanced at Penelope, who was staring at him. "Perhaps a turn around the dance floor would do you some good. Some champagne."

Her brows quivered. "Yes, perhaps. You know, you seem—quite different tonight, your lordship. Quite unlike an aristocrat—very much a gentleman. Even your voice—it's changed somewhat."

The message seemed to burn in Dominic's hand. "Excuse me." He turned his back, flipped the message open, and felt the floor under his feet tilt. He turned back to Penelope. "Damned business matter," he muttered, barely seeing her through the haze clouding his vision.

Anger was a consuming red fog in the mind. Or was it fear?

Penelope Merriweather said something to him but he didn't hear it as he ran from the house into pouring rain.

Chapter 29

Lightning flashed. Savannah's eyes darted to the frayed curtain hanging close beside her head. Fat drops of rain splattered, one by one, then faster, against the pane. Thunder rumbled low and ominous and distant. She swallowed and glanced at Hyde-Gilbert.

He was slouched in a chair against the wall, watching her. He held a glass of liquor in one hand, his pistol in the other, pointed at the door. His cravat hung loose, his coat open, displaying a slight paunch and a sunken chest beneath a shirt front that looked splattered with food. A lock of greased hair fell over his forehead.

After he'd shoved her up the stairs to the hotel's second floor, he'd bound her hands in her lap and her feet at her ankles and pushed her into a hard chair with one teetering leg and a sagging back. The place smelled of mildew and must. The bed shoved into the corner next to her was rumpled. She didn't want to look at it. Hyde-Gilbert looked at it every now and again, and the look on his face as he did made her taste bilious terror.

"I think you should know something," she said, tasting the first traces of raw fear on her tongue when the rain started to pound harder on the window. "About New York storms."

Hyde-Gilbert snorted and drained his glass. "Rain. A few loud booms. Not quite an American invention. We English have them too." Thunder shook the walls. He narrowed his eyes as he reached for the bottle on the table beside him. "So pale you are. Ah—you're frightened, but oddly enough, not of me." Glass slid against glass and liquid splashed. "Yes, now I remember. You were frightened at the inn by the storm. I didn't take you for such a child." He looked at her breasts over the rim of his glass.

"There are storms here that tear roofs off buildings."

"Tear them right off, eh?" Hyde-Gilbert smirked into his glass.

"And suck the people out of their homes. Winds that can twist steel and send wooden beams flying through the air like spears."

"You've quite an imagination."

A thunderous boom rattled the panes. Savannah swallowed a shriek. Her palms were instantly slick. Her heart raced. A trickle of perspiration wove down her temple. But she was cold, shivering-to-her-bones cold. Terrified.

No . . . she couldn't let this happen, not now.

"I've seen it firsthand. There are things I've seen that I can't ever forget. Do you know what becomes of a man when he's sucked through barbed wire fencing by wind?"

Hyde-Gilbert's head snapped up. He sat very still, watching her with distinct wariness in his eyes. As if she were a wild animal . . . a skittish horse he couldn't control.

Yes, very good.

Savannah blocked out the sound of the wind. Was that ice pellets pounding against the window? No . . . Her words tumbled over each other they came out so fast. "Or when glass is blown in by the force and the world becomes a sea of flying shards? The air changes when it comes—you can almost feel it popping in your ears—but you have to know what to listen for."

Hyde-Gilbert frowned and opened his mouth as if he was clearing his ears. When lightning sizzled beyond the glass, his head jerked to the window. He seemed straighter in his chair, his eyes wider, his face paler.

"Those are ice pellets hitting the panes. The rain is coming down from so high, so hard and fast, it can't melt. That's the way it is before the big winds come." She tried not to look at the window so close beside her, tried not to feel the room trembling in the wind. The window—she had to get him to come to the window—close enough beside her. "The room will explode from the pressure. I've seen it happen. Everything in this room will explode."

He looked at her so intently, with such doubt she felt her heart plummet. She tasted sweat on her lips and knew that her face and chest were bathed in it. "Look at me," she breathed, her chest jerking with her breaths. "I'm terrified for good reason. Please—open the window. It could save us."

Hyde-Gilbert looked at the window, then at her, again at the window, then snarled something under his breath and lurched from the chair. Savannah stared at the pistol dangling from one hand. He held it carelessly, his attention on the window.

He moved so close beside her his leg brushed hers. She forced herself to breathe regularly, to be the docile prisoner, to wait for just the right moment . . .

"Bloody hell." He snarled, trying to lift the window with one hand. A blinding blue-white flash lit the room. Hyde-Gilbert cried out, then turned and laid the pistol on a table well beyond Savannah's reach. With both hands he tried to lift the window, straining, veins popping at his temple.

Savannah gathered all her strength and lurched sideways out of her chair, driving all her weight into Hyde-

Gilbert's side. They fell heavily against a chair that gave beneath them in a splintering crash. For an instant Savannah sprawled on top of Hyde-Gilbert, then rolled to her belly onto the floor and spotted the pistol on the table above her head, beyond reach. In this dress she'd never get to her feet in time.

"Damned fat bitch, you broke my arm! And I'm bleeding!"

She spotted the liquor bottle sitting on the floor, swung her bound hands in front of her, and crawled on her side like a frantic seal toward it. She stretched until her arms felt as if they'd come out of their sockets. Fingers touched the neck, curled, grasped, pulled closer. Hyde-Gilbert grabbed her leg. Tulle and satin gave an ominous tear. He swore, then tried to trap her legs with his knee. She thrashed and squirmed, then, garnering the last of her strength, twisted her torso up and around, and brought her arms and the liquor bottle swinging in a blind arc. By luck alone she found the side of Hyde-Gilbert's head.

There was an ominous clunk of skull meeting glass. Shards and liquor sprayed over Savannah's face and chest. She twisted her face away and heard Hyde-Gilbert groan, then topple to the floor.

Chest heaving with her breaths, she stared at him lying on the floor.

"Oh, God," she said, peering closer at him. "Mr. Hyde-Gilbert? Please tell me you're not dead—"

The door burst open behind her. "God almighty—"

She closed her eyes and almost slumped over with relief. "Dominic," she whispered, and then she was in his arms, her face smashed against his chest, and his strong arms were trembling they held her so tight. "You're all wet," she managed.

"God almighty," he said again, his voice barely recognizable it was so thick. "I'm so sorry—if anything—I couldn't have lived with myself if anything had happened to you. How could I have been so—"

"No. It was me. I believed him when he said—oh, God, I think I killed him."

"Bastard's still alive."

Savannah turned her head and saw Bonnie bent over Hyde-Gilbert. He looked at her and grinned. "Glad to be of service, miss, though ye dinna need us, by the looks of it."

"I need you," she whispered, as Dominic yanked the rope from around her wrists and ankles. "No, I can stand."

But he didn't listen to her. With great ease he scooped her up and cradled her high and close to his chest, then turned to the door. "Tend to him, will you, Bonnie?"

"Glad te do it, Nino. Kidnappin', attempted murder—anythin' else the police should know?"

"Jewel thievery," Savannah said, looking up at Dominic. She was certain her heart would burst from her chest. "Tell them to notify the English authorities that he was the man who stole the Crimson Fire necklace. It's time Dominic Dare's name was cleared."

Dominic stopped just outside the building's front door and lowered his mouth to hers in a kiss that touched her soul. He lifted his head, looked up, as the rain fell all around them. "You're not afraid?"

"Never again," she murmured, resting her head against his heart. "For as long as I'm with you, never again."

"Let's go home."

"Yes."

The rest of the world could wait one more night.

Epilogue

"Your lips are moving."

Savannah looked up into the dressing table mirror and smiled at the silhouette stirring the velvety shadows behind her. "Ah, you're interested, are you? Perhaps I should read it out loud."

A broad hand cupped over her shoulder. Candlelight glinted off the gold band encircling one long finger. "Don't take too long."

Savannah drew the paper closer and began to read.

Town Topics is pleased to be the first to report that James Atwood, internationally known art agent and consultant to New York's Four Hundred, was arrested in his studio the day after the Nesbit masked ball. Close sources report he confessed to the murder of a Boothby's agent, theft, embezzlement, fraud, and customs evasion. Mr. Dominic Dare, New York artist and businessman, and Miss Savannah Rose Merriweather, heiress to the much-ballyhooed fortune of Mr. Stuyvesant Merriweather of New York City, and lately of

Newport, are heralded by all with uncovering Mr. Atwood's black market scheme.

Savannah beamed with satisfaction. "Now aren't you glad we went to him instead of the police? Things surely would have turned out differently."

His palm smoothed over her shoulder. "We wouldn't be here."

"I shudder to think what would have happened. The press really does have an inordinate amount of power. The ability to twist a story, to give it a slant, to show things in a certain light—it's quite uncanny. I never thought I'd be so grateful for it, or feel so beholden to a man like Colonel Sharpe."

"We needn't go that far, my dear."

"Yes, but he saw you as I do, as a hero. Everything you did to uncover Atwood's scheme, the thefts—"

"Quite illegal from a policeman's point of view."

"Quite noble, according to Colonel Sharpe. He paints a picture of a man so devoted to his memory of his family, so bound to do the honorable thing, he risks everything. What better way was there to focus attention on Atwood? Sharpe makes it sound like a scheme cunningly hatched and perfectly executed."

"Now what makes you think it wasn't?"

"I believe Aunt Maxine still thinks we were in on it together from the very beginning."

"Weren't we?" A muscular length of hip and thigh appeared from behind her chair. The hand at her shoulder slid to her upper arm, then reached for the ribbon laced through the top of her chemise and tied in a small bow.

"Perhaps she's been swayed in her thinking lately."

"Indeed, Silvestro can sway a woman."

"He's threatening to paint her and make her the sensation she deserves to be."

"Silvestro always makes good on his threats. Maxine is in trouble."

"Even my father believes it was some brilliant scheme to save all of New York society from embarrassment—so brilliant he even forgave you for not being an earl and me for lying to him."

"They all forgave us, love."

"You knew they would."

"I wasn't thinking about anyone but you."

"The Four Hundred will be forever grateful. You exposed a traitor among them. And you retrieved every last one of your father's paintings."

"Rosy, sweet, stop talking." Long fingers tugged gently on the ribbon. It fell loose. Fingers nudged. Cambric gapped.

Savannah swam in heady pleasure. "There's more."

"Mmmm." His lips were warm on the side of her neck, his hands tender on her breasts. "Read on."

"It's—it's on the following page—here—Mother will be so pleased. Remind me to send her a postcard. 'Mr. and Mrs. Stuyvesant Merriweather are delighted to announce the marriage of their daughter—' "

"I know the girl." He was on his knees in front of her, dark and boldly impassioned. "I love her, you know."

"Yes, I know."

He lowered his head to her breasts. "Go on."

"It says after the ceremony the couple enjoyed a champagne dinner hosted by Mrs. Astor. And that they'll reside near St. Augustine, Florida, where Mr. Dare intends to paint." A breeze tossed the sheer drapery at a window. Beyond it, in the darkness, came the rush of surf over sand.

"And what will the adventuress do? Does the paper say?"

Savannah gathered him into her arms and closed her eyes. Her smile felt as whimsical as a dream, her heart as full as an ocean. "Yes. It says she's embarked on a new course in life. And to all the suffragists of the world she has only one thing to say: the greatest of all a woman's gifts is the power of love."

"Come show me."

And she did.